TROJANS

PHILIP PURSER-HALLARD

Proudly Published by Snowbooks in 2016

Copyright © 2016 Philip Purser-Hallard

Snowbooks Ltd.
email: info@snowbooks.com
www.snowbooks.com

British Library Cataloguing in Publication Data
A catalogue record for this book is available from the
British Library.

E-book ISBN 978-1-911390-84-8
Paperback ISBN 978-1-911390-83-1

Printed in Denmark by Nørhaven

**BOOK THREE OF
THE DEVICES TRILOGY**

To Mum and Dad. Sorry about the language.

Note: Lists of characters and devices appearing in Trojans can be found in the final pages.

i

CAMELOT

1. SIR BEDIVERE

The High King of Britain, the Pendragon, heir to King Arthur, arrives at the newly extended Southbank Centre in the familiar motorcade.

Two Knights of the Circle in full armour lead the procession, riding at a measured jogging pace on the Triumph motorbikes supplied exclusively for the Circle's use. There are contexts when horses just don't cut it in the modern world, and the M4 from Windsor into central London just now was certainly one of them.

The riders' armour matches the dull urban grey of the bikes' chunky bodywork, like the hide of some robotic centaur. Their carbon-steel swords hang sheathed at their hips; their toughened polyester riot-shields are slung at their sides. Aside from the clear panel at the top, both riders' shields are predominantly gold: the left-hand one bears the red-and-black lynx emblem of Sir Lucan, and the right the three-pronged red banner of Sir Bedivere.

Behind them comes the High King's customised Bentley Badon limo. Sleek, black and bulletproof, it hums along behind its motorcycle escort, its electric motor all but silent. On its bonnet is mounted a flying golden dragon, and on its roof flaps a blue pennant bearing a yellow dragon's head. At the High King's insistence, his tinted, reinforced window has been wound down so he can acknowledge the cheering crowds lining Belvedere Road, many of them waving their own Pendragon banners alongside the Union Jacks. At the monarch's side, a Circle man-at-arms with an unholstered Webley 2020 sub-machine gun maintains a watchful eye on the throng.

Behind the royal limousine comes another Bentley, then a Rolls-Royce Revenant, bearing the second- and third-rank dignitaries attending today's festivities. The fourth car is a gleaming black Range Rover, carrying more men-at-arms of the Circle's Regal Protection Detail.

The cars are followed by two more Knightly motorcycles, the shields on their riders' backs displaying the abstract gold-and-green patterning of Sir Safir and the silver-on-green armoured arm of Sir Brastias. Behind them comes the secular police's Special Escort Group, represented by a car and two outriders, and looking rather surplus to requirements.

The motorcade draws to a precision-timed halt in front of the steps of the National Centre for Oral Storytelling, the plush new arts facility the Pendragon is here to open. A glass-and-steel structure in the style which predictably gets called New Arthurian, its corner staircases in their glass tubes suggest turrets and it boasts a crenellated roof-garden. Inside are multiple performance spaces in sizes ranging from intimate to cavernous, rehearsal rooms, a restaurant-cum-performance-café, and an extensive multimedia library.

(Not that you really need me to describe the building to you, of course. I think it's safe to say you're all familiar with it by now.)

The Knights park up their bikes and dismount, forming an honour guard. The man-at-arms who rode with the High King comes round and opens the streetside door just as the Director of the Centre herself, a performance poet of national reputation who's slightly bemused to have this greatness thrust upon her, steps forward to greet the monarch.

The crowd crane their necks for a sight of their sovereign: the man who, seven years ago at Stonehenge, took on the Pendragon device and thereby became the rightful High King of Britain, in the process ending the catastrophic War of the Devices and saving these same citizens from the internecine struggle between their increasingly out-of-control and savage mythologies.

No British monarch in recorded history – none, perhaps, since the days of Arthur himself – has been as well-loved by the populace as High King Jordan.

The man who steps from the car is at the tail-end of his thirties, blond, well-built, physically still fit despite his radical change in lifestyle, wearing an unfussy but extremely expensive Savile Row suit in sober blue, with a gold tie. The slim gold band encircling his head – created by the Alexander McQueen design house to convey a sense of restrained, modestly regal dignity – is the only outward sign of his status.

You don't really need outward signs, though, when you're inhabited by the semi-autonomous culturally-inflected archetypal memeplex of Arthur Pendragon, King of the Britons, the Once and Present King. The Director bows with instinctive reverence, as do the various functionaries and colleagues surrounding her, while a ripple of awe that spreads out amongst the crowd acknowledges that this tall, mildly handsome but otherwise unexceptional-looking middle-aged man is the nearest thing Britain has produced to a homegrown messiah.

For some of the foreigners in the crowd – the ones who aren't here because of rampant anglophilia, at least – it all looks a bit disconcerting and neo-Stalinist. The Brits here are attuned to subtleties they miss, though, and we (because yes, I'm here too) see beyond the regal mask. Beneath that golden circlet, behind the beard he's cultivated since his coronation, the face of Jordan Taylor betrays a slightly rueful self-awareness – an ironic detachment full of amusement at the situation in which he now finds himself, which comes from the *other* device he hosts.

The other VIPs are released from their own limos now, and step forward behind the High King in order of precedence. A couple of minor royals (from the UK's previously existing royal family, Jordan being unique in his sovereignty); the Minister for Culture and Devicial Affairs; the Seneschal of the Circle, Sir David Stafford, fifty and balding, wearing an ordinary suit rather than his armour and with his own device, the red cross of Sir Galahad, emblazoned on a lapel-pin. He's followed by the Poet Laureate; a representative from the BBC Trust; and… well, the High King's bard and faithful chronicler.

(That would be me, of course. Hello.

Dale's the name I like to go by, although these days people keep expecting me to use what's on my birth certificate instead. I'm kind of duty-bound to tag along to these ceremonial things, so I can tell people about them afterwards – and this time, what with oral storytelling being basically a bard's job spec, the Pendragon was most insistent.)

As we reach the top of the steps into the new Centre, High King Jordan raises his hand and stops. We all cluster around him as he turns to talk to the crowd. There'll be a formal speech later, of course, in the restaurant they've laid out like an Ikea-furnished banqueting-hall, but that will be for selected guests only. Most of the crowd here won't be invited, and the Pendragon obviously thinks they merit the abridged version.

The High King clears his throat, and the crowd instantly quietens down.

'I'm delighted to see so many people here today,' he tells them warmly. 'Not long ago, few people in this country appreciated the vital importance of telling one another stories. It's heartening to see how far we've come since then.'

As the Pendragon launches into edited highlights of the speech he's practiced, I notice a worried-looking Sergeant-at-Arms Robert Thackett, in charge of the protection detail, having a quiet word with the four Knightly outriders – the device-bearers of Lucan, Bedivere, Brastias and Safir. A moment later, the five of them slip away through the big double doors into the Centre.

I stay put, of course. I know where my talents lie.

Behind us, in the building's roomy, glassy lobby, the bondsman of Sir Lucan (King Arthur's butler, so the legends say, not that the title meant quite the same thing back then) pushes up his helmet visor and asks, 'What's this about, Thackett?'

'Possible security breach, sir,' Bob Thackett tells him. 'One of the staff found a cleaning cupboard unlocked.'

'What, you reckon someone hid in there overnight?' the Knight bearing Sir Bedivere's device asks at once. Bedivere was Arthur's marshal and standard-bearer, hence the three-pointed pennant – heraldically speaking, a *gonfanon* – on his shield.

'Surely the cleaner just forgot –' puts in Sir Brastias's device-bearer, but Thackett interrupts.

'I don't think so, sir,' he says impassively. 'The staff are under strict instructions to follow health and safety procedures today. Those cupboards are kept locked because they contain hazardous cleaning chemicals.'

'Cleaning chemicals? Come on,' Sir Brastias's bondsman scoffs. All four of the Knights here are young, but he's the youngest: a recent acclaimee to Knighthood, and the first to bear the punning arms of the reclusive Sir Brastias since the device's previous bondsman was killed in the final suppression of the Red Ravagers half a decade ago. 'Some minimum-wager leaves a cupboard open by mistake and you call in four Knights of the Circle? This is your department, Thackett, not ours.' Like many such lads – though the Seneschal's been doing his best recently to change the Circle's recruitment demographic – he's cocky, full of himself and disinclined to defer much to the judgement of a non-commissioned officer, even one more than twice his age.

Bob Thackett opens his mouth to say something tactful but extremely firm, but Bedivere's device-bearer gets there first. 'Don't be an arse, Andy, OK? You say it's probably a cleaner, and yeah, probably it is. D'you want to trust the High King's life to that "probably"?'

Andy looks like he's going to argue, but doesn't. 'Well, I suppose. But surely your people, Thackett –'

'Not if the intruder's got a device, sir,' Thackett says.

It's not a trivial danger, as these Knights know. The Pendragon's reign has seen unprecedented success on the Circle's part in suppressing mythological manifestations hostile to the Round Table. Still, it's in the nature of the devices that they don't stay suppressed for long. If a dragon or belligerent ogre or gigantic savage wildcat – that is to say, a member of the public who's been suborned by one of those devices – is lurking undetected somewhere in the building, then ordinary men-at-arms might be unable to stop them. And then the consequences for the High King, and the realm, could be catastrophic.

'Makes sense to me,' says the fourth Knight – the device-bearer of Sir Safir, the Saracen knight who's known mainly for being the brother of the more famous Sir Palamedes.

'Right, then.' Bedivere's device-bearer takes charge. 'We'll sweep the building. Andy, Amal, you take the ground floor then head up to the roof garden, OK? Johnny and I'll take the lifts to the second floor, cover that one and the first. We'll meet up back here. Bob, you and your blokes guard the stairs, right?'

Thackett salutes, obviously relieved that someone other than him has got some basic sense around here. Unshouldering their shields and unsheathing their swords, the four Knights of the Circle go about the urgent business of protecting the Circle's Head.

Quickly, they fan out through the building, passing from the glassed-in lobby into the honeycomb of rooms beyond. Stepping out on the second floor, the bearers of Bedivere and Lucan make a circuit of the performance and rehearsal spaces surrounding the Great Hall. The largest of the Centre's performance spaces, the Hall takes up much of the first floor and extends up to the roof, where multiple light wells set among the shrubs of the garden supply it with daytime illumination. These smaller spaces each have windows looking down into the Great Hall, and could make excellent sniper positions.

Some of them have a small stage or dais, some circles of chairs. In some of them nervous performers are rehearsing, awaiting their forthcoming royal command performance; others are empty. A few questions, or a swift flick of a light switch – because they all have blinds which are closed if they're not going to be used today – and a visual sweep, checking behind any obstructions as necessary, is all it takes.

* * *

'Seven years ago,' the High King is saying, 'things looked very bleak for this country. Britain was emerging from a devastating struggle: our first civil war in three and a half centuries, and the first fought with modern weapons; a war in which our most enduring cultural archetypes – our stories – had turned against and fought one another. I know that many of us then were still coming to terms with learning that the heroes and villains of those stories lived on in the minds of modern Britons in more literal ways than most of us had believed possible, directing and motivating citizens from our most respected law enforcement agency to our most principled underground activists.'

(He's being euphemistic with the 'activists' line. Ten years ago when I first met him, the Circle had interdicted the Green Chapel as a terrorist organisation. Since I was a hanger-on at the Chapel and Jory Taylor was a Knight of the Circle at the time – bearing the device of Sir Gawain of Orkney, now in abeyance – it caused a certain amount of friction between us.)

'We've worked hard since then,' the Pendragon says, 'every one of us, to restore our country to what it was before. In industry, economy, research and academia, in our politics at home and in our relations with the outside world – even in sport, as we intend to demonstrate at the Olympics this year – we've made enormous strides as a country and a people.

7

'I think it's no exaggeration,' the Pendragon suggests, 'to say that that world wouldn't recognise that battle-scarred, impoverished nation in what we've become today.'

The High King's modesty is one of his most popular qualities, so he's not bothering to mention that without his leadership, his wisdom and – crucially – his willingness to trust the experts, very little of this could have happened. Seven years ago, with the help of the best advisors he could assemble, he set the bulk of the armies who'd been fighting the war – and who were now unswervingly loyal to him, their new sovereign – to good use harvesting neglected crops, helping out in overworked hospitals, repairing torn-down bridges and torn-up roads, rebuilding ruined housing and reopening abandoned factories, and generally doing whatever was necessary to re-establish and maintain the civic life of the nation.

While the High King himself was leading the elite of the Circle against that realm's surviving enemies – the Circle Knights so dedicated to the idea of King Arthur that the reality would never suffice for them; the Black Knights who'd fought with the Chapel but would never serve the Pendragon; the opportunist troublemakers like the Saxon Shield and the Sons of Gore – this skilled and unskilled manpower was beavering loyally away until, by the time those enemies had all been killed, arrested, pacified or brought into the fold, the country's infrastructure was in a stable state once more.

Since then, most of our serious devicial threats have been foreign rather than domestic – and since then, thanks to steady injections of cash brought in by selling off half the Crown's portable assets and mortgaging half its capital holdings, Britain has thrived. Our manufacturing, banks, media, universities, tourist industry, farms, hospitals – all are as efficient and effective, and as profitable, as they were before the War of the Devices: in many cases, much more so. The term 'Golden Age', which usually only means some imaginary time in the distant past, has been applied to the present day so much in the past few years it's become a media cliché.

'But during all of this,' the Pendragon says, 'British culture continued. A little muted perhaps, but as vital to our national identity as ever. We might have been a bit suspicious of our stories, back then – some of us felt they'd turned against us, that they were more trouble than they were worth, perhaps that we'd be better off without them. But in the end, storytelling is part of what makes us human.'

* * *

The Knights with the lynx and gonfanon shields take the lifts down to the first floor and check out the Media Library. It's a bigger job, filled as it is with ranks of shelving for books, discs and assorted storytelling props from placards to puppets, and banks of computer terminals. The two librarians in charge goggle at the newcomers.

'ID, now,' the bearer of Sir Bedivere's shield insists, and the pair hastily show their cards.

'Seen anyone you don't know?' Sir Lucan's device-bearer asks, and they shake their heads, nervous and bewildered as the Knights jog quickly up and down the gangways, checking in every nook and study cubicle.

From the library they pass into the Great Hall itself – a gigantic space built to seat eight hundred. Later the High King will stand here to give his speech in full, then sit to listen to stories told by the most prestigious actors, stand-up comedians and performance poets the Director's been able to procure (including, God knows why, yours truly).

For now there are just a couple of Circle men-at-arms here, as well as the Centre's meeters and greeters and some backstage techy types: seven or eight people in all.

'Surely no-one's got in here,' Sir Lucan's device-bearer says.

His fellow Knight shrugs. 'Got to check.'

The entrance the Knights have come in through is

midway along one side of the Hall. One end of the space is taken up with a triangular stage – not curtained off, because of course this isn't a theatre, and with no wings or doors leading from it, but raised up so the audience can see what's going on. The seats, like the stage, can be moved around to give the room different configurations, but at the moment they're in rows, thirty or so of them, angled parallel with the sides of the stage like the fronds of a fern.

The rear wall of the room is painted with a mural intended to suggest the sea, an abstract of swirls and jags in grey, green and blue. Much of the high ceiling that isn't glass is taken up with lights for night-time use, but – again – this isn't a theatre, and there are no gantries up there for anyone to hide in.

Lucan's man Johnny nods. 'Let's just walk the perimeter, then.'

'Then we'll get downstairs and meet the others,' his colleague agrees, and they separate, peering at walls and seats for signs of tampering as they move further apart along the left wall.

At the front of the Hall, Bedivere's device-bearer steps up onto the dais. The front wall is hung with a black velvet drape, and the Knight twitches it back to see how much dead space there is behind. It's just five centimetres or so: anybody hiding behind the curtain would have to be two-dimensional. *Unless there's an alcove or something,* the Knight thinks. *Or they could have planted a bomb. Better see…*

The Knight looks back to see how the other man's getting on. He's nearing the rear of the hall, checking the seats rather perfunctorily as he fiddles with the strap on his shield. Just up ahead of him where he's not looking yet, part of the green-grey mural blurs.

The Knight gasps, then shouts, 'Johnny, look out!'

The sound of a shot echoes around the room, and Lucan's device-bearer falls to the floor.

* * *

10

'So the stories we tell our children, one another and ourselves,' the Head of the Circle insists, 'aren't just British stories – they're the very thing that makes us British. A single vibrant people, rather than a ragtag collection of Celts, Saxons, Normans, Asians, Africans, eastern Europeans and others who all just happen to live together on the same few islands. And not just stories about King Arthur, but other stories, too: the tales of King Alfred and Hereward the Wake, Sir Francis Drake and Lord Nelson, Rob Roy and Owain Glyndŵr, Richard III and Falstaff, Dunkirk and the Blitz, Ambridge and Albert Square.'

Maybe that's last bit's taking the piss a tad, I'm not sure. (Oh – I wrote the speech. Didn't I say?) I wanted to include Cú Chulainn, who's definitely an Ulster hero rather than a generic Irish one, but the friction with the Children of Oisín makes that too dicey just at the moment. The High King vetoed it, and who am I to argue?

'This new facility, our National Centre for Oral Storytelling,' says the High King, 'will help us to keep and preserve these and all our stories as a living tradition – as tales we pass from friend to friend, from grandparent to grandchild, from local to newcomer, while other media come and go. Whether our descendants a century from now will be reading books or going to the theatre or streaming TV shows I can't say – but I know for certain they'll be telling each other stories.'

(To be perfectly honest, I reckon having a special place you go for storytelling kind of misses the point. It doesn't need a venue – it's something you can literally do anywhere. But nobody asked me.)

* * *

'Get down!' the standing Knight yells to the Centre staff, most of whom have had the sense to do just that. Again a small area of the ocean mural hazes, and Bedivere's device-bearer dives off the stage just in time to hear the bang, the

11

muffled thud of a bullet hitting a wall through a thick velvet curtain. The men-at-arms the Knights found here have flung themselves right back against the wall opposite the door. They've got their guns out, and are looking frantically for something to shoot.

There's another blur, another report, and one of them falls, bleeding badly from the chest as his gun spins away across the dark-blue carpet. A couple of the civilians on the floor scream.

Down the far end of the room, Lucan's man groans. He has to be considered out of the fight for the moment. The sniper had a lucky shot, or knew exactly what they were doing: there aren't many weak points in a Knight's ceramic-polyamide armour where a bullet can burrow through to vulnerable flesh.

That makes covering your face and torso with your shield, drawing your sword and charging as fast as you can towards the enemy – which is what the Knight does next – a bit of a gamble, but not a disastrous one. The room echoes and rebounds with the thud of heavy boots on carpet as the armoured figure thunders towards the painted wall.

There is of course the slight issue of 'towards the enemy' being an inexact quantity just at the moment, but the Knight will deal with that in good time.

* * *

His pep talk concluded, the Pendragon turns to enter the Centre – but Sir David Stafford halts him with a gentle pressure on his arm.

The Seneschal peers at his phone as he receives an update from inside the building. 'My lord, there's some kind of incident,' he says. 'We need to leave.'

'No, David,' the High King says, with quiet but unanswerable authority. 'I didn't come all this way to miss the show. Besides, I meant all that. Today is important.'

12

Stafford sighs: he expected this, of course. 'In that case, my lord, I have to insist we stay outside for the moment.'

The Pendragon looks defiant for a moment, but then nods shortly. He looks over to where the public are pressed against the rope-line bisecting the pavement.

'Not worth it, my lord,' Stafford says quickly. 'Under the circumstances, my men and women can't guarantee –'

'Understood,' the High King says. Then he sweeps down the steps towards the citizenry, and starts shaking hands and chatting.

Sir David groans. 'Stick to him like fleas!' he yells to the High King's protection detail, then turns and trots into the building.

* * *

The other man-at-arms is firing now, evidently working his way along the wall on the basis that the would-be-assassin has to be standing there *somewhere*. Paint applied last month with painstaking care by a Turner Prize winner chips and flies, a line of black starfish appearing across the sea's surface. The mural blurs again, there's another shot, and the second man-at-arms falls, clutching at his thigh.

'Shitty bollocks buggery,' opines Sir Bedivere's device-bearer. Approaching the far end of the room, passing the rearmost row of chairs, the Knight goes suddenly into a dive, hits the floor and rolls.

Active optical camouflage is making great strides these days, but even the latest military prototypes – which this would-be-assassin's outfit surely has to be – have distinct limitations. The millions of tiny cameras embedded in the full-body cloak which record the colouration behind the wearer, and project it onto the millions of tiny LEDs studding the opposite side, can only manage so much resolution: this kit does its best work against a broken, randomly-patterned field like the painted wall. Against one of the bookshelves in the library, say, the distortion would be too obvious and there'd be no possibility of hiding in plain sight.

Ultimately, too, there's always going to be a directional component to the camouflage: given that complete transparency is impossible, the image has to be presented for the benefit of a particular viewer. As well as assuming that people are most likely to glance this way when they come in the door, this array is working on the reasonable basis that they'll be looking at it from eye-height.

From floor-level, then, and further away from the door, the distortion should be maximal – and from the point the Knight's reached on the carpet, it is indeed quite clear that there's a human figure there in front of the mural, a rounded, legged-and-armed bulge compromising the artist's oceanic vision.

'Got you, you fucker,' breathes the device-bearer of Sir Bedivere. Even the gun's quite visible now, along with the hand that holds it, though from side-on they'd still be concealed by the cloak's wide sleeve.

This means, of course, that the gun is now being pointed at the Knight, who hurriedly brings up the shield as another shot rings out around the room.

A Circle riot-shield can stop a bullet, but those tiny bastards have a lot of momentum. The shield bucks in the Knight's stinging hands as the scarlet gonfanon emblem crazes and scars.

The Knight has a location now, though, and diving forward, slashes out with the sword as where the figure's feet must be. The mural shimmers and unfocuses as the assassin dances away. Eyes fixed on the figure's location, the Knight leaps up again and thrusts, as another bullet screeches past the hardened plastic of the helmet. The Knight reels, but swings the sword again in a vicious downward arc.

The intruder's optical array goes crazy for a moment, rainbows arcing from the impact point on the sleeve as its wearer drops the weapon. The gun hits the floor by the Knight's feet as the assassin clutches the injured arm, and the

Knight swings in for another blow, this time to the indistinct blur that's the figure's nearer leg.

The Knight snatches the pistol up from the floor as the figure falls, the greens and greys of the wall chasing themselves wildly across the human shape before settling into the navy-blue of the carpet.

Too late, the Knight realises that one of the men-at-arms's Webley 2020s has at some point been kicked across the room, and has also ended up here. Specifically, it's within reach of the collapsed sniper, who's busy retrieving it in a shimmer of carpet-colour. The camouflaged sleeves fall away revealing bare arms, one of them smeared with blood, as the desperate man (because the hairy arms are clearly male) raises the weapon towards the Knight's visored face.

'Oi!' yells a voice, and Sergeant-at-Arms Thackett is standing in the doorway, Webley in hand. At once the hands move and the floor hazes as the assassin starts to roll again, bringing the borrowed firearm to bear against this new threat.

Without a moment's thought, the Knight discharges the sniper's weapon into the centre of the indistinct figure, then kicks the gun out of his hands as his camouflage rig strobes violently and goes offline.

Now clearly visible in a silvery-grey cloak that shimmers like fish-skin, the figure shrieks and convulses, then lies still, twitching slightly.

Thackett reholsters his own weapon, wiping his brow. He nods his thanks to his armoured superior, who pants 'Christ on a bike,' to the room at large.

The Centre staff are moving now, checking up on the fallen men-at-arms – one of them clearly dead – and the device-bearer of Sir Lucan, who's still breathing. A greeter runs to get the first-aid box. On the way out she passes Sir David Stafford, slightly out of breath himself. He stops and takes stock, slightly stunned at the chaos that's surrounding him.

'Laing?' he asks, seeing Bedivere's shield.

'Yes, sir,' the Knight replies. She removes her helmet and

her hair flops, slick with sweat, down the gorget and backplate of her armour. 'Bloke was armed, sir,' she reports. 'Wearing a bloody impressive camouflage rig. Good shot, too – I'd say he had a device, although it'll be difficult to confirm now. He killed Stavers, sir, wounded Johnny and Bryce. If we hadn't checked, he could've sat quiet while everyone came in and sat down, then killed the Head during his speech.'

'Good work,' Stafford says. The assassin's stopped twitching now, and blood is seeping slowly out from his body to purple the carpet. The Seneschal's eyes narrow as he takes in the gun in his Knight's hand. 'You didn't *shoot* him, did you, Laing?'

Projectile weapons are for men-at-arms (including women-at-arms, these days, but the Circle's old-fashioned enough to stick to the familiar terminology). Knights of the Circle fight face-to-face, in full and open view of their opponent: they use swords and shields, or lances when mounted; or failing that, whatever other contact weapon may come to hand.

'Bloody right I did, sir,' says Bedivere's bondswoman decisively. 'I was protecting High King Jordan, sir, remember?'

For a Knight to wield a gun, even in the direst emergency to save a life, is to invite dishonour and disgrace. It's been a matter of principle for the Circle for far longer than there have been firearms – even in Arthur's time, you wouldn't have caught a Knight of the Round Table dead shooting an arrow. That stuff was for *peasants*.

The Seneschal's illustrious predecessor would never have let this go, not for a moment.

Stafford sighs. He looks around the room – at the two dead men, at the unconscious Knight and man-at-arms, at the innocent civilian staff of the Centre who are merely relieved to be alive… and at Bob Thackett, who returns his gaze gravely.

Sir David nods to himself. His predecessor would never have allowed Laing to be acclaimed as a Knight in the first place. 'Jolly good work, Bonnie,' he tells her again.

2. SIR GALAHAD

The opening goes ahead as planned, 'out of respect' (as the High King explains) 'for Roy Stavers, the man-at-arms of the Circle who gave his life to ensure that it could.' There's not many heads of state who'd get away with that, but when the High King says it, his sincerity's clear for all to see.

Sir David Stafford doesn't get to stay, of course. The bodies have been taken back to the morgue at Kelliwick House, the Circle's central London fortress now universally known as the Fastness; but assassination attempts – and deaths in service – are bastards for paperwork. The Seneschal will be tied up back at the office for the rest of the afternoon. He had an appointment later on, after this afternoon's festivities, but he should be able to make it still.

While he waits for his personal car and driver to collect him for the mile-and-a-half drive to the Fastness, the Seneschal gives the High King a full confidential briefing on the incident – including Bonnie Laing's coup de grace, which he otherwise intends to keep quiet. The Head of the Circle looks grave, then thoughtful. Just as the Seneschal's leaving the building, he calls him aside.

'Bonnie showed a lot of courage today,' Jory says. 'I'd like to have her on my personal staff. Can you arrange it?'

'Of course, my lord,' says Sir David. The High King has half-a-dozen Knights on continual deployment at Windsor

Castle. At present one's on permanent secondment, but most go through a regular rotation. Laing's too junior a Knight as yet to warrant a squire, which simplifies things. Stafford recalls that Laing and the Pendragon already know one another, a little: Bedivere's bondswoman grew up with the Green Chapel before she opted to join the Circle as a page a few years ago. Those of us who were there still remember thirteen-year-old Bonnie handing out bottles of homebrew at the party for Jory Taylor's first night at our encampment.

In any case... when you're as popular as High King Jordan, simple loyalty's cheap, but a Knight who'll unhesitatingly risk her honour for her sovereign bears keeping an eye on.

Slightly twitchy now at the delay, Stafford briefs Laing, telling her the full quest parameters will be waiting for her at Windsor Castle. Then he leaves for the Fastness.

In his office on the ninth floor of the central keep, filled with the sunlight that filters down through the glass roof, Sir David writes a letter to Roy Stavers' widowed father, offering the Circle's condolences for his son's loss, plus the usual peacetime death-in-service pension. This upsetting duty concluded, he emails Laing her standing orders, then contacts one of the Circle's secular advisors on devicial matters and sets him to analysing the afternoon's shenanigans.

A full afternoon of admin later, the Seneschal emerges from the Fastness with a nod to the men-at-arms on door duty, just as the streets are filling up with freed office-workers rushing to pubs, shops or trains and buses home. He lets the throng pull him along the south bank of the Thames, past London Bridge and the Globe, the Tate Modern and the Oxo Tower, and passes the Southbank Centre a little after the High King's limousine has departed once more, in convoy with Laing and her fellow Knights. After passing the National Theatre and the Royal Festival Hall, Stafford climbs the stairs to Hungerford Bridge and crosses the Thames, strolling up Northumberland Avenue to Charing Cross.

Deep in thought, the Seneschal enters Trafalgar Square, the site of the first battle in the War of the Devices – in which David Stafford, caught up in the chaos of that time like everybody else, fought on the Green Chapel's side against many of the men he now commands. He's been here many times since then, of course, and has become desensitised to its associations. When he's distracted, as he is today, he can walk through the square and barely hear the shrieks and sobs of the crowd, the rhythms of charging hooves and discharging machine-guns, the bellows and defiant choruses of 'The Green Flag'. The David who rallied the Chapel protestors here, the man who temporarily forsook the device of Sir Galahad for that of Richard the Lionheart returned from the Crusades, is a distant memory to the Seneschal – even if the flagstones still show the scars from that day, and Landseer's bronze lions bear its bullet-tracks.

Sir David pauses briefly to gaze up at Anthony Gormley's statue of Big Jack Bennett, now permanently installed on the fourth plinth. A towering, stylised figure in bronze, half-crouched, its quarterstaff raised in defiance of the admiral, king and generals on their own column and podia, it's a fitting tribute to the spirit of Little John's ally, who died that day within spitting distance of this very spot. Stafford imagines that Jack himself would have considered it a poncy pile of shite.

A separate memorial in the centre of the promenade in front of the National Gallery lists the names of those who perished in the battle – Chapel, Circle and civilians listed alphabetically, with no note made of their allegiance. Even the neo-fascist Saxon Shieldsmen who decided to pick that day for suicide-by-opposing-army are honoured here, because, as the High King said when dedicating it, 'Why should we extend division into death?' It's exactly what they wouldn't have wanted, and for many people that's enough.

Sir David heads north, through Leicester Square and the heraldic reds and golds of Chinatown, and into Soho, where he makes his way purposefully through a maze of backstreets, past coffee-shops and sushi-bars, sex shops and start-ups, to reach a particular bar on a particular corner. In the window, a lean and sly-looking man sits, older than Stafford's fifty years. He's reading a magazine and nursing a vodka, but when he sees Stafford he looks up and smiles a predatory smile. With a nervous glance across the street, the Seneschal sits down next to him.

They talk, but not for long.

* * *

In a darkened room in a sleazy hotel across the street, a man named Harding Steele is waiting for David Stafford, armed only with his tablet, a muscular henchwoman and the persuasive power of the almighty dollar.

Steele is twenty-three, an MIT electronic engineering and computer science graduate from New Haven, Connecticut, and he's one of those non-domestic threats I was telling you about. He's in the UK under the auspices of the Founding Frontiersmen, the United States' own homegrown devicial order – although unlike their more chivalric counterparts in Britain, Ireland and France, they prefer the term 'agency'. Legally and constitutionally they're an organ of the US Government, just as the Circle in the UK has always enjoyed Crown protection, but they're no more answerable to the public, and if anything they're even more secretive, than the CIA.

There are also fewer of them. While the legends of Paul Revere, Davy Crockett, Wyatt Earp and their ilk haven't stood the same tests of time as those of the Round Table, they've certainly persisted to the present day. Still, a certain parochial paranoia – exacerbated, perhaps, by their formal inception as a Government agency during the first years of the Cold War – has always prevented the Frontiersmen from harnessing the rich resources of African-American, Hispanic or Native American folklore. Accordingly, their philosophy and demographic are still as conservative in US terms as the old-school Circle was under Sir Charles Raymond.

Steele's own primary may be an upstart compared with

the likes of Daniel Boone and Paul Bunyan, but it's one that gained a certain amount of traction during the twentieth century – and that's uniquely suited, or so the agency's bosses believe, to handle the Frontiersmen's interests (which are, it goes without saying, those of the American people) in twenty-first-century New Arthurian Britain.

The King Arthur device is not only more powerful in archetypal terms than any other active in the world at present, but its unique position as de facto head of state gives it an influence on global politics quite out of proportion to Britain's usual enfeeblement on the world stage. The Frontiersmen's chief problem with this – and they aren't unique in finding it difficult to get their heads around – is that despite operating as an absolute monarch, advised but not ruled by Parliament, High King Jordan's actual agenda in power has been progressive, liberal, at times even approaching socialist. The fact that this programme has actually been working rather well, and enjoys widespread popular support, is to the Frontiersmen a particularly dangerous species of anathema.

Add in the vexed issue of Arthur's historical claim to the island of Ireland (and to Brittany, although the French can take care of themselves as far as the Frontiersmen are concerned) and it's fair to say that not only the USA but several of Britain's nearer neighbours are checking the news more nervously these days. Which is why the Frontiersmen are keen to do anything they can to make High King Jordan's behaviour more predictable and compliant.

In addition to his technical skills, Harding Steele's a student of popular versions of the Arthurian myth, from Lerner and Loewe's *Camelot* to Disney's *The Sword in the Stone* – he'd never have got his current gig otherwise – and since his arrival he's been compiling extensive dossiers on the holders of the primary Arthurian devices in the UK.

Some he's had to dismiss. Dr Malory Wendiman, the long-term girlfriend of the pre-Pendragon Jory Taylor who's now believed to bear the Morgan le Fay device, vanished at the time of her ex's Stonehenge apotheosis, and has surfaced only once, and briefly, since then. Despite his best efforts, Steele's been unable to trace her. Sir Charles, David Stafford's predecessor as Seneschal of the Circle, still bears the device of Arthur's foster-brother Sir Kay but is now retired: his influence at Windsor is minimal. And since Taylor so far refuses to marry, the promisingly unfaithful figure of Queen Guinevere seems to be out of the picture for the time being.

This by Steele's reckoning leaves four key Arthurian players in British public life, aside from the High King himself: Bernard Maddox, the avatar of Merlin and one of Taylor's closest advisors; Paul Parsons, the device-bearer of Sir Lancelot, who started out as Taylor's squire and has a cult following among the UK's many chivalry fans; Jason Smith, a former aspirant to the Pendragon device who's now content to hold the device of Sir Gareth, and acts as the High King's personal envoy; and the Circle's current Seneschal, Sir David Stafford.

Maddox and Smith have criminal records dating to their respective times with the Green Chapel, but since joining the Circle they've kept themselves clean. Their histories are known to the High King – who was himself affiliated with the Chapel, after all, and committed a number of criminal acts you don't hear so much about these days – and don't seem to be an issue. Although Steele's primary has a particular antipathy towards Merlin, there's not a great deal to work with there.

Parsons is a sore loser with his own questionable taste in girlfriends, but High King Jordan arranged some kind of device-based therapy for him after he suffered a breakdown years ago, and his loyalty to the man doesn't seem to have wavered since. Again, if Guinevere was in the picture Lancelot's loyalty might be easier to compromise, but Steele has to work with what he's got.

Which leaves Stafford. His history's equally complex: a Knight since the age of twenty-two, his rebellion against the Circle came after a quest ordered by Raymond led to the death of his secret homosexual lover ten years ago. This is particularly interesting to Steele because, as Galahad's bondsman, Stafford is supposed to derive enhanced abilities from his celibacy.

Though openly gay these days, Stafford has seemingly stuck to this ascetic regime since the newly-created Pendragon appointed him Seneschal – but in Steele's view, a man who can enter into a clandestine same-sex affair once can do it again. And while Steele personally finds the stuff queers get up to in bed together kind of disgusting, it's the 'clandestine' part of this that interests him.

* * *

Ten minutes after Stafford's meeting with the guy in the bar, Steele watches on his tablet via a feed from the lobby CCTV, as the Seneschal checks in with a much younger man, an effeminate pretty-boy in his early twenties. The black Brit on reception doesn't register surprise or disapproval as she books them both into a room on the first floor, or as she takes their room service order for champagne.

'Classy,' opines Steele. The female bouncer he recruited outside a local bar the night before, in return for a great deal of Frontiersman money, grunts her disinterest. She's about Stafford's age, burly with close-cropped grey hair. She looks ex-military, but definitely not officer material.

A moment later, whispers and giggles tell Steele that the men have arrived on their floor. If the receptionist has done her job, they'll be in the room opposite. And if the elderly pimp who Steele added to the payroll months ago has done *his* job, the hustler he's set him up with will be getting down to business right away.

The hardest part, of course, was setting Stafford up for this – getting him the pimp's contact details in a way he wouldn't suspect, along with a personal recommendation emphasising the man's discreetness. It took a closeted Member of Parliament, a favour from his Mossad handler and hacked seating plans for the Lord Mayor's banquet to arrange that – but so far Stafford doesn't seem to have suspected a thing.

A minute after the lovers have gone into their room, a maid turns up with the champagne. She hands it over, face utterly impassive even as Sir David hands her a substantial tip, then as he closes the door she crosses and raps quietly at the door of the room where Steele's sitting.

The bouncer opens it. 'You got it in there,' Steele observes as she closes the door. 'Good girl.' His tablet's now showing a view of the room from inside the champagne bottle, tinged green and subtly distorted by the curved glass, but otherwise as clear as HD. 'We're doing great so far.'

'Is good,' the maid says. Her accent's heavily eastern European. 'I go back working now?'

'Not just yet, sweetheart,' Steele replies. He doesn't want anyone talking to anybody until this is in the can. He's wary enough about trusting the sister on reception, but someone needs to intercept the room's outbound calls. He doesn't want Stafford getting spooked and calling the cops – or worse still, his loyal Knights. 'No, you sit quiet for now. I've squared it with your boss.'

Expression neutral, the maid sits down on the bed.

On the screen, the two green-tinted men are kissing and peeling off each other's clothes. Steele laughs gleefully, then, realising it came out a bit high-pitched, corrects it to something a bit more masculine. 'This is what we came here for, all right,' he gloats. 'Goddamn fags,' he adds for clarity's sake, in case either of the women thought he was enjoying this in a personal capacity.

It's quite clear Stafford's taken the bait, and damn the consequences. Steele guesses an English public-school education will do that for you.

'They no breaking law,' the maid observes neutrally.

'Aye,' the bouncer says, her disapproval evident.

Steels glares at them, displeased. 'I don't recall asking for your opinions, ladies. But since you bring it up, I think that High King Jordan would like to know one of his senior

24

government officials has been visiting queer prostitutes, don't you?' He gestures at the screen, where the couple are now getting it on in earnest. 'Yeah, I reckon he'd like to know about *that*. I'm doing this country a public service.'

The women refrain from offering any further reactions. On screen, the silent figures lick and pump and thrust.

Half an hour of repetitive viewing later, there's a pause in the proceedings, and the room phone rings. 'They've called for tea,' the receptionist relays brightly.

'You're up.' Steele grins at the maid. 'Go get it from the kitchen. When you come back up, we'll be right there behind you.'

* * *

The men are wearing matching dressing-gowns and finishing off the champagne as the maid enters the room. The Seneschal looks up in alarm as Steele and the bouncer follow.

'What —' he says. 'What are you d-doing here?'

'Why, Sir David,' Harding Steele tells him nonchalantly, 'I reckon High King Jordan may soon be asking you that self-same question.' He holds up the tablet and gives Stafford the benefit of a few seconds' playback. 'All backed up, of course,' he adds as Stafford weighs up the option of grabbing the tablet from him. 'Great performance you gave there, Carl,' he adds with a nod at the hustler.

'C-Carl?' stammers the Seneschal. 'You t-told me your name was Bruce!'

'Yeah. Sorry about that, big boy,' Carl/Bruce shrugs, and pours himself a cup of tea.

'A lot of things aren't quite how they seemed, Sir David,' Steele says. 'Hey — since we're going to be real good friends, how about I call you Dave?'

'What do you want?' Sir David asks, his face hard now. 'I've got money. Not the sort of money you're p-probably imagining, but some. Is that it? Is that what you want?'

'Oh no, Dave.' Steele's enjoying himself now. 'That

would make this whole thing go away. That's not going to be an option, not for quite some time.'

'What, then?' Stafford's still trying to figure it out. It would be cute, Steele thinks, if it wasn't so pathetic. 'It's obvious you've got a device. You wouldn't have been able to take me in otherwise. So who is it? Someone known for their cunning, I suppose, and their ingenuity.'

'Oh yeah,' Steele gloats. 'I've got a "device" all right. It's custom-built for outfoxing people like you, Sir Dave. Getting one up on the fusty old Brits by superior Yankee knowhow is pretty much the name of the game.' The Seneschal slumps back in despair, so he carries on. 'It's an old story you may have heard of. They've made a movie or ten out of it. Keep changing the plot, mind, and the central figure. One minute he's an astronaut, the next he's a black schoolgirl. You might have heard of some old writer called Mark Twain? And a little book he wrote called *A Connecticut Yankee in King Arthur's Court*?'

The Seneschal groans. 'Of course. A modern-day American ends up in King Arthur's court and outwits everybody. The details keep changing, but the central idea remains the same. It's young even by American standards, but it could be a d-device all right. And it's just the sort of vainglorious boasting the Founding Frontiersmen love.'

'Hey, Dave.' Steele's voice is abruptly harsh. 'Don't go badmouthing the Frontiersmen, hey? You work for us now, and don't you forget it.'

There's silence for a moment as Sir David sits up straight. 'Thank you, Mr Steele,' he says. 'That's what we needed to confirm.'

The maid (who's stronger than she looks) and the bouncer (who's exactly as strong as he imagined) grab Harding Steele from behind.

* * *

Thirty seconds later, he's being held down in a chair by the bouncer.

'I've called her,' the tall black receptionist tells them, coming into the room followed by the disreputable old pimp. 'How'd it go then, Ron?'

'Amazing,' grins Carl/Bruce/Ron, and Sir David looks abashed all over again.

'You're telling me this has *all* been a sting?' Steele's incredulity is epochal. 'And you're *all* in on it? Fuck me sideways.'

'We were in on it before it even started, kiddo,' says the pimp. Whereas before his accent was deepest London, it's now a husky Anglo-Californian hybrid. 'We figured a while back that Dave here might look a tempting target for some of the less LGBT-friendly elements of the international intelligence community. We've been watching out for signs someone was planning to set him up.'

'What we really wanted to know,' Stafford supplements crisply, 'was *who*. And that you were kind enough to tell us. Rather shoddy espionage protocol, if you don't mind me saying so.' There's no sign of his stammer now.

'You can't prove anything –' Steele begins, but the maid's produced a tablet of her own. *'Don't go badmouthing the Frontiersmen, hey? You work for us now,'* says Steele's voice from the speaker.

'You made it very easy for us, Mr Steele,' the maid tells him. Her English is perfect, with only the faintest hint of an accent.

'Aye, you're an idiot as well as a homophobic dickhead,' the bouncer, whose Glaswegian tones haven't changed in the slightest, concurs. She gives his shoulders a painful squeeze, then figuring he's sufficiently surrounded for escape not to be an option, steps aside and slips an arm round the maid's waist.

Steele rallies slightly. 'OK. Let's talk, then. I uploaded that footage, don't forget. I don't check in, my bosses will know where to look for it. And the High King will still be pretty interested to see his Seneschal romping with a rent-boy, aren't I right?'

'Rent-boy,' muses Ron/Bruce/Carl. 'That's flattering, that is. I've not got called *that* for a good few years.'

'You'd need to talk to our Eric about that,' the receptionist tells Steele. 'He hacked into your camera and fed it a bunch of false images. He had David and Ron's faces, he had the layout of the room, and gay porn's not exactly hard to find, like. The lads here had to make sure they were dressed right – to start off with, at any rate – but that were all.'

'So no-one'll ever know what really happened in this room this last half-hour.' The old pimp cackles at Sir David, who goes bright red. 'What your bosses have, though, is *faked* footage of the Seneschal of the Circle fucking a prostitute. *We* have a record of every stage of the faking process. So, you leak yours and we'll leak ours. It won't be Dave who comes out looking like a jerk.'

Steele is aghast again. 'But… shit, how did you guys pull this off? Hank Morgan – my primary –'

'That'll be this Yankee fella, aye?' asks the bouncer. ''Cause I never read that book.'

'It's not bad,' the pimp concedes judiciously. 'Lampoons the Arthurian myths pretty good. Before the Pendragon came back, it'd have been just our kind of thing.'

In general, devices have to work hard to interact with those of another culture: finding common assumptions, matching up archetypes, adapting or integrating so that their narrative gears mesh. Hank Morgan, though, was created in the context of Arthurian legend, albeit viewed from another country's perspective. Today's operation was pretty much what he was made for; he just wasn't up to the job.

'Oh, stop keeping the poor lad in suspense, Rev,' laughs the receptionist. 'Just tell him.'

'There's nothing wrong with your primary, kid,' the man called Rev tells Steele. 'And if it had been *just* King Arthur's court you were up against… well, let's just say that's a fight I'd have paid to see. But it wasn't. You made the same mistake a lot of other people have.'

Steele groans. 'Fuck me,' he says again. 'You're the Green Chapel. Everyone thinks you guys disbanded after the war.'

'That's the way the High King likes it,' Rev agrees mildly.

Sir David obviously feels its time to reassert his authority. 'You see, the Green Chapel operate under a different remit from the Circle,' he tells Steele. 'The High King restricts their public profile, so he can keep them in reserve. When a foreign agent – or a domestic criminal – thinks they're going up against King Arthur and the Knights of the Round Table, they have certain expectations. The Chapel can confound those.'

'Yeah, Robin Hood's Merry Men are tricksters, criminals and dirty fighters,' says Rev, 'not paragons of chivalry like Sir Galahad and his pals. That fits us pretty neatly for this kind of work.'

'OK,' says Steele. 'So what's the process here? What happens next? You want me to spy on the Frontiersmen for you, is that it? I can do that, sure – if the price is right. I've had enough of those assholes anyway, thinking they're better than me because my primary's fictional and wasn't around for the War of Independence.'

'It's a kind offer,' says Sir David, 'but the High King prefers not to employ traitors. Partly out of principle, partly because it's not a very clever thing to do.'

'Plus,' says Rev, 'and don't take this the wrong way, your ally's kind of an asshole too.' The receptionist chuckles.

Stafford continues, 'No, you'll be processed through the standard criminal channels, I'm afraid. Blackmail, conspiracy, espionage, failure to declare a mythic device – between them, they should add up to a good few years in prison.'

There's a peremptory knock at the door, and Stafford and Rev shout 'Come in!' simultaneously, before exchanging an exasperated glance. Outside stand two uniformed officers of the Metropolitan police.

'Sergeant Jenkins,' says one of them to Steele. 'Device

Squad. I'm afraid I'm going to have to ask you to come with us.'

* * *

Leaving the Seneschal to get dressed, the Chapel people retire downstairs, where the real hotel staff are at their posts once more. They repair to the bar, Ron unselfconscious in his dressing-gown, and order drinks on their civil service expense account.

'It's grand to see you, Rev,' says the erstwhile receptionist – in actuality Janene Long, Big Jack Bennett's successor as the ally of Little John. 'It's been a while.'

Rev Cantrell, the avatar of Robin Hood's fat, bald friend Friar Tuck, acknowledges this with a gracious tilt of his gin. He's as thin as a whippet, with a pretty good head of hair for his age.

'You sticking around this time, aye?' the bouncer asks bluntly. Her name's Scar, and she's inherited the plain speaking of her ally, Will Scarlet.

'There's going to be a party later,' the maid adds, resting a hand lightly on her girlfriend's shoulder as she comes back from the ladies. 'Back at the camp.' Zara is the ally of the Saracen, the variously-named Muslim outlaw in Robin Hood's band.

'There's always a party back at the camp,' Cantrell grins. Then he adds regretfully: 'No, amigos, no can do. I'm getting a ride to Windsor with David.' Although he doesn't appear in public, Rev is at the High King's side more than ever these days, advising and encouraging him. 'Now we've finally got proof the Founding Frontiersmen are moving against us, HK's going to want to talk things over – and Dave says there was an incident at the Southbank Centre opening, too. An assassination attempt. It's been a busy day for enemies of the Pendragon.'

Janene's eyes widen. 'Assassination? Is HK OK?'

'Sure he is,' Cantrell reassures her. 'In fact it was Bonnie who got the bastard.'

'That's our girl,' says Scar.

Rev nods approvingly. 'But he was using some kind of high-grade military gear. Could be the Frontiersmen again.'

'Well, all that's beyond our pay scale, innit?' Ron Byron says. (His ally's Much the Miller's Son, if you're keeping a spreadsheet.) 'We just miss you, Rev. We could do with you back with us sometimes. "You can't have a Chapel without a holy man", isn't that accurate?'

Rev shrugs ruefully. 'The High King says "jump", you don't ask for a parachute. I miss the parties, too. Things used to be different, we all know that. But HK needs us all to play our parts, and today shows why.'

Ron smirks. 'Well, I reckon he'll appreciate *my* part. 'Cause David did.'

And the conversation moves on to other topics.

3. ELAINE OF CORBENIC

There's something about perfectly straight roads that people in authoritarian cultures get off on. The Romans started it off, of course, imposing the geometrical perfection they learned from the Greeks across the landscapes they conquered, their highways radiating out from Rome like the arms of the crosses they used in their executions. Before they arrived in these parts, everyone wanted labyrinths, preserving the prestige of the destination through secrecy and concealment. To the Neolithic Britons, power lay in inaccessibility.

The Romans, like Americans today, understood that straight lines reinforce authority, making it seem inevitable. Where you can see where you're going for miles ahead, the thought of going somewhere else feels like an aberration, a whim you consider but quickly discard. A long straight road with a palace at the end of it – or a Capitol, or a vast domed Volkshalle designed by Albert Speer – is a subliminal message that the people who occupy those buildings aren't going anywhere, that their dominance is as unavoidable as their workplace.

It's early evening by the time the High King's motorcade turns off the M4, to coast along through Windsor Great Park, eventually turning off onto the Long Walk, the three-mile dead-straight path which leads north to Windsor Castle. (And south to... well, a large hillock with an equestrian statue of George III on top of it. That end's not the important one.) They drive between regimented rows of chestnut and plane trees towards the main gates of the castle. It glows rosily in the sunset as they approach, the gold-and-blue Pendragon banner fluttering from the flagpole on the twelfth-century Round Tower.

This royal residence has loomed above the little town of Windsor for a thousand years, its solid walls and squat turrets – and the gothic windows and Georgian chimneys which show its more recent architectural modifications – utterly dominating the local landscape. For centuries – and especially since it became literally true in the early twentieth – this castle's name has been synonymous with Britain's ruling dynasty. High King Jordan's residence here is as potent a symbol of what's changed in Britain since the Pendragon Settlement as the restoration of the common land, the conversion of Regent Street into social housing, or the repurposing of Kensington Palace into an exclusive – and massively lucrative – state-owned tourist hotel.

The walls of the Upper Ward stretch wide as Bonnie Laing and the other outriders approach the castle proper, and the towers flanking the entrance gate stretch high towards the sky. There's no need for an honour guard here at the High King's home, but Bonnie and the other Knights dismount and stand respectfully by while they wait for the Pendragon to get out of his Bentley.

'Good luck with the new quest, Laing,' Amal Samadi, Sir Safir's bondswoman, says. She lowers her voice out of respect rather than nervousness – the Pendragon's not known for standing on ceremony, except when the occasion warrants it. Her voice betrays no sign of any jealousy at Bonnie's prestigious new appointment.

'Yeah, cheers.' Bonnie's sincere enough, but she doesn't really know what to expect. Is she here as a security guard, or a domestic servant, or a royal envoy – what? The Knights who've been assigned to this gig in the past have always come back tight-lipped about the goings-on at the royal residence. Which is as it should be, of course.

She adds, 'Hey, tell Johnny to get well from me, OK?' Sir Lucan's device-bearer's awake and stable, according to the doctors at St Thomas's, and likely to be moved soon to the Circle's recuperative facility on the Norfolk coast. Andy and Amal will be visiting him when they get back to London.

'Quiet now,' admonishes Jerry Transom, the older Knight assigned from the Fastness to take Johnny's place on the homeward run, as the High King emerges from the limbo of his limo.

He walks past them, absent-mindedly tapping at a tablet as he goes, until he remembers them and turns. The men-at-arms following him stop obediently.

'Thank you all,' he tells the Knights, with luminous sincerity. His eyes flick down to the screen for a moment. 'Andrew, Amal – I'm grateful for your courage today. If you'd been the ones to meet our friend back at the Centre, I know I could have relied on you.'

'My lord.' The Knights in question accede to this, hiding whatever private doubts they may have about it.

'Good to see you, Jerry.' The Head nods at Transom, but doesn't have any especial praise for his outrider skills. Then, 'Bonnie – you're with me, I believe?'

Laing swallows. 'Yes, my lord.'

'That's good. Come on, then,' he instructs her, and sweeps away quickly through the gates.

With a quick wave of farewell to her friends, Bonnie follows her monarch into the castle.

* * *

Seven years and a couple of months ago, Jory Taylor stood in an entirely different royal residence. It had been two days since the Stonehenge Summit, and the High King's new order was still asserting itself. The Queen, who'd reluctantly retreated to weather the civil war at Balmoral in the Highlands, had returned to Buckingham Palace the moment peace broke out.

Technically Jory could have summoned her to meet him at his temporary headquarters in Salisbury, but bossing around a ninety-year-old woman didn't seem like the best way to start his reign, so instead he made the journey to London, in an RAF Chinook the Circle had requisitioned some months previously. He came to the palace direct from a hastily-recalled Parliament, whose vote to accept his claim to sovereignty had been passed near-unanimously, only a handful of die-hard republicans respectfully dissenting.

She received him in the throne room, beneath a gilded ceiling hung with a chandelier like an interstellar spacecraft. The satin walls and perfect double-glazing muffled the sounds of the crowd who stood beyond the railings at the front of the building, some of whom had travelled up from Salisbury ahead of the High King's arrival.

She sat on the throne atop its podium, red velvet drapes her backdrop, a frail old lady with a crown pressing down on her head and the weight of a scarlet train and of a nation on her back. She was supported by loyal Scots Guards, alert for any sudden moves on the part of the newcomer or his supporters.

For symbolism's sake, High King Jordan had entered flanked by a fully-armoured Knight of the Circle – Theo Harte, recently Sir Charles Raymond's adjutant, trying desperately not to fidget – and a green-hooded follower of the Green Chapel. I'd argued that the latter should be me, since I'd be able to recount the historic meeting afterwards, but Jory had felt that this particular meeting shouldn't be minuted. Instead he'd picked Janene Long, who provided not only gender and ethnic balance but an intimidating amount of tallness (and who proved exceedingly garrulous about the whole occasion when I plied her with Lambrusco later).

He approached the throne steadily, calmly, the enormity of the occasion causing him no obvious nervousness. He had a suit on, but not an expensive one: as yet he had no official crown, but wore a makeshift construction one of the Chapel's camp followers had hurriedly pliered together from copper, gold and silver wire. It had looked pretty cool in a battlefield context, but it could hardly compete with the jewel-encrusted, orb-surmounted, silver-purple-ermine construction the elderly monarch wore.

He stood before her throne and did not bow.

'Mr Taylor, we believe,' the monarch told him. She looked every year of her age.

'Two days ago that would have been correct, your majesty,' he replied. 'Since then I've been bound to the Pendragon device, and acclaimed as the High King of all the lands of the Britons. Since that territory includes the modern United Kingdom, I'm here to claim your fealty, according to the ancient compact between the Crown and the Circle.'

There was a stately, pregnant pause.

'The compact of which you speak,' the Queen replied carefully, neither acknowledging nor repudiating his correction, 'was made long before the Crown, the United Kingdom, or even England existed in their present forms. None of one's family were involved in its institution. Why should we or our subjects be bound by such an agreement now?'

She'd been rehearsing this, of course. Since the emergence of the first Pendragon pretender nine months previously, she'd known that a day like this might come – if, indeed, her kingdom hadn't disintegrated utterly before it was reached. She couldn't seriously think after all this time that a status quo without the newly-emerged High King could be achieved.

'Because I can bring peace,' he replied, biting back the monosyllable his tongue tried automatically to append. *Your majesty* was a factual description, but a *ma'am* would imply a power relationship, and not in his favour. 'As the Circle has done on a smaller scale for the whole of your reign, and the fourteen centuries preceding it.'

She inclined her head, graciously conceding his point. 'We

respect the Circle's traditions and beliefs, and we understand that these are extraordinary times. We're grateful for your efforts in calming the storm. The Circle has provided loyal service to this country for many generations, and it is our hope that you will continue to serve us all.'

That was her angle, then. She knew the Pendragon's ascendancy was inevitable, but she still hoped to make Jory subservient to her, rather than vice versa. To make him her regent, her viceroy, her general – rather than her High King and her rightful liege lord.

'I'll serve,' he said, 'as every monarch serves his or her people. As you have served throughout your reign. I will serve them, but I will not serve you. I must be High King in title and reality, or the name "Pendragon" is meaningless. And I must ask you to call me "my lord".'

'"My lord?"' she repeated, lips pursed. 'No, I don't think so.'

She felt the power of his device, of course – must do, because for all her unique status she belonged as much to the culture of the nation, partook as much of its collective unconscious, as any of her subjects. More so, perhaps. For her, as much as for the schoolboy Jory Taylor who'd eagerly devoured the works of TH White and Rosemary Sutcliff twenty years earlier, King Arthur was an archetype of unparalleled potency. Standing up to his avatar in this way must have taken enormous willpower.

But then, of course, she'd known a great many kings, some of them in her immediate family.

She said, 'I've read your file, Mr Taylor. The staff who remain at MI5 were kind enough to supply it to me. You're a commoner, are you not? Your father used to be some kind of sports coach, I believe, while your mother works at a library. There's not a drop of noble blood in your family, let alone royal blood.'

He nodded. 'You're right. I've never claimed sovereignty in my own right – nor even, as you say, nobility. I was a Knight once, but even that feels like a long time ago now. I've been called a thief and a domestic terrorist and a murderer, none of them without justification. I certainly betrayed the Circle, which means betraying the Crown. For two years I was an outlaw. None of this has any bearing on my claim by virtue of the device of King Arthur Pendragon, who evidently isn't choosy.

'Your personal wealth,' he told her, 'which I'm told is enormous, is none of my concern. You'll retain the title of Queen over the United Kingdom. Your son and his descendants will still inherit. I haven't the least interest in the Commonwealth – you'll still be sovereign over Canada, Australia, New Zealand and the rest, or rather that choice will be for them to make. All I ask is that, in your capacity as monarch of the UK, you defer to me as High King – as your ministers of state have already agreed to do.

'Oh – and I'll be taking some of the Crown holdings,' he added, 'including the royal art collection and the Duchies of Cornwall and Lancaster. I don't think that's especially unreasonable.'

For a long time there was silence in the throne room. Then the Queen said quietly, 'Some people think I lack practical skills. They consider me a figurehead. I used to be a lorry driver, you know.'

Jory tried not to show his startlement. 'I didn't know that,' he offered warily.

'You think I'm going dotty, I dare say. But it's true.' Her crown bobbed with her nod. 'I served with the Women's Auxiliary Territorial Service during the War.' For her, unlike most of her subjects, *the War* still meant World War II. 'They trained me up. I was rather good at it. One sometimes wonders whether, in another life, one mightn't have made a proper go of it.'

She stood. 'Come with me, Mr Taylor,' she said. An unobtrusive footman and maid relieved her of the crown and robe of state, and she led the way, slowly but with dignity, out of the throne room.

Jory followed, Janene and Theo coming after with the

Scots Guards, as she led him through arched doorways and portrait-hung corridors, past statues on pedestals and ormolu clocks, between gilded mirrors and marble pillars, into a room startlingly decorated in Oriental style – or at least a Regency attempt to approximate it. The paintings here were of mandarins and other people in Chinese dress, and porcelain and lacquer were much in evidence. Golden dragons adorned the ceiling, while a stone one was carved into the mantelpiece. The Pendragon chose to take this as an auspicious sign.

The noise of the crowd was louder here, and Jory realised with a jolt that they were at the front of the palace, facing the Mall. Indeed, as two Scots Guards stepped forward and unlocked a pair of French windows set between two massive vases, he understood suddenly which room this was.

'Shall we?' the Queen asked, as the guardsmen opened the door and stepped out, ready to protect their monarch.

The crowd outside were ordinary Londoners, their numbers swollen into tens of thousands by the visitors from the camps at Salisbury, and by those from all over the country who had followed the rumours and broadcasts in the hope of seeing history made. There were Circle and Chapel veterans, Britons from all nations and of all ethnicities, manual labourers and City stockbrokers, babies in slings and pensioners older than the monarch herself. Their voices, which had been creating an excited hubbub outside the palace now for hours, rose in pitch and volume as the doors were opened, thrilling deafeningly louder as the tiny woman and the large man appeared framed in the doors.

Jordan Taylor followed the woman who had been his sovereign out onto the balcony of Buckingham Palace, on which he had, so many times in photos and on TV, seen her and her family emerge and greet the people.

The crowd hushed at once. The Queen stepped forward and waved, and every single member of it cheered. It was a rousing cheer, relieved and triumphant, the jubilation of a people who had been through a devastating trial and found themselves strengthened by it. The sight of this woman, so long unseen except in broadcasts to the nation, invigorated and enthused them.

Then Jory stepped forward to join her.

At the sight of him the eager cheer became a full-throated yell of frenzied adulation. At first inchoate, it quickly settled into a meter, a trisyllabic chant whose single word became ever clearer as the rhythm established itself across the many thousands of voices in the crowd.

'PEN-DRAGON! PEN-DRAGON! PEN-DRAGON! PEN-DRAGON!'

From the Victoria Memorial to Admiralty Arch, the Mall – another long, straight road leading to a place of authority – rang out in praise of a Romano-British chieftain whose name was older than that of England.

The woman at the High King's side drew in a long, slow breath. She said, 'You were right to say that the monarch serves the people. And the people, it seems, have made their choice… my lord.'

And as the crowd continued to chant the name of her supplanter, the ninety-year-old woman began, very carefully, to kneel.

* * *

The room the High King's adopted as his conference chamber belongs to the private apartments in the East Wing of the Castle. It looks out across his pet building project, the New Quadrangle, which when complete will entirely enclose the seventeenth-century East Terrace, preserving all its features intact. The room itself is lavish, with intact Georgian wallpaper and chandeliers, but the High King's furnished it in modern corporate style, with a meeting-table selected for its lack of roundness, and surprisingly comfy boardroom chairs.

Pages of both genders (because Jory is a strictly equal opportunity employer) serve the assembled advisors with a simple supper and a very fine Beaujolais from the castle's labyrinthine cellars. Servants aside, those present are the

Pendragon himself; David Stafford and Rev Cantrell; Chief Superintendent Kinsey of the Device Squad, Sergeant Jenkins's boss; Merlin's bondsman Bernard Maddox, better known as 'Blaze'; Bonnie Laing; and – doing my best to pull my weight in conversation with the big boys – me.

Blaze is a black South Londoner in his late twenties, who used to be a street conjurer and retains a flamboyant taste in clothes and jewellery: he wears a silver dragon's head ring and a baggy aubergine suit from some designer you're not cool enough to have heard of. He and Rev live here, intermittently at least, their main duties being to advise the High King on mythopolitical affairs.

Stafford and Kinsey are based in London, and will be heading back there later this evening in their respective company cars. Jade Kinsey's a short, short-haired, short-tempered woman in her mid-forties, who despite continuing and heroic efforts has entirely failed to moderate her industrial-grade profanity in the presence of the monarch. Apart from the servants she's the only person here without a device; but she's been dealing with them in her professional life since a decade ago, when Jory, then bearing the shield of Sir Gawain, seriously annoyed her by beheading the bondsman of a cannibalistic giant named Retho of Arvaius on her patch.

I live here too. This would certainly have surprised my younger self, who wouldn't have known a quality Beaujolais from a Welsh table wine, and would have preferred a pint to either, but I'm the High King's official bard – the bondsman of Taliesin or ally of Alan a'Dale, whichever you prefer – and that kind of entails being on hand most of the time. My apartments in the South Wing aren't the most lavish by any means, but they're a good few steps up from a draughty tent at the Green Chapel encampment, a dank bedsit over a hardware store in Slough, or even my Auntie Ginnie's flat in Eastbourne.

Bonnie stands guard at the door, a hurried half-hour being all the time she's had to stow her gear and discover that the barracks provided for the half-dozen Knights in residence are considerably less plush.

'We've searched Brewster's house,' Kinsey's reporting. Valentine Brewster is the name her team have managed to attach to the dead assassin at the Southbank Centre: a sales executive, twenty-eight years old, no dependants, no previous. 'Textbook stuff, literally. Bastard had *Morte D'Arthur* and *Idylls of the King* on his Kindle, and a volume of post-Vulgate nicked from the UCL library. Every last bloody reference to Sir Garlon the Red bookmarked and highlighted. Doesn't get much more open-and-shut than that, sir.'

Ten years ago Kinsey had barely heard of Tennyson, let alone the Old French post-Vulgate texts, but she's, if not a quick learner, then at least a dogged one.

'Sir Garlon?' The High King tries to recall. When he was with the Circle he read avidly from the Arthurian canon, but that was years ago. These days, on the rare occasions he gets the time to read, he usually dips into a Ken Follett or an Ian Rankin. (I happen to know he's had *Arms and the Dead* on the go for a year now.) 'I assume he was…'

'Invisible. Yes,' agrees Kinsey.

'Dude could *make* himself invisible,' Blaze corrects her. 'Couldn't be "the Red" if no-one ever saw him, could he?' These days Blaze spends a lot of his time reading Arthurian texts, which again is something that would have surprised him at one time. 'Sources don't say how. But he went round killing Arthur's knights while no-one could see him. There's a bunch of other stuff about the Spear of Longinus and shit, but the headline's "Knight makes himself invisible, kills other knights". Then Sir Balin ran into him when he was visible at some party, and killed him there.'

He grins at the Knight by the door. 'Bonnie here beat that, though. She killed Brewster when she couldn't even see him.'

* * *

The first women Knights of the Circle were acclaimed during the first year after Jory's coronation as High King. Despite the fact that such a thing had never happened, despite it violating every one of the Circle's most sacred traditions, and despite the loyal but strenuous reservations of ex-Seneschal Charles Raymond and a large proportion of the existing Knights, it turned out that, if a woman went through all the usual ceremonies for an acclamation, a Knightly device would adopt her just as happily as it would have one of her male counterparts.

Seven years later female Knights are still a minority, but that's largely because the Circle's panicked over-recruitment during the War of the Devices – even given the large attrition rate the war itself imposed – hasn't left many devices to go round. As they fall free, though, a strict quota system allocates half to women, and Amal and Bonnie are part of a growing number of Britons who possess both a chivalric device and internal gonads.

Although the High King himself welcomed Kate Blackwood, the bondswoman of Sir Lamorak and the Circle's first female Knight, to her new status – indeed, she was the second of the Circle, after Jason Smith at Stonehenge, to be knighted by his own hand – he had had, as it happens, rather different plans.

Jory met Laney Wardsley during that same visit to London following the Stonehenge Summit, in an upper room at the pub near Marble Arch which he'd commissioned as his temporary headquarters. He'd sent Scar to collect her from work, with instructions to be as polite and sympathetic as she could manage – which, being Scar, wasn't overwhelmingly – and to stress to her and her employers that she wasn't in trouble.

Laney had been, over the years preceding Jory's acquisition of the Pendragon device, a student at a highly prestigious girls' boarding school, a teenage runaway, an unallied member of the Green Chapel, the girlfriend of Sir Lancelot's device-bearer Paul Parsons, and the tool used by a former secular advisor to the Circle to provoke the War of the Devices, causing the deaths of tens of thousands of British citizens and bringing the country to its knees. In these last two capacities she'd been motivated – charitably, you might say blinded – firstly by her longing for revenge against Parsons, who'd been responsible for the death of her best friend Liss Dashwood during a raid on a squat named Mystic Villas, and secondly, possibly (though the question had never been settled) by the device of Elaine of Corbenic, who Sir Lancelot saved from a boiling bath where she'd been placed by Morgan le Fay, and whose ill-starred seduction of her rescuer had provided the model for said revenge.

By the time of the Pendragon Settlement, Wardsley had been arrested by the then Chief Inspector Kinsey and charged with conspiracy and theft. Unfortunately, the conspiracy was too bound up with the workings of the devices for that fragment of the Crown Prosecution Service that remained during the war to get a proper grip on it, and with the revelation that the artefact Wardsley had 'stolen' had in fact been previously illegally appropriated from the British Museum, the trial collapsed. Laney, whose parents had never been short of a bob or two, had waited out the remainder of the civil conflict as a secretarial temp living – albeit under close Circle monitoring – in a studio flat in Chelsea.

She entered the upper room of the pub to find the Pendragon sitting in a snug directly opposite the stairs, a pot of coffee steaming on the table in front of him. She arrived indignant at being shanghaied by Scar, determined resolutely to be unimpressed by the High King's majesty, and was taken aback at once by the charisma radiating from his device.

'What –' she began, then cleared her throat. The unspoken *the hell do you want?* echoed around the room. 'What… can I do for you, your majesty?' she asked, injecting a slightly desperate sarcasm into her voice. 'Or should I still call you Dan?'

Though known to most of his friends as 'Jory', Taylor had always been 'Dan' to the Green Chapel.

Laney had always been a social chameleon, her dress sense and appearance reflecting the company she was keeping. Coming directly from work she wore a plain blouse and skirt, her hair short and well-kempt. Discreet pearl earrings were cushioned in her earlobes, while the other piercings Jory knew her face was dotted with were well concealed by foundation.

'I don't think people can do that now, Laney,' he replied with genuine regret. He made an apologetic gesture at a woman sitting behind the bar – it would be a while before being waited on came naturally to him – and she came over to pour coffee for them both. 'Leave us alone now, please,' he told her. Then, addressing himself again to Laney: '*Sir* is fine, if the other options feel over-the-top.'

Laney nodded quickly. 'OK. What was it you wanted from me then?' The lack of a final word dragged on for several seconds before she reluctantly added, '...Sir?'

The Pendragon sighed. 'Two things,' he said. 'Firstly, Laney, I want to forgive you.'

For just a moment, Laney's eyes blazed with anger and her knuckles whitened on the handle of her teacup. Then she spoke lightly again. 'That's big of you, *sir*, but you should know I stand by everything I did. Paul Parsons killed my best friend.'

The High King nodded gravely. 'I said I *wanted* to forgive you. I understand it may not be possible. What happened between you and Paul is your own business –'

'It was,' Laney interrupted fiercely, 'before you interfered. *Sir.*'

The specific form Laney's revenge on Paul had taken was that she'd tipped off certain enemies of the Circle that the Knight would be travelling alone at night to a particular location, allowing them to divert him and subject him to the form of devicial assault that's been termed a Wendiman Derangement. The subject becomes severely befuddled, distressed and volatile, and remains incapable of functioning properly for as long as their device remains affected.

In Paul's case, the newly-minted High King had been

able to arrange a form of bespoke devicial therapy, to which Parsons had responded positively, and Sir Lancelot's bondsman was on the mend. It seemed the news of this had reached his ex.

'He's suffered enough,' replied Jory firmly. 'By which I don't mean that he didn't deserve to suffer. As far as I'm concerned, though, the matter's over. I'll be telling Paul to treat it as such, and I'd appreciate it if you'd do likewise. The more important point is that your act of revenge provided the leverage for enemies of this realm to set the Circle and the Chapel at each other's throats. That conflict has injured and killed countless people who'd done you no harm at all.'

For some time Laney stared into her coffee-cup. Then she said, 'You know, I could say I didn't know that would happen. And I didn't, not at first. But I knew who I was helping, and I carried on helping them even after the war had started. Because I owed them for what they did to Paul. Like I say, Paul fucking Parsons killed Liss Dashwood. And I bloody worshipped Liss, sir.'

That time the form of address had just slipped out, and Laney looked a little startled by it. 'I don't mean...' she went on, 'it wasn't, like, you know, a gay thing. Not that I... Well. Liss may have been into that kind of thing, a little bit. I never was. But I still needed her, like she needed me. She showed me what I could have been like if I'd dared. I showed her what she'd be like if she kept her feet on the ground. We made each other... complete people, you know? We kept each other sane. Well, ish. Other friends come and go, but me and Liss... we'd have stayed together, I know it. The rest of our lives. Boyfriends, marriages, divorces; kids, grandkids; menopause, old age... till we ended up holding hands in some fucking nursing home with no idea who we were or why we were there, but knowing we had a friend there with us. *That's* what Paul *shitting* Parsons took away from me.'

She was sobbing now. The High King stood up, stepped around the table, and held her as she wept.

When at last she quietened, he said gently, 'Paul let

everyone down, that day in Bristol. He failed the Circle, and he failed himself. He failed in his duty to protect the innocent and the undeviced. He failed to keep his vows as a Knight.' He paused. 'You could show him how it's supposed to be done.'

Laney stared at him. Then she blew her nose noisily and stared some more. 'No, sorry. Haven't a clue what you're getting at.'

'You're brave,' said Jory. 'You're determined and loyal, you believe in justice, and you can certainly be ruthless. These are all qualities a Knight needs. It's true you've made mistakes, but so did many of Arthur's knights. If there's one virtue the Circle practices in abundance, it's forgiveness. I'm asking you to become the first woman Knight of the Circle.'

Laney sipped her coffee, but continued to stare at him.

If you know anything at all about Arthurian myth – and by now I'd hope you would, to be honest – you'll have spotted that the women just don't fight. It doesn't seem to have occurred to them, or to the men around them, that they could. Sure, women like Elaine of Corbenic may transgress against society's expectations of them, but it's always in ways which preserve their feminine role.

Generally, this means shagging someone other than their husbands – so, in the case of the unmarried ones, anyone at all. As often as not it's Sir Lancelot.

'You know the Chapel's allies are pretty much gender-blind,' the Pendragon reminded her. 'Scar and Zara have male allies, and so does Janene. From what I'm told, the '60s Chapel had a gay Robin and a male Maid Marian. The Paladins de la République let women become *porteuses du blason* in the late '80s. It's sort of embarrassing when the French are ahead of you in feminism.'

(As it happens, the real trailblazers in this area were the pan-Scandinavian Ragnars Synir Loðbrókar, who started letting women join in the 1950s, and elected their first female chair, the then runeholder of Ivar the Boneless, in 1972. The Sons have opened up their archives, since the existence of

47

devices became public knowledge, and living at the castle leaves me a lot of time for looking stuff up on the internet.)

'The Circle's time for equality has come,' Jory declared. 'They just need to accept the fact.'

Laney was still frowning at him, her coffee-cup forgotten in her hand.

'We never did establish whether you were carrying Elaine of Corbenic's device, I know,' said Jory. 'But we're in a time of flux. So many people have changed their devices recently. In fact, I think I might have the authority to change them by fiat. It worked with David Stafford.' It had been a word from the High King at Stonehenge which reverted David from his warlike Lionheart persona to the chivalrous Sir Galahad.

Laney blinked several times, and shook her head like a moist dog. 'Well, thank you for the offer, sir,' she said, carefully returning her cup to the table. 'And good luck with reforming the Circle. But frankly, and all due respect and so on, I wouldn't piss on them if they were on fire. You'll have to find your warrior maiden somewhere else.'

'Well, it's your choice.' The High King sighed. 'I suppose I can't really blame you. But Laney, keep in touch. I'd like to know that you're doing OK.'

And, for a while, she did.

* * *

'Not to criticise your investigative approach, Jade,' David Stafford ventures (a little diffidently, because if Kinsey decides he's having a go it's likely to prompt some choice invective), 'but could someone have planted all that reading-matter in Brewster's flat? Without the psychometric tests we can't be certain he was a device-bearer.'

'Bonnie thinks he was,' says Rev quickly. 'Isn't that right, Bonnie?'

'Um, yeah,' Bonnie says from by the door, not quite sure who she's meant to be addressing now, but disinclined to 'sir'

Cantrell, who she's known since she was nine. 'I mean, he was a really good shot...'

'Lots of people are good shots, Laing,' Stafford observes. 'And the camouflage could have been a bigger advantage than any device.'

'So what's your theory, Stafford?' Kinsey wants to know. 'You think someone set him up? Why the f... why the hell would they do that?'

'Get someone else blamed, maybe?' Rev suggests. 'Say I'm a foreign agency, or even a bunch of homegrown anti-device terrorists. Wouldn't it be smart to recruit an unallied assassin, then plant evidence to put a local device in the picture so I won't look guilty?'

Kinsey is sceptical. 'That's pretty fucking convoluted, Cantrell.'

'What can I say?' Rev shrugs. 'The Green Chapel aren't the only trickster archetypes around.'

'My lord, beg pardon and that,' says Bonnie.

The Head nods graciously. 'Go ahead, Bonnie,' he says.

She does. 'Thanks, my lord. It's not just the shooting, is it? If a normal person wanted to kill you, they'd've hid in the crowd with a gun. Lots of cover, plenty of opportunity. They'd've got caught, but it's not like Brewster was gonna get away with it either. What Brewster did? Get hold of military-grade camouflage, go and stand right where the High King's coming and just wait? That's not normal, that's making a statement – *I'm gonna kill you by being invisible*. Only someone with an ally – sorry – with a device is going to do that. Sounds to me like Sir Garlon fits the spec, my lord.'

'She's got a point,' I say, and everyone else is nodding too.

'All right. So why now?' Jory asks. 'Why did Brewster pick today to try and kill me? Was it because of David's meeting with Steele, or is that just coincidence? Is this about Scotland?'

'Scotland's got the Fianna and the Paladins pretty jumpy,' says Blaze. 'That's gonna get their friends interested too.'

It's been a decade since the question of Scotland's

independence from the UK was supposedly settled, at least for the foreseeable future; at the time, though, the UK's coming constitutional revamp under the Pendragon Settlement hardly fell into the category of 'foreseeable'. In the new context, the alternatives have changed: as well as the status quo (and, I suppose, open rebellion against their new liege lord), the Scots have the option of becoming an independent realm under the protection of the Pendragon.

This would in effect restore the old kingdom of Scotland – albeit under an elected President – and for the first time ratify Jory's claim to the title of High King, a ruler over many rulers as Arthur himself was. And it's the option fifty-four per cent of Scottish people voted for, a week ago today.

The UK deciding that its traditional head of state would now be answerable to a third party has been viewed internationally as an eccentric choice, but basically an internal matter. With Jordan Taylor made High King over two separate nations – an independent Scotland and a residual United Kingdom of England, Wales and Northern Ireland – his claims to sovereignty over the Republic of Ireland and the French historical region of Brittany would come one step closer to credibility.

And – of course – his death, with the associated question-mark over the future of the Pendragon device, would be one of a very few things that might induce the Scottish Parliament to reverse that decision. This is the main reason why relations with the Paladins de la République and the Children of Oisín, the Irish device-bearers also known as the Fianna – not to mention their allies such as the Founding Frontiersmen and the Nibelungentreue – are especially dodgy just now.

'It's not like this is even the first time,' Rev Cantrell reminds us.

* * *

In the months following Jordan Taylor's coronation, the media fawned on him like Elvis fans who'd found their hero alive and looking like he'd been cutting right back on the fried snacks.

The British press and broadcast media have always had a special relationship with royalty, sycophantic yet prurient like a dog reverently sniffing its owner's crotch, and here all at once there was a new subject for their obsequious curiosity – one about whom nothing had previously been known, and who was, if not young exactly, at least still handsome and conspicuously single. His long-term relationship with Malory 'Merry' Wendiman (formerly the Green Chapel's Maid Marian and the Circle's Lady of the Lake, but now generally considered the avatar of Morgan le Fay) had ended acrimoniously some months before his bonding to the Pendragon device, and he was generally considered fair game for speculation. A number of names were romantically linked with his that first year – including Laney Wardsley's, which may have been why she stopped meeting him – but there's one story that never made it into any news outlet.

We were staying in a hotel in Leeds, the High King and his retinue, one rainy night in September, in the late stages of an attempt to recreate the old-fashioned tradition of a 'royal progress': a kind of morale-building tour of the country, but one where all the travelling was part of the attraction rather than a behind-the-scenes detail. The Pendragon claimed – and, for the most part, had – the loyalty of Britons from Scilly to Shetland, but most of them had only seen him, only felt the power of his device-enhanced charisma, over the TV and radio. If the war-shredded nation was to rebuild itself, if was vital we cement these people's bond with their distant sovereign and his device.

At this stage his entourage was small: a couple of Knights and squires, a dozen men-at-arms, a valet (because while Jory never paid much attention to his own appearance, given his newfound status somebody had to), and me. We'd taken over a whole floor of the hotel, with the High King in a luxury suite at the end of the corridor. I was in bed at the time, so I only have the details the Pendragon told me, and I have to admit the story's oddly similar to another he told me, about a very different period of his life. Whatever the exact particulars, the incident was a startling one.

Jory was troubled by some intractable problem about deploying resources between industry sectors – he did tell me the details, but they were so dull they fell out of my head immediately, and I won't inflict them on you. The point is, he was awake well after midnight, pacing his living-room in pyjamas and dressing-gown and jabbing irritably at a tablet, lights dimmed in an effort to persuade his furiously rampaging brain that it was actually night-time.

He heard the door click open, and turned – surprised, because it was months since anyone had walked in on him without knocking – to see a woman in a long raincoat enter the room.

Her coat was wet, which suggested either that she'd just come in out of the rain or that she took a pretty unorthodox approach to showering. The former possibility was obviously more likely, and the only reason he didn't dismiss the latter out of hand was that underneath the coat she appeared to be wearing nothing at all.

'Jory,' she said. Her flame-red hair was purplish in the shadow-light, and her eyes gleamed darkly behind steel-rimmed glasses. 'It's been ages.'

It was, indeed, nearly a year since he'd seen Malory.

'You shouldn't be here,' he told her, bewildered. 'How did you even manage to get in?'

'It doesn't matter,' she said. 'Your itinerary was published weeks ago. It wasn't difficult to arrange.'

'You said I'd never see you again,' he reminded her.

'I've changed my mind,' she said. 'I thought what you were doing was stupid, yes, and hideously risky. I didn't realise how successful you were going to be. But you shouldn't be doing it alone. You need me, sweetheart. Like you always have.'

She unbuttoned her raincoat and tossed it onto a chair, confirming Jory's impression regarding her clothing choices.

Jory – who had in fact been simply too busy over the past year for anything resembling a romantic relationship, and had been feeling the lack of one quite keenly – found his breath catching in his throat.

'How does it feel?' she asked him quietly. 'To carry *that* device? To have that power surging through your psyche, overwhelming everything? Every word, every gesture, every breath an expression of majesty? To know that everything you do is right, and ordained so by God? You must be so bloody *bored*.'

She walked towards him, freckled skin pale as candlewax beneath the flame of her hair. Her body was older, of course: the first time he'd seen Malory naked, they'd been in their early twenties, and nobody stays in that springtime state forever. But the memories it stirred were easily powerful enough to cause other, more intimate stirrings.

'I want to share this with you,' she told him. 'I want to be your queen. I know –' she added, touching a finger to his lips as she planted her bare feet before his, '– that's for you to decide, not me. And you must. We've got so much to catch up on.' She reached out, took his free hand, and placed it on the cool dry skin of her hip. 'First, though – my darling Jory, I've missed you so very much…'

For just a moment, as she leaned in to kiss him, Jory seriously considered the possibility that he was dreaming and should make the most of it before she turned into a pangolin or something.

Then he thumbed the panic icon on his tablet, and the Knights came running.

Two minutes later with the lights on, the differences between Malory Wendiman and the woman now held between the armoured bondsmen of Sir Lanval and Sir Kahedins were somewhat clearer. Her face had slightly more freckles than he'd have expected of Malory at this time of year, and her upper ears had rather different whorls and ridges. The lie of her body-hair was subtly different. They'd made a creditable attempt to reproduce the mole he used to kiss on her left breast, but it hadn't quite the same beloved double-lobed shape.

'Sweetheart,' the woman said acidly, and her voice was still an eerily close match for Malory's, 'please tell the nice Knights to take their hands off me. Or at least give me my coat back, no?'

The High King nodded, and Sir Lanval's device-bearer went to fetch the woman's coat.

Immediately she dived for the sword in her other captor's scabbard, but Sir Kahedins's bondsman was too fast for her. He turned away sharply, twisting her wrist, and Jory stepped in to hold her still while the other Knight settled the raincoat around her shoulders. The Pendragon himself closed it over her chest and fastened the belt, gratefully covering up the heartbreaking facsimile.

'Who are you working for?' he asked. 'Who sent you? Was it the Paladins?' The French were, at the time, our biggest worry, making indignant diplomatic noises about the High King's overtures to the Regional Council of Britanny both through their ambassador and at the UN.

The woman glared at him. 'I'm here for myself, Jory. Myself and you. I told you that.'

'Stop that,' he told her sharply. 'You don't need to act any more.'

'Oh, for the love of –' She exhaled heavily. Her mimicry of Malory's mannerisms was uncanny. 'I can't decide whether you're suffering from Capgras Syndrome, or whether you've really become this much of an arse.' She shook her head. 'Whatever, my love – you're the High King.'

'Take her away,' Jory told his Knights. 'Lock her in one of the rooms, then call the Seneschal and ask him to send a van. We're going to get to the bottom of this.'

'You've missed your chance there,' she said caustically, and the Knights frogmarched her away.

I never saw the intruder, myself – I'd had a fair bit to drink the night before, and to be honest I slept through the whole shebang. A couple of hours later, she was gone – off in the van to the Fastness.

Except that along the way, while it was stopped at traffic lights, some bastards shot out the tyres, incapacitated the driver and guards with gas canisters and made off with the prisoner, who's never been recaptured. So I never did get the chance to have a proper look at her.

If I had… well, obviously I didn't know Merry as well as Jory did. And maybe, if she was that good an imposter, she might have fooled the rest of us as well, not just a man in an unprecedentedly pressured job desperately missing the one person who actually understood what he was going though.

It's just that… Well. I trust the High King, obviously. But on this question, he wasn't exactly in a position to be neutral. And if I'd seen her, I'd have been able to make my own judgement.

That's all.

* * *

'Our best clue to Brewster's agenda,' says David Stafford, 'may be where he got that camouflage array from. If it's American then that would point to the Frontiersmen, but I doubt they'd be quite that blatant. If it came through British military contacts, then that points to domestic terrorists. Our people are pulling it apart to find out. It's probably a prototype, but they should be able to trace the provenance of the components.'

'We're going through all his address books,' the Chief Superintendent counters. 'Brewster wasn't military – well, he was in something called the combined cadet force at school, but not since then. He belonged to a shooting range, but no-one there thought much of him. He worked in international sales for a Silicon Vale software company – that could have put him in contact with foreign agents. We pulled some photos of Paris off his phone, dated two weeks ago. There are older ones of New York, plus Amsterdam, Dubai and Madrid.'

'Well, I don't think we've annoyed the Compañeros Del Cid recently, at least,' the High King smiles. 'And I'm not sure the Emirates even have a devicial order, though they could certainly afford a freelance. Could Brewster have brought the array back in his luggage?'

David frowns. 'I doubt it. It was light enough to wear, so obviously he could have carried it, but I don't see how he could have got it through customs. It wasn't good enough for him to walk through without being seen.'

'It would be a hell of a lot easier for a company or a government,' Kinsey agrees. 'I'm guessing it was delivered to him here in the UK.'

Jory considers. 'We ought to cover all the possibilities. Jade, follow up the domestic leads, but I think we'll put a Knight on the overseas quest.'

Kinsey nods curtly, obviously not trusting herself to speak. Rev, rarely one to pass up a chance to needle a cop, chuckles, 'I guess you won't be getting that weekend in Paris, Jade.'

'With respect, my lord,' says David, 'wouldn't it make more sense to send a Green Chapel agent? The Knights aren't trained for covert work. Unless you were thinking of Jason Smith, of course.'

It's been a point of contention for some time that Jason, the bearer of the device of Sir Gareth – and David's former rival for the position of Pendragon, before Jory took that particular contest into his own hands – is on effectively permanent secondment to the High King's staff. The Seneschal respects the Head's authority, naturally, and wouldn't dream of actually objecting to the arrangement, but there's such a thing as the chain of command, which is why he brings Jason's name up now and again.

For several years Smith's been out of the loop on a top-secret quest the Pendragon assigned him, checking in with the Fastness only occasionally for assistance and to collect his salary. Jason's like Bonnie in that he joined the Circle from the Green Chapel, and in that prior life – known by his graffiti handle of 'Squig' – he was an expert burglar and spy. If any Knight has the skills to investigate the Paladins or the Frontiersmen in their own capitals, it's Jason Smith. Although I'm not sure his French is up to much.

The High King pretends to be oblivious to all of this. 'Oh, I think there are Knights who could manage it. You know your men and women better than I do, David, but who's holding the device of Sir Menw at the moment?'

I recall that Menw son of Teirwaedd was another invisible knight, but one who was on Arthur's side. He could turn an entire war-party invisible, and disguise himself as a bird. He'd be ideal for a covert quest.

Stafford nods, accepting the High King's deflection of his request. 'It's Zoe Bramwell. She's a good woman. Excellent suggestion, my lord, I'll put her onto it straight away.'

* * *

In the absence of their absconding semi-naked prisoner, the Circle's analysts didn't have a great deal to go on, but in the end, based on the High King's testimony that she'd been impersonating Malory (and doing it rather well), they narrowed their devicial analysis down to two possibilities.

Much the less likely of these was that the woman was the ally of the Witch of Papplewick, an entirely obscure character who was probably made up in the 1630s by Ben Jonson for a Robin Hood play he never got round to finishing, but who does succeed, in the fragment that survives, in posing magically as Maid Marian.

Far more probable was that she was the bondswoman of Queen Morgause, whose device the Circle's archivists had recorded manifesting a handful of times over the past millennium. Morgause was one of those women who seem to be related to everyone you know: Uther Pendragon's stepdaughter, Morgan le Fay's sister, Arthur's half-sister, wife to King Lot of Orkney, lover of Sir Lamorak, and the mother of Sirs Gawain, Agravaine, Gaheris, Gareth and Mordred. Mordred, of course, was also Arthur's son – the others being Lot's, at least according to Morgause – and yes, this does mean that Morgause seduced her own half-brother to conceive his eventual betrayer and murderer. Like her colleague in Papplewick, she was enough of a sorceress to spin herself an illusory appearance – in her case of the one person Arthur could have had blameless sex with, Queen Guinevere.

(OK, so in some versions of the legends it's Morgan le Fay who does this, but the general consensus was that her device was taken at the moment. And, while for this very reason none of Jory's subjects would for a moment have suggested equating Malory Wendiman with Guinevere, the modus operandi was too similar to be ignored.)

Whether the false Malory had intended to kill the High King on the spot, or to play a longer, more subtle game of infiltration, wasn't something the Circle could guess without more data. Luckily Jory had been canny enough, and alert enough to this kind of mythical subterfuge, to rumble her before she could do either.

What was obvious, though, was that whoever she'd been working for had extensive info about Malory (though presumably not access to Malory herself, or why send an imposter?), and could tailor someone's appearance to mimic her as closely as possible. This was something the analysts had previously assumed only happened in James Bond films, but it was clearly possible given enough determination and cash, and a suitable subject (because even plastic surgery has its limits). It pointed to her employers being a first-world government or multinational corporation with a well-established tradition of espionage, but that was about as far as anyone could speculate.

The morning after his disconcerting encounter, the High King called me to his suite. It wouldn't always be the case, but in those days he confided in me as much as anyone, and although he'd talk to Blaze, Rev and David about it later I was the one he told first. (I'm not saying this to boast, you understand, although obviously that's a handy side benefit. It's a chronicler's job to be accurate, and this is how it was.)

'I've come to a decision,' the Pendragon told me. 'Or a realisation, perhaps. Have you ever noticed, Dale – I mean, I'm sure you have, you think about these things – that an awful lot of the trouble in the Arthurian myths comes from women? Sometimes it feels as if the women are there mainly to create problems for the men to sort out. Mostly through marital infidelity, in fact.'

'It's been observed, boss,' I said. 'Feminist critics have written huge books about it, in fact.'

'Well, that's obviously fair enough,' Jory said. 'I mean, I think the whole thing's pretty dubious myself. After my time in the Green Chapel, I think I'm about as egalitarian as any man in my position could sensibly hope to be. But still, those are the myths we're stuck with, and I have to be practical.'

'OK,' I said, wondering where all this was going and whether they sold aspirin there. As I've mentioned, I'd had a heavy night.

'As the device-bearer of King Arthur,' he said – sounding, as he always did, a little uncomfortable as he said it – 'it's likely I'm going to end up repeating his death, unless I'm very careful indeed. I've been thinking about that a lot since… well, since Stonehenge, and last night helped clarify things for me.

'Arthur's downfall comes down to two causes,' he suggested. 'His wife's infidelity with Lancelot, and Mordred's conception, which he was tricked into by Morgause. Guinevere and Morgause, both women. With me so far?'

I thought it was a bit rich not to let Lancelot share some of the blame there – not to mention Arthur himself, who really can't have been paying attention if he failed to notice that his wife was talking and acting like his sister all of a sudden – but the High King was still talking, so I let it pass.

'I'm only High King by virtue of my device,' he reminded

59

me. 'I couldn't establish a dynasty if I wanted to. Any kid I had could well end up channelling Mordred anyway, assuming they had any affinity for the devices at all. I don't think that would be good for family life, do you?'

'OK,' I said again. 'But boss, you can't only let men come near you. Superintendent Kinsey'd have your balls, if you'll excuse me saying, and so would Scar and Zara and Janene.' Besides, it was only a few weeks since Kate Blackwood had been acclaimed as a Knight.

He shook his head. 'It's not about women as such. If I was gay, I could hardly avoid seeing men – although I suppose there'd be no risk of fathering a Mordred, at least. But no, what I need to do is take a vow of celibacy. A solemn promise not to marry or sleep with anyone – woman or man, I've never been tempted in that direction but best to spell it out – until... oh, let's say while the realm, *my* realm, lasts. I'll take an oath with witnesses and a legal record of proceedings and so on – perhaps the Archbishop of Canterbury there too, to show I'm taking it seriously. And the Chief Rabbi and someone from the Muslim Council of Britain, I suppose. Do you think I should invite some Buddhists and Hindus too?'

'Erm,' I said.

It was, perhaps, a bit of a leap. A vow of celibacy is no guarantee of actual abstention, after all (as the Catholic Church keeps discovering to its eternal astonishment), and while Arthur may have been a paragon in all sorts of ways, the Morgause incident shows he wasn't actually infallible.

Still, it's probably easier to have sex by mistake with someone you think is your wife than to have sex by mistake when you've promised not to have any at all. Well, maybe. And it would certainly be reasonable to assume that, once the bearer of the Pendragon device gave his word, it would take exceptional circumstances to make him break it.

But... well. 'Isn't that a bit extreme, boss?' I asked. 'I mean, obviously there's no-one in the picture at the moment. And I get that having your ex's evil twin – her *equally* evil twin, I mean – turn up and try and shag you would put anyone off.

But still, do you really want to make a promise like that just for safety's sake? What if you meet someone really nice, you find out they like you, you go for a meal together and you hit it off, then you want to move things on to the next level and…'

'That's *enough*, Dale,' the Pendragon told me sharply, and up I shut.

After a moment, he said more gently, 'There's no likelihood of any of that. Not now I'm High King. Not since… well. Let's just say there's nobody I'm likely to be interested in, in that way.'

I knew perfectly well what he meant: *Nobody since Malory*. And the two of them had split up months before he got hold of the Pendragon device. Something about something she'd confessed to him, something that painted her in a bad light and first got him thinking that maybe she was Morgan le Fay. (Well, that was my understanding at the time. I wouldn't get the full story until a good many years later.) Whatever, Jory had burned his bridges there, even before events at Stonehenge turned the two of them into archenemies. That was a love that wasn't merely star-crossed, but galaxy- or possibly even supercluster-crossed.

There was a long pause while the Pendragon pondered, and I wondered whether I should go. Technically you're supposed to wait for the High King to dismiss you, but Jory had never been a stickler for protocol. I stuck around, though.

'Ha!' he said eventually and rather suddenly, after musing for a while. 'I've just realised I'm going to rather enjoy my next press interview.'

* * *

In the conference chamber at Windsor, we finish dissecting the events of the day and move on to other matters: the approaching visit by a prison reform charity to the Circle's Benwick Institute facility; Paul Parsons' recent set-to in Norwich with the bondswoman of the sorceress Hellawes;

the situation in the Duchy of Cornwall ('Send a couple of Knights down to escort the others back to the Fastness,' the High King advises Sir David, 'and have them carry out a covert assessment while they're there').

Soon, it drifts away from business altogether and becomes more sociable: the latest gossip from the Circle and the Chapel, events we've been to, films we've seen, the vestigial traces of our private lives. Blaze has somehow found the time to acquire a new girlfriend – she even got through the security vetting without turning out to be an evil enchantress – and we get some mileage out of that. Rev describes to us, in altogether too much detail, the strapping young farmer he picked up in one of the Windsor pubs over the weekend. David resolutely refuses to be drawn on what went on between him and Ron at the hotel. (In theory he's as celibate as the High King himself – his chaste virtue, or possibly his pent-up sexual frustration, is supposed to imbue the Sir Galahad device with much of its power – but it's not like he gets to see much of the more confrontational kind of action these days.)

Throughout it all, Jory greases the social wheel, teasing others, mocking himself and making everyone, even poor Bonnie, feel reasonably comfortable. It helps of course, that all of us here – Bonnie included – knew him before he became the Pendragon, and certainly his personality isn't so subsumed in that of King Arthur that it's unrecognisable. The Pendragon device itself, of course, has a certain jovial affability, a gift for putting subordinates at their ease, but that doesn't go far enough to explain what's happening here.

No, this is down to the other device Jordan Taylor holds: the second most prominent legendary hero of Great Britain, whose unification in Jory's person with the Arthur device healed the breach between the Circle and the Chapel seven years ago.

This ally's sense of fun is more disrespectful, more mischievous and biting than the kingly humour of the Pendragon, and without him this would be a very different social gathering. Robin Hood may have retired from outlawry these days to serve the rightful King, but he remains a perennially merry man.

...But still. When the gilded clock on the mantelpiece chimes some horrendously late hour, and the guests start to make their excuses and their moves, Kinsey to share a car with David back to London, Bonnie to the guardroom for the rest of her shift, Rev and Blaze and me to various bedrooms around the castle... the many masks that Jory's wearing begin to slip, and I – because I think I'm the only one still paying attention – get a glimpse of the man inside, the man who promised away his future chances of romantic happiness and didn't much care. The man who, fundamentally, doesn't believe his chances of *any* happiness amount to much, the man who's embraced a duty more lofty and isolating than any other, yet who's still sufficiently alert to the possibilities of hostile narrative imperatives that he refuses to find a companion to comfort him in it.

The thing is, that was altogether *too* self-aware. There's a thing called story-blindness, which afflicts all of us with a device, at least potentially. It's part of the way they change our bodies and brains. Intimately familiar though we all are with our allies' stories, we still find ourselves repeating their mistakes – or their heroic acts, in contexts which for us are mistakes – without any self-awareness at all. It shouldn't be possible for the bearer of the Pendragon device to decide, as Jory did that night in Leeds, that he'd better not take this King Arthur thing too far.

We know, of course, that Jory's carrying the devices of King Arthur and Robin Hood. It's the fact which resolved the War of the Devices, the foundation of the Pendragon Settlement, and the continuing basis of the peace, security and prosperity of the entire realm.

The thing is... after accompanying him everywhere for seven years, I've come to realise the High King himself doesn't believe it at all.

I think he thinks – wrongly, of course – that he's pulling

off the most audacious con trick in British history. Oh yes, he puts on a good act (not that it *is* an act, but that's how it feels to him), but all the time, inside, he reckons all this guff about knights and outlaws from the past guiding and fortifying us in the present is exactly as ludicrous as it sounds.

In point of fact, Jory hasn't really believed in his own device since he was carrying Sir Gawain. He pretty much lost his faith in all the devices – as a theory, even – around when he lost Malory. He's a romantic soul, and her betrayal is a blow he's never quite recovered from. It's affected the entire world as he sees it, and his actions in it.

He thinks that everything the rest of us believe – the reason the Circle and the Chapel exist, the reason his subjects try to kill him and his friends every so often, the reason Malory's off-limits to him – is all just mass hysteria, a vast collective delusion that the British populace has bought into en masse.

Which explains what he's doing, of course. If the lunatics have taken over the asylum, the only way a sane man can keep them under control is to pretend he's Napoleon.

He's wrong, of course. I mean, obviously.

But still.

4. WAYLAND SMITH

A few days after she's assigned to the castle, Bonnie Laing goes ahead as the advanced guard for the High King's visit to his old university. She leaves Windsor on her Triumph after a scant few hours' sleep, and drives through the steadily lightening morning until she reaches the beautiful medieval city where Jordan Taylor – and for that matter Malory Wendiman – spent their formative years.

There was a time when the grandeur of the university buildings would have intimidated her, child of the greenwood that she is: they would have seemed vertiginous and sterile, and horribly, irresponsibly permanent. (Her time at the Fastness has cured her of that, of course – Windsor isn't even the first castle she's lived in.)

The city's already under discreet Circle occupation, with men-at-arms cordoning off parts of the major streets where the High King's motorcade will pass, and occupying – as politely as possible, but forcibly where necessary – the student rooms overlooking the archways and courtyards where he'll walk. Supervising them is Paul Parsons, the bondsman of Sir Lancelot: it's a bit of a change of pace for one of the Circle's top men, but the Seneschal's assigned him to light duties after his run-in with Hellawes.

It's unusual, in fact, for Paul to have this much contact with his liege lord. As Parsons's sovereign it goes without saying that Jory commands his unswerving loyalty... but unlike the Arthur and Lancelot of legend, who were BFFs before predictably falling out over a girl, they don't actually get on that well. When Paul was his squire Jory found him petty, snobbish and self-righteous, and the Knight didn't disguise his distaste terribly well. Although High King Jordan's unfailingly gracious to him now, of course, Paul's a proud man and the niggling memory has prevented them ever becoming close.

'Actually, Laing, we've got it all under control,' Parsons assures Bonnie cheerily, shortly after she's dismounted and removed her helmet. 'Nothing for you to fret about.' Paul's squire takes her Triumph discreetly, and parks it between two Circle troop-carriers across the High Street.

'Head wants me to judge that,' Laing replies. 'Talk me through the arrangements, Paul, OK?'

Parsons gives her a supercilious look, but she still stares at him defiantly. In the end – woman though she is, and younger than him, and despite his continuing reservations after working alongside younger women Knights for half a decade – she's here at the High King's command, so he can hardly argue.

He takes her around the brand new sports facility the High King's due to open, and then to Jory's old college where he'll shake the hands of various academics, students and support staff. At the venerable building where the High King's to receive his honorary degree, they debate the best approach to safeguarding VIPs in a venue which was never built with security in mind, but the conversation's details are technical and its tone largely amicable.

'Heard you had a spot of bother with Sir Garlon the Red,' Parsons observes as they proceed on foot to the remaining venue. 'Never had any dealings, myself. Cause you much trouble, yeah?'

'Not once I'd killed him,' Bonnie replies.

Eventually, they reach the glossy New Arthurian building that houses the university's state-of-the-art Mythopolitical

Research Facility. Security here is tighter than a male model's boxers at the best of times, and even Bonnie and Paul have to show ID before they can be admitted.

They're met by Craig McCutcheon, the Knight currently in charge of the Circle security detail assigned to the MRF. A middle-aged Scot with a dry sense of humour, he's one of the few Knights with an academic background, holding a PhD in software engineering, and actually joined the Circle as a man-at-arms in the technical division before being talent-spotted by Sir Charles Raymond, who was capable on rare occasions of a certain pragmatic wisdom. McCutcheon bears the twin-serpent device of King Arthur's one-time hunting buddy, Sir Accolon of Gaul.

'Everything ticking over as normal, McCutcheon?' Paul asks him blandly.

'The researchers are scurrying around like squirrels on a sugar high,' McCutcheon replies. 'After the Southbank Centre, nobody wants anything going bottoms-up. But yes, we're sound.'

The work that's done here is top secret: the researchers, and the postgrads who assist them, have gone through several layers of security vetting, signed the Official Secrets Act and sworn an oath of fealty before the throne of the High King. Much though he enjoyed his student years, visiting the city always brings back some poignant memories for Jory, and it's doubtful he'd be coming today if it wasn't an effective cover for his visit here.

Since the MRF's inception four years ago it's been the subject of various rumours in the university and city – a popular one being that it's working to create new, bespoke devices, an army of British superheroes to protect the High King's realm. There's a strong consensus that, whatever the details, the Facility's primary purpose is to make Britain the first country in the world to develop devicial weaponry.

The rumour-mongers are closer to the truth than they know.

* * *

The High King's itinerary brings him to the MRF in the mid-afternoon. The meet-and-greet at the college went off without incident (unless you count the bursar dropping a champagne glass and getting his shoes sticky), and so did the opening of the new Centre for Chivalric Arts. That one came with a demonstration of the spanking new archery range and tiltyard by the university's archery team and Tournament Society – transparently designed to appeal to the High King's nostalgia (and, presumably, wallet) since he was a member of both. Someone's obviously been reading a biography.

There's still a couple of hours to go before the honorary degree ceremony, and the second, probably somewhat boozier, drinks reception back at the college, so the Pendragon's taking advantage of the downtime – officially speaking, anyway – to drop in and visit an old friend at the Facility. This cover story is, of course, believed by precisely nobody, but the niceties must be observed.

The Pendragon turns up, with Bonnie and Paul in tow, having left me catching up on my reading at the university library. I may be his official chronicler, but there are limits to what he wants chronicled, and my security clearance reflects them.

They're greeted by the Facility's Director, Professor Freda Tate-Hendricks, a plumpish, fortyish woman in a pristine lab coat that was probably fresh on half an hour ago. Four years ago, Dr Tate-Hendricks was a junior academic viewed by most of her colleagues in the social sciences as easily distracted and lacking in focus, before her background in political science, her specialism in virtual data modelling, her hobby of historical re-enactment and her secondary career writing Arthurian-themed romance novels suddenly made her the ideal surprise candidate to run the new Facility.

Paul Parsons nods coolly to Craig McCutcheon, who's taking over the High King's security inside the building, and goes to wait in the limo. Bonnie stays at the Pendragon's side

68

like an armoured terrier. The Director introduces him to her deputy, an older man with profuse curly hair and beard that serve to render his head effectively spherical. He enthuses at the High King for several minutes about his project to categorise all known devices, British and foreign, into a complex taxonomy like an evolutionary tree diagram.

After the High King extracts himself, Prof Tate-Hendricks takes him on a tour of the labs, which blend elements of library, computer room and clinic in unexpected and exotic combinations. He sees the neuroimaging equipment one set of researchers are using to map the brains of supplicants for Knighthood before and after they acquire their devices. He nods in feigned understanding of the 'inframemetic interfaces' another group are developing, which will use subliminal sounds and images to communicate directly with devicial structures in the brain. He takes more interest in the software a third team are designing for surveillance systems, which will enable them to detect characteristically device-driven body-language among the population at large.

In total, they visit fourteen labs. All have strict security, consisting of passcards and keypads and CCTV cameras. They account for all the visible areas of the building.

After an hour of this, Tate-Hendricks leads Jory to a lift on the ground floor, which she unlocks with her own passcard, code and palmprint. 'We won't be long,' the High King reassures Bonnie as he and the Director step inside, and she glances at McCutcheon in dismay.

'My lord —' Bonnie objects, but the Pendragon has anticipated her.

'Professor Tate-Hendricks has the highest clearance of anyone in the country, other than a few select members of the Circle and Chapel,' he reassures her. 'Higher than Chief Superintendent Kinsey. Higher than Dale, in fact, who you may recall actually lives with me.' (Yeah, thanks boss.) 'If *she* can't be trusted then we may as well hand the country over to the French, because they'll make a better job of the security arrangements.'

'…OK, my lord,' Bonnie grudgingly agrees, and the Director thumbs a button on the lift panel – one which, Bonnie notices as the doors slide closed, has only two buttons on it.

'What's down there, anyway?' she asks McCutcheon.

McCutcheon winks at her. 'Oh, horrors unimaginable,' he deadpans. 'But I reckon if the Head wanted you to see them he'd have taken you down there.'

Bonnie can't argue with that, obviously.

* * *

Below them, Jory and Tate-Hendricks step out of the lift into a workshop taking up most of the concrete bunker that is the building's sub-sub-basement. The space itself is laid out methodically, with manufacturing facilities ranging from a state-of-the-art ceramic forge and boron-carbide anvil to the latest in 3-D printers. The workbenches are set at waist height, and are messily strewn with papers, models and machinery, from tiny toy robots to a full-size motorbike frame, next to which a welding-mask and blowtorch lie.

In one corner stands an entire garden shed snapped together from printed panels. It looks as if someone's been using it as a bedroom.

An old man in a wheelchair sits at one of the workbenches, soldering a circuit in a bespoke motherboard. He looks up and groans as the High King enters. Putting down his hot iron, he rolls himself back from the bench, pulls out an e-cigarette from his labcoat, and takes a grateful drag.

'Well, Schmidt,' demands the High King without preamble, 'what progress with the Excalibur Programme?'

* * *

This isn't the first time the High King's visited the Mythopolitical Research Facility. Four years ago he was here to declare the place open, and last year he found time for

70

a flying visit between judging a young entrepreneurs' award and inspecting an RAF base.

Those were the planned visits. Between the two, he had to come here in full force as the Head of the Circle, with Knights and squires and men-at-arms in tow.

The MRF's been a high-security facility from the beginning, but the High King's enemies are cunning – and one of them particularly so. Five months after the Facility opened, a new researcher arrived, a neurologist called Alison Sedgwater. A dark-haired, tanned woman in her late thirties, she had impeccable credentials and a commendable enthusiasm for the job. In her case, that job was to measure the physical responses of undeviced volunteers in the presence of a device-bearer. She was an exemplary worker, and her results were impeccable; they've been amply confirmed since by other mythopolitical researchers, and are still considered a landmark in the field.

At that point, the MRF's security was run by the university's usual contractors rather than by the Circle, so the device Dr Sedgwater used in her research was that of Sir Urre, borne by an elderly retired Knight of the Circle named Darius Beddowes who happened to live in the area and found himself at a loose end most weekday afternoons. Beddowes was seventy-eight, had become extremely short-sighted (the Circle had had to turn him down a number of times for active service in the War of the Devices), and Dr Sedgwater's relationship with him was briskly, even brusquely, professional. The fact that she left her assistants to handle Beddowes while she monitored the volunteers was why it took several months before it dawned on the elderly Knight that there was something rather familiar about her.

A number of weeks after that, one night when he was eating a ruminative slice of cheese-on-toast before bed, it occurred to him exactly what the thing was.

Beddowes might have been getting on, but he was a Knight of the Circle and a device-bearer, and when he knew something needed to be done his determination was stubborn and irresistible. It took him an hour to get put through to the Pendragon's personal staff, but barely five minutes after that for Jason Smith to pull the High King out of a formal banquet with the Norwegian Ambassador and the Chair of the Ragnars Synir. Ten minutes late they, and a bunch of other personnel deployed from the Fastness, were on their way to the university town in one of the early Westland Catuvellauni helicopters.

By the time they arrived, to no-one's great surprise, Alison Sedgewater was gone. It would turn out later that she'd had Beddowes's phone tapped, on the basis that if anyone was going to recognise her, it would be a Knight who, however elderly and visually impaired he was, had known her vaguely before his retirement, during her early days at the Circle as a secular advisor.

Her digs had been systematically emptied of any clues as to where it was she'd gone, and her desk at the MRF only contained stuff relating to her official research – but the autowipe she'd set on her workstation wasn't quite sufficient to outfox the Circle's dogged techie men-at-arms. The data they managed to salvage was patchy and corrupted, but it was enough to confirm Beddowes' suspicions, and reveal some thing that he – and everyone else, to be fair – had never imagined.

Firstly, as I'm sure I hardly need to spell out at this point, 'Dr Alison Sedgwater' was the High King's ex, Dr Malory Wendiman. While she hadn't, of course, been dense enough to leave that name on the computer, the IT guys were able to reconstruct a partial photo of a paler, redder-haired Dr Sedgwater whose appearance was more immediately familiar.

Secondly, in her spare time 'Dr Sedgwater' had been using data and specialist software from the MRF systems to develop a subtler and more vicious form of the Wendiman Derangement, although the information about how that might have worked was also partial.

And thirdly… thirdly, there was the *other* person in the photograph.

'It's not exactly piss-easy, my lord,' Prof Tate-Hendricks reminds the High King, slightly peevishly. 'Like I've said before, it's a multi-stage project, and we're still at a fairly early...'

'I realise that,' says Jory, addressing himself both to the Director and the man Schmidt. 'But we don't have the luxury of time. The Founding Frontiersmen have made a move against my Seneschal, and I'm facing a potential rebellion in Cornwall of all places. These are hostile times. If I'm to defend Britain effectively against our enemies, I'm going to need Excalibur *soon*.'

It's understandable enough that the absence, in this New Arthurian Age of wonders, of any equivalent to King Arthur's iconic sword would be a source of continuing embarrassment to Jory. It's been the source of interminable jokes in the foreign satirical media, who generally relate it humorously to his commitment to celibacy, their hilarious implication being that he doesn't have a penis either.

It's not like it's impossible for such an object to exist. (Excalibur, I mean, not... OK, you knew that.) As Malory told Jory long ago, artefacts can carry the devices we imbue them with, and there are certainly modern items which parallel particular mythic originals. Many of them played a significant part in the war: the Round Table (aka the circular boardroom table on the eighth floor of the Circle's Fastness), Robin Hood's silver arrow (smelted from Shafiq Rashid's Olympic archery medal and now on public display in the British Museum) and the Holy Grail itself (a wooden Roman drinking-vessel dug up in the eighteenth century and supposedly displayed alongside the arrow, but in fact replaced with an exact replica and now sitting on a bench in the corner of Schmidt's workshop overflowing with small screws), to name but three.

In all the recorded history of the Circle, though – and it goes back at least a thousand years before it gets too entangled in its own myth to be reliable – there's been no instance of Excalibur appearing as a device. On the other hand, until seven years ago, the Pendragon had never reappeared either. It seems to many people, Jory included, that the return of the King should have been accompanied by the reappearance of the sword... but if that's happened, nobody's yet discovered the stone or lake it's hiding in.

Meanwhile, the High King of the Britons has battles to fight.

The man in the chair spreads his hands. 'It won't be ready,' he says. 'Our understanding is increasing, yes, one day we may be able to make this thing, but now...' His voice is strong, his able English clearly learned from Americans, his accent unmistakeably Germanic. He's healthy still, with the broad shoulders and developed chest that can come from forever pushing around your own body-weight. 'Your weapon may not be ready for *years*.'

The issue, in a nutshell, is this. Excalibur's a sword with a specific provenance. It's *not* the sword Arthur pulls from the stone, although for simplicity's sake some versions of the legend combine the two. Excalibur's the sword he gets from the water, the one that's handed to him by the hand of the Lady of the Lake, and the one she takes back after he's mortally wounded at Camlann, when Sir Bedivere finally, after much nagging on the dying Arthur's part, chucks it back in. Amazing cinematic imagery for an ancient culture to have come up with, hilarious basis for a Python sketch, but not much use when your pond hasn't got a strange woman lying at the bottom of it.

These days, of course, everyone accepts that Malory Wendiman's the avatar of Morgan le Fay. But during her time with the Circle she was believed to be carrying the device of Nimue, that same titular Lady, and since her enforced retirement no other contender for the identity has been forthcoming. With no-one in the traditional role to grant the High King his appointed weapon, he's had to turn to other channels.

'I'm amazed you can even find your notes in here,' says Jory, staring around at the chaos. Schmidt shrugs and takes a deeper drag.

'We're getting places with *other* types of devicial weaponry,' Tate-Hendricks points out. 'Not that, you know, any of the others...' She trails ambiguously off. 'Still, we've isolated the Wendiman Derangement to the point where we're pretty bloody confident we can reproduce it via an inframemetic interface. Not that we can *test* that, but... And we're working on a humane variant, too – give us time and we might be able to detach someone from their SCAM instead of crippling them both.' (A 'SCAM' is a semi-autonomous culturally-inflected archetypal memeplex – to you and me, an ally or device.)

'Jesus – no offence, Ernst,' she adds, realising that her last sentence contained a verbal faux pas. Schmidt rolls his eyes.

She scowls. 'But it all takes time. And what you've asked for, my lord – none of us are convinced it's even *possible*. If it is... well, like Dr Schmidt says it could be years away.'

'From a strictly scientific standpoint, I'm sure you're right,' the Pendragon says shortly. 'But I'd expected more from *you*, Schmidt.'

Tate-Hendricks said just now that the quest for Excalibur has many stages, and she wasn't kidding. The first stage consisted of combing British mythology for any *other* figure who might have been able to create Excalibur, or a sword of equivalent power. The second was tracking him down and offering him a job.

The invention or acquisition of ironworking seems to be a vitally important rite-of-passage for a young culture, and a good many of them seem to have ended up with a god of blacksmithing as a result. These embodiments of the divine fire range from omnipotent creators to put-upon dwarves, and there are a lot of variants where they're ugly or physically disabled, to contrast with the beauty and perfection of their metalwork. If you know your mythology it's easy to think of examples.

The Germanic tribes and their descendants across Europe, including the Anglo-Saxons, had a folk-hero called Wayland the Smith. He's mentioned in various Old English poems including *Beowulf*, where the hero boasts that Wayland made his mail-coat, and he makes a bunch of appearances in the visual art of the period. Admittedly none of the stories about him are set in Britain, but it's clear that Wayland was a cultural touchstone in Anglo-Saxon England.

Modern myth-telling tends to ignore Wayland's personal story (which is complicated and bloodthirsty, involving swan-maidens, hamstring-slicing and skulls repurposed as drinking-vessels), and to use him the way *Beowulf* does, as a kind of hallmark of quality in weapon-forging. In the TV series *Robin of Sherwood*, the 'Swords of Wayland' include both Excalibur and Robin's sword Albion.

Since there's no smith character native to either Arthurian myth or Robin Hood lore, there was only one real candidate to develop Jory's modern devicial weapon. Not being part of Arthurian myth or Robin Hood lore though, Wayland, like Beowulf, has never manifested as part of the British national deviceplex. It took some time for the Circle's archivists – never at their best when it comes to foreign history – to track down where he *had* manifested, and longer still for the Green Chapel's hackers to break into the Berlin records of the Nibelungentreue, Germany's devicial order, and identify his current avatar.

After that the Chapel's direct action to kidnap him from his toy-design consultancy in Dusseldorf, and bring him back so the High King could make him a job offer he couldn't refuse, was relatively simple.

Now Schmidt inhales another lungful of cool nicotine vapour, and says: 'I can only do so much. Even with *Wieland der Schmied* to call on I'm just an inventor, and what you need is highly theoretical. I have the craft, but what's really needed is the knowledge.'

The Director scowls. 'Which we're doing our best to supply, of course... But scientific hypotheses aren't formed and tested overnight, my lord. That happens in Hollywood, not in academia.'

'You see?' Schmidt sighs, and shrugs theatrically. 'I've said I'll stay here for as long as you pay me, High King. I have no family, the Nibelungentreue never had any use for me, and I enjoy the work. But I can't pretend I think it's worth your money.'

* * *

Three and a half years ago, when Jason Smith showed the Pendragon the photo that the Circle's IT people had reconstructed from 'Alison Sedgewater''s workstation, the High King wept.

Not immediately, of course. His first words were, 'Oh my Christ. When was that taken?'

'They couldn't read the time-stamp, my lord,' Jason replied. If he was surprised by the High King's blasphemy, he knew better than to show it.

'How old would you say...' the High King asked, his voice going slightly hoarse.

Jason peered appraisingly at the picture. 'Three, my lord? Four maybe, I dunno.' He wasn't an expert on kids.

'We last...' the High King said, after a long pause. 'We last... spent time together at her dad's bungalow in Prestatyn. That night when Laney came to steal the Grail.' (Yeah, the thing Laney stole was the Grail, some time after Jory himself did. Things got a bit complicated during the war.) 'Six months before Stonehenge. But surely we'd have noticed then if...' He tried to remember. 'No, she was wearing a big baggy jumper. It was cold out at the stones. She's always been a slim woman. She could have been...'

All this was a long way above Jason's pay grade, but he could tell Jory needed him to say something. 'There's nothing to say it's her kid, my lord,' he said. 'Or, well, erm.'

The background was fuzzy, as was the foreground, but it looked like Malory and the three- or four-year-old were on a sunny hillside somewhere. The child was wearing purple trousers, and a T-shirt with a cartoon character of some kind — was it a dinosaur or a dragon? Its bright ginger hair was cut short, and it gazed warily at the camera, as if expecting it to do something disconcerting. Malory crouched behind in sensible jeans and a blouse, her hands on the kid's shoulders, a smile on her face that could only be described as proud.

'It could be…' Merry had no brothers or sisters, Jason knew that. 'Her godchild?' he hazarded.

'For fuck's sake Jason, look at his *hair*,' snapped the Pendragon, and Jason physically flinched.

A number of counterarguments came into his head, but he knew better than to say more than, 'Yes, my lord. Sorry.'

It was at that point, of course, that the High King cried. It lasted for a full thirty seconds, then he closed his eyes, counted silently, opened them again and wiped them with a handkerchief.

'I'm sorry, Jason,' he said. Unlike the Knight, he'd seen his family's old photos. He knew full well what he'd looked like himself at that age. (He knew, too, that his own mother was a redhead.) 'This has taken me by surprise a bit. It seems I took that oath of chastity too late.'

The next thing he said was pardonable under the circumstances, but completely unwarranted.

Most modern retellings leave them out — again, for brevity's sake as much as anything — but the fact is, in the various legends King Arthur fathers a prodigious number of sons. There's Loholt, who helped to rescue his mother Guinevere after one of her several abductions; he later killed a giant, and may have been slain in turn by his foster-uncle Kay. There's Amr, who Arthur himself apparently killed (well, they were a violent family), and Gwydre who was gored to death by the giant boar Twrch Trwyth. There's his bastard son Arthur the Less, one of the noblest of the lot, who was knighted by Sir Tristan and bested both Gawain and Percival

78

in combat. There's Llachei, and Borre, and Adeluf, and Garnot, and the rampantly implausible Tom a-Lincoln, who roams the world in a seventeenth-century story assiduously providing Arthur with grandsons, one of whom's also the grandson of the legendary oriental potentate Prester John.

But Jory wasn't thinking about any of them, of course. He didn't even consider whether the kid would even have a device yet.

Because what he said next was: 'Well, it looks as if we've found our Mordred.'

5. LITTLE JOHN

Now, three and a half years later, Jason Smith is still on the quest he was given that day, of tracking down the High King's son by Malory Wendiman.

Assuming that everyone's assumptions about the kid are right, he should be turning seven right around now. Jason assumes he's in school somewhere, but even if Merry's gone down the home-schooling route, everyone leaves traces. You can't just bring a child into the world without generating midwives' records, doctors' notes, local council population data.

The trouble is, without a name or anything other than a description of the mother, it's not exactly easy to track such things down. It took Jason nearly eighteen months to check up personally on all the Arthurs born that year – it was, for obvious reasons, a massively popular choice of name – plus the inflated numbers named after Gawain (whose device Jory used to carry) or Lancelot (Nimue's foster-son), and the handful of unfortunate small boys whose parents had, with more enthusiasm than good judgement, christened their sons Mordred. Even with the full force of the High King's authority opening doors for him, that achieved nothing.

Nor have any of the less obvious approaches he's thought of for finding the lad – from checking all the premature births on the first of May that year (that being Mordred's traditional birthday, though it would have been about six weeks early for this kid) to sponsoring and judging a nationwide poetry competition with an Arthurian theme for under-eights. He never wants to go through *that* again.

Short of DNA-testing every six-year-old child in Britain – and he's actively looking into the logistics and ethics of that – Jason is basically out of ideas.

Which is why he's decided to go the other direction, and try to find Malory's father instead. It's trickier to disappear when you've got seventy years' of financial, employment and medical records behind you – and when, being nearly ninety now, you're likely to need medical attention more frequently anyway. It's a set of hospital records – a recent stay for a nasty bout of flu, to be precise – that have led him to a low-rise block of sheltered housing in Strathclyde, and the door of a man allegedly named Hamish McTaggart. Dr Edward Wendiman is no more Scottish than Jason is, which makes the Knight think he'll be needing all his marbles still, especially with pro-independence feeling running high. Jason wouldn't fancy it, maintaining a false identity day and night, but then he's not in hiding to protect his family.

He quite fancies having a family himself, one of these days, but if he does he hopes it doesn't turn out like this.

He realises he's probably making a spectacle of himself, standing here. He's out of armour, in slacks and an open-necked shirt, and looks (he hopes) like a relative or family friend visiting on a day off. No point alarming anybody else here. An ancient-looking Chinese lady is watching him intently from a window opposite. Her flat and its next-door neighbour still have 'YES' and 'NO' stickers up from the vote a few weeks ago.

Jason presses the doorbell. What he'll say if Hamish McTaggart turns out not to be Edward Wendiman he doesn't really know, but if he's not Wendiman it won't really matter.

There's a long pause, as of a very old man hoisting himself out of a chair and shuffling across a carpeted floor to his front door, and then it opens. The figure who answers the door is thin, with a stoop that means he's barely taller than Jason. His white hair's wispy and his face deeply lined, but there's no doubt about his identity.

He stares at the younger man. 'Ach,' he says, after the briefest pause. 'Ye'd best come in, then.'

Inside the flat with the door closed, he reverts to his natural voice, which is that of an antiquated BBC announcer from the home counties. 'Sit down, please. Can I offer you some tea?' Though his movements are slow and quavery, the old man's tone is perfectly businesslike.

Jason sits in the wooden chair he guesses is for guests. 'Yes please, Dr Wendiman,' he replies politely.

'You're Jason Smith, the device-holder of Sir Gareth,' Edward Wendiman acknowledges as he busies himself with the teapot and kettle. 'We met briefly at Stonehenge. I knew your face before that, of course.'

Jason's unsurprised. As the slightly more official of the two rival (and, as it turned out, completely fraudulent) Pendragon claimants, his likeness was common currency at the time. He's in his mid-twenties now, and he's grown a beard (something he'd never have considered if circumstances had been different, although it suits his Sir Gareth persona), but when he's in civvies he still gets recognised in the street. A lot.

'I was a mate of Merry's, before the war,' says Jason. 'Malory's, I mean. I was Green Chapel before I was ever Circle. I went by Squig then. Not a lot of people know that.'

'I was aware,' says Wendiman. 'I don't imagine that's why you're here today, though. One sugar or two?'

'Three please,' says Jason promptly, because there are some habits even the Circle can't eradicate.

'I haven't been in contact with my daughter for years, I'm afraid,' the old man says as he carries Jason's mug over with great care. 'We both agreed that it was best if I knew nothing about her life. All things being equal, I imagine I'll die without seeing her again. We've reconciled ourselves to that.'

Jason takes the tea and sips it appreciatively. It's sweet,

strong and milky, just the way he likes it. He waits while Wendiman shuffles back to his armchair and makes himself comfortable. 'So what about your grandson, then?' he asks.

'Ah.' Wendiman looks at him carefully. 'So you know about that, do you?'

'He'd be, what, nearly seven now?' Jason asks cheerfully. Wendiman doesn't reply. 'High King's pretty keen to meet him,' he adds. 'Like you'd expect.'

Edward nods, then he sips from his own mug. 'I haven't deceived you,' he says. 'I haven't seen or spoken to Malory since she settled me in here. I've never met her son, which is another thing I've had to reconcile myself to. When you reach old age, you accustom yourself to never seeing many of the people you know again. At least Malory and the boy are alive, as far as I know.' His tone's resigned. 'I imagine you'll be arresting me now. I hope we can finish our tea first.'

Jason takes a bigger swallow and thinks carefully. He's pretty sure the bloke's telling him the truth – after all, the last thing Merry would have wanted would have been for the Circle to come after her through her old man. Which makes it troubling that he's here doing just that.

He knows Merry's the bad guy in all of this – that's pretty much a given, though it sometimes occurs to him to wonder whether he's got himself unwittingly involved in the world's most acrimonious breakup saga – but he still remembers her as a kind, funny person who always had time for his awkward teenage self. She's obviously still a thoughtful daughter, and she probably makes a good mum and all.

He doesn't see a lot of point bringing the old man in. Nobody's going to force him to talk – the Circle's not the CIA, after all – and failing that, what's it going to achieve? He'll be locked up for perverting the course of justice or fraud or some bollocks charge, and that's all. He'll have his ninetieth birthday behind bars, with not a lot of hope of seeing outside again.

No, Jason doesn't want to be responsible for that.

'I believe you,' he tells Wendiman, sincerely. He adds: 'I

expect she didn't give you any way to get her a message in an emergency either, did she?'

'Certainly not,' the old man replies quickly. 'Too easy for you people to set up an ambush, she said.'

Jason nods to himself, noting the way Edward's eyes dropped to his teacup as he replied. Yeah, he thought as much.

'Well, I'll let you finish your tea in peace and quiet, Dr Wendiman,' he says, standing. 'I've got other places to be.'

He crosses to the door. He turns there, a bit like a TV detective with a final thought-that-might-be-a-threat, but all he says is, 'We used to get on all right, you know. Me and Merry.'

Then he leaves.

* * *

'Are there lots of giants' devices about the place, then?' Stephen Mukherjee asks his colleague, with professional interest. 'Can't say I've run into any myself.'

'I've met a handful,' says Woodville, studiedly casual. Outside their train the Devon countryside rolls by, all dark and light greens – hedge-lined fields, wooded hills – with smatterings of livestock to break the routine. Both Knights are in civvies, their armour stacked neatly in their suitcases. Their swords and riot-shields sit in the luggage-rack above their heads. They have the first-class carriage to themselves, not because they planned it that way – the Circle's keeping tighter controls on its expenditure these days, at Sir David's insistence – but because few people want to travel this route first-class on a Tuesday morning.

Their squires, of course, are back in second class. The Circle may be more democratic these days, but there are certain basic standards to be maintained.

'There's Retho of Arvaius, of course,' Stephen says. 'I remember the High King, Taylor as he was then, crossing paths with him. Cut his bally head off, as I recall. The old

84

Seneschal, Sir Charles, was furious. Taylor made a bit of a habit of that sort of thing, truth be told.'

Stephen is the bondsman of Sir Palamedes, the Saracen knight who's Sir Safir's older brother, and he, like so many people in this story, is an old friend of Jory's. Woodville is rather younger: Sir Tristan's device-bearer would have been at school during the High King's days as the bondsman of Sir Gawain.

'I've met Retho.' Woodville's words surprise Stephen, even though Sir Tristan's notoriety as a slayer of giants is the reason the subject's come up. He'd missed this particular piece of gossip.

Gratified by his attention, his colleague continues. 'He appeared a couple of years ago in Dundee. Hitched to a man named Bob McTeague — a barber, appropriately enough.' Apart from being huge and murderous, Retho of Arvaius's USP was his cloak of beards, sewn together from the facial hair of the kings he'd killed. 'Of course McTeague didn't just hang on to the hair he shaved off his customers — that wouldn't have been Retho's style. No, our boy followed them home afterwards and did them in there. The boys and girls in Devicial Analysis eventually spotted a pattern in the local police reports, put one and three together, and sent me. I managed to bring him back alive,' Woodville concludes, not unsmugly. 'He's in the Benwick now.'

'One better than the High King, then,' Stephen observes neutrally. The Circle's arcanely complex code of honour doesn't actually include a stipulation of modesty, and Stephen understands — few male Knights better, in fact — why Tania Woodville might be tempted to talk up her accomplishments to her colleagues. Even so (and he'd be quite upset if you suggested he was trying to take a mouthy woman down a peg or two), Stephen feels that a reminder of the virtue of humility can't do the younger Knight any harm.

'You know that's not what I meant, Mukherjee.' Tania looks annoyed. 'Obviously I read the files on Retho. The High King was responding to a danger to an undevved bystander, and acted in the heat of the moment. Yes, he was disciplined afterwards, but I hardly think you or I would have fared any better. Giants' devs enhance the strength like nobody's business, you know.' (They do so through entirely non-supernatural means, of course – encouraging their bearers to take up body-building being the main one – but her point remains.) 'Taking one on solo's not an easy ask. In fact, since it was King Arthur who brought down the original Retho, the fact that Jordan Taylor did it might have clued some you in that there was something special going on there.'

Stephen is struck by this. 'Suppose you're right,' he concedes. 'None of us thought much of it at the time.'

'Giants' devices don't always pick big blokes,' Woodville concedes, 'but McTeague was huge, the biggest hitch I've met since I joined the Circus.' (A 'hitch' is an unauthorised device-bearer; the 'Circus', obviously, the Circle. Like many of the younger, more gung-ho Knights – not that she's among the Circle's youngest, by any means – Tania makes Stephen feel terrifically old.) 'Sir Tristan offed six, including a giantess, but I've only run into three – Retho, Lucanor the Great and Urgan the Hairy. Had to take out Lucanor's hitch, which is why his brother – the bondsman's, that is – cuffed himself to Lucanor's brother Urgan and came after me. Him I managed to stick in the Benwick. He's had to learn to eat with his left hand, mind.

'Lucky he's not a Muslim,' observes Stephen. 'Or is he?'

Woodville frowns. 'I don't suppose so. His name's Ryan Murphy. Anyway, in the myths Urgan and Lucanor had two more brothers, but there aren't any more Murphy siblings. So I'm not expecting any comeback from that one.'

'Unless Lucanor gets himself another bondsman,' Stephen observes. 'That's the trouble with killing the device-bearers – the devices can come back at you later.' He ponders. 'That happened to the High King, too, though not with Retho. Hmm. Although come to think of it, isn't the Green Knight supposed to be a giant?'

Tania shrugs. 'Suppose so,' she says. 'Maybe the High

King should have come down himself. Anyway, the Seneschal thought the giant-slayer thing might give me something in common with the Duke – something for his device and mine to talk about, sort of effort. Not that the Duke's met a hostile dev in his life, but Corineus was quite the boy with the giants, apparently. Gogmagog's the one everyone's heard of, but he slaughtered stacks of others, in Cornwall and abroad.'

Woodville's being a touch disingenuous here. The most important reason she was sent on this quest is that her family are upper-crust even by the exacting standards of the Circle's traditional constituency. Although she doesn't use the title any more, by rights she's the Honourable Titania Tamsin Elizabeth Woodville, and her mama in particular knows the Duke's family very well. She's the first of her family to join the Circle since the eighteenth century, and Stephen doesn't envy her the conversation where she told her parents she was going to be a Knight. As the youngest child in a family of six brothers and a sister, though, it's easy to see how she ended up there.

'I suppose there's the Cornish connection too,' Mukherjee adds as an afterthought.

Outside their carriage, the rolling hills are beginning to change character, with granite outcrops beginning to appear. One of the High King's public spending priorities has been the renationalised railways, and the London-to-Penzance high-speed rail link has drastically cut travel times to the Duchy. The public benefit is obvious, but as with so many of Jory's directives, there may be an ulterior motive.

'I suppose,' echoes Tania. 'It's Tristan who comes from Cornwall, though, not me. I've been to St Ives and the Eden Project, but that's about it.'

'Oh well, I expect it's just like anywhere else,' says Stephen, whose experience of this part of the country is equally limited. 'It's all England, isn't it?'

* * *

As Stephen's well aware – what with it being the reason for their current quest and all – there are those who'd take issue with those last words, to the extent that if they had their way they might not remain true for very much longer.

After that conversation of theirs at Buckingham Palace, the Queen (who, in the absence of anyone else to take that title, remains in most people's minds *the* Queen) raised no objection to the new Pendragon's appropriation of the royal duchies, and these days Jory holds the title of Duke of Lancaster as well as his various other honours.

He's not, however, the Duke of Cornwall. Her majesty's oldest son, who counted the dukedom among his *ex officio* holdings as heir to the throne, took a different view. While stopping short of denying the High King's authority or disrespecting the Pendragon in any way, he made it clear that he intended – purely out of a loyal sense of duty to the people of Cornwall, of course – to hang on to his ducal lands and title, if it was all the same to the interfering common-born upstart.

It was an early, critical decision for Jory whether he should accept this refusal gracefully or kick up a fuss. Unlike his always studiedly neutral mother, the Duke had been a stout Circle partisan in public throughout the civil war, while mumbling in private to anyone who'd listen that these Green Chapel johnnies may have been bolshies but they had the right idea about the environment, and what were the Circle going to do about that? The High King could have compelled his obedience – in the end, with even his mother backing the Pendragon, the Duke would have had to capitulate – but it would have caused unpleasantness and alienated a significant segment of his newfound support, so in the end they worked out a face-saving solution whereby the High King took title of the dukedom and straight away ceded it graciously back to its previous holder.

The compromise hasn't brought the harmony the High King might have hoped for, however. The Duke's position in relation to the Circle's Cornish garrison is also anomalous:

the four Knights, with associated squires and men-at-arms, started off as his protection detail during the war but were, by its end, following his orders in weeding out Chapelist resistance throughout the (officially) staunchly Circlist lands of Cornwall.

After the war the Duke had new premises built so they could stay there permanently, and their status remains awkwardly ambivalent. Officially, of course, they're commanded by the Seneschal in London, on behalf of the Head of the Circle, High King Jordan, but there've been troubling rumours of the Duke using them, in small ways, as his own private army, and he's certainly exerted pressure to prevent their redeployment to other duties or quests.

Since the rumours also suggest that the Duke privately opposes the Pendragon Settlement, hankering for the days when he looked forward to a reign of his own, rather than succession to a nominal throne subservient to a higher authority, the loyalties of these men have been the subject of some discussion among the High King's advisors. The Duke isn't a young man though, or even a middle-aged one, and as long as his mother (now nearing a hundred and the inevitable awkwardness of sending herself a telegram) retains the robust health typical of the women in their family, his covert disloyalty hasn't been considered a pressing issue.

Meanwhile, the Duke's spent the time since the war building himself a spanking new official residence, in the centre of a new town development built by the Duchy just outside Newquay. (Quite a lot of the Duchy's original plans for the development had to be shelved when its owner announced this.) Arthurian placenames have naturally made a huge comeback over the past seven years, and legendary rulers of Cornwall made for as good a naming convention as any. In the context of a suburb named Tregorlois, containing the Circle barracks called Fort Cador – after Arthur's mother's first husband and his maternal half-brother respectively – calling the new ducal seat 'Corineus House' didn't strike anyone as especially noteworthy.

Just recently, though, the Duke announced to a rather bemused press conference that this chappie Corineus – one of the refugees from the fall of Troy who founded Britain along with the legendary Brutus, and after whom Cornwall was supposedly named in the first place – had actually appeared to him on a number of occasions while he'd been pottering about in the grounds, that they'd had some fruitful and constructive chats about the deplorable state of modern Britain and how the Duchy might act as an example in certain respects, that over the course of these conversations they'd become firm friends, and that, having read up a bit on these device thingies, the Duke rather wondered whether he hadn't managed to stumble upon one of his own.

There is, it has to be said, considerable scepticism about this at Windsor. Quite apart from the political expediency of claiming a device in a country when politics has become largely a question of mythic status and influence, it's rare for such a thing to happen to a man of the Duke's age – particularly with a device noted for its strength and vigour, as the giganticidal Corineus was. Nonetheless, the claim is a concerning one – not least because popular perception is exactly what drives the devices, and a false claim publicised widely enough (as this one's bound to be) can become true just by being generally accepted.

Not that Corineus is the equal of the Pendragon, of course. But he's not just any old device either.

For a start, he's the joint oldest in the Matter of Britain – one of the founders of the nation, according to the bunch of medieval historians who (while knowing nothing of such modern archaeological revelations as Doggerland, the Younger Dryas or the Beaker People, preferring by far to make up stuff because it sounded cool) once heavily influenced that very popular perception.

Before the Trojans, according to Nennius and Geoffrey of Monmouth and their pals, nobody lived here but a bunch of savage giants – and you don't see their descendants writing history books, do you? (Well no, you don't, because Corineus mostly killed them.)

First-generation British devices like Corineus and Brutus rarely manifest themselves at all, and only at momentous times in history. In all the Circle's annals, there are only four credible precedents, all disputed. One avant-garde school of devicial analysis, which proposes that some characters in the Matter of Britain themselves carried the devices of their predecessors, considers that King Mark of Cornwall, Sir Tristan's liege lord and an enemy (in some versions of the myth, at least) to Arthur, may himself have borne the Corineus device.

A Duke of Cornwall with a yen for his own crown, claiming the identity of the first ruler of Cornwall, with even a small body of device-bearing Knights at his command, might well decide that it was time to secede from the UK altogether and return the duchy to the independence it enjoyed before the ninth century or thereabouts. And there's no guarantee that the Duke would feel, as the Scots people do, that it was to his advantage to remain under the High King's rule.

The last full-scale Cornish uprising was the Prayer-Book Rebellion of 1549, which Edward VI's generals had to put down using imported German mercenaries, leading to thousands of Cornish deaths. That's not the sort of thing Jory wants his reign to be remembered for.

* * *

While Mukherjee and Woodville are taking their politically freighted train journey, Janene Long of the Green Chapel – the long-term ally of Little John, recent undercover receptionist, and occasional armed robber – is standing on the pitch at a football stadium somewhere in the Midlands, in a quite uncharacteristic ensemble of a Cath Kidston floral dress and a straw hat with flowers on it, surrounded by a couple of thousand people and listening to a popular American evangelist fulminating.

'...Because *sin*, my friends, is what separates us from God, *sin* is the one thing God cannot stand, and *sin* is the thing that's holding us back from the life God wills for us!' is the succession of words he's currently spouting.

The fat white bloke's voice is loud, and his delivery fiery, as he explains the precise nature of the Lord's displeasure with feminists, prostitutes, homosexuals, drug users and a number of Janene's other friends. (Thieves seem to come fairly low on his list of priorities, oddly enough.)

Still, he seems to be avoiding the trap a number of his compatriot and co-religionists have fallen into over the past seven years, of denouncing the devices as false gods created by Satan to lead the people of Britain astray. To hear some of them tell it, any myth even remotely tainted by traditional British folk culture has to be satanic in origin (because, look, a couple of the Celtic gods were sometimes pictured with horns).

Admittedly some preachers achieved a certain popularity with that message during the war, when the damage the devices were doing to lives and property was tangible and tragic, but these days they'd get booed off the stage pretty quickly – Britain's evangelical Christians being, as a group, as loyal to the High King as everybody else.

(There are exceptions, of course. One pastor in particular, named Bill Spink, has been hugely critical of Jory – but then he's allied to the device of St Gildas, a critic of King Arthur, and was locked up in the Benwick Institute until the High King's coronation amnesty for non-violent devicial prisoners, so he's hardly an impartial voice. It's difficult to quantify, but in general there's a percentage of Brits – a very small one – who seem unmoved by the near-universal loyalty Jory commands, and who become fertile ground for the hostile devices the Circle continues to battle. But such people are viewed with understandable suspicion and hostility by the populace at large, and any foreign preacher pandering to their prejudices is likely to end up being quietly deported back where he came from.)

The man's still thundering on: '…because it's the state that tells us what a *crime* is, but God – only God – can tell us what *sin* is! *God* is the sovereign of the world, not any man, and all the nations are as one in his sight, brothers and sisters!'

As anti-Pendragon rhetoric goes it's subtler, and less likely to ring alarm bells: the message is that the High King's claim to authority, and the quite understandable British exceptionalism which his reign's ushered in, are groundless in God's eyes. The preacher goes on to discuss how all men (and women presumably, although he doesn't see fit to mention them now), no matter how exalted, are steeped in sin and will have to kneel before the throne of God on Judgement Day, etcetera etcetera etcetera.

It's all designed to plant seeds of doubt, rather than inciting open revolution… but in some ways that approach, if successful, could prove even more dangerous. As I say, popular belief has a powerful influence on how the drama of the devices plays out, and if such doubts became widespread, the basis of the High King's authority might come into question. Janene, who was fond of Jory even before his ascendancy, wouldn't want that.

That's not why Janene's here, though. Yes, there was a fear, when the guy first arrived in the UK on his world tour, with his big stadium meetings and his limo, that he might be an agent of the Founding Frontiersmen. That's been a suspicion of every even slightly influential American visiting these shores these past few years, though, from the ambassador down, and Janene doesn't reckon it in his case. No-one with Rev Cantrell for a friend could believe that all preachers are insincere – not even all American ones – but she reckons his secret's a lot more shabby.

This guy advertises his revival meetings on the basis of the miraculous healings which he (or rather, of course, the power of the Lord Jesus Christ working through him) boasts of being able to carry out at the drop of a hat. Janene's been keeping a watchful eye on him during this tour, and a number of things have become clear to her.

Firstly, around the same number of people – four or five – are allegedly healed at each meeting, of everything from slight limps to bladder cancer. Secondly, there's always a larger number of people – twenty or thirty – who aren't healed, a fact which the preacher, and they, regretfully put down to their sad lack of faith. Some of these are the same people every time.

Thirdly, though both the media and Janene herself have tried, the subjects of successful healings are never around to talk to after the meetings. It's almost as if the organisers are deliberately keeping them out of any potential limelight.

And fourthly, the preacher, whose name is Roberto Schultz, makes a hell of a lot of cash out of these events. The ticket price is steep in itself, but there are also multiple calls for donations to further the Lord's work, particularly from those participants selected to go up on stage as candidates for healing. Janene's no accountant, but she reckons he must be making tens of thousand of pounds extra out of every meeting, purely from the generosity of his congregation. That's not bad for a couple of hours' ranting.

Anyone with an ally knows, of course, that belief can affect the body in remarkable ways, but curing an actual physical disease seems to Janene to go way beyond that. Admittedly she's no doctor either, but she's pretty sure her parents, who've worked their whole lives as NHS nurses in Carlisle and still attend church every Sunday, wouldn't even give that thought the time of day.

And since her considered view since the age of thirteen has been that Christianity's a load of old toss, she doesn't believe God's doing it either.

Schultz disagrees: '*God* is the sovereign, not of any nation, but of the whole creation – and that includes our bodies, brothers and sisters, the bodies *he* gave us, and the diseases that Satan uses to afflict them. God can heal us with a *word*, my friends, if only we believe in him.'

The preacher's demanding, and distracting, company, insisting on the congregation joining in with prayers and choruses and frequent rousing shouts of 'Hallelujah' – quite apart from the frequent passing-round of collection-plates – but since he's carefully avoiding anything that might engage the brain, Janene's been able to pay close attention to what he's doing. She's seen that every time he glances round the stadium, beaming beatifically or frowning in condemnation as his rhetoric demands, his gaze lingers for a fraction of a second on a few – say four or five – specific people in the crowd.

The people here aren't rich, just desperate. Some of them have been spending their life savings to follow Schultz around the country, buying tickets and making larger donations at every session. Honest thieving from those who can afford it is something Janene can admire – she'd hardly be in the Green Chapel otherwise – but this is something different. The idea of playing on people's gullibility this way sickens her, as it would many an honest armed robber, to the core.

She's going to put a stop to it.

* * *

Mukherjee, Woodville and their squires disembark at the sparkly new Newquay Tenvantius Station, the last stop before the Atlantic Flyer reaches its Penzance terminus.

They're met by Patrick Sullivan, the device-bearer of Sir Marhaus: a big Northumbrian of about Stephen's age, surly by temperament and rarely talkative. He seems pleased to see Stephen and to meet Tania, but not effusively so. Like them, he's in civilian clothes. He has his squire bundle their luggage out to a Circle-issue Range Rover, and stow it and their weapons in the boot. Sullivan's riot-shield is already in the fitted rack, a red lion rampant against blue-and-silver stripes, and Tania's, the same heraldic animal in gold on green, slides in neatly on top of it. By comparison Stephen's monochrome chequerboard design looks drab, but he gets that a lot.

Stephen gets in the front, their squires pile into the back, and Tania sits in the middle seats with Sullivan's own squire.

Tregorlois, the new suburb in whose outskirts Fort Cador lies, is one of the Duke of Cornwall's pet projects, constructed over the past decade from locally-sourced materials, in slightly twee imitation of traditional fishing-cottages. The Fort itself is made from Bodmin granite, and looks more like a Victorian castle folly than a functional military installation.

To Stephen's surprise, though, the Circle barracks aren't where they're going. Wordlessly Sullivan drives past the turning for Fort Cador, and continues up an incline towards the mock-Georgian new-build mansion standing on the rise above the model village, surveying the locals from inside its walled grounds like a priest in a spacious and comfortable pulpit.

'Where are we off to, Sullivan?' asks Stephen. The answer's obvious, but he wants to hear Sullivan's justification.

'Duke knows you'll need to talk to him while you're here,' Sullivan replies. 'You won't reassign us all to London without at least telling him in person.'

Which is true as far as it goes. If dealing with the Duke wasn't on the agenda then the Seneschal wouldn't have given so much thought to assigning Woodville to the quest, not that Sullivan will know that. (He won't know, either, that part of the quest is to covertly assess the Duke's devicial allegiance while they're here.)

But: 'The plan was to speak to you fellows first, and to the men,' Stephen points out. 'Seeing the Duke is just a courtesy call. He's not your commanding officer.'

Sullivan shrugs massively. 'He said you should stay with him while you're here. Wants to put his case, I shouldn't wonder. Stein, Rudge and Hithers are up at the house already.'

The wrought-iron gates open smoothly and automatically to the Rover as the Knights drive in. The drive's nowhere near as majestic as the one at Windsor, but it makes the most of what it has, winding a picturesque path past a stand of

96

Cornish oaks and an ornamental lake with ducks, before approaching the stately home in the centre of the grounds.

The Duke is standing there, hands thrust awkwardly into the jacket of his customary grey suit, the Duchess at his side in twinset and pearls. Behind them are the three Knights Sullivan mentioned, each in full armour, carrying the shields of Sir Sadoc, Sir Licanor and Sir Andret, and each accompanied by his own squire.

We're not only unarmed, then, Stephen thinks coolly, *but outnumbered two to one* – and that's leaving aside the men-at-arms on whose services the local Knights and their squires can call. To him – and, he can see from a glance in his sunshade mirror, to Tania – this is starting to look an awful lot like an abduction.

* * *

Janene's been watching Roberto Schultz like a vulture waiting for its lunch to stop crawling, and she's now sure that she's pinned down some of the worshippers he's been checking up on with his occasional reflexive glances. An elderly white man, wearing dark glasses and accompanied by a younger woman who's holding his arm protectively; a white woman in a wheelchair with a rainbow fish emblem painted on the back; a black teenager leaning on a pair of crutches. These have to be the people who'll be 'cured' today.

Muttering apologies and 'excuse me's, Janene's worked her way through the crowd on the pitch until she's standing at the front, right next to the nearest gangway. She checks her handbag – just to be sure she's got the cash she withdrew from the Chapel's expense account this morning, together with the other item she'll need – and mimes putting a note in the collection plate as it comes past her yet another time.

It doesn't take long. Schultz is building to a climax now, talking about how those who would be healed by miracles where human medicine has failed must trust in the sanctity and authority – and sovereignty, obviously – of Christ Jesus.

And so on. It's all claptrap, in the fine old Victorian sense of the word – and the people around her are indeed applauding, as well as moaning, raising their arms and intoning 'Amen'. Janene, who does her best to believe in the dignity of all human beings, can't help finding it pretty depressing.

Eventually the call goes out, for 'all those here who are troubled by ailments that socialised medicine cannot cure' – a dig at the huge proportion of Crown revenue the High King's gifted in perpetuity to the NHS – to come up to the stage for the laying-on of hands. As always, Schultz is careful to make no guarantees: only those 'whose faith is pure', 'who really hold Jesus in their hearts' will be cured. He doesn't mention anything about unprincipled out-of-work actors, but Janene's sure they'll be getting special attention from the Almighty today.

She approaches the stage when called, along with the other petitioners for healing. Superficially, some appear as healthy as she does; some are visibly disabled; a few look so ill they probably shouldn't be here. Janene feels herself – and within her, the huge and glowering presence of Little John – getting more and more incensed at the way these people are being exploited. They're all required to murmur their health issues to an usher, who's armed with the inevitable collection plate and expects people to use it, before they're allowed up on the stage. When it's her turn Janene slips a handful of tenners into the plate and murmurs, 'I've been having some bad trouble with my waterworks. Don't mind if I don't go into detail, do you?' The embarrassed man hurries her along.

Soon there are about thirty of them ranged along the back of the stage, the stooges interspersed with the genuinely needy. Janene keeps her eye on the three she identified, and waits her chance.

It doesn't take long. As she knows from reading up on him in blogs and forums, it's Schultz's practice to start off with a spectacular success, to encourage the others and keep the audience keen to see more. After the inevitable preparatory prayers and false humility, he calls forward the bloke with the dark glasses. His carer takes him forward to the front of the stage, passes his arm to Schultz, then steps discreetly aside.

'What's your name, brother?' Schultz asks the notionally blind man.

'I'm Edgar,' the man in the glasses replies, speaking carefully so that the mike can pick his voice up.

'And what are you bringing to Jesus today, Edgar?' the preacher asks.

'I'm blind,' explains the old man, for the benefit of the hard of thinking – which, to be fair, covers a lot of his audience. 'I had an accident when I was nineteen. I haven't been able to see since.' There's a sympathetic murmur among the crowd.

Janene sighs, pulls her handgun from her handbag, steps forward and brandishes it at Edgar's face.

The alacrity with which the self-proclaimed blind man recoils from the sight of the weapon is gratifying to see. The preacher cries out in panic and cowers, covering his head as Janene grabs the microphone from its stand.

'You see that, brothers and sisters?' she shouts. 'It's a bloody miracle! Except… I didn't see any laying-on of hands, did you? Nobody prayed to the baby Jesus for brother Edgar's sight to come back, either. It *has* come back, right Edgar?' The old man, realising the gig's up, rips off his dark glasses and tosses them away in disgust before stalking off the stage, followed rapidly by his 'carer'.

'Let's see if we can scare up a couple more miracles,' Janene suggests. 'How are your legs feeling, laddie?' she asks, turning her gaze – and her gun – on the kid on crutches. He looks defiant for a moment, then drops them and dashes away. He's followed by the woman from the wheelchair, who can see the way this is heading.

Janene rakes the line with her eyes, and spots another congregant looking guilty and trying to back away. She walks up to him with long strides, all six foot six of her incandescent with righteous anger. I imagine she looks pretty bloody magnificent.

'And what,' she asks him, still speaking into the mike, 'did our mate Roberto – who I see shifting towards the edge of the stage, by the way, so you can stay *right* were you are, my lad – what did that smooth-talking sod of a preacher man tell *you* to say was wrong with you?'

The man swallows. 'I was supposed to have a speech impediment,' he says, clearly for all the crowd to hear.

Janene turns to the congregation, raising the gun above her head. 'Well that says it all, doesn't it?' she asks rhetorically. 'You lot there, with the cash – I'd say these good people deserve it back, wouldn't you? Send it round, there's good lads, let everyone take what they put in. We're all honest Christians here, aren't we? No – hold on a mo.' She marches forward to Schultz, still huddled on the floor near the edge of the stage, and drags him upright. 'Give us your wallet.'

The preacher whimpers, but hands it over. Janene whistles at the contents, takes back the amount she put in the collection tin, then shakes the rest of the notes out into the nearest collection plate. 'Bit of a bonus,' she suggests to the congregation. 'Compensation like, for wasting everyone's time. I expect everyone here will be getting their tickets refunded too, won't they, aye? Before you cancel the rest of your tour and head back home to the States.'

Mutely, his legs unsteady, his eyes blurry with tears of panic, Roberto Schultz can only nod.

* * *

'My dear Titania, it's delightful to see you again,' says the Duke of Cornwall, shaking Tania's hand firmly at the door. 'It must have been, what, ten years? How is your mother? And Mr Mukherjee, delighted to meet you. Welcome to Corineus House.'

He doesn't sound delighted. In fact his voice sounds strangulated, as if he's swallowing marbles, but Stephen's heard the man and his imitators enough times on TV to know that this is more or less normal.

Stephen exchanges platitudes and a handshake with the Duchess, then says, 'We bring good wishes, sir, from the Circle and from the High King.'

'Delighted to hear it,' grimaces the Duke. 'Won't you come inside?' With his right hand, he gestures through the open door into the hallway.

Stephen glances at Stein, Rudge and Hithers – all men of course, ranging from thirty-five to fifty, acclaimed as Knights long before the civil war. They nod, in a friendly enough manner, and Rudge, the youngest, says, 'Mukherjee.' None have their hands anywhere near their swords.

It's notable, though, that Sullivan, while still unarmoured, has retrieved his own sword and lion-rampant shield from the car, while Mukherjee's and Woodville's remain in the boot. Seeing Tania's glance, he says, 'Someone will bring them in. Get into the house, girl.'

Woodville bristles at that, but has the sense to let it pass for the moment. Stephen has time to mutter to the squires, 'Stay outside for now,' before he and Woodville follow the Duke though the hallway and up a flight of carpeted granite stairs and round, into a large study full of glass-fronted bookshelves.

Most of the books are leather- or clothbound and largely there for decoration: only a few shelves near the desk, of dictionaries, encyclopaedias, Debrett's, *Who's Who* and some agricultural and architectural textbooks, look like they get some use. Stephen's not much of a reader himself, but he's been trained to observe these things, books being one thing the Circle has no choice but to take seriously. He also notes the Victorian editions of Geoffrey of Monmouth's *History of the Kings of Britain* and Thomas Malory's *Le Morte D'Arthur* lying on the desk.

'I thought we'd have a bit of a chat,' says the Duke, gesturing for Stephen and Tania to sit. 'Get a few things straight between us before someone shows you to your rooms.' Patrick Sullivan's entered the room behind the

Knights, and stands solidly in front of the door, gazing at the fine view through the picture windows.

'That's very kind,' Stephen replies. 'But honestly, sir, the Knights' quarters at Fort Cador will suit us nicely.'

'Not at all,' insists the older man. 'I won't hear of it.'

'You might change your mind after hearing what we've got to say, sir,' Tania suggests boldly.

'I doubt that, Tania,' muses the Duke. 'I doubt that very much. But do go on.'

'We're here with orders for the Knights and men here to head back to London,' Stephen says. 'There've only been two devicial outbreaks in Devon and Cornwall so far this year, and with the new rail link we can send chaps down at a couple of hours' notice – faster still by chopper. The Fastness can't justify the manpower any more.'

'Yes, I see,' swallows the Duke. 'Yes, they told me you'd probably say that.'

'We realise you've got used to having them around, sir,' Tania adds, 'but really you've not been under threat here for quite a while now. And with a dev of your own, well…'

'Quite so, quite so,' the Duke agrees. 'And this comes directly from your Head, I suppose?'

Tania glances at Stephen, who replies smoothly. 'Our orders are from the Seneschal, sir. The politics of it aren't our concern.'

'Indeed.' The Duke exposes his teeth in a nervous non-grin. 'Well, perhaps after enjoying our hospitality here you'll reconsider.'

'It's not our place to reconsider,' Stephen reminds him. 'We have a quest here. With your own military background, sir, you surely understand that we must follow our orders.'

'I see,' the Duke repeats. He's fiddling with his shirt-cuffs now. 'Yes, I see. Well, it seems there's no helping it. Your High King may have his Knights back, Mukherjee, on one condition.'

'Sir, we can't possibly agree –' Tania begins, but Stephen interrupts her.

'I'm sure that once we've returned with the others, sir,' he says, 'the Head will be grateful for your help with our quest. I'm certain he'll look favourably one any reasonable request you care to make. On the other hand, I'd imagine he might feel rather put out by having conditions imposed on him. Forgive me, sir, but wouldn't you? Tell me what you need, though, and I promise I'll put it directly to the High King.'

He can guess, of course. This bee that's arrived in the Duke's bonnet has pollinated an idea that he's made known to the High King's advisors on several occasions now. Both Knights were fully briefed on Geoffrey of Monmouth's account of Corineus' behaviour after Brutus died.

'Oh, I don't think there's any need for that,' the Duke replies. 'We have telephones in Cornwall, you know.' He gives a little laugh. 'We'll leave it for a few days first, to set him wondering. But in the end I imagine he'll be rather keen to get his Knights back.'

He stares at the bookshelves as he says this, leaving Stephen in little doubt about which Knights he means. 'Since you ask, though…,' the Duke adds, looking back at them, somewhat defiant now. 'I really think it's time we formalised his arrangement with my family, don't you? My granddaughter's only nine, of course, but I have a perfectly marriageable niece. It doesn't seem that much to ask of the ghastly bloody fellow, does it? I mean, really.'

6. SIR KAY

The High King's working in his study at the castle, reading a civil service draft report on the timeline for Scottish independence, when the call comes through that afternoon.

The study's panelled in teak, with tall arched windows opposite a giant oak desk. One wall is taken up with bookshelves, the venerable leatherbound volumes alternating with box files, optical storage media and cheap paperbacks of the essential Arthurian texts: on the other side, the shelves have been stripped out to install a giant screen display that the High King keeps permanently switched off. Across the carpet, big green leather armchairs stake out their territory like beached walruses.

'Oh, I suppose so,' the Pendragon says, when his secretary asks him if he'll take the call. It's a break from the routine, at least.

His secretary brings the tablet over and places it on the desk-stand. The face on the screen looks impatient. 'Damned stupid things,' it says. 'Why people want to see each other when they're talking I'll never know. What happened to phones you just talk to each other on, damn it?'

'Charles,' says Jory, keeping his sigh as internal as he can. 'It's good to hear from you.'

'Yes, well,' harrumphs the old man. 'Just wanted to check in, m'lord. See how everything's going. Whether there's anything I can do to help.' Sir Charles Raymond, David's predecessor as the Seneschal of the Circle, is seventy-seven now. He's been officially retired since the Stonehenge Summit, but that hasn't stopped him offering his services at every turn, whether they're wanted or (as has more generally been the case) not. Out of consideration for his device, Arthur's foster-brother Sir Kay, and for his half-century of service to the Chapel, the Pendragon usually tolerates him at least.

'Everything's going well, thank you,' the High King says.

'Heard you had a spot of bother at the Southbank Centre,' Raymond confides. Jory knows the old man still has sources at the Fastness, but all this demonstrates is that he has access to news outlets.

'Nothing the Knights couldn't handle,' Jory replies smoothly. There's no need for Sir Charles to know about Bonnie's temporary lapse of honour: Raymond would only use it as the latest in his line of tedious arguments against there being women Knights at all. 'They acquitted themselves admirably.'

Sir Charles grunts. 'Pleased to hear it,' he says. 'Stafford holding up well, is he?' He always asks this, despite the fact that David has run the Circle with considerably more competence and efficiency than he ever did.

'I'm very pleased with his service, Charles,' the Pendragon replies. 'He's a credit to your legacy.'

Raymond bristles. 'No need to patronise me, m'lord,' he says. 'May be old. Not bonkers yet.'

'No, of course not.' Jory sighs slightly less inwardly. 'Well, I do have work to do, so…'

'Reason I called, m'lord.' Raymond interrupts him out of habit. He's so used to taking precedence over other people that he sometimes forgets that it doesn't apply to everyone. 'Wanted a word. Heard Parsons had a tangle with Hellawes of Castle Nigramous.'

'That's right,' the High King confirms. It was a fairly routine encounter for that device – a woman named Sharon Brain had developed a dangerous fetish for the Knights of the Circle, had lured Paul Parsons to her house with a false rescue mission, and then tried to keep him prisoner for her gratification. Brain had set up an impressive bondage dungeon in her garage, but Paul had been able to escape his shackles the moment her back was turned by simply popping off the prosthetic hand he's worn for nearly a decade. He survived with his honour intact, and was able to persuade the woman to accept being chained up herself with surprising ease. As hostile devices go Hellawes is more pathetic than dangerous, and Brain is in the Benwick for her own protection as much as anyone else's.

'Wanted to say, keep an eye on her,' Sir Charles goes on. 'Not as helpless as she seems. We had a Hellawes back in the '90s. Killed two Knights before we caught her. She worked as a taxidermist in Bradford. Stuffed both bodies, and kept them in the wardrobe for... well, you get the idea. Can't trust her, that's all. Like the rest of these damn sorceresses.' He pauses, uncharacteristically hesitant. 'I don't suppose...'

'No, Charles.' This time Jory's sigh is pointedly outward. 'We've no new leads on Malory Wendiman.' He's not going to share Jason's latest discoveries with a retired civil servant, no matter how distinguished.

'Shame,' Raymond tuts. 'Have to forgive my asking, m'lord. Unfinished business.'

'I'm afraid all your business with the Circle is finished now, Charles,' the High King reminds him, not for the first time. 'Now, if there's nothing else...'

'I say,' Raymond interrupts again, as impervious to hints as ever. 'I saw Miss Long on the television earlier. Fine girl, what?' The ex-Seneschal goes misty-eyed for a moment, presumably at the memory of wrestling Janene at Stonehenge, in those moments when the ceasefire failed and it seemed everything was about to go finally and apocalyptically pear-shaped. It's as close a bond as he's formed with a woman for quite a number of years. 'Sounded like she gave that Yank the fright of his life.'

'She's a good woman,' Jory agrees. 'Now, Charles, I'm

very sorry but I'm quite busy today. I'll have to say goodbye now.'

He cuts the connection before Raymond can blunder down yet another conversational avenue. The retired Knight's lonely, that's the problem – he lives on his own in a cottage in Worcestershire, and misses the bustle and the busyness of the Fastness. Jory supposes he should do something about ensuring the old boy gets more visitors.

The High King turns with a sigh back to the report. Then frowns.

'Bonnie,' he says to Laing, who's been standing guard at his study door during this conversation. 'Find out what Janene Long's been up to, would you? I'm afraid we may have to ask her to stop it.'

* * *

Tania Woodville is sitting on the bed in the guest room on the second floor of Corineus House, breathing deeply to control her anger. The door isn't locked, as far as she knows, and in practice she suspects she'll be allowed the run of the house as much as any other guest – maybe even the grounds, under careful supervision of course. The four local Knights are keeping tabs on her and Mukherjee, though, and it's clear enough to everyone – without anyone having been so vulgar as to actually spell it out at any point – that they won't be leaving until the Head accedes to the Duke's demands. Not that he seems in a hurry to make them.

('Your niece?' Mukherjee asked the Duke earlier, after he dropped his conversational depth-charge. 'With all due respect, sir, why would the High King marry any of your relatives?'

'Because it's the way these things are done!' insisted the Duke. 'The dreadful fellow doesn't seem to understand that. When one's ancestor Henry VII conquered the Yorkists, he didn't just barge in and take the place over without so much as a by-your-leave, did he? He married Elizabeth of York, so that his heirs would be descended from the House of York and there'd be no need to spend another hundred years fighting over the throne. Even William the Conqueror's wife was a descendant of King Alfred, don't you know?'

'But…' said Stephen. 'Are you saying you'd give up the throne for –'

'Of course not!' the Duke exploded. 'Don't be so bloody stupid, man. If people really believe this awful man's the rightful High King, a marriage would make me his uncle, and my son his cousin. That would legitimise him too, of course, but it would make my family his heirs. The fellow's not planning to have children himself, is he? He's always said he isn't.'

'He's always said he isn't going to marry, sir,' Tania observed.)

The idea's ridiculous, of course, based in an ancient model of dynastic politics which can't possibly apply in the age of the devices, however relevant it may have seemed when the Duke learned his history in the 1950s. But his sudden obdurate insistence on the point backs up his claim to have been adopted by the Corineus device. According to Geoffrey of Monmouth, Cornwall's first ruler outlived his friend Brutus, but made his support for the king's successor Locrinus conditional on the young man marrying his daughter Gwendolen. The Duke doesn't have a daughter, and his granddaughter's clearly too young, so he's settled on the nearest marriageable relative.

In the event, although Locrinus married Gwendolen as promised, he carried on an affair with a woman called Estrildis until Corineus' death, whereupon he ditched Gwendolen and made Estrildis his official wife. There's a parallel there with the Duke's own life, Tania thinks – except it's with Locrinus's story, not Corineus's, so perhaps that's not a useful observation. Or perhaps some cross-contamination between devices is possible – Woodville's no expert on these matters.

In any case, the war which followed ended up with Locrinus getting an arrow in his face, Gwendolen ruling

Britain as its first queen regnant, and Estrildis and her daughter at the bottom of the river Severn. From the High King's point of view, this is hardly reassuring... not that the situation's going to arise in any case, because however impeccably-sourced the Duke's current wheeze may be, the Pendragon is widely known to have sworn never to marry, no matter how royal the nominated bride may be.

...all of which makes Woodville suspect that she and Mukherjee may be here for the long haul. Their squires have been sent with the others back to Fort Cador, where Tania imagines their movements are just as constrained as her own.

Impatiently, she stands. After some time spent pacing, kicking furniture and staring out of the window at the admittedly magnificent view across the rooftops of the town down to the Egyptian-blue Atlantic, she hears a peremptory rap at the door.

She doesn't answer. A moment later the rap's repeated, and then the Duke himself opens the door.

'Tania,' he says. 'I'm hoping we can have a chat.'

'It's your house, sir,' Woodville replies, none too politely. 'And I'd prefer "Woodville", if you don't mind.'

The Duke frowns. He pulls at his shirt cuffs, puts his hands in his jacket pockets and stares out of the window. 'You know Tania, I first met you when you were three. You were wearing red dungarees and playing with one of those plush toys – some sort of horsey fellow, as I recall. It does seem peculiar for us to be so formal now.'

Tania shrugs fiercely. 'That's not my doing, *sir*.'

The Duke grimaces. 'Very well then, Woodville. I've an offer to make. Rather than being my... well, hostage I suppose, for want of a better word... how would you feel about coming to work for me?'

She stares at him, aghast.

* * *

Rev Cantrell arrives at the Green Chapel camp just as Janene is telling her story for the third time.

After the war, when the Chapel found itself not only newly legal after years of enforced nomadism but positively endorsed by the new High King, there was talk of building a permanent settlement in Sherwood Forest – a village, or even a small town, for whoever of the tens of thousands who'd fought on the Chapel's side wanted to remain together as a community.

Jory nixed that, of course, with his plan that the Chapel should become his covert intelligence service, the Baker Street Irregulars to the Circle's Diogenes Club. These days the thirty or so core members of the group, with about as many ever-shifting hangers-on, live the same peripatetic existence as always, moving from forest to forest around the country – though this time with a special arrangement between the High King and the Forestry Commission that stops them getting kicked out. A larger community of Chapel loyalists – several thousand at least, though not all on the High King's payroll – remain active still, keeping in touch through chatrooms, online forums and mailing lists. These days the Chapel's a distributed community, most of whose members live their own independent lives.

Cantrell finds Janene perched on a trestle-table among the tents and yurts and tepees, assiduously depleting the white wine in the communal store-tent and recounting her victory over Roberto Schultz to an admiring crowd. Scar and Zara are there, and Ron, and Lee and Ahmed who carry the obscure allies Gilbert Whitehand and Arthur a'Bland, as well as a dozen unallied Chapelgoers, all hanging on her every word.

'You should have seen his face when I took his wallet!' she laughs. 'I've never seen someone so upset at parting with their cash. Hey, I wouldn't have liked to be him after I left. What do you think those Christians would have done to him, eh? Turned the other cheek, like? I don't bloody think so!'

'They goddamn near lynched him, Janene,' says Rev, and

everyone turns to look at him. 'The police had to be called. There's CCTV footage of you all over the news.'

'Aye, I saw that.' Janene tries not to look delighted, and entirely fails. 'It's no more than that bastard deserved. All them poor ill sods he were taking for a ride. He ought to be bloody ashamed of himself.'

'He'll be a hero in the States,' says Rev. 'Once he's recovered enough to travel back, at least. Most of the evangelicals there think the whole UK's possessed by communist demons anyway. He'll make a million from TV interviews his first week back.'

Janene looks uncomfortable. 'Aye, well. Can't change everything, can we? I'm just glad he won't be conning people here any more.'

Rev makes a pursed-lip face. 'Guys,' he says to the company at large, gesturing around the clearing. 'Can we have the room?'

'Aw, come on Rev,' Scar protests. Since her stint of undercover work in Soho she's dyed her hair back to its habitual scarlet, though it's a fast-washing dye that she can get shot of at half an hour's notice. 'We're settled down for a party here.'

'I'll never get in the way of a party,' Cantrell assures her. 'Five minutes, I promise.'

Grumpily, the rest of the Chapel people troop away to their tents, leaving Janene sitting on the table, glaring at him. 'You're here to bollock me, then, like?' she asks.

'Janene –' Rev begins.

'That tosser deserved it!' she insists. 'You should have seen them, Rev. Them poor bastards, coming to him with all that hope…'

'The guy's a piece of shit,' says Cantrell. 'You won't find me arguing with that.'

'What's your problem, then?' Janene asks. 'We're the Green Chapel! This is what we do.'

Rev sighs. 'Not like this, kid. Not any more. We keep a low profile, remember? The High King needs us out of sight for the big direct actions. Your face is all the way across the national news right now. And it's not like people can't join the dots. There are pics of us all from the war. A couple of websites are already running with "Green Chapel open for business". It'll be all over the papers tomorrow.'

Janene looks abashed. 'Bugger. I never thought of that. But –'

Cantrell says, 'Look kid, I understand why you did it, maybe better than you do. What went on back there was pretty much a re-enactment of a ballad called "Little John A-Begging". I'm guessing you've read it?'

The story Rev's talking about is first recorded in the seventeenth century, but like all of them it's probably older than that. The Merry Men are temporarily strapped for cash, so Robin sends Little John out to beg – but he meets a gang of crippled beggars who object to him muscling in on their territory. They attack him despite their supposed disabilities, and being Little John he beats them easily, proving in the process that the lot of them are fakes: 'John nipped the dumb, and made him to roar / and the blind that could not see / and he that a cripple had been seven years / he made him run faster than he'. Then he takes all the money they've conned out of people and takes it back to the others, although nobody in this particular ballad mentions sharing it with the poor.

'Little John…' Janene's shocked. 'Oh my God, you're right. I hadn't even –'

'It's the story-blindness, kid.' The scrawny man sighs again. 'Gets the best of us at times. You see someone with an ally acting like a dick who isn't a dick, chances are it's the ally in the driving seat. You found yourself in a place where Little John could act out a story he's the hero of, so he went for it.'

The story-blindness is a studied and researched phenomenon these days. The best-known example, just because of who it involves, is Jory and successive representatives of the Green Knight trying to decapitate each other when Jory was bound to Gawain, but it covers everything from Stephen Mukherjee's one-time obsession with capturing the avatar of the Questing Beast, to Paul Parsons starting a disastrous relationship with a woman called Elaine.

'Listen,' Rev says now. 'We can't stop the rumours, but we'll do what we can to sit on the official media – the Circle have a stack of experience with that. You need to lie low for a bit, though, kid – we can't risk using you in direct actions till this fuss has been forgotten about.'

'Rev?' Janene asks. 'You came from Windsor, aye? Does HK – is he pissed off about this, like?'

Cantrell wags his head. 'Kind of,' he says. 'He sees the funny side. And he understands the story-blindness, natch. But he needs us on top of our game right now, and this has tossed a wrench in the works. He says be more careful in future, that's all. OK?'

* * *

At Corineus House, the Duke's still trying to recruit Tania to his dubious cause.

He tells her, 'My four Knights are fine men, of course, but you see none of them are really *gifted*. Sullivan has a certain forcefulness to him, I suppose, but I'm afraid the rest are rather lacklustre, really. I've heard great things about you, though, Woodville. They say you're the best Knight of your generation – you know, of either sex. Of course I don't mind about that, but you might say we could do with a woman Knight here, to make our whole operation seem more modern. Balance things out, what?'

Tania still can't bring herself to speak. For all her making light of 'the Circus' and its traditions, she wouldn't have overcome the obstacles she has to become a Knight if she didn't believe passionately in the virtues it espouses. And those include stuff like constancy, loyalty, steadfastness and generally not running off to serve rival rulers.

'Don't worry about, you know, the money, if that's a

113

consideration,' says the Duke, 'or anything like that. It's all taken care of. Have a chat to Sullivan or the others if you like, ask them what it's been like working for me. The squires too. Good grief, ask the men-at-arms if you want to.' He waves a hand magnanimously.

'You may be asking, why you and not Mukherjee,' the Duke goes on, apparently interpreting her continued silence as an openness to the idea. 'I'm sure he's a fine fellow – these British Indians often are – but it's you I want. I was rather hoping they'd send you down, as a matter of fact. Not just because our families know each other, though that's helpful of course – it's always useful to have someone with a personal loyalty to one. But it's your device, you see. Sir Tristan was a Cornishman, he's well known for it. And he was loyal to the King of Cornwall, too, except for that unfortunate business with Queen Isolde.'

In the myths (and they've gained some impressive currency separately from the Arthurian legend, as anyone who's sat through the Wagner opera or that film with Sophia Myles in won't need me to point out), Isolde or Iseult is Tristan's lover, and the wife of his uncle, King Mark of Cornwall. Mark's a character of varying degrees of villainy: sometimes a justifiably jealous husband, sometimes an all-out murderer and rapist who ravages Arthur's kingdom after the High King's safely dead.

The Duke chuckles suddenly. 'I, ah,' he says. 'Well, I don't know what your preferences are of course, but I can't see my wife coming between us, Woodville, can you?' He pauses, as if to assess her reaction to his little joke.

It's true enough that Sir Tristan, though a Knight of the Round Table, was also Mark's loyal champion (or henchman, if you prefer) before the latter's beautiful Irish wife made her appearance. The attraction between Tristan and his aunt by marriage is sometimes tactfully ascribed to a love potion drunk by mistake, but in most versions they don't need any magical aid before they're at it like bunnies. (The Welsh *Triad* poems call Tristan one of the Three Amorous Men of the

Island of Britain, but then they call him one of the Three Powerful Swineherds of the Island of Britain too. The *Triads* are always saying stuff like that – the Three Prominent Oxen of the Island of Britain are my favourite.)

Tania takes a deep breath, then releases it slowly. 'Sir,' she says. 'Sir Tristan was a Knight of the Round Table, one of King Arthur's bravest, loyallest men. He'd not have supported a Cornish uprising any than Gawain would have an Orkney one, or Percival a Welsh one. As for me, I'm a sworn Knight of the Circle, and I serve its Head. Frankly sir, trying to persuade me to turn traitor is an insult to Sir Tristan's honour and mine.'

'Oh, but he *was* a traitor,' insists the Duke angrily. 'A traitor to his rightful lord King Mark. Sleeping with his wife, putting Arthur above him… Tristan's the biggest traitor in the *Morte D'Arthur*. I'd hoped that you might both be persuaded to betray the right side this time.'

'Forgive me, sir,' says Woodville flatly, in the tone of someone about to say something absolutely unforgiveable, 'but you're not exactly in a position to take the moral high ground when it comes to adultery.'

The Duke flinches. 'Young lady,' he says, 'I'm not at all accustomed –'

'Oh my fuck,' adds Tania, and he goes an interesting beetroot colour. 'I've just realised,' she informs him. 'Everything you said there. You're not hitched to the Corineus device at all, are you? For all I know there isn't even a Corineus dev. All that tedious yawn about wanting the Head to marry your niece – that's all a bluff. You've been letting him think you're Corineus's hitch, while all the time… you're actually King Mark's. You must have been planning to betray the High King for *years*.'

The Duke stares at her like a gutted fish. He splutters slightly. Then he turns on his heel and stalks out of the room.

This time, he locks it.

* * *

'So Rev, you staying for the festivities this time?' Ron asks, feigning indifference, when the others emerge from their tents. (A lot of them have heard the whole thing, of course – a camp's no place for covert conversations – but the Chapel have conventions about respecting other people's right to privacy, even if it involves a lot of pretending.)

Rev sighs. 'Soon kid, I promise. There's nothing I'd like more right now. But HK needs me back at Windsor, to talk through the ramifications of… well, all today's stuff. This is just a flying visit, and now I need to fly back. But you guys are grownups, you can get by without your mother hen.'

Zara says, 'Maybe if you'd been here, Rev, Janene might not have made her mistake. Did you think of that?'

The Chapel have always had issues with authority – historically, it's their raison d'être – but the Pendragon's is of a different order. Nobody here resents working for him, not as such… but still, that makes them anarchists working to further the aims of a monarch. That's bound to create some cognitive dissonance.

The result is that they sometimes shoot the messenger. Cantrell looks hurt. 'Hey Za, that's harsh. Like I say, you're grownups. You guys can make your own choices.'

'Yeah, we know HK needs you,' says Ron. 'We need you too, you great twat. Can't you divide your time between Windsor and here?'

'Guys,' Rev Cantrell says. 'Guys. What can I do? HK calls the shots. My hands are tied. When there's time I'll be back, OK, and then we'll all spend some quality time. Especially you and me, Ron.' He waggles his eyebrows suggestively, and the younger man tuts, exasperated. 'Now, duty calls. I've got to go.'

'Back to the palace in your chauffeur-driven car, aye?' Scar observes flatly.

'Jesus, Scar – what do you want me to do, cycle there?' Rev asks, uncharacteristically annoyed. 'I'm needed back in Windsor in an hour. I guess I could drive myself, but…'

'The limo's got a minibar,' says Scar. 'We get the idea.'

'Stop being a cow, Scar,' Janene says, unexpectedly. 'None of this is Rev's fault. Leave him be.'

Scar glares at her for a moment, then realises she's looking a little tearful. 'Ah well, if that's what he wants,' she mutters, and turns away.

'OK,' says Rev. 'I'll be back soon, I promise. I miss you guys.' He turns and lopes away through the trees, a rangy coyote experimenting with bipedalism.

'We should get ourselves a new holy man,' mutters Zara.

'Don't be so hard on him,' says Janene. 'He's doing his duty to the High King, same as us all.'

'She's right,' says Ron. '"Sides, it's not like we've got a plethora of candidates to pick from, is it? Rev's Friar Tuck's ally, and Tuck's the only holy man the Merry Men have got. What are we going to do, ask HK to appoint us a chaplain?'

'He's no the only one,' replies Scar, obscurely.

7. SIR MARHAUS

Roughly once a month, High King Jordan has to persuade a production company not to make a film or TV drama about his life story. It's a tedious cycle, which varies in frequency depending on arcane fluctuations in the industry, but after seven years Jory's mostly got it down to a fine art. The trick is to seem cooperative, but to impose so many reasonable-sounding restrictions that in the end they decide it isn't worth their while, and so persuading them to change their minds without coming across as a tyrant with skeletons in his closet. This particular consortium are being unusually pushy, though, and what with all the recent distractions Jory's not been on form today. 'Honestly,' he tells them implausibly for the fifth time, 'I can't see that it would be all that interesting. Before I became High King I was nobody, really.'

'All due respect, your majesty, but that's bullsh – that's unnecessarily modest.' The director's enthusiasm is feverish, but non-contagious. (You can tell a lot about the production these people would be likely to make by their mode of address. 'Your majesty' – a title Jory never uses – means it'd likely end up looking like a costume drama. 'Sir' suggests a political thriller, while 'sire' implies outright fantasy. 'My lordship' means the producer is American and doesn't have a bleeding clue.) 'You were one of the Circle's top Knights, then the leader of the Green Chapel –'

'The Chapel doesn't really have leaders,' Jory puts in. 'And I'm pretty sure nobody thought of me as a "top Knight" at the time.'

He fails to deflect the momentum of the director, who enthuses: '– Chair of the Shantih Foundation, and that's before we even get to High King! Warrior to outlaw to peacemaker to monarch – it's the story of a lifetime. And that's leaving aside the personal side of things.'

'Which I presume you would,' the Pendragon says lightly.

The director's wrongfooted, but the producer steps in smoothly. 'We feel a fictionalised version of the truth will serve us best there,' she informs him. 'We'd establish your vow of chastity back when you were a Knight, steer clear of the whole issue. All very tasteful. Nothing invasive or, erm, salacious.'

'I see,' says Jory. 'But if you're fictionalising *that*, my make it about me at all?' he asks. 'Why not go the whole hog and make a series about a fictional High King?'

The pair exchange a puzzled look. 'Well, sir,' the producer says. 'Given you're the only High King in modern history, it would be tricky to do that and not have people think it was about you.'

At this point Bonnie appears at the door of the High King's reception room and clears her throat. ''Scuse me, my lord, but there's this urgent phone call, yeah?'

'Well, we'd better wrap it up there for today,' Jory beams. 'Perhaps you could have a word with my secretary about another appointment.'

After the duo have filed out, he adds: 'I appreciate the gesture, Bonnie, but I'm used to handling these people. I'd have been fine.'

Bonnie frowns. 'No, my lord,' she says. 'There's this urgent call, really. From that Professor Tate-Thingy at the MRF. Priority one, she said.' She hands him a tablet and activates a window.

'Are we secure, my lord?' Tate-Hendricks asks. Her face is etched with concern.

'Wait outside please, Bonnie,' says the High King sharply. 'What is it, Freda?' he asks as she closes the door.

'We've got a security issue,' the professor says. 'A fucking breach... Down in the basement, I'm afraid.'

'Schmidt?' asks the Pendragon, sitting up straight in alarm.

'Afraid so,' says the Director. 'He's fine, but some of his research is gone. The daft bastard only kept one copy... on a USB stick.'

'How can he be sure it's gone?' the High King asks, recalling the scale of the mess in Schmidt's domain.

'He's not completely,' she concedes. 'Craig's men and women are going through the place now.' McCutcheon is the only Knight at the Facility, but he has a squire and eight men-at-arms under his command. 'He didn't think we needed to tell you yet – Craig I mean – but I know the rules.'

'You did the right thing,' the Pendragon confirms. 'Keep me posted if you find anything. Meanwhile I'll send Chief Superintendent Kinsey up to co-ordinate the local police. She won't thank me if you do find it in an ashtray somewhere, but I'd rather she was on site if you need her.'

'Schmidt vapes,' Tate-Hendricks reminds him, with the useless precision that's pandemic among academics. 'No ashtrays.'

'Nonetheless, Freda,' Jory sighs. 'Tell me, what was it that was taken? Was it...'

'A devicial mine,' the Director says, wincing. 'Or, well... the specifications for a prototype. You'd need to be an expert coder, or have one on your payroll, to turn it into anything functional, and we weren't... we're not there yet, my lord.'

'But if someone else was...?' the Pendragon prompts her.

'Jesus,' Tate-Hendricks says. 'In theory, if you could build the software and find a way to deliver it... well, it would set up an inframemetic interface and –'

'Tell me about inframemetic interfaces,' the High King commands.

'Inf-int? Well,' Tate-Hendricks begins, 'it's basically kind of a kind of hypercompressed storytelling. A bit like subliminal advertising? Well, except that it's not complete bollocks. What we have... what we're working on... is a way of telling stories via, kind of, flashcards and squirts of sound that we *hope* can directly interact with and reprogram the brain's devicial constructs.'

'And this weapon uses that how?' Jory asks.

'Christ, it's not a weapon yet,' Tate-Hendricks says. 'But when it's finished... well, it sets up an inf-int via a computer network, and when someone activates it... well, flash, crackle, pop and bye-bye that someone's device.'

'"Bye-bye"?' Jory repeats grimly. 'As in a Wendiman Derangement?'

'That's one possible payload, yes,' the Director admits miserably. 'The design allows for... others.'

'Right, well,' Jory says decisively. 'We'll need to – what is it *now*, Bonnie?' He speaks quite sharply, although the Knight knocked before opening the reception room door. 'I thought I was clear I wasn't to be disturbed.'

'Yeah, but I think you might want to be now, my lord,' Bonnie replies. 'Sorry. Jamie and Darren have just arrived – Steve and Tania's squires – and they've got a message from the Duke of Cornwall. I asked them about it though, and it's just bollocks. I mean, 'scuse the language my lord, but it sounds like his lordship's gone completely off his twat.'

* * *

Last night, before a brief but welcome bout of sleep, Bonnie sat in on another conversation between the High King and his advisors.

'So, do you think she was set up?' the Head asked Blaze, as he poured him a twenty-year-old Islay malt.

'Could be,' Merlin's avatar replied coolly. 'People using pretend disabilities to blag money off people – that's kind of a specific situation, innit? Sounds like they even matched the disabilities in the ballad. Looks a lot like someone built a trap just for Little John.'

'Damn, I'm glad to hear you both say that,' Rev confided. He'd only got back from the Chapel encampment an hour or so before, and had been drinking steadily ever since, with no observable effect. 'I thought I was getting paranoid.'

'Just 'cause they're out to get you, it doesn't mean you're not,' I suggested, but no-one was in the mood.

'But they didn't catch her, did they?' Bonnie objected. We were all in the conference room again, this time just those of us who live here – no David or Kinsey, just me, Blaze, Rev, Bonnie and the High King. 'Not to kidnap her or whatever. Was it all just about getting her face on Google?'

'Could be,' Blaze agreed. 'Like Rev says, raise the Chapel's profile and it's no good as a secret weapon. Tell everyone it's back in the picture and suddenly it ain't no more.'

'So was it the Frontiersmen?' I asked, but all three men shook their heads. (Bonnie said nothing.)

'Don't see how it can be,' Rev replied. 'Schultz has been in the country a month already, so it's not retaliation for Harding Steele. And Steele was *their* secret weapon – they'd have sent him in after torpedoing the Chapel, not before. He had no idea we were still around, which means his bosses didn't know either.'

'The Oisín crew, then,' suggested Blaze. 'Or the Paladins. Maybe the Nibelungentreue, they've got a grudge against us.'

'Could be someone homegrown,' Cantrell countered. 'Could be the Sons of Gore are back in business, or the Children of the May. The Saxon Shield, even.'

'Or it could be someone we're not expecting at all,' Jory sighed. 'Like, I don't know, the Brotherhood of Haroun Al-Raschid. Or the Yamato No Senshi.'

It could be Malory, I thought, but didn't say it. Best not to go there, not just now but generally. 'Any progress on finding out where that camouflage suit came from?' I asked instead.

'Not that David's told me,' the Pendragon replied. 'It might be the same people, or it might be different ones.

That's the problem with hosting the most powerful devicial entity currently active in the world,' he concluded gloomily, pouring himself another whisky. 'It makes you a target for pretty much everyone.

'If Schultz was working for someone,' Blaze said, 'there's gonna be some trace of it. Some dude bankrolling him, or inviting him here, or that he was reporting to. Who do we know with church connections?'

The High King frowned. 'Well, her majesty's still the Head of the Church of England,' he said. 'But I can't imagine Roberto Schultz is C of E. There's Bill Spink, St Gildas' bondsman, but he's always seemed fairly honest – I doubt he'd tolerate a fraudster like Schultz. Besides, the Chapel have people keeping tabs on him. We'll look into any possible connection, though, just in case. And I'll have David pull all Schultz's emails and bank transactions since he arrived in the country. A Knight can go through them and see whether anything jumps out.'

The meeting broke up there, and we all started heading back to bed (in my case), to a bunk in the guardroom (in Bonnie's), to do more work (in Jory's), or for a vigorous bout of sexting (in Blaze's), or last orders at the Crown and Cushion (in Rev's).

'Hey – any word from Stephen and that Tania woman?' Blaze asked as we were all leaving.

'David had a message from Patrick Sullivan saying they'd arrived safely,' the High King replied. 'Nothing since then. It sounds as if that's going smoothly, at least.'

* * *

It's technically the third day of Tania Woodville's confinement at Corineus House, although in fact she's been here less than forty-eight hours. Since the Duke locked the door on her she's been let out six times – mostly for meals, which she's eaten in the spacious kitchens under the supervision of Patrick Sullivan or one of the other Knights, but once yesterday for exercise. This meant a morning jog around the grounds, following Hugh Stein and with Sandy Hithers close on her heels, each of them armed with sword and shield (though armoured only by tracksuits) while she took with her nothing more dangerous than her Nikes.

She's been kept carefully separate from Mukherjee, who she hasn't seen since that 'chat' in the Duke's study on Tuesday afternoon. They've heard nothing from the squires.

She's exhausted all the reading matter that was left in her second-floor guestroom – mostly back issues of *Country Life* magazine, which didn't keep her occupied for very long – and is lying across the bed like a sulking teenager when the knock at the door comes.

She's already dismissed all the likely escape plans. The window's locked, the wall outside smooth; it's highly unlikely that they'll miss her hiding under the bed and conclude she's escaped already; or that if she feigns some unspecific illness whoever arrives to investigate will be so unprepared she can overpower them. There's nothing in the room to start a fire with – no matches, no lighter, no magnifying-glass, even. She might just get a spark from the mains, but she doesn't have any wire-strippers on her either.

She's just wondering whether the mattress would be enough to break her fall, if she smashed the window and heaved it out ahead of her, when Sullivan bangs on the door, unlocks it and sticks his head round.

'Exercise,' he tells her curtly. Yes, it's about that time of the morning. Woodville sighs, gets up off the bed and follows him.

Ken Rudge is waiting outside. Like Stein and Hithers yesterday, both Knights are dressed in Circle-issue blue tracksuits. It makes their shields – Sullivan's red lion on blue and silver, and Rudge's more restrained black wavy bar on silver – look drastically incongruous, but their swords dissuade Woodville from laughing.

The Knights escort her down the servants' stairs to a side-door, and step out into the mid-morning sunshine. Without further conversation, Sullivan sets off at a brisk jog towards the little copse, and Woodville follows his broad back, matching his pace. She hears Rudge keeping up behind them.

She wonders whether Stephen's getting this treatment, too. Are these concessions motivated by purely humanitarian concerns, or is the Duke still hoping she'll come over to his side? He hasn't spoken to her since their conversation that first night, when he accused her device, accurately enough but with little self-awareness, of treachery and adultery.

She wonders whether, if it came down to it, she could kill a brother – or sister, though that's a more theoretical question for the moment – Knight. Tania's one of those Knights who, though normally careful and deliberate in their decisions, are occasionally overcome by near-irresistible compulsions from their devices, and ever since meeting Sullivan – even before he betrayed them to the Duke – she's been ruthlessly suppressing an urge to murder the bastard.

She assumes this is because of the legends in which Tristan and Sir Marhaus are mortal enemies. The enormous Irish knight is Iseult's uncle as Mark is Tristan's, and his exact allegiance (like his name, which is variously Sir Moraunt, Sir Marholt or even 'The Morholt') changes from story to story. Even so, it's invariably by Tristan's hand that he meets his end. Of course many Knights of the Circle have devices with this kind of bloody backstory – Arthurian legend is nothing if not violent – and most of them manage to maintain perfectly civil professional relationships. Still, finding herself in actual opposition to Sullivan has made her device's homicidal impulses feel an awful lot more justifiable.

Spring's been unreasonably hot this year, and northern Cornwall hasn't seen rain for a few weeks. The Duke's grass, though, has been watered well. It's green and springy underfoot. The trees ahead have an equally healthy look to them, their leaves sleek and waxy. Woodville wonders whether the stand predates the landscaped garden, or whether the trees were transplanted here. The path they're taking winds through the tiny wood, and Tania – on the lookout still for potential escape routes – takes note of where the line of sight from the house ends. They pass it shortly before the point where Sullivan stops abruptly and turns, grabs her around the waist as she hurtles into him, and swings his sword at the startled Rudge.

He uses the flat, but he's a powerful man and Circle swords are built for business. Rudge goes down instantly and lies still, his head unbloodied but with what's going to be a hell of a bruise when he eventually comes to. Sullivan checks his injury quickly and professionally, lifts him with ease and moves him carefully between the trees, to rest out of sight of the path.

In this dazed moment Woodville recalls that, in many of the legends, Marhaus was also the sworn enemy of King Mark.

'This isn't right,' says Sullivan by way of explanation, returning with Tania's own sword, sheathed, and her gold-on-green lion shield. 'None of it is.'

'No argument there,' Woodville replies, taking the weapons gratefully. The tracksuit she's wearing has a waistband, so she quickly threads her scabbard through it. She checks the sword, to be sure it'll slide in and out easily. 'What about Mukherjee?' she asks.

Sullivan shakes his head. 'Too risky,' he says. 'Duke was going to contact the High King this morning. He's sent your squires up to Windsor with a couple of our men-at-arms. It won't be long before we're missed. We get away from here, come back for Mukherjee when we've got help.'

'What about your squire?' asks Tania. She can't remember the young man's name, but knows he was assigned from the Fastness relatively recently – the squires Sullivan and his comrades had during the war have long since been promoted to Knight, or shunted into desk jobs back at the Fastness.

Sullivan shakes his head. 'Don't trust him,' he says. 'The Duke requested him from the Fastness. Family connections, just like your lot. I wouldn't trust you either, if he hadn't locked you up.'

Tania considers. 'OK,' she says. Sullivan may have rescued her, very belatedly, but she's buggered if that's going to put him in charge. 'We go into town, contact the Circus from there. Have you got a phone?'

'Didn't want them tracing me,' Sullivan says.

'Never mind,' she says, 'we can rustle up one in town if we need to. Now, let's go.'

They check for anyone in view, then – keeping the stand of oak between them and the house – they set off at a run for the perimeter wall.

* * *

The pace has picked up at Windsor, too, over the past hour. Since the message arrived from the Duke of Cornwall, spelling out the terms on which he's happy to give up the Knights now in his custody (those who joined him willingly having seemingly been taken off the table for the moment), things have been moving at a frantic pace.

Those terms, by the time they reached the High King, had nothing to do with matrimony. The Corineus feint has apparently served its purpose of luring the Knights into the Duke's trap (perhaps specifically the Tristan device, though that would show an uncommonly acute level of devicial thinking for a newcomer). In his message – relayed verbatim by a quaking Jamie, with occasional corrections from Darren – he addressed the Pendragon king-to-king, as the bondsman of King Mark. His demand is now nothing less than a Cornish independence referendum to echo the Scottish one, with a binding commitment that the High King's government will abide by the result, and unfettered scope for the Duke to lobby the electorate for his own favoured outcome.

Just over an hour ago, the worst the Pendragon had to face was TV hacks invading his privacy. Now one of his subjects is determined to create a subsidiary state within the High King's own realm, as a clear preliminary to overturning the

Pendragon Settlement and establishing his own sovereignty over the peninsula, quite possibly with aid from overseas.

It's rare to see the High King quite this incandescently cross. His face has a colour to it that I don't recall seeing since... well, the incident with the Malory impersonator, actually. The wrath of the Pendragon is awesome to behold, as majestic and terrifying as a charging lion. He hasn't actually said, 'Will anyone rid me of this turbulent duke?', but it feels like it might be just a matter of time.

In fact, though, what he's saying is a lot more practical. 'We'll need the latest aerial imagery of Corineus House's grounds. Plus architectural blueprints, and some drones in the air.'

We're all in the reception room now. Through the vaulted Norman-arched windows we can clearly see the courtyard where those men-at-arms stationed at the Castle are loading arms and equipment into vans and FV452 Brachet Armoured Personnel Carriers, overseen by those Knights who aren't Bonnie. Up in the room, the High King is embroiled in urgent conference with Blaze, Sergeant-at-Arms Thackett and a widescreen tablet in whose panes Chief Superintendent Jade Kinsey, Sir David Stafford and Professor Freda Tate-Hendricks appear like a medieval altar triptych. Bonnie and I are also in attendance, but on this occasion we're silent partners. Rev Cantrell's at the Green Chapel encampment, finally making good on his promise to get down and party.

As the Pendragon speaks, pages scamper around us, expertly encasing his body in the ceramic-polyamide armour of the Circle. It reminds me of one of his early official portraits, the Claire Phillips that hangs in the National Portrait Gallery, where he's shown unguardedly half-armoured, as if dressing in preparation for a more traditional portrait in fullest pomp.

'I can't sanction your joining us in this action, my lord,' the Seneschal's insisting over the phone link, without a great deal of optimism. He's in the Fastness courtyard, and behind him similarly hectic preparations are under way. 'It's shockingly risky. Tell him, Thackett.'

'I think he knows, Sir David,' Bob Thackett replies drily. 'For the record, my lord, we can't promise to keep you safe if you go into combat. No-one could.'

'Yeah boss, so let the Knights deal with it,' Blaze pipes up. 'You're worth too much for us to lose, yeah?'

'Thank you all.' Jory's voice is clipped. 'The obvious has been stated. Now David, what have your people found out in the last hour?'

'The Duke's implicated in the Brewster and Schultz affairs, at least,' the Seneschal confirms. 'His tracks were obvious once we knew what we were looking for. He owns shares in Tarnhelm System GmbH, a German firm which specialises in cutting-edge battlefield camouflage among other things.' He's diverted Zoe Bramwell, Menw son of Teirwaedd's bondswoman, to Stuttgart to investigate after she drew a blank in Paris. 'As the name suggests, they do some work for the Nibelungentreue, but they're an industry leader so that may not be significant. We've also established that the evangelical charity who invited Schultz to the UK were given a big donation from a Duchy-run charitable foundation, in return for which they introduced Schultz himself to a ducal envoy. We're trying to get a description of the man, but I strongly suspect it's one of our errant Knights.'

'What about Schdmidt's missing research?' Freda Tate-Hendricks asks. She's alone in her office at the MRF, but we can guess from her stressed demeanour that police and men-at-arms are blundering about offscreen, disrupting the smooth running of several dozen research projects.

'It's too early to tell,' David says. 'There's nothing to connect the Duke to Harding Steele's blackmail attempt either.'

'Yeah, guessed that,' Blaze observed. 'Those Frontiersmen aren't big fans of the royals. They'd rather sell Mount Rushmore to al-Qaeda than work with them.'

'My people are helping McCutcheon,' Kinsey reports, 'but

we're certain the USB's not in the lab.' She's in the passenger seat of a police car, travelling at great speed down a motorway. Her tablet pane is responsible for the constant low-volume siren noise that's permeating the room and making every one of us a couple of degrees more tense. 'I'll be taking charge of the operation as soon as I manage to *fucking get there*.' The comment is aimed squarely at her driver. 'We'll find out then whether it's a clever break-in or an opportunist.'

'Well, then,' the Pendragon says. 'We'd better assume for now that the Duke has acquired Schmidt's prototype. When we end this call we should revert to old-fashioned phones and walkie-talkies, avoid any more sophisticated networking for the moment. Just to be on the safe side,' he adds as Tate-Hendricks begins to protest.

He's armoured now, his body expertly clad in ceramic plating from gorget to sabatons; only his head is not yet helmed, instead bearing the gold circlet which is the outward signifier of his majesty. 'Send a reply to the Duke now,' he tells one of his flapping secretaries. 'Inform him that his terms are not acceptable, and nor is his defiance of my authority. I'm taking personal steps to rectify the matter, and he should expect me to call on him shortly.'

His left hand leans on his riot-shield, blazoned in azure blue with a golden dragon's-head design; his right rests on the hilt of the sword, sheathed at his hip, which is not Excalibur but is the finest polymer-coated carbon-steel the Circle's traditional armourers can provide.

The High King gives us all a grim smile, one not without a certain predatory joy. He says, 'The Duke's house is in Tregorlois, which he himself named after Gorlois, his predecessor as the Duke of Cornwall. Gorlois was the father of Morgause and Morgan le Fay, who Uther Pendragon killed before fathering King Arthur on his wife Igraine. It's not an incident that does the family much credit, of course, but if I were the present Duke the omen would make me feel rather nervous.'

His armour is fitted to the highest standard, as all the

Knights' are, but his is uniquely surmounted by a velvet surcoat. Royal blue, it bears that same dragon's head picked out in thread of gold. His helmet with its inlaid crown stands on a nearby table. Again I'm reminded of a portrait, but this time those slightly scary paintings of medieval kings in full military majesty.

The High King turns to the tablet. 'Seneschal,' he says briskly. 'Have Harte contact the Highways Agency and get them to close the M4, M5 and A30 all the way from here to Newquay. Tell them the Pendragon is riding west.'

8. KING MARK

Woodville and Sullivan arrive in Newquay town centre at a casual jog. They've stashed their swords and shields in the hedge of a pretty bungalow back in Tregorlois, after they realised they weren't going to help them look inconspicuous to any passing Knight or man-at-arms loyal to the Duke.

The situation in the town amply justifies their caution. The streets are crawling – not literally crawling, of course, but liberally dotted – with the Duchy of Cornwall's men-at-arms.

They're wearing standard Circle combat fatigues and berets, as Woodville would have expected, but the gold-on-blue ring insignia has been replaced with the fifteen golden bezants – circles representing coins, arranged in an inverted triangle – of the Duchy's coat of arms. All of them are carrying guns… which before the war, on a street in mainland Britain, would simply have looked surreal, but these days is just liable to give a lot of citizens unpleasant flashbacks.

'Your boss is off his rocker,' Tania marvels from behind a parked van, as they watch the men-at-arms set up a roadblock, supervised from horseback by Hugh Stein and his squire. Stein is in full Circle armour, his riot-shield bearing the wavy black-on-white stripe of Sir Sadoc. 'This isn't a political disagreement, it's an attempted coup.'

'He's not my boss,' grunts Sullivan. 'Not any more.'

'This is because of me,' Woodville realises. 'Flitting, I mean. We've tipped their hand.'

Sullivan nods sullenly.

'Well,' Tania muses. 'It's miles to the next town, and they'll have search teams out. They'll have locked down the train station already, and they'll be watching the docks and the airport. Probably the phone shops too, and anywhere with wi-fi. By now they'll be telling the civvies to look out for anyone asking for a lift or to borrow a phone. What does that leave?'

'Mug someone and nick their mobile?' suggests Sullivan gruffly. 'Sarcasm,' he adds curtly, in response to Tania's contemptuous look. 'Duke's been my commanding officer for years, but I'm still Sir Marhaus' bondsman.'

Exactly how reassuring this is, Woodville thinks privately, might well depend on which version of Sir Marhaus Sullivan believes in. The *Morte D'Arthur* portrays Iseult's uncle as a bit of a bruiser, but basically one of the good guys: a Knight of the Round Table, an ally of Sir Lancelot, a chivalrous warrior and courtly lover whose fatal conflict with Sir Tristan arises, not from personal animosity, but from a cruel twist of Kerno-Hibernian diplomatic relations. In other sources, though, 'the Morholt' is a far more sinister figure – a brutal armoured giant, Goliath to Tristan's David. Even in Malory, Sir Marhaus's strength increases with sunset (in precise counterpoint to the heroic Sir Gawain's solar-powered muscles), and he wields a poisoned weapon for no reason but the extra bastard points.

This means that, while obviously Woodville has to trust Sullivan for the time being, she's reserving judgement on his device's long-term reliability.

In the meantime, her brain's been turning the current problem over. 'The Duke will have all his men out here looking for us,' she realises. 'He doesn't have any spare capacity – which means the Fort will be practically deserted. Can you get us in there?'

As inconspicuously as they can, the pair retrace their steps through quiet back-alleys to Tregorlois, and through its broad and pleasant avenues to Fort Cador, in the shadow of Corineus House, retrieving their swords and shields en route.

The miniature Gothic castle of the Circle barracks shows no signs of occupation as they approach. The car park's empty, and so is the sentry-booth next to the gates. No lights are on inside, but at lunchtime on a sunny day it would be odd if they were.

The flagpole's brazenly flying the Duchy flag in place of the High King's golden dragon. Woodville finds the emblem of a pile of cash vulgar and showy, a boast about the Duchy's wealth (a view she can afford to take with her family background, of course). If this is a Cornish uprising, where's the white-on-black cross of St Piran? But of course that one belongs to the Cornish people, and makes no gesture towards the Duke's patronage.

They're not expecting Sullivan's access codes to be still working, obviously – even if they're assuming Woodville knocked out Rudge herself and took Sullivan prisoner, the Duke's men would be daft to take the risk. Still, Fort Cador was designed by the Duke's pet architects, and has none of the military rigour of the Fastness proper. Sullivan knows the place's vulnerabilities: a back entrance to the compound behind the stable-block where the bins are kept; a security camera mounted where a well-heaved brick can knock it askew; an access code reserved for contractors which someone's forgotten to rescind.

Once inside, a quick sweep of the building turns up two unsuspecting men-at-arms, one of whom gets as far as hollering 'Oi!' before Tania knocks him senseless. The Knights lock them in a storeroom next to the ops room, then try to work out how to put through a priority call to the Fastness.

* * *

Rev Cantrell surfaces from his tent at a little after eleven, a time by which the more enthusiastic risers in the Green

Chapel encampment have been up a good six hours. Indeed, he met a handful of them on his way to bed.

Rev's vowed several times recently to make it up to the Chapel camp for a proper get-together and pow-wow, and he's a man who takes his promises seriously. Besides, he gets the sense that there's some actual dissatisfaction among the Chapel (which him turning up the other day with the express purpose of scolding Janene probably didn't help with), and it's clearly part of his function as Friar Tuck's ally, as well as his nebulously-defined official job, to resolve that kind of thing before it festers.

Accordingly, he rolled up last night in his government limo, with a case of rare vintage port, a bucket and a ladle, and announced to everyone in earshot that the party was now in session.

There's nothing the Green Chapel does better than an impromptu bash – given the opportunity, they could organise a piss-up in a Saudi embassy – and it wasn't long before the music was banging, the drink and various other mood-affecting substances flowing, and the assembled company bouncing around each other like maize kernels in a popcorn machine. Rev's recollection of it all is predictably hazy, but he does recall Twink, a member of the Chapel who compensates for his unallied status by being built like an exceptionally muscular bulldozer, dancing on a table with half the partygoers earnestly begging him not to and the other half egging him on, the traumatised trestles creaking beneath him like a galleon in a storm. Cantrell doesn't have a clear memory of how that ended up, but he guesses the Chapel won't be short of firewood today.

He came to bed alone – by now he's sampled every willing adult male in the Chapel, and he knows himself well enough not to even try sustaining a liaison over the long haul. It's like the Groucho paradox in reverse: he doesn't want to inflict that kind of grief on anyone he likes enough to be boyfriend material. He has other outlets these days, although he does seem to be getting through the young farmers of Berkshire at an alarming rate.

Knowing Rev as they do, the Chapel keep a large and well-appointed guest tent on standby, and he's spent a comfortable night on a camp bed. He rises, relieves himself copiously into some empty pint glasses, pops a couple of paracetamol as he does most mornings, throws on some clothes and leaves the tent. Outside, he finds Janene waiting for him.

Also Scar, Zara, Ron, Ahmed and Lee. Twink's there too, and Vicks, the Chapel's explosives expert, and Shell, who's allied to the other minor Merry Man, David of Doncaster. They're sitting around on camp chairs and upturned logs, sharing a pot of coffee and – in a few cases – clearly nursing nasty hangovers. They're not talking, and aside from the ten of them, the camp seems to be deserted, which perhaps explains why he didn't wake up earlier.

Well, no, because that's not something that particularly needs explaining. But still, the absence of everyone else has to mean something.

Cantrell says, 'Can I get some of that coffee?' Wordlessly Ron, who's sitting nearest to his tent door, pours him a mug.

'Well, this is nice,' says Rev, settling into the seat they've left for him. 'Feels like months since anyone threw me an intervention.'

Janene says, 'Rev, we need to talk.'

'Hey,' he says affably. 'Don't tell me all of you are breaking up with me.'

He grins, as winningly as he can manage. Behind the smile, though, it's clear to him that that's pretty much what's about to happen.

* * *

'Bloody hell, this is hopeless,' Tania Woodville concludes after five minutes of trying to get an outside line. 'Those tossers must have done something to the landlines.' In the absence of advice from the Fastness – if not the Seneschal's own orders, then at least some guidance from his adjutant Harte – she and Sullivan face a dilemma.

Sullivan shrugs. 'We could lock down the security and sit tight. We'll be safe enough for now.' He's been sifting through the day logs on the Fort's systems, and found out about the High King's challenge to the Duke. It leaves little doubt that the Pendragon's on his way with the Circle's forces in tow. 'Someone will get to us sooner or later.'

'Yes?' Woodville says. 'And what if it's the home team? We already know what the security's like here. I don't think we can hold the place against everyone else who actually lives here, do you?'

Sullivan weighs that up. 'What, then?'

Tania considers, but not for long. 'We question the men we found. Work out what the Duke's planning, and stop it. He must have known this could happen when he snatched Mukherjee and me. He has to have some military response up his sleeve.'

'Be realistic, Woodville,' Sullivan says. 'Man's in his seventies. He's not fighting anyone.'

'He doesn't need to,' she says tartly. His tone's a bit *Get into the house, girl* for her liking. 'He's still got your three pals on his side, not to mention a barracksful of men-at-arms.'

Sullivan nods slowly. 'OK,' he says. 'We talk to those two men, find out if there's anything we can achieve here. Otherwise we find an empty house somewhere, and hole up until the Circle get here. Town this size there's bound to be some people away on holiday, even in May.'

'Agreed,' says Woodville. She's about to go and get their prisoners, but stops. She still doesn't know if Sullivan can be trusted. She needs to shift the balance of power here.

She says, 'Listen, this change of heart of yours. Awfully convenient, isn't it, with the Pendragon on his way with a superior force?'

Sullivan looks annoyed, but he can hardly deny her point. 'That's not it. I realised the Duke had gone off the rails when

137

he looked you up, but I couldn't do much with the other three around. Got you out the first opportunity I had.'

'So Rudge, Stein and Hithers are all on the Duke's side?' Tania presses him. 'And all four of your squires? Just not you.'

'Far as I know,' Sullivan agrees. 'If they had doubts, they kept them to themselves.'

'So did you, I assume,' Woodville shrugs. 'I need to know, though, Sullivan. When we're out there together, can I trust you not to shop me to your former chums? More than that, can I rely on you to fight them with me?'

Sullivan looks mutinous. 'Rescued you, didn't I?' he grumbles.

'And that's the only reason I haven't arrested you so far,' she tells him crisply. 'I'll be making my rep to the High King when he arrives. If I can tell him you put yourself at my command and followed my orders, I should think that will go better for you, don't you?'

He looks almost impressed by this. 'Can't argue with that,' he admits grudgingly.

'Your word of honour, then?' she insists. 'You'll fight with me – under my command – against the Duke for the duration?'

Sullivan nods. 'Sure. Word of honour,' he says shortly.

In the storeroom, the man-at-arms Tania knocked out is awake again, though looking groggy. His colleague is more alert, but massaging his temple where Sullivan hit him with his sword-hilt. Both of them look up nervously as she enters.

'We know the Head's on his way,' she tells them briskly. 'He has several hundred Knights of the Circle at his disposal: the Duke has three. The High King's include the bondsmen of Sir Lancelot, Sir Percival, Sir Galahad and my device, Sir Tristan. Remind me, who do you have on your side? Oh yes, Sir Sadoc, Sir Licanor and Sir Andret. He'll also be bringing a couple of hundred men-at-arms at least, to your forty or so. The Pendragon's going to smack your Duke's arse like the slipper of God.'

She smiles sweetly. 'So – when he gets here, do you two want to be tied to chairs with Duchy insignia on your kit, or would you rather be on the side of the angels?'

The man Sullivan took down looks keen to please, but her own man is scornful. 'The Pendragon's not going to get here,' he tells her, slurring his words slightly through the concussion. 'He won't make it past Quintrell Downs.'

'Oh really?' Woodville asks. She turns her attention to the other man, who's now looking positively eager to co-operate. 'Fancy telling me what's going on at Quintrell Downs?'

* * *

'You know us, Rev,' Janene tells him. 'You know we love HK as much as anyone else.' She sounds a bit awkward saying it – Cantrell's suspected for a while that she harboured certain feelings for Jory Taylor before she became his subject – but there's no doubting her sincerity.

'Big Jack Bennett would skelp the lot of us for it,' Scar confirms, 'but we're all King's men now.' There's a general murmuring of assent, albeit a slightly embarrassed one.

'All that contretemps and argy-bargy between us and the Circle,' Ron says, 'that's in the past now. None of us want that again, do we? We've got no problem with HK, none of us.'

'OK,' Cantrell says patiently. Waiting for the Green Chapel to get to the point can feel like debating with Ents. 'I'm hearing that nobody's got a problem with the High King, which is great. What I'm not hearing is why we're even talking about this.'

Zara, whose impatience with stuff like diplomacy, tact and basic politeness gives her a (sometimes) admirable directness, has her answer ready for him. 'We don't like what's happened to the Chapel,' she says. 'We're not what we were. You know this, Rev. You've been part of it for longer than any of us, even Scar.'

It's true enough. Rev shrugs. 'What can I say? Times change. And us, we live in interesting times. But listen –

the Chapel's always changed. The Circle may be all about stability and the status quo, but we reinvent ourselves from one generation to the next. Didn't you ever listen to Brian's stories about the Chapel in the '60s?' Brian was the last ally of Will Stuteley, before he died and passed the mantle to the reclusive computer-imaging guy Eric. Brian's tendency towards name-dropping is legendary among the Chapel. 'Those guys used to drop acid with the Beatles,' Cantrell recalls. 'Well, according to Brian anyway.'

'Aye – we reinvent *ourselves*,' says Scar, ignoring the extraneous flannel and cutting to the chase as usual. 'That's the way it should be. That's *evolution*. This...'

'We don't like what he wants us to be,' Zara says flatly. 'None of us will betray him, Rev, but we can't betray our allies either.'

'HK reckons we're his personal black ops unit,' opines Ron. 'Which – yeah, obviously he's entitled to one, being High King and all. But it doesn't seem right that it's us.'

'Nobody minds stuff like catching that American agent,' says Janene. 'He were a right nasty piece of work. But spying on that Knight's wife who was shagging that other fellow, that were shabby.'

This was about three years ago. The Knight in question, Nigel Roth, carried the device of Sir Marrok, whose unfaithful wife cursed him with lycanthropy. Roth was therefore more paranoid about such things than most married Knights.

(One exception is Harry Plaice, the bondsman of Sir Geraint, but since the point of *that* legend is that his suspicions were unfounded, people tend to groan and tell him to shut up when he starts on about it... although it's possible his wife's cleverer than people imagine. After all, if you wanted to be promiscuously married to a Knight of the Circle, Harry would be the obvious one to go for.)

Jory – who's still acutely aware that infidelity is a major catalyst of crisis in the Arthurian myths, and didn't want any of his Knights turned into a werewolf, however metaphorically – detailed the Chapel to find out whether Roth's suspicions were true. The Chapel, whose sexual morals are, to say the least of it, less rigidly traditional, were quite indignant about being used as Roth's private detective agency.

Although it did turn out in the end that Valerie Roth was having an affair, with an author who tended to write people he knew into his teenage supernatural romances.

'Aye, and I had to dig up dirt on that Paladin woman,' Shell supplied. One of the least recognisable of the Chapel, and fluent in French by the fluke of her mother being Guyanese, Shell spent several months working for the British Embassy in Paris while covertly investigating the background of the Paladins' occasional liaison to the Circle, Marie-Odile Laclos. It turned out that Laclos had been something of a teenage vigilante at around the time the mayor of Bordeaux's son, widely believed to be an unconvicted serial rapist, had gone missing. The Chapel had planned to blackmail her, but instead she'd gone straight to her bosses and told them the truth about the incident, before being reassigned elsewhere. We didn't emerge from that one with much credit, it has to be said.

'There was getting that inventor bloke out of Germany, and all,' says Ron. 'That was sort of fundamentally your actual state-sanctioned kidnapping, basically.'

'Well,' Rev says heartily, 'while it's great we all feel free to talk so frankly and openly about the highly sensitive secret missions we've been on –'

'It's just no what the Chapel's for, Rev,' says Scar. 'It's no what our allies are for.'

Zara adds, 'But when one of us does something that her ally would do, that there's an actual story about him doing, you come down and tell her to stop doing that.'

'You got me there,' Cantrell says. 'Fact is, though, all this happened on the High King's say-so, so if we're *not* talking about disobeying him from now on, I can't see –'

'You said yourself, though, Rev,' Janene says. 'He can't use us for anything right now, can he? We're all over the blogs and the news sites. "On His Majesty's Secret Sherwood." "High King Hood and His Merry G-Men.'"

'Don't forget "Friar, Miller, Tanner, Spy,"' Ron puts in. 'That was a good one.'

'There's pics of us everywhere, even,' Janene says. 'And yeah, I know that's sort of my fault, like, but we can't do secret stuff when everyone knows it's us, can we?'

All this is, of course, true. At first the UK's print and broadcast media toed the Pendragon line and kept their mouths shut, but with the blogosphere and social media sites full of the recent revelations – which were soon appearing across the foreign news from Fox to Al-Jazeera – the lack of official domestic coverage became embarrassing enough that the High King relaxed his prohibition. Since then the tabloids have been having a field day.

'We reckon it's time to sit down and have a proper cogitate,' Ron tells Rev. 'Commune with our allies and all that. Decide whether all this is really what we should be doing or... well, not.'

'If we and our allies decide that we shouldn't be doing this kind of work, will the High King respect that?' Zara asks. 'This is what we need to know, Rev.'

Cantrell sighs. 'Beats me. Like you say, the Chapel's not much use to him right now, so I guess he'll deal. He won't like it, though. You know him – *dedicated* is the word. Always working to secure the realm. You may have a fight on your hands.'

'No-one's fighting anyone,' Janene says. 'He can depend on us in a scrap, he knows that. Like I said, we're loyal. Just... not unquestioningly. He knows us well enough he won't expect it, I reckon.'

'And if we no longer work for the High King, what will you do, Rev?' asks Zara.

'That's easy,' Ron says at once. 'He belongs with us, don't you, Rev?'

Cantrell feels terribly weary suddenly. He's sixty-six now,

hard though he tries not to act his age, and it feels like he's been having this conversation for a long, long time.

He says, 'That won't be for me to choose, kid. We none of us get to decide our destinies. That's not the world we live in any more.'

He sighs. 'Look, guys… you don't need me, not so much. A Chapel needs a holy man or woman, sure, but I'm not the only one out there. Now, Friar Tuck and me have got a good understanding, so he's not going anywhere – but who says a holy man has to have an ally anyway? There are plenty of priests and rabbis and gurus in this country who believe the sort of stuff we do. If you need you can fix yourselves up with a new guy, no problem.'

It's like the Groucho paradox, he thinks again. Any club Rev cares to belong to shouldn't have to deal with him as a member.

'But hey – it not like it's going to come to that.' He smiles broadly, ignoring the ache inside him. 'Now, did we leave any of that port, or am I going to have to rehydrate myself with goddamn water?'

* * *

Quintrell Downs is where the A392 into Newquay crosses the new express railway line that brings the Atlantic Flyer down from London Paddington. While Jory's reign has brought determined efforts to improve the rail links to all the furthest-flung corners of his realm, strong environmental arguments (which, for once, the Duke of Cornwall is fully on board with) have discouraged an equivalent expansion of the road networks.

Even so, the widening of the railway required a new road bridge, built – at the Duke's insistence and expense – from Cornish granite rather than the conventional concrete.

The Duke's stubbornness has certainly made the bridge pleasanter to look at. It also, according to the man-at-arms who's sitting behind Woodville on the horse she borrowed from the Fort's stables, allowed him to select the builders.

He chose his own preferred contractors, ones who worked closely with him on the construction of Corineus House – and who, apparently, he was able to persuade to make some modifications to the official plans. It seems the Duke's been planning for this day for quite some time.

Granite's pretty solid, of course – far more so than concrete. Woodville wonders how much of the quarrying explosives they had to pack in there to be sure the bridge will collapse on cue.

From where the Knights sit on their horses, in armour they liberated from the Fort, under the cover of a stand of trees to the north of the bridge, it's difficult to work out where Sandy Hithers might have concealed himself. According to the man-at-arms, all he needs is line-of-sight – along with a short-range radio transmitter and the necessary detonation codes – but Tania suspects he'll have positioned himself pretty close.

This is because, in itself, taking out the roadway won't stop the Circle forces descending on Tregorlois –the A392 is the obvious route for them to come by, but others are possible. What most certainly would throw the attackers into disarray, though, would be if one of the Duke's Knights waited for them to arrive, then blew the bridge up while the Pendragon himself was crossing it.

To do that, Hithers will need a decent vantage point from which to time his detonation, one where he himself is unlikely to be spotted. There are a handful of buildings near the bridge – old farm structures long ago converted into expensive holiday cottages – but only two where any such viewpoint is likely to be available.

'I'll take the barn, you take the farmhouse,' Woodville tells Sullivan. 'Oh, buggeration,' she adds a moment later, as she realises what the sound she's been subconsciously hearing for the past few seconds must be.

It's a low growl of serious-sounding motors, proceeding at a medium pace along the main road from the east. It sounds pretty much like what it is – a sizeable military convoy.

Without knowing its exact complement it's difficult to tell, but she guesses it'll be here in a couple of minutes.

'Move!' she shouts. She unceremoniously sets down the man-at-arms and spurs her horse across the fields towards the barn. She'd hoped they could to do this without making themselves too conspicuous, but if her suspicions are correct, Hithers panicking and blowing up the bridge before the High King's arrival would count as a win.

Off to her side Sullivan's galloping towards the farmhouse. Tania's mount hurdles the hedge that surrounds the barn – it's lucky they were in too much of a hurry to armour the horses, as an animal carrying more weight would have had trouble clearing it – and canters to a crunching stop in the gravel car park.

The barn has been converted into three holiday properties, two of whose current occupiers are staring at her in amazement, frozen in the act of climbing into their car.

'Someone came to look at the roofs this morning,' Woodville guesses hurriedly. 'Where is he?'

The nearer of the elderly couple gestures towards the far end of the building, where a tall ladder has been set up against the roof. Tania feels like kicking herself for being so unobservant, but at the moment she simply doesn't have the leisure. The sound of the approaching convoy's getting louder all the time.

'Thanks,' she shouts over her shoulder as she rushes to the ladder's foot, ditches her shield and starts to climb.

She wonders as she does so whether there was a better option. She won't get anywhere if Hithers spots that she's on her way and, say, gives the ladder a hefty kick as she nears the top. Even in her armour, the fall would mean spectacular bruising at least. But the only other thing she can think of is burning the building down, and the timescale hardly favours that.

She couldn't see Hithers from the car park. That probably means he's on the far side of the barn's shallow sloping roof. She climbs up past a frosted window from which clean-smelling steam is billowing, then a few metres more and she's scrambling on to the roof itself.

From here she has a good view of the bridge, and the road stretching away towards White Cross. The convoy's trundling alarmingly close now: the Brachet APCs, the Circle's vans, a formation of armoured horseboxes and the High King's bulletproof Bentley, accompanied by two of the new BAE Castellan tanks – scrambled from the army camps on Salisbury Plain, she guesses – and perhaps twenty Knightly outriders on motorcycles. They're near enough that Tania can almost recognise their shields – she's pretty sure she can see Laing's gonfanon and three red stripes which, from this distance, could be any device of Sir Lancelot's family.

She wonders whether she can attract their attention and stop the convoy, but there are all kinds of ways that could backfire. Instead she strides towards the figure sitting on a corner of the roof, wearing an ordinary boiler suit and resting his arms on a metal box as he stares over at the approaching military machinery.

'Hithers!' she shouts, drawing her sword, and the man looks around in alarm.

It isn't Hithers. It's someone she's never met, with 'PENDENNIS ROOF AND TILING' printed on the pocket of his outfit. The metal thing's a lunchbox, judging by the ball of clingfilm and half-eaten sandwich resting on top of it.

'Who the hell are you?' the man asks, taking in her armour and sword. He has the strongest Cornish accent Tania's heard since her arrival here. He nods at the approaching Circle phalanx. 'Are you with that lot?'

The first Castellan is trundling onto the bridge, closely followed by two of the Brachets.

'Oh, damn and sod it!' Woodville yells petulantly, and whirls round to stare at the roof of the neighbouring farmhouse.

On its nearest gable, two Knights are locked in combat. From here she can't tell which is which – Sullivan and Hithers are both big strapping blokes, and they didn't bother carrying their shields up onto the rooftop. In the gutter between them, something's been dropped that could well be a short-range radio transmitter.

Their swords are flailing wildly, as they fight not only for dominance but for their balance on the awkwardly angled surface. Woodville can't hear the sounds they're making over the noise of the convoy, but they're both powerfully strong, and they're landing some fearful blows. One of their breastplates has a visible crack in it.

There's nothing Woodville can do now, except try to stop the convoy – but now she realises the Pendragon's Bentley's followed the APCs onto the bridge, and stopping them there is the last thing she should be doing. Tania yells with frustration, therefore, as Bonnie Laing halts her bike and stares at the farmhouse roof, then gestures to the other vehicles, which start to slow down.

Over on the other rooftop, one of the Knights aims a mighty swing at his opponent, who at the same moment loses his footing and stumbles against the tiles. The attacking Knight's blow misses, and thrown off balance by his own momentum he steps too close to the gutter, which gives way beneath him. As he topples from the roof, his fallen opponent lunges for the transmitter and manages to hold onto it, stopping it from following him to the ground.

'Keep moving, you bloody idiots!' Woodville screams at the convoy, but her voice can't carry over the idling motors.

The Knight on the roof pushes back his visor and gives her a thumbs-up. Then he takes off a gauntlet and carefully pops the batteries out of the transmitter, before dropping it and crushing it under his boot.

'Are they with you as well?' asks the roofer who's come to stand beside her, but she ignores him, sagging with relief. Sullivan's climbing down the ladder now, presumably to go and see how badly Hithers is hurt.

Despite her relief at his success, though, Tania can't help feeling just the tiniest bit cheated.

'OK Scar, time to divulge,' Ron tells the older woman after they've all bid Rev goodbye. 'You said Friar Tuck wasn't the only holy man the Merry Men had. So who's the other?'

Scar scowls at him for a few seconds, then sighs. 'You're too young to have seen *Robin of Sherwood*, aye Ron?'

Ron bristles. 'Of course not! I loved that show when I was a kid. I had a massive crush on Jonas Armstrong.'

Scar tuts. 'No that one, you daft wee child. I'm talking the '80s one, with that Jason Connery. Lived in a forest but always had perfect fucking hair. On every week when I was a girl.'

'Well prior to my time, then,' Ron says dismissively.

'I've seen some of it,' Janene says. 'We've got these old DVDs around somewhere. Rev says the people who made it must've known about the allies. The first Robin gets killed halfway through, but then Jason Connery comes along and it's like the Robin ally chooses him to carry on, like.'

'That's the one,' says Scar.

Zara says, 'It's the first version with the Saracen in it. They invented him, or discovered him perhaps, and now all of the later versions use him. Now he's a fixture.'

Janene frowns. 'Friar Tuck were in that one, though, right?'

'Aye,' Scar agrees, 'but he's no the holy man I mean. There's that shaman guy. Lives in a cave, wears antlers on his head. Gives them prophecies and tells them what to do and shite.'

'His name's Herne the Hunter,' adds Zara. 'He's played by John Abineri. What?' she adds, seeing the look Ron gives her. 'I read the credits and I have a good memory.'

'Shaun used to wear antlers,' Lee recalls suddenly. 'When he was doing stuff and the Circle might be near. Shaf too. Used to say it was a Green Knight thing.' Lee doesn't talk much, so when he does people tend to listen.

'See?' Janene says. 'It's like the TV people had someone from the Chapel giving them advice or some such.'

'Probably Brian,' says Vicks, which gets a laugh.

'Herne's an actual legend though,' Scar says. ''Za looked him up. He's no part of the Robin Hood story, but there are these proper stories about him. He's even in some Shakespeare thing.'

'*The Merry Wives of Windsor*,' Zara says. She reads a lot of classics now her English is good enough. 'He doesn't appear, but he's spoken about. Like Scar says, there have been stories for a long time. He's said to be the ghost of an executed gamekeeper, but some people think he came from long before that, from one of the gods the old British legends talk about. ' She's picking her words carefully. There are, after all, no gods but Allah, and however she's chosen to live her life she continues to believe that.

'Aye,' says Scar. 'Horny bastard with antlers living in the forest, that's who the Celts worshipped. A nature god. Cernunnos.' Scar herself is an atheist, but she's done her time at various women's communes, many of whose residents have had a distinctly neopagan bent. 'All I'm saying is, if we're looking for a new holy man, we could do worse.'

'You reckon there might be a properly actual Herne the Hunter ally?' Ron purses his lips. 'But how could we get in touch with it?'

'Far as that goes,' Scar says, 'I'd say one of us should talk to Burn.'

'Burn?' Ron repeats. 'Who's… Oh,' he says, remembering. 'You mean Blaze.'

* * *

The Circle convoy waits while Woodville explains breathlessly to Bonnie what's going on, then while the High King's evacuated from the Bentley with impressive dispatch.

'Good work, Woodville,' the Seneschal tells her, as everyone else withdraws to a safe distance and sappers are sent in to check out the bridge. 'You've saved the Pendragon's life today.'

'Actually, sir, it was Sullivan,' Tania admits, still feeling the injustice of this, but certainly not about to lie to her boss over it. 'He stopped Hithers fragging the bridge, not me.' Sandy Hithers has a broken ankle and a fractured arm, and is being cared for by the Circle's field medics.

'Sullivan,' Sir David acknowledges warily.

'Just following orders, sir,' Sullivan replies, a little piously. 'Surrendered myself to Woodville's command when I realised what the Duke was about.'

Sir David nods. 'Quite right. We'll discuss your future when time allows. For now, you're dismissed from duty.'

The sappers take soundings of the bridge to locate the charges, then make a variety of worried noises and faces. Eventually their sergeant-at-arms comes back and reports that the explosives can't be removed without effectively dismantling the structure. Theo Harte, the perpetually harried bondsman of Sir Ector who's stayed behind at the Fastness to co-ordinate the necessary logistics and fretting, has been working on alternative routes – but all of them are either too winding and narrow for the military vehicles, or else unbelievably circuitous and likely to introduce unacceptable delay.

That's not the only factor to be considered, though. If the bridge, designed and built by appointment to his grace the Duke, could hold deadly booby-traps, then what of the streets of Tregorlois, the little fiefdom created at his behest? It could be that the Circle troops are entering territory more dangerous than anyone's previously guessed.

A conversation ensues between the High King and his Seneschal, which threatens to get heated until both Bonnie Laing and Sergeant-at-Arms Thackett intervene to back Sir David up. The upshot is that Stafford will take the main body of the convoy across the bridge at speed, having carefully scouted the surrounding area for anyone else lurking with a radio transmitter. Meanwhile, and under protest, the High

King and a smaller force of Knights and men-at-arms will hold back and await safe passage.

The Seneschal presses on, then, with the two Castellan tanks, the Brachets and the Knights and horses in the transports. They breast the bridge successfully, and press on to Tregorlois, but find the little suburb's streets effectively impassable. A number of houses in strategic positions have been demolished, evidently by more explosives, and the locals are out in force. These aren't the mutinous men-at-arms from Fort Cador, but ordinary residents loyal to the Duke, carrying illegal firearms and prepared to defend their homes against all comers. With the chocolate-box prettiness of the houses, and the efficient ruthlessness of the populace, it's disconcertingly like trying to invade Switzerland.

The Seneschal and his men have by far the superior force, of course, but their vehicles – except the tanks, which can get over pretty much anything – are barred from the town. It's down to hand-to-hand fighting in the streets, with the onus on the Circle forces to minimise civilian casualties despite the fact that these 'civilians' are currently enemy combatants.

Sir David orders the non-lethal weaponry brought out, and soon the air is full of smoke, disorientating flashes and shrill ultrasonic whines.

The Knights go in with their shields and the flats of their swords to pacify the befuddled civilians, while the men-at-arms restrict themselves to picking off the snipers on the roofs and upper floors of the houses – without, wherever possible, actually killing them. Everyone's all too aware there'll be an independent inquiry about this later, and the High King does not tolerate cover-ups.

Tregorlois isn't large, but the going is hard, and it'll take Sir David's forces an hour or so to fight their way through to Corineus House.

By the time they get there, the High King will be waiting for them.

* * *

As soon as the Seneschal's force was out of sight, High King Jordan put a call in to RAF Benson in Oxfordshire and ordered a flight of three Catuvellauni CV-2 heavy-duty troop-carrying helicopters and two Dunmonii DN-8 gunships. It took them about forty minutes to arrive at Quintrell Downs.

Sir David left two vanfuls of men-at-arms, the motorcycle outriders and Woodville, who's been rather hoping the High King would pull a trick like this. Leaving a token guard for Sullivan and Hithers, they all troop aboard the choppers and belt up for the short hop to the grounds of Corineus House.

The Pendragon and his troops emerge from the Catuvellauni next to the ornamental lake, and the men-at-arms set up a defensive cordon around the Knights. As the third helicopter lifts away, the High King's forces begin their advance.

The first assault they face is from Hugh Stein, Ken Rudge and the four squires, charging in on their horses from the cover of a nearby ha-ha. Ignoring the enlisted troops, on the basis that well-trained Circle men-at-arms would never fire on a Knight, they do their level best to fight their way through the High King's Knights to attack Jordan himself. They're outnumbered, of course, but the Pendragon's Knights are horseless (and the motorbikes were too heavy to bring). A surprisingly brutal struggle follows, with the Duke's cavalry hacking and slicing viciously at their erstwhile comrades and the High King's doing their level best to remove the attackers' advantage by disabling their horses.

Tania finds herself at the mercy of Rudge's steed as it rears up in panic and prepares to crush her with its hooves. She tries to fall back, but Sir Lionel's bondsman Doug Felton is in the way, fighting hand-to-hand with Sullivan's unseated squire.

A desperate spring – assisted by Sir Tristan, one of whose fortes was the spectacular evasive leap – places her momentarily on the startled squire's shoulders as Rudge's horse's hooves come crashing down, and then another jump has her in the saddle, facing Rudge and wrestling to unhorse him.

By the time Rudge is on the ground and Tania sitting backwards on his horse, the skirmish is over. Felton puts the point of his blade at Rudge's throat, as Laing withdraws her messy sword from somewhere inside Hugh Stein's torso. Three of the squires are captive, and the fourth is fleeing on horseback towards the gates.

The High King's advance on the house begins again, and the thirty-odd men-at-arms concealed in the copse open fire.

These men were once well-trained too, of course, but now they've been hopelessly corrupted. Their bullets come in a horizontal hail, bouncing from shields and armour, scoring the occasional lucky hit at a join.

The Pendragon gestures, and a man-at-arms hands him a megaphone. He raises it – his surcoat tattering with the impact of the rounds – and such is the authority of his device that, for the moment, the enemy troops hold fire to hear what he says.

The Pendragon clears his throat, and speaks mildly into the megaphone. 'You understand, of course, that now you've shot at us, my men-at-arms are entitled to shoot you back. You feel comfortable with that, I'm sure – you have the cover of those trees, and there aren't as many men in my party as yours. But as far as I recall, there's no stipulation in the honour code about the firearms we use being handheld ones.'

From behind Corineus House, their rotors thrumming, the two Dunmonii gunships rise up ominously, and hover in the sunny sky like murderous heavy-duty hummingbirds.

The men-at-arms' surrender follows rather quickly after that, and the High King's party continue on their way into the Duke's House.

Inside there's a little more resistance from the few men-at-arms left on interior guard duty, but nothing the Pendragon's troops can't handle. It isn't long before he's in the Duke of Cornwall's study, facing the man himself.

The High King coolly eyes the Duke's last line of

defence, the big burly men from the Met's Special Escort Group assigned to royal protection duty.

'You chaps can stand down now,' he says. 'I'll take full responsibility for his grace's safety.' And, to a man, they do.

The Duke seems calm. Like most of the male royals, he spent a few years in the military, but he never saw anything resembling active service. After the life he's led, it's probably inconceivable to him that he might be in actual physical danger.

He says, 'I don't recognise your authority, Taylor, you know. My claim to kingship's older than yours.' His voice sounds even tighter than usual, but that's all the tension he displays.

The High King says, 'What you recognise is utterly immaterial. I don't care if you're carrying the device of Brutus himself, I'm the High King of Britain. You'll kneel to me or you'll end your life a prisoner.'

The Duke glares defiance at him, but he's been bettered and he knows it. The Pendragon's threat is far from an empty one – even if history will not prove it altogether accurate.

* * *

'My God sir, he wanted you to *get married!*' Stephen Mukherjee exclaims indignantly when he's brought before the Pendragon. The Knights found him within a few minutes of taking the house, locked in the attic, frustrated but unharmed. The idea that the High King might be induced to break his vow of celibacy obviously offends him as much as his imprisonment.

'My word,' says the High King gravely, a merry robber's smile playing around his lips. 'If that should happen, I can only think of one line of defence. I trust I could rely on you, Stephen, to safeguard everyone's honour by standing in for me.'

Stephen looks suitably appalled.

9. SIR GARETH

So that he won't look like the kind of adult who hangs round furtively outside the gates of schools, Jason Smith has borrowed a surveillance van from the Circle's depot outside York, and is hanging around furtively inside that instead.

The school themselves are fine with him being here, of course (or if not fine, are at least going along with it when presented with his Circle ID and an ultimatum), but that won't help him with the overprotective nosiness of the parents, which is the kind of attention he most needs to avoid.

Since this particular quest is off the radar of the Circle proper – and has to stay that way, unless Jason wants to see Edward Wendiman arrested and chucked into prison – he had to tail the old man himself. The day after his visit to his flat, Jason followed Merry's dad onto a bus into Glasgow, and then trailed him around an astonishing number of payphones, post offices, internet booths, public libraries, wi-fi-enabled public spaces and park benches, before the ex-academic quietly went home to his flat. Jason's still going through the lists of Wendiman's communications from all those places – including the park benches, where Jason photographed then carefully refolded and left several pieces of paper containing gibberish alphanumeric sequences – but it hardly seems likely that any of the information that emerges from this process will lead him successfully to Malory.

That, though, was never the plan.

Malory, you see, is clever – and she's had a lot of experience of hiding herself away. For years she led a triple life, her colleagues in the university psychology department having no more idea that she was secretly a secular advisor to the Circle than the Knights had that she was covertly re-establishing the Green Chapel on their watch.

She'd know full well that one day the Circle might get round to tracking her as far as her dad. That would be why she gave him her emergency contact details, after all, whatever they might have been. She'll also have had an escape plan in place for when that day came.

Jason's willing to bet that it involves some third (or possibly fourth or fifth) identity: one she's carefully prepared so she can up sticks and step into a new life whenever it's needed. One day she might be, say, a brunette Liverpudlian travel agent with a pierced nose living in Portsmouth; the next, a blonde, tattoooed freelance illustrator who's just moved from Cork to Fort William. Or wherever. The point is, Merry can be whoever she wants to be – as far as anyone around her knows, at least – and there's no way he can obtain a list of every fortyish woman who's moved house over the past week.

With the kid, though, she doesn't have so many options. Keeping a seven-year-old boy at home in the middle of term – that the neighbours *would* notice. She'll have to send the lad to school, or teach him herself – he'll appear somewhere on the local authority records, in either case.

Using the High King's own pool of office support people instead of the Circle's, Jason put out instructions to every primary school in the country, to report directly to him any six- or seven-year-old boys arriving via an unexpected mid-term transfer. (He also asked them for details of any who unexpectedly didn't turn up for school, but there turn out to be shedloads of the little buggers. Picking out the ones who've moved without notice from those who've been ill or playing hooky, or whisked away by irresponsible middle-class parents to the south of France at termtime prices, looks like a big job. And how much would it tell him, except about Malory's past life in a place she's now abandoned?)

Three possibilities popped up. One had the surname 'Oshiro', and Jason dismissed him after a quick chat with the school secretary established that the family was indeed Japanese. (Well… he did consider the idea of really convincing makeup, but he couldn't see it reliably surviving a day after day of school rough-and-tumble.)

The second lad he trailed home from school yesterday in Maidstone: his mum, though, looked nothing at all like Merry and both parents appeared to be violent alcoholics – no way would Merry have exposed her kid to that, even as a cover story. After a very brief conversation with his conscience, Jason phoned the local social services before moving on.

Today, at 8:45am, he's outside a Church of England primary school in Halifax, where a single mother called Harriet Stoke is dropping off her son, Bradley. The surveillance van's CCTV – whose basic workings a long-suffering techie man-at-arms insisted on explaining before Jason drove the vehicle away – feeds onto a massive, high-definition touchscreen taking up most of one wall of the van. It's so clear it gives the impression of a picture window on the street outside – a zoomable, tappable, multimedia-capable interactive picture window. Jason can zoom in on Harriet Stoke's face, and gets a good look at her eyes, the curve of her nose, the quirk of her lips…

…And yes, all of those are Merry's. Admittedly her hair is black, not ginger, and he thinks she may have padded out her bra a bit (unless that comes from having had a baby, the effects of which on the female body Jason is hazy about), but if he had to put numbers on it like the Circle are always making him do, he'd say he was eighty per cent certain this is her. Given the circumstances that brought him here, that has to be chalked up as a yes.

'Harriet Stoke' bustles young Bradley – whose face Jason doesn't get a decent look at – into the main gates of the school, and presumably to his classroom door. The kid's starting out fresh, after all, he probably needs a bit of parental support.

Jason settles back in his seat, watching the images of the fathers and mothers as they leave their children and head off for work or home or the shops, and waits for his quarry to emerge.

* * *

The High King's staring moodily out of the window of his study at Windsor, his hands clasped behind his back.

Outside, the Long Walk rolls from the castle forecourt like a shockingly faded red carpet, down through the gatehouse and the avenue of trees, past skittering deer and trudging tourists and into the Great Park. From here the deer look like a herd of delicately articulated insects, and George III on his horse is as tiny as a Lilliputian's toy soldier.

For a good few minutes Jory stands still and silent, staring down at the Long Walk. 'We're really privileged to live here, Blaze,' he concludes eventually.

'Well, yeah,' Blaze agrees absently. He's sitting with one leg draped over the arm of a green leather armchair, practicing producing and vanishing coins using different combinations of fingers. The suit he's wearing is a different, vibrantly clashing shade of green. 'It's a palace, innit?'

'I know,' says Jory. 'I just don't want to end up taking it for granted.' He frowns, and goes over to the door. 'Bonnie,' he calls, 'some swine's trying to carve his initials in one of my trees. Send someone to stop him, will you?' Blaze smirks, but doesn't pause in his sleight of hand.

The High King returns to the window. 'I still can't work out what he was trying to achieve,' he tells Blaze abruptly. 'He isn't talking, the stubborn man.'

'The Duke?' asks Blaze after a moment, as the Pendragon's meaning percolates through to his awareness. 'Yeah, me neither.'

'Ex-Duke soon,' says Jory, 'if Parliament have their

way.' With the fabric of the ancient Palace of Westminster increasingly close to collapse, the Houses of Commons and Lords are keen to curry favour with the High King in the hope of being moved to new premises (rather than, say, abolished as an anachronism in this bold New Arthurian Age). The Duke will be impeached before the Lords, and the Commons will probably strip him of his title along with his freedom. 'Even so, I've got half the Commonwealth denouncing me for arresting him. A number of old-school royalists here, too, though they're being more polite about it. Even her majesty's been a bit distant since it happened. And I still have no idea why it did.'

Blaze shrugs. 'Don't ask me, boss. Don't make any sense. Fingers in all the pies, no joined-up thinking, that's his problem.' He finally vanishes the three coins into his pocket and sits up straight.

'He funded Roberto Schultz's visit,' muses Jory, 'with, we think, the express intention of exposing Janene and putting the Green Chapel beyond use. That's clever. It shows the ability to plan a scenario to fit some fairly obscure details of Robin Hood folklore. Does that sound like the Duke to you?'

'Don't know the dude,' Blaze points out equably. 'Don't fit his public image, though.'

'Exactly,' says the High King. 'I'm not sure he'd have had the patience for it. The Brewster business, on the other hand, was a proper attempt to kill me, using a rogue device. That must have taken some forward planning, especially to get hold of the camo gear, but to find and contact Brewster too. The Duke can hardly have done that himself, not without attracting attention.'

'Sullivan and the others were helping him,' Blaze reminds the Pendragon. 'They've admitted it.' He heaves himself upright and crosses to the High King's desk, where he starts jotting something down on a piece of paper.

Hugh Stein is dead, of course, skewered by Bonnie at Tregorlois. Hithers and Rudge have been cashiered and are each facing a court martial when they've recovered.

They're likely to be the first Knights to be stripped of their commissions since Clifford Chalmers, the last confirmed avatar of Sir Mordred, twenty years ago. There's serious talk at the Circle of shutting them up in the Benwick Institute to keep their devices from going rogue.

Patrick Sullivan's situation is more ambivalent: up to the morning of the Battle of Tregorlois he'd done nothing to distinguish himself from the other three, but saving the Pendragon's life at Quintrell Downs is quite a sizeable distinction. The talk in his case is of a disciplinary hearing only, although it's likely to be quite a severe one.

The tablet propped on Jory's desk chimes. Over at the window, the Pendragon tuts.

Blaze pauses in his scribbling to squint at the screen. 'Urgent message from Freda at the MRF. Top priority, it says. "Your eyes only."'

The High King sighs. 'I've had enough of James Bond film titles, with all those idiotic headlines. "Sherwood Is Not Enough", did you see that one? "The Man with the Golden Arrow." I don't know where the papers find these subs.'

'You want me to open it?' Blaze asks. 'We've got the same security clearance.'

The High King shakes his head wearily. 'No, let me think about this for a moment. Schultz and Brewster are two strands: the other's Woodville. The house, the interviews and so forth, all making the Duke's claim to the Corineus device… all designed to get us to send someone down to Tregorlois, but specifically targeted at Tania. I think the Duke seriously thought he'd get her on his side. That shows terrible judgement on his part.'

'Well, yeah,' says Blaze again. 'That's why the whole thing went to cock.'

'Quite,' the Pendragon says. 'And I can't see how the three schemes were meant to fit together at all.'

Outside, the morning sun brightens the clouds like brushed-steel statues of ragged ghosts. In the study, the tablet emits another tinging noise, reminding them of the message.

'Yeah, that's been bugging me,' agrees Blaze. He finishes his scrawling and sits back. 'So he's trying to get his Duchy independent, right? That's his endgame. Except maybe what he *really* wants is the old status quo back, so he gets to be king properly when his old mum dies. So maybe snuffing you at Southbank's his best option, and the rest is just Plan B. But it's pretty bleeding elaborate for a contingency plan. Also,' he adds, flapping his notes in the air, 'the timings are shagged right up.'

'Hmm?' says the Pendragon. 'Oh, yes. He's been planning this a long time. He bought the shares in Tarnhelm System not long after the war, which is about when he named Corineus House.'

'It's not just that,' says Blaze. 'The Duke couldn't control when Janene went off-brand at Schultz, so did he want the Chapel out of action for the Tania thing, or the Brewster thing, or what? But then he couldn't control when Dave would send Steve and Tania down to Cornwall, either. How was it all meant to fit together?'

'I haven't a clue,' the High King admits. 'Unless their main goal was just to annoy the hell out of me.'

'So maybe it was,' says Blaze, as the tablet peals for a third time. 'Look, d'you want me to open this or not?'

The icon's flashing insistently, waiting for an index finger to jab at it and open up the message from the Mythopolitical Research Facility. And…

Well. You know I'm not one for being unnecessarily portentous. I prefer to let events speak for themselves.

If I was writing a Welsh *Triad*, though, I wouldn't be exaggerating if I said that what happens next will be one of the Three Fateful Touchscreen Interactions of the Island of Britain.

(I haven't a clue what the other two would be, mind you. I'll have to get back to you about that.)

* * *

161

The woman Jason's identified as Malory leaves the school a few minutes later, and heads off briskly up the road, in the direction of the slightly more upmarket houses.

Jason picks up his shield, which he's wrapped in brown paper and stuck in a black binbag, then checks his sword in its concealed shoulder-scabbard. He's wearing a donkey jacket and jeans, but Malory of all people knows what he looks like. Still, it's the best he can do. He puts on his sunglasses, fluffs out his hair and beard a bit, then slips out of the van and follows his quarry.

He trails her as he trailed Dr Wendiman senior a few days before, between the yellow-brick and grey-roofed houses of the town, past the local Britomart and the crimson-and-teal splash of a Post Office, to a three-storey terraced house on the very edge of the school's catchment area. He can see from the intercom panel at the front door that it's been split into flats, and shortly after 'Harriet Stoke' enters he sees movement on the second floor.

Jason considers his options. He's here without backup – the covert nature of the quest the High King gave him has ensured that. He has his sword and shield but he's unarmoured, and Merry might well have a gun. He doesn't think she'd shoot him deliberately, but she might not realise it was him until it was too late.

He doesn't know what the back of the building is like – if he rings the doorbell, she might be able to climb down a tree or something and head off into the sunset, and then he'll be stuck with going back to the school and seeing who comes for the kid. On the other hand, if he goes round the back himself and tries to get in that way, she can leave a lot more easily by the front door.

He should scout the back out, really. But what if she heads off out again while he's doing it?

Jason decides to go for the direct approach – or fairly direct, at least. First he texts Blaze – the High King's notorious for never carrying a phone – to let him know what's going on. Then, pulling the wrapped shield out of its bag, he strides up to the house and rings the doorbell for the second floor. When a distorted female voice answers with an unintelligible squawk, he calls out a chirpy, 'Parcel for Ms Stoke?'

She buzzes him up. Inside the hall, he climbs the stairs to the first floor landing. The fact she's doing it this way rather than coming down to meet him is ringing a number of alarm bells, but in the end Jason's a Knight of the Circle, and with them bravery trumps caution every time.

He wrapped the shield-parcel with extra loops of parcel tape, arranged such that he can still hold it defensively. It hardly offers the security of its usual sturdy strapping, though, so he pauses to draw his sword, slit open the packaging and strap the shield on. Then he climbs the rest of the stairs and raps on the door of the second-floor flat. 'Got your parcel, Ms Stoke,' he cries cheerily.

The door opens and 'Harriet Stoke' stands there. She smiles, and he remembers how much he's missed a smile very like that one. 'Jason,' she says warmly. 'It's so lovely to see you. Why don't you come in?'

* * *

The library at Windsor houses the Taylor Collection, the most comprehensive archive of Arthurian and Robinian texts in the UK (I assembled a lot of the modern pop-culture end of it myself, although that mostly involved faffing about on Amazon and eBay), but there are some titles, like the digital facsimiles of the chronicles created by successive generations of Circle archivists for internal consumption, which Sir David insists are too sensitive to be held there. Those are kept on a stack of optical disks locked in a glass-fronted bookcase in Jory's study, and I'm one of the few people with borrowing privileges.

I've been looking into the supposed past manifestations of the Corineus and King Mark devices, and there are some details of the Circle's involvement in suppressing the Cornish Rebellion in 1497 that I need to confirm. There's no answer when I knock on the door of the High King's study, so I head on inside. He's often somewhere else, even when he's at the Castle during the working day – plus as I've said, he's pretty informal, and generally perfectly capable of telling me to bugger off when he's busy. (Though more genteelly, obviously. Well, usually.)

I expect to find the big, wood-panelled room empty except for the smell of old books and leather armchairs. I'm not prepared for seeing the High King slumped at his desk, groaning as if in pain, while Blaze leans heavily against the dark teak panelling, looking like he's about to be sick. There's a sound like babbling voices filling the room, though the windows are closed.

'Bonnie! Get here quick!' I yell through the door.

I cross to the desk to help the High King, but he raises a hand to stop me. 'No!' he mutters urgently, flapping it about like a panicked bird.

'Yeah,' grunts Blaze, without moving. 'Don't... look at that... fucking screen, bruv.'

The tablet display's angled away from me, but I can see from the light it's casting on the desk that it's flashing and strobing brightly with saturated colours. The burbling sound is coming from the machine's speakers. Moving as if with superhuman effort, Jory leans forward and shoves it off his desk. It topples, falls like a brick and hits the floor with a crack. The screen goes dead, as do the speakers.

Bonnie arrives at the door, breathless, and gasps in shock as she takes in the tableau.

'Bonnie,' the High King orders her in what's little more than a whisper, 'destroy that tablet.' She stomps in, lifts an obliging armoured boot and crushes it to shards.

'Are you OK, my lord?' she asks when she's finished. 'Can I get help? And what the fuck, if you don't mind me asking?'

'Just... close... the door,' grimaces Blaze, pushing himself bodily away from the wall. He takes a deep breath

164

and tries to stand without wobbling. 'Just close it, Bonnie, yeah?'

'Can I just echo Bonnie's "What the fuck"?' I ask as she does so, quite seriously concerned by now. 'What's happened, are you both ill? Did someone poison you or something?'

'Devicial mine, you berk,' snarls Blaze. 'Inframemetic inter... Fuck.' He bends double in pain, then straightens out slowly and with much scowling. 'Exactly what Freda T-H warned us about, but... sent from her own account.'

He shambles over to the Pendragon and heaves him upright, staring into his eyes. Jory reacts at once, batting him irritably away. 'I'm fine,' the High King insists. 'I'll live, anyway.' He hauls himself straight in his chair. 'We haven't the time to waste.'

'Devicial mine?' Bonnie repeats, wide-eyed. 'So one of you –'

'Never mind that for now,' snaps Jory. 'We need to put a stop to this before he does the same thing to anyone else.'

'Put a stop to who?' I ask. 'You said Freda –'

'Not Freda,' Blaze growls. 'She wouldn't send it from her own account. She's an academic, but she's not totally fucking stupid.'

Bonnie's lips are moving as she works it out. 'Must be Craig,' she realises. 'Runs all the security at MRF, doesn't he? Tate-Hendricks could have done it, but why tip us off? Schmidt too. Craig didn't want them to tell us they'd lost the USB.'

'Craig *McCutcheon*?' I repeat, aghast. 'Oh, for pity's sake.'

I wasn't there when they went to the MRF, if you recall, nor am I even vaguely privy to its inner workings. If I was – and sorry if it sounds like I'm boasting here, but honestly – this whole appalling cock-up would never have occurred.

Because I know who Craig McCutcheon is, even if I haven't seen him around much recently.

'You're seriously telling me,' I ask, incredulous, 'that you two, bearing between you the two wisest devices in British mythology –' (I realise that may have been tactless as they both wince at it, but I press on anyway) '– that you agreed to put the *bondsman of Sir Accolon* in charge of *security* at a sodding *weapons research installation?*'

Blaze groans again, and puts both arms over his head as if he's suffering from the worst hangover yet invented. Jory just looks upset and a bit cross-eyed.

'I mean,' I elaborate, 'there's story-blindness and there's just plain mind-buggering stupidity. My lord,' I add, remembering suddenly who pays my salary.

* * *

Jason follows his quarry through the door into the flat. The main room's bare and all but empty, with no curtains, not even a carpet on the floor: two cheap dining-chairs and a coffee-table from Argos stand in its centre. The walls, doors and window-frames have been painted a glossy white, very recently by the look of it. The door leading to the rest of the flat's rooms is closed.

It's a nice space though, clean and roomy, with big windows giving them a view out across a leafy garden. Jason supposes anywhere would feel like that, if you took out the furniture and gave it a proper hoover and a lick of paint.

'Tea?' 'Harriet Stoke' asks him. There's a pot waiting hot on the table, with two matching mugs, a milk jug and a sugar bowl. He doesn't think she'd have had time to boil the kettle since getting back. Again he feels like someone's a few steps ahead of him.

He supposes there's no reason not to be polite, though. 'All right,' he says. 'Thanks.' He watches her for a minute as she pours.

'Cheers,' he adds as she passes him his tea. Both his hands have weapons in, though, and they feel unnecessary and awkward under the circumstances, like a colleague who's turned up at the wrong meeting and is too embarrassed to admit it. He lowers the sword and pushes the point carefully into the gap between two floorboards, so that it's standing upright next to him, the hilt within easy reach. Then he leans his shield against one of the chairs. Finally, he takes the teacup and sits, facing the door to the bedrooms.

'Thanks,' he says again. He takes a sip of the tea, which is good stuff. 'So,' he says. 'You called me Jason.'

'Ah,' says the woman. 'Would she have called you Squig? I wasn't sure.'

Her voice is no longer Malory's. It's deeper and less melodious, with a touch of a foreign accent. She drops the 'h' of 'have', but not in the careless way a Brit might, more as if she just doesn't much care for it.

'Yeah, I reckon,' Squig says. It's how he secretly still thinks of himself inside, and he reckons Merry would have got that. 'We haven't really seen each other since I started using Jason instead. Just that once at Stonehenge, and we didn't get to talk.'

The woman nods. She still hasn't touched her tea.

'So you must be the other one,' he informs her redundantly. 'The double they sent to kill High King Jordan.' The woman, though, has got up and is crossing to the bedroom door. Jason stands warily, and puts his hand on his sword again.

Malory's double disappears through the door to the bedrooms, leaving him sitting there with his tea.

Behind him, the flat door opens and a female voice says, 'Her name's Claudine, not that you give a shit.'

Quick as a scorpion's strike, Squig's crouching behind his shield facing the door, his sword at the ready, his tea pooling on the bare floorboards. Then he sees who's standing there, and he relaxes very slightly.

This woman isn't Malory Wendiman either. For some reason it's Laney Wardsley. She walks over to the coffee-table, sits and picks up the mug the Malory impersonator didn't touch. She picks up Squig's cup and refills it calmly.

She takes a sip, then goes on. 'Claudine used to work for the Paladins de la République. They found this actor who looked a bit like Merry, gave her plastic surgery and intensive, I don't know, coaching? Conditioning? Not full-on brainwashing – because the Paladins still think they're the good guys, just like you lot do – but as good as. In the end she practically thought she *was* Merry. Then they sent her to get into bed with High King Dan, who rumbled her straight away.'

'It was a stupid plan,' Squig opines. He's stood up gingerly while she's been talking, which she hasn't shown any alarm at. Now he sits, leaning his shield against his legs and balancing the sword across his knees. 'The High King knows Merry. Even I could spot she wasn't her.'

'Yeah, well,' agrees Laney. She's gone back to her old look, more or less, with the facial piercings and dreadlocks, a pair of not especially flattering dungarees and big clomping boots. 'The fuckers didn't even rescue her when the Circle arrested her. It was us who did that that. That's why she works for us know.'

'Who's "us"?' Squig asks.

She looks at him as if he's mentally deficient. 'Well, Merry's people, obviously. Who did you think I was working for?'

'Merry's got people?' Squig asks. 'OK.' He guesses it makes sense – she pretty much founded the modern version of the Chapel under the Circle's noses, after all. She must have just done the same again. 'What about the lad?' he asks. 'I'm guessing his name's not Bradley.'

'He's just some kid,' says Laney sharply. 'Tomorrow he'll be back home with his parents, back at his normal school after a bad tummy bug. You leave him the fuck out of this.'

'OK, sure,' says Squig, wondering what exactly 'this' is. 'So Merry's actual kid, right...?'

'You're not getting near, now or ever,' Laney replies. 'So just don't even, OK?'

'Right,' Squig nods. 'You used fake-Bradley as a decoy then? Just so I'd follow fake-Merry here? All right, well, that worked. I'm here. What happens now, Lanes?'

Laney sighs. 'Well, we're not going to kill you, or take you prisoner or shit like that. See you, Claudine,' she adds as

168

the Frenchwoman passes back through from the bedroom, wearing a different dress and with what looks awfully like a different wig on.

Malory's double gives Laney a quick peck on the cheek, says 'Goodbye, Jason,' and leaves the flat. It sounds sexier in a French accent than 'Goodbye, Squig' probably would.

'Basically,' says Laney with precision, 'what happens now is you leave us the fuck alone. Do you think you can manage that, Squiggles?'

* * *

So I suppose you'll be wanting me to tell you about Sir Accolon of Gaul.

Well, he was a Knight of the Round Table, obviously. The stories make him out to be a decent enough bloke – a good fighter who kept his promises, pally enough with the High King that the two of them went hunting together with Arthur's brother-in-law King Uriens.

Unfortunately – for Accolon, and arguably for Uriens, and in the end for Arthur and a large number of other people – Sir Accolon was in love with King Uriens' wife, Morgan le Fay. With hindsight, anyone could have told him that wasn't going to work out well, but at the time Morgan hadn't been outed as a villainous enchantress, and was widely revered as the King's loyal and loving half-sister.

The sources aren't clear about whether Morgan and Accolon were actually shagging (well, the ancient sources aren't anyway; most modern retellings have them at it like bunnies), but it seems that Morgan fancied him right back and was planning to leave – by which I mean 'kill' – Uriens for him. But not before Accolon had done her a favour.

Why exactly Morgan hated her half-brother isn't altogether clear – indeed, her attitude to him seems to have been ambivalent right up to the end, because she's one of the three (or possibly nine) queens who carry him off in a barge to Avalon after he's fatally wounded, with a view to healing him and enabling his triumphant and vaguely messianic return. For whatever reason, though – because his father basically raped their mother, or because Queen Guinevere broke up Morgan's early affair with Guinevere's cousin Sir Guiomar, or because (as some modern authors would have it, and it makes sense of some of the complexities of her character) she was a champion of traditional British paganism against the Christianising influences Arthur allied himself with – Morgan wanted her kid brother gone. And with him and her own inconvenient husband out of the picture, she intended to rule as queen in her own right, with Accolon as her consort.

Getting rid of Arthur was tricky, of course, given that he had Excalibur, a sword notorious for being able to cut through other swords, and Excalibur's scabbard, worth ten of the sword because it protected the wearer magically against any loss of blood from wounds sustained while wearing it. So Morgan hatched a plan – an unnecessarily complicated one, of course, that being always the way of such things – which ended in Accolon and Arthur reluctantly fighting one another as the champions of two rival knights, each of them unaware of who the other was.

That wasn't the really clever part, obviously. The really clever part was that Morgan had also made replicas of Excalibur and its scabbard, and had them switched so that Sir Accolon was fighting with the real ones while Arthur had been given the fakes.

Naturally the fight didn't go well for Arthur, who ended up horribly wounded and with his sword broken – until the Lady of the Lake intervened with her own magic, making Accolon drop Excalibur so Arthur could grab it and, pausing only to rip off his opponent's scabbard, give him a fatal head injury. Once he realised who his opponent was, Sir Accolon – who'd obviously known he was fighting with Excalibur, but thought that was because he had the High King's blessing – managed to confess before he died that it was Morgan le Fay who'd given it to him, and thus was the sorceress's treachery revealed.

Morgan tried to kill Uriens but was foiled by their son, Sir Uwaine, and had to flee the court. She did, however, pause en route to stop off at the nunnery where Arthur was recovering, nick Excalibur's scabbard again, and chuck it into a well. Which is, of course, how he came to be vulnerable enough at the Battle of Camlann that he could be fatally wounded at all.

And that was the end of the whole sordid episode. (It's fiddlier than that, of course – it always is. There's stuff about a ship full of fair damosels, and twenty knights who've been imprisoned for seven years, and the actual cause of the dispute between Sir Ontzlake and Sir Damas, which is something to do with land inheritance and terribly dull, but...) The salient point here is that Sir Accolon of Gaul is the knight who tries to use Excalibur to kill King Arthur.

So – like I say, *I* wouldn't have put his device-bearer in charge of the High King's weapons facility. But maybe that's just me.

* * *

'I don't reckon so, really,' Squig tells Laney honestly. 'I don't really think I can leave you the fuck alone, Lanes. I got given this quest by the High King, see.' He takes a gulp of tea, but this time she's forgotten to put the sugar in.

'Yeah, we know,' Laney says. 'He wants to see Merry. Can't he understand she's over him now? She has been for years. He may be the High King and all, but he's not all that.'

'It's not just 'cause they used to be together,' Squig protests. 'I mean, it might be a bit, but it's not just that. She got into this top-secret research place and sabotaged it. That's why I'm supposed to arrest her. There needs to be a trial and that.'

'Sabotaged, my arse,' Laney says scornfully. '*She* says she set them off on some line of research they're still following now. They should be thanking her for the kickstart. Besides,

171

when did *you* decide breaking into places and sabotaging them was a bad thing? It used to be what you were best at.'

Squig sighs. 'Yeah, I know,' he agrees. 'But I'm different now. I've got Sir Gareth's device. There's rules I've got to follow, stuff like that. That Ron's your Much the Miller's Son ally now.' For some reason Jason always thinks of his successor as 'That Ron'. He puts down the tea. It's not worth sweetening it now.

'Jesus,' sneers Laney, 'you're no better than Paul. Just because you're a Knight and have your Knightly honour to think of and shit, Merry has to suffer for it? Does her kid have to suffer, Squig? Does her dad?'

'I never hurt her dad,' Squig protests.

Laney says, 'He's nearly ninety, you dick. Why can't you leave her and her family alone?'

Squig's getting annoyed now. 'She sent you here to say that to me, did she?' he asks. 'Why didn't she come herself? All that bollocks with getting me to follow that Claudette.'

'*Claudine,*' Laney corrects him.

'Whatever,' he snaps. 'Why couldn't that have just been her? Why couldn't she have told me all this out of her own mouth?'

He realises he's sounding sulky, whiney even. The truth is, he used to be really, really fond of Merry. Not in a sexy way, it wasn't like that. It was more like she was an older sister, one who always took an interest, always had time for him.

That's how it was, back in the old days in the Green Chapel – Merry took an interest in everyone, and we all loved her for it. Squig perhaps didn't realise it till now, but for all his loyalty to the Pendragon, the main reason he's been so diligent in following this quest of the High King's is that he really wants to see his old friend again.

Perhaps Laney senses this, a bit, because her voice is slightly softer when she answers. 'She couldn't take the risk, Squig. She hasn't seen you for years, has she, and like you say you've changed. What if you arrested her anyway? I mean, she's a mum now. She can't risk leaving –' she almost says a

172

name, but checks herself in time '– leaving the poor kid all alone with a mother in the Benwick, can she?

'And what the fuck were you going to do about *that* if you arrested her?' she adds, angry again suddenly. 'Leave that poor little sod waiting at the school gate for a mum that never turned up?'

'No! 'Course not.' He's upset at the very suggestion, although of course he realises that taking the boy home to a dad he'd never met – and who, as it turns out, isn't actually even his dad – wouldn't have been a perfect solution either.

'Well, whatever,' Laney says, conceding the point. 'This is us asking, anyway. You used to be Merry's friend. Shit Squig, you used to be *my* friend. You warned me off that time the Circle were gunning for my arse, when Paul got hurt and they thought I did it, remember that?' (She *did* do it, of course, or rather she set him up so someone else could, but Squig doesn't bring that up for now.) 'Well, I'm asking you as a friend now, and so's she. Leave us alone. Tell King Dan you couldn't find us. Or say you followed a false trail and it went dead. That would be the truth, wouldn't it? I know how keen you Knights are on truth. Christ, I should be – I spent six months lying to one of you.'

'The trail's not gone dead, though, has it?' Squig says stubbornly. 'I've still got a lead.'

'What, Claudine?' Laney's scornful. 'She's long gone, bitch. She's been trained in covert ops by the Paladins *and* Merry Wendiman. You're not going to find her.'

'Yeah, maybe,' Squig says lightly, settling his hand on the hilt of his sword. 'But I've got you.'

'Me?' Laney rolls her eyes. 'Yeah, right. You know how I feel about the fucking Circle. You helped me get away the last time they were after me. You're not going to arrest me know. You're not that much of an arsehole.'

Jason doesn't think he's much of an arsehole, really. It's just that he's come all this way – not just from Windsor to Glasgow to Maidstone to Halifax, but from petty thief and graffiti artist to Knight of the Circle and confidant of the

High King himself. He's worked through plan after plan, he's bullied and schemed and snuck around after old men, he's followed lead after useless lead – he's even judged a bloody poetry competition – all to find Merry and this kid of hers… and ended up here, in this flat, with nothing to show for it except a cup of unsweetened PG Tips that's going cold already.

Yeah, well. Arsehole or not, he's buggered if he's going to leave it at that. 'Sorry, Lanes,' he mutters. 'It's my duty, isn't it?'

He stands and raises his sword. 'Elaine Wardsley,' he tells her, 'I'm taking you into custody, in the name of the Circle and its Head, High King Jordan of Britain.'

Laney glares at him, her eyes full of caustic hatred. She takes a final sip of tea, then slowly stands. 'Liss told me all about you and her, you know,' she says. 'That time after the party at the squat in Leytonstone, the one to see you off when you were going undercover at the Circle. We were all seventeen, and you'd both taken those Es that boy Waz brought round. She said you weren't much cop, but she felt sorry for you. I bet if she'd known you were this much of a dick, she'd have had a wank instead.'

'Probably,' the bondsman of Sir Gareth concedes. 'Sounds about right, yeah.'

He leads her at swordpoint out of the flat and down the stairs.

10. SIR ACCOLON

As they begin their descent, Bonnie does her best to put aside her worries about the High King and enjoy the moment. Tregorlois was some serious combat, even by her standards, but it was over quickly, and the Pendragon's spent the few days since fretting about how it happened. It's possible today may be more of an anticlimax, of course – and any excitement that does happen may not involve her at all – but for the moment it's all feeling pretty dramatic.

She's in the Catuvellauni with Jory as it prepares for landing in the university playing-field. There are a bunch of other Knights with them in the helicopter's gigantic metal belly, as well as Bob Thackett and the men-at-arms of the Regal Protection Detail. The squires and horses are coming with some more men-at-arms in a second helicopter – mercifully, because however well you train them not to panic, the smell of ten or twenty nervous nags in a confined space is not conducive to enjoying your flight. (There are pages too, whose job it will be to muck out the copter afterwards.)

'Are we really hoping he'll have stayed put, my lord?' Stephen Mukherjee yells as they approach the city. 'I'd expect him to have buzzed off long ago.' To Bonnie he doesn't seem much the worse for his imprisonment at the hands of a villainous aristocrat, but what does she know about post-traumatic stress and stuff like that?

'He's as likely to be here as anywhere else,' the High King replies. He's strapped in as they all are, the webbing harness obscuring the gold dragon on his new surcoat. 'Besides, I have a feeling he'll want to face me.'

Stephen nods respectfully at this regal insight, but Bonnie, who was there when I went off on my little rant, knows Jory's basing it on nothing more concrete than the story of Sir Accolon's contest with King Arthur. She guesses it makes sense for the High King to show the world that his device is still inspiring him, though, and hasn't been crippled by the devicial mine.

Whether it's actually true or not she still doesn't know, but it's a no-brainer that that's what the Circle forces need to believe. The High King could have ridden in his personal chopper – one of the first new Iceni IC-1 military transports off the production line, which has been set aside for his sole use – but he said it would be better for morale if he rode with his men and women. It's following behind, though, in case he needs it later.

'Another rogue Knight!' Amal Samadi exclaims next to Bonnie. Sir Safir's bondswoman is terrifically and slightly squeakily overexcited by this entire situation. 'It almost never happens except the Mordreds. This is the fifth in a week!'

'Not all the Cornish ones count as rogues, necessarily,' asserts Andy Burridge, Sir Brastias's device-bearer, from Amal's other side. 'One of them changed his mind, remember. And we're not even sure about McCutcheon yet.' His work as a man done, he turns back to Chris Timms, the bondsman of Sir Aglavale, and starts critiquing the pilot's handling of the chopper. Bonnie rolls her eyes.

'Has McCutcheon any family?' Theo Harte bellows from the other side of the helicopter's innards. He's making notes on a tablet: presumably he wants to know for whoever ends up having to contact the rogue Knight's relatives. Next to him are Ross Cornish, who sports the device of Sir Percival, and Nigel Roth – the bondsman of the lycanthropic Sir Marrok, who's been happily divorced for some time now.

176

'A daughter,' shouts Jory, who checked all this with David before they left. 'Adopted. She's at a boarding school in Somerset – I've sent Woodville there. He's not married, or otherwise attached as far as we know.' Harte nods and taps his screen thoughtfully.

'Don't open any emails, Theo!' Bonnie shouts at him helpfully. She realises the thrill is getting to her after all, though it hasn't stopped her worrying about her liege lord.

The contradiction's making her feel slightly manic. Theo frowns at her and she blows him a kiss.

* * *

It's rare that the Circle's mobilised so quickly or so comprehensively in peacetime. For it to happen twice in a week is so unprecedented – not just during Jory's reign, but in the annals of the Circle leading up to the War of the Devices – that a couple of the edgier media pundits are arguing that this no longer counts as peacetime at all. Others are asserting that this is what you have to expect with an actual Pendragon on the throne, and with no historical precedent since the sixth century it's hard to argue the point.

Within minutes of their arrival on the playing-field, the men-at-arms have erected a pop-up marquee to act as the High King's temporary HQ. He waits there – Bonnie sticking to his side like a particularly devoted limpet – while the other Knights set about their work. Chief Inspector Kinsey, who met him as he disembarked, had been liaising directly with Craig McCutcheon after the robbery at the MRF, and is seething at having missed any sign he might have given of his imminent derailment.

Her people are out scouring the city for him, of course; but ultimately they're undeviced, and he's a Knight. If they find him, it'll be because he wants to be found. The Pendragon sends Amal, Andy and Ross out on horses to search for likely boltholes. He has Kinsey hold off on sending a forensic team to search McCutcheon's accommodation, and details

Stephen to head there instead, with some of the Circle's CSI-trained men-at-arms. Kinsey swears more than might seem reasonable, but there's very little she can do about it. McCutcheon's the Circle's own, and the Circle and its Head are dealing with him in their own way.

Meanwhile, Theo takes slightly stressed but otherwise competent control of security at the MRF. He relieves the men-at-arms on duty, and McCutcheon's squire, on the basis that they may still feel some residual loyalty to McCutcheon, and the Circle's had enough of its personnel going native in regional silos. He installs two new teams – one to search the building for any clues the errant Knight may have left behind, while the others lock down the security as tight as the hemispheres of a golf-ball. Professor Tate-Hendricks he debriefs – sympathetically enough, but with a certain wary distance: she has to understand that she, as the person whose email the devicial mine was sent from, can't be considered in the clear yet. Like everyone, she's on tenterhooks to find out what effect the weapon had on the High King, but in her case the interest is professional as well as political.

By now Roth and Timms are installed respectively at the city's rail and coach stations, vetting all departing passengers for their resemblance to a disguised McCutcheon. Elsewhere across the country, other Knights are on similar quests, hoping to intercept the traitor leaving the UK: at every international airport, every overseas ferry terminal, each train station where the Eurostar express calls – even, in the interests of slightly pedantic thoroughness, at the commercial spaceport on the Isle of Lewis – RAF Dunmonii are depositing Knights with their squires and men-at-arms, to take up positions of surveillance over any departing travellers. Other Knights patrol with the coastguard, watching for boats heading into international waters. A division of twenty under Kate Blackwood, the device-bearer of Sir Lamorak, patrols the Northern Irish border, on the offchance that McCutcheon left the mainland for the province before the lockdown and is now trying to cross over into Fianna territory.

Paul Parsons, who as ill luck would have it was on his way from the Fastness to Windsor when the balloon went up, has been hastily diverted to Heathrow, where he stands scanning the faces in the Terminal Two departures lounge. He knows it's sheer happenstance that's placed him here, miles from the High King's side, where it's statistically almost unthinkable that the rogue Knight will appear... but still, it rankles. It doesn't help his mood that this is the very place – give or take a few hundred metres – where the then-outlaw Jory Taylor, on behalf of the Green Chapel, once kidnapped a distinguished foreign visitor from underneath his nose. Paul clenches his non-prosthetic fist, remembering past humiliations.

Woodville, meanwhile, is at a girls' boarding-school in Wells, keeping a discreet eye on McCutcheon's daughter Izzy. It hardly seems likely that the thirteen-year-old's dad would try to pick her up before fleeing the country – she's well looked after at the school, after all, and he'd find it easier to make his escape first and extract her by some covert means later – but they can't leave any avenue unexplored. Tania, who only really enjoyed her schooldays when she was out on the sports field, finds the place gloomily familiar, while the headmistress for her part recognises the Knight as exactly the sort of girl the school aspires to export into the wider world. She agrees to keep Izzy McCutcheon in the dark about Tania's presence, and what's going on generally, on the condition that Tania comes back at some point and gives a careers talk to the sixth form. Nobody really has a clue what to tell the girl anyway: as Andy Burridge says, it's still possible that her father's been framed by some other party.

Back at the Fastness Johnny Quayle, the bondsman of Sir Lucan the Butler, is supervising a roomful of the men-at-arms' technical division. The men and women are doing the best they can to track McCutcheon electronically – through financial records, patterns of net usage, phone taps, surveillance cameras, speech and facial recognition software, all the tools available to a modern surveillance state. Johnny, who like McCutcheon happens to be one of the few Knights with some degree of technical expertise, was recalled in haste, still aching from Valentine Brewster's gunshot wound, from the Circle's recuperative facility at Tud House. He listens to the reassuring taps and clicks of keyboards and mice, and wonders what Bonnie's doing right now.

From his office in the Fastness keep, Sir David Stafford co-ordinates the whole vast network of quests, a mug of coffee stone-cold at his elbow, a dozen tablet screens open on his desk. He's in his element: the fighting he did as a younger man, whether as the bondsman of Sir Galahad or the ally of the now abeyant Richard the Lionheart, feels distant and alien to him. He's served his turn; best to leave all that sort of thing to the younger men and women who have an actual passion for it. If necessary he'll grit his teeth and muck in, as he did in Tregorlois, but this – chivvying, encouraging, organising, dealing with crises of ability and tactics and logistics as they arrive – is his calling now.

Nine floors beneath him, in the cells under the curtain wall (redesigned during the war to allow for the holding of medium-term prisoners), Sandy Hithers sits, his leg propped up and his arm in a cast, playing an irritable game of Scrabble through the bars with Ken Rudge. Elsewhere, in the London home he's visited only fleetingly during the past seven years, Patrick Sullivan is moodily watching daytime soaps and drinking cheap whisky. At this moment the three of them are the only Knights of the Circle without duties.

And Jason Smith, who's spent the journey from Halifax in a conversation so acrimoniously engrossing he hasn't heard a thing about the current flap, draws up at the service gates of Windsor Castle in the Circle surveillance van. The men-at-arms on the gate raise their eyebrows at the sight of Laney Wardsley handcuffed in the passenger seat, frown at her stream of invective and smile patronisingly at her insistence that she's been kidnapped and that they should call the police immediately. They wave Jason through. He drives in through the Castle's tradesmen's entrance, still trying to work out where he's going to stick his prisoner when he gets her inside.

If he wasn't so nice, he thinks wearily as she calls him a 'slimy little shitweasel' for the thirteenth time since Milton Keynes, he might look into whether the Castle had any dungeons that were still usable.

* * *

Craig McCutcheon's abandoned flat – at least, everyone's assuming it's abandoned – is in a new-build housing block on the outskirts of the university town. All brick and glass with solar panel ceilings, it's part of a national drive to build affordable and eco-friendly accommodation in areas where housing's been under pressure this century, which is basically everywhere remotely urban. The Device Squad have been camped outside since Bonnie phoned through from Windsor. They've evacuated the rest of the block, and confirmed McCutcheon's home is unoccupied using heat-imaging cameras, but at the High King's command nobody's yet gone inside.

The fear, of course, is that McCutcheon – who clearly managed in short order, thanks to his software engineering knowhow and the special aptitudes of his device, to appropriate, repurpose and weaponise Ernst Schmidt's experimental research prototype – may have planted booby-traps in his flat that could harm other devices.

You might think that under such circumstances it would make more sense for undeviced civilians, or at least men-at-arms, to enter and deal with anything they might find there without any devices present... but there's also the possibility that McCutcheon might have set more conventional traps as well. Besides, you'd be reckoning without the stipulations of the Circle's honour code. Asking an ordinary soldier – let alone a police officer – to do a Knight's work is dishonourable, however sensible it might be under specific circumstances.

It's Stephen Mukherjee himself, then, who leads the men-at-arms into the flat, after one of Kinsey's constables has opened it up with a skeleton key. He lowers his visor before proceeding into the living room, on the theory that it might impede his vision and hearing slightly, and anything's worth trying in defence against a devicial mine. (He supposes, given time, the Circle will devise a form of protection against this class of attack. Some kind of goggle-and-earmuff arrangement, possibly.)

Stephen, too, is grateful to be seeing some sort of action – however Bonnie may feel about it, Tregorlois was a lot more frustrating for him – but that doesn't mean he plans on being reckless.

They find the place clean and tidy, homely even; certainly more comfortable and less minimalist than Stephen's used to in his own flat, or those of other unmarried Knights he's visited. Evidently McCutcheon makes an effort for his daughter, or perhaps she's taken him in hand. Either way, some of the media on the shelves, the posters on the wall and the mugs on the mug-tree must belong to Izzy rather than her father, unless the bondsman of Sir Accolon's a closet fan of the *Frozen* trilogy and the music of Boy To Let.

The effect of abandoned domesticity is more than a little creepy, in fact. In a huge poster above the sofa, Izzy McCutcheon's favourite boyband smiles down at Stephen from five winning faces, their dead eyes seeming to follow him around the room. Opposite it, on a shelf below the TV, a rank of fluorescent-haired gonks or trolls, whatever people are calling them these days, seem to be grimacing and gurning wrinklily whenever he looks away from them. The men-at-arms fan out behind him as he walks, nervously menacing the inanimate occupants.

Stephen's approaching the kitchen counter, where an expensive high-end tablet's sitting on the wipe-clean plastic surface, its silence pregnant with menace. It's folded shut against its slot-in keyboard, with a sticky note on top suggesting 'OPEN ME'.

He pauses to take stock. He's as gung-ho as any Knight of the Circle when it comes to danger to life and limb, and has cheerfully ridden, abseiled and hang-glided into battle against enemies from the Saxon Shield to the Gormund Boys, without a thought for his own personal wellbeing. This, though, is a different class of danger. To die with a sword in one's hand and a device on one's shield is very different from being stripped of one's device altogether. Sir Palamedes has led him into some strange places over the years – and given him a few obsessions he could have done without, to be perfectly honest – but without him Stephen has no idea who he'd be. This threat is far more philosophical than the ones he's used to.

Still, he thinks, there's no point shilly-shallying. There's every chance that any booby-trap will instead be physical, using actual explosives – so that's all right. I mean, how much of those can you fit inside a tablet, realistically speaking?

'Best get outside, chaps,' he tells the men-at-arms. The sergeant-at-arms dutifully protests, but Stephen just as dutifully – and a touch impatiently – overrules him. The men and women clatter out and close the door behind them.

Quickly, Stephen steps forward and opens the tablet. He waits, grateful not to have been instantly exploded, as it boots up. He composes himself for a mind-altering onslaught of psychedelic noise and imagery, but instead a simple text window pops open.

He reads it through twice carefully, then phones the High King's temporary HQ.

* * *

Simultaneously, miles away in London, a man sitting in a café receives a automated text message on his tablet. He finishes the latest in the succession of espressos he's spent the last few hours consuming, and lugs his heavy valise to the gents.

Ten minutes later, he emerges in the full armour of a Knight of the Circle. He wears a sheathed sword, and carries a tough polyester shield on which two serpents, wavy azure, sport palewise on an argent field.

Ignoring the stares of his fellow patrons, Craig

McCutcheon tramps heavily out of the café and marches the short distance to Piccadilly Circus, where the takes up his stand amidst the bustling swarm of human bodies, on the steps in front of the fountain topped by the statue of Eros. Assuming he's some kind of Arthurian-themed performance art, a couple of them stop to watch, but are disappointed by his immobility and soon move on.

Very shortly afterwards, two vans full of men-at-arms arrive at speed from the Fastness, and start endeavouring to clear one of the busiest junctions in London of traffic and people. It's quite a challenge, but they manage it in the end.

* * *

The High King arrives a little while later, his Iceni touching down on the flat triangular roof of the old London Pavilion, now part of the Trocadero Centre. Even so far above their heads, its downdraft plays havoc with the hair and clothes of the crowds – tourists and shoppers, Londoners and visitors, police assisting the men-at-arms with crowd control and reporters trying to break it – crammed into the six roads surrounding the awkward set-square triangle of Piccadilly Circus. Inside the rigid cordon of men-at-arms keeping back the populace, all the Knights the Seneschal's been able to assemble at this notice have gathered under the massive video hoardings on the north side.

The Trocadero itself has been evacuated, along with the Criterion Theatre and the other buildings surrounding the junction, and the Tube station beneath their feet is closed. Most of the public who were in them at the time are now the other side of the Circle cordon, gawping at the scene.

The helicopter disgorges the High King and Bonnie, the only Knight who was on hand to leave with him at once, along with Thackett and his second-in-command, a woman called Jacqui Parkes. The Catuvellaunis are half-an-hour behind, carrying Stephen and the other Knights (except Theo, who's stayed behind to secure the MRF because someone has to).

By the time they get here, this whole business may well be settled.

It takes a few minutes for Jory, Bonnie, Thackett and Parkes to descend to street level through the abandoned Trocadero. They emerge into the empty street across from the Criterion Restaurant, and hurry across Shaftesbury Avenue to join the Seneschal and his Knights.

'My lord,' urges David, indecently soon after the Pendragon greets him, 'you don't have to do this. McCutcheon's dishonoured himself by abandoning his quest and turning against his High King. He isn't entitled to ask you to meet him in an honourable contest.'

Jory turns slowly, looking at who's assembled here: his Knights and squires; the ordinary men-at-arms holding back the public; the foreigners who came here for a glimpse of the New Arthurian Age (they're getting their money's worth, at least); the ordinary Brits eager to catch a glimpse of their sovereign; the reporters from every media outlet in the world, with their cameras and microphones and drones.

McCutcheon's standing alone and alert beneath the fountain, his sword drawn at the ready. It rises up above him, three tiers bearing concentrically smaller basins, with Eros above them all, aiming his bow up Piccadilly proper. It looks as if the god of love is defending McCutcheon's back.

'I don't think it will impress people very much if I back out now, do you?' the Pendragon asks mildly.

'Quite right, my lord,' Paul Parsons agrees at once. 'As per your orders no-one's approached McCutcheon, but we've looked him over pretty closely with the HD imaging, and we don't think you'll be finding any hidden surprises.'

Bob Thackett's been conferring with the sergeant-at-arms. 'He's got a standard Circle-issue sword and shield, sir, and his armour's well maintained. He ain't wearing much underneath – you can see he's been standing there in the sun for a while and he ain't sweating much. He's drank a lot of coffee today, so he's probably a bit jittery and he must have a bladder like a balloon. That's all we've got, sir.'

McCutcheon himself interrupts them from his position on the steps. 'Are you a penguin, Taylor?' he cries, and the crowd gasps at his lack of respect. 'Because you seem to be getting cold feet.' His voice is brash, full of bravado, the way rogue device-bearers sound when they've a strong suspicion their device is about to get them killed but they're going ahead with it anyway. 'Maybe you're not quite the man they think you are, eh?' The assembled throng murmurs in thrilled indignation.

'I'm talking, McCutcheon. Wait your turn, please,' Jory shouts back, to sniggers from the crowd. 'Devicial assessment,' he orders Sir David, all business now.

'We're ninety-five per cent confident he hasn't been misdeviced,' Stafford replies. 'We haven't seen this behaviour from previous device-bearers of Sir Accolon, but they haven't had a Pendragon to trigger it. That matches the pattern with Hithers' device – Sir Andret's been docile enough in the absence of a King Mark, but becomes dangerous with that device around to catalyse it. Given Accolon's role in the legends, it seems clear enough that he's doing this because he believes he has an advantage over you in combat, equivalent to the original Accolon acquiring Excalibur. My lord, I must ask –'

'We haven't time, David,' replies the High King.

'Jory,' says the Seneschal, low enough that only the High King can hear. 'I need your orders. In case you d-don't –'

'No, David,' says the Pendragon firmly. 'Believe me, that's the last thing any of us need. Any room for doubt now could get me killed.'

McCutcheon's climbed onto the lower rim of the fountain now, putting his feet above the onlookers' heads. 'The Pendragon is gone!' he yells to the crowd from his precarious perch. 'Your High King's device has been erased like a corrupt file, like a dirty browsing history! There's no great man to protect you now, no demigod to pray to! *King Arthur is a myth!*'

'Right,' Jory mutters, 'that's quite enough of that.'

He strides out across the tarmac towards the rebel Knight.

* * *

The journalists' drones, which have been hovering at a respectful distance while the High King's conferred with his advisors – their operators would've been stripped of their press accreditation on the spot if they hadn't – swoop in now to capture the best images and sound they possibly can, as the High King marches across to stand in the centre of the road.

'King Arthur *is* a myth, McCutcheon!' he shouts from the middle of the box junction markings. 'He's a myth who's standing right in front of you now. I may not have Excalibur, but nor do you – and by God, I carry the device of the High King of the Britons. Let's see my dragon make short work of your serpents, bondsman of Sir Accolon!'

(OK, so the dialogue's a bit cheesy, but that's kind of expected under the circumstances. Besides, when you've got armour with a velvet surcoat and a helmet with a crown on top you can get away with a lot.)

McCutcheon climbs off the fountain and stomps down the steps onto the pavement. One news network, more enterprising than most, succeeds in buying a real-time feed to the video wall on the north side of the square, and all at once the view from behind and above the rogue Knight's shoulder is lit up above them both in ten-metre tall HD, the company's logo prominently displayed.

'What's this about, Craig?' Jory asks more quietly – though still loud enough to be picked up by the drones' mikes – as McCutcheon approaches him. For now he keeps his hand on his sword-hilt, but doesn't draw the weapon. 'As far as I know I've never done anything to hurt you. I trusted you to be loyal. I put you in charge of a secure facility. Wasn't that enough for you?'

'You're a glitch, Taylor,' growls McCutcheon. 'A bug in

the code. The Circle worked fine before you came along to disrupt it. Boast all you like about ending the war, but if you hadn't stolen the Grail it would never have started. And now look at them all, dancing attendance like your farts are the voice of God. Without a Head, the Circle's fit for purpose. With one, it's a tool of tyranny. We're overdue a decapitation here.'

'Then I can only suggest,' says Jory grimly, 'that you try.'

He draws his sword, as McCutcheon rushes at him with a deep-throated yell.

* * *

At Windsor, Rev, Blaze and I are in the High King's study, watching the BBC's live feed on that wall-sized screen as the gigantic figures – currently about four metres tall from the waist up, though obviously this is changing frequently – finally come to blows.

Although they're made of steel, the Circle's swords are, as I suspect I've mentioned, polymer-coated, so when they're clashed together they don't ring resoundingly so much as clatter. The sound of sword on plastic riot-shield is dull as well, more of a thud than anything. Nor do either of them glint in the sun to speak of, although you can get a bit of a gleam from the ceramic outer plating of the armour.

Still, when the combatants get going, the skill, speed and ferocity make up for the lack of the traditional lighting and sound effects. The swords swing left and right and round and up and down in rapid arcs, as arms and legs twist and thrust and recoil and jostle for position. Blow after blow targets some vulnerable point in the armour with what should be devastating force, only to be deflected by the opponent's shield, or parried by his sword, or dodged through some lithe piece of footwork.

For many minutes they seem well matched, the High King and the rogue Knight, circling in place within the yellow crosshatched road-markings, neither man gaining nor losing ground. Even running security in a university town, McCutcheon's kept himself in the peak of health. He may be older than Jory, and Jory may – or may, of course, at this point not – be carrying the Pendragon device, but this conflict is the climax of Sir Accolon's story, and at such times the devices bring their bearers to the very apex of their potential.

Indeed, the first blood goes to McCutcheon, with a feint towards the High King's left hip that turns into a low, and lucky, slash to the join at the knee between the High King's cuisse and his greave. It's obvious even from Windsor that Jory's tendon and muscle aren't damaged: it's not even a flesh-wound, just a cut, but the Scotsman's sword comes away bloodied nonetheless. The crowd give an impressed gasp.

'That's gonna annoy him,' Rev observes placidly.

'I don't know,' I say. 'I wouldn't put it past him to do it deliberately. Piece of theatre, kind of thing.'

Blaze says nothing.

* * *

Across the road from the fight, David and Paul watch as McCutcheon presses his advantage. Jory steps back, losing ground, and then again. He's favouring his unhurt leg. The way they've oriented themselves by now, the Eros statue's to the High King's rear. He rallies, aiming blow after blow towards McCutcheon, but the Scotsman turns them all away. Then Jory overcommits himself and McCutcheon dives in again, landing a blow on the Pendragon's torso. This time the armour isn't breached, but there's a thwack like a car being hit with a small tree, and Jory hurries back a few more steps, gasping.

'Is he bluffing?' Parsons wonders aloud, in a tone of detached interest. 'I actually can't tell.'

'The High King knows what he's doing,' Sir David replies, his voice firm.

And indeed, at this point Jory rallies again, more fiercely this time, closing in for another exchange of blows and another circling dance which ends with him facing the fountain once more, the video-hoardings at his back. From where McCutcheon stands, the High King's attack is reduplicated beyond him, magnified hugely. Indeed, the drone currently has the hoarding in shot, creating an infinite-regressing mise-en-abyme effect which everyone who's watching the screen finds dizzyingly disorientating.

As the drone closes in slightly and the image inflates, the Knight takes an involuntary step backwards, and Jory follows up with a flurry of sword-thrusts. A moment later he's trapped McCutcheon into defending himself against a low blow that never comes. Instead the Pendragon him high, between the spaulder and rerebrace, bloodying McCutcheon's upper arm on his shield side. McCutcheon recoils, retreating a few steps, and Jory charges at him, his sword outstretched towards the visor of the rogue Knight's helmet.

McCutcheon turns and runs.

'Yeah, a bluff,' drawls Paul. 'I thought so.'

* * *

'Some sneaky moves,' observes Zara, watching the action on Scar's phone at the Green Chapel camp site. 'Our High King is a tricky one.' She's been feeling uncharacteristically restless for most of the day. Normally self-contained and undemonstrative to an extent that some people are disturbed by, she's instead found herself snapping at people, though once or twice something has amused her enough that she's responded with a rare, thin smile. She puts it down to their enforced inactivity since Janene's public exposure. She imagines they've all been feeling pent-up to some extent.

Some of the others are following the action in Piccadilly on their phones, but Lee's produced a laptop so old it might as well have a cathode ray tube, and many of them are watching along on that.

On the various screens Craig McCutcheon turns his rout into a tactical withdrawal, climbing the steps up to the fountain and then onto the rim of the lower basin once more. From there he has an advantage of height, and although Jory climbs the steps after him he's still able to thrust down at the High King's head and neck while Jory has to angle his sword up awkwardly. The Scotsman's foothold is moist and precarious, though, and Jory clearly knows it.

'Stab him in the bollocks!' Janene yells helpfully from over by the laptop.

For half a minute they continue that way, trading unequal blows – then the Pendragon suddenly dances left along his step and turns, slashing backhandedly at McCutcheon's ankles, hoping to make him stumble back into the water.

Instead, McCutcheon jumps back onto the central pedestal, turning awkwardly to grab the rim of the next basin up, and circles away around the structure, walking on the wet heads of the ornamental dolphins. Then, astonishingly, he hauls himself and his weighty armour up onto the middle basin of the fountain, where he crouches precariously, aiming a wide slice of his sword downwards at Jory's head. Above him, the water pours down from the uppermost container, the one from which Eros himself rises, standing atop another dolphin's tail.

'That's no very bright,' Scar observes. It's obvious from the drone's view as it rises to follow McCutcheon that the rim of the fountain is wet, and slippery with pigeon shit. The Knight has overreached himself. His position's more precarious than ever, and the height he's gained is countered by the need to keep his balance.

Which is why he's crouching. His shins and ankles are exposed, and it's almost impossible for him, especially with his wounded shoulder, to angle his shield to protect them. Zara watches as Jory, who's leapt into the lower bowl and stands in the water there, continues to slash and hack, until McCutcheon's forced to stand to avoid a leg injury.

His feet are now at Jory's head height. Jory throws his own sword aside, leaps directly upwards and grabs on to

McCutcheon's serpent shield. The Green Chapel 'Ooh' in unison.

* * *

The crowd watches, in actual and magnified views, as McCutcheon's balance is fatally thrown. He struggles for a moment with the extra weight, but when he goes, he falls spectacularly, a great forward dive propelled by the considerable weight of Jory and his armour.

Jory falls too, of course – the short distance into the lower fountain bowl. He does his best to turn McCutcheon's momentum into an overarm throw, letting go of the Knight's shield as his arm swings out towards the street. McCutcheon's propelled away from the fountain, down onto its lowest steps, which he hits head-first.

The Circle's armourers build strong, but their wares simply aren't designed to protect against a fall of six metres onto hard, sharp-cornered concrete. There's a crunch whose timbre suggests that more than McCutcheon's helmet has been broken, and after a moment blood begins to trickle down the final steps onto the pavement.

Jory climbs, panting and dripping, from the fountain and drops onto the steps. He pulls off his own helmet, then marches down to crouch at McCutcheon's side.

The Scotsman's conscious still – though only just, and certainly not for much longer. He clasps his traitorous shield tenaciously, as if it's a talisman.

'It didn't work,' he mutters to the High King, staring up at him as his life recedes. 'The bloody thing didn't work. I was sure…'

'Oh, it worked, Craig,' the Pendragon replies, his voice firm and declarative for the benefit of the nearby drones. 'Your weapon worked very well indeed – but it wasn't me who opened it. Blaze did. You severed his device from him. Thanks to you, Britain is without a Merlin.'

('Ah,' Parsons murmurs to the Seneschal, across the square. 'Good news and bad news, then.')

(In Windsor, Blaze stands quickly and half-runs from the room.)

('Suppose he might be up for that consultancy work,' Ron observes callously at the Green Chapel camp.)

There'll be much debate later on across the media as to whether a smile skims across McCutcheon's dying lips at this point. Certainly the High King's revelation elicits a reaction from the crowd, most of whom are getting the audio feed on their phones and tablets. Their gasp is like a wave pulling away fast from the shore, before returning with even greater force.

'But that...' McCutcheon whispers to the Pendragon. His voice is very weak now. 'I thought...'

'You were stupid to,' says Jory, not without compassion. 'Did you really think the device of Arthur Pendragon, the High King of all Britain, could be banished by *technology*? By a computer virus?'

McCutcheon frowns, troubled by this. 'Not... a virus,' he gasps. 'It was... a trojan.' The breath he lets out doesn't return to his body.

As last words go, they get more points for pedantry than pathos.

11. MERLIN

I look for Blaze in his room – his suite, I should say, as it's as opulent and well-appointed a set of guest chambers as this royal palace can boast, with a lavish view across the greenery of the castle's Home Park down to the River Thames. To be honest, from my smaller rooms with a dull view of the courtyard I've always been a little jealous of it. But he's the High King's closest advisor; I'm just the entertainment.

I find him in his bedroom, packing.

'Hey mate,' I say, a little awkwardly. What do you say to someone who's had his whole function, the thing that's defined him for the past nine years, stripped away from him like that?

It's true that he only became Merlin in the first place because he happened to be around at the time – the elaborate ritual Merry concocted to transfer the device to another party was primarily intended to free her father from the Wendiman Derangement she'd imposed on him (accidentally or otherwise). His presence at that historic ritual's the main reason why Ron and the others want to talk to him about inviting particular allies into your life. Still, in the years since he's grown to inhabit the role as fully as Edward ever did. I can't imagine how it must feel to have that taken away from you.

Inadequately, I ask, 'How are you holding up?'

He glares at me. 'How the fuck d'you think?' I can't tell whether his anger's directed at McCutcheon, Jory or himself, but I'm the one here to get the brunt of it.

'Well, yeah,' I say, meaninglessly. I watch him stuffing clothes into a holdall for a bit. I notice he isn't taking any of his brightly-coloured suits with him. He's not wearing his silver dragon ring either, although I can't see it lying around anywhere. 'Do you need a hand with that?'

He looks at me again, slightly more calmly this time. 'You're not gonna try and get me to stay?'

I shake my head. 'If you've got to go, you've got to go. I understand the impulse, believe me.' There are three ways people join the Green Chapel: having always been shut out of the kind of safe, comfortable, predictable life most people in this country lead most of the time; having one of those but losing it through no fault of your own; and walking away from it deliberately. I took the third route. 'Not that he'll want you to go, but you know that.'

He shakes his head and stares at his holdall. 'Man, that's why I've got to go now. He'll be back soon. If *he* asks me to stay, I can't say no to him. Maybe I could've before, I don't know. But not now.'

He's right, of course – the High King will want him to stay. Jory won't care that Blaze is no longer as useful to him as he was before. (Well, he'll *care*, of course, because he knows that every asset is important, but he won't want the guy to leave his home of seven years because of it. He'll find another role for him, somehow, although his pre-Merlin CV as a street conjurer doesn't exactly mark him out as a high-flyer.) I say, 'Blaze, if you're doing this because –'

'Not Blaze, you twat,' he says, and this time it's definitely not me he's angry with. 'My name's Burn, for fuck's sake. Blaze was *his* name.'

Different *he* this time, of course. 'Well, technically Blaise was his tutor's name,' I remind him. 'And he spelt it with an "I" and an "S". But yeah, point taken. Even so –'

'Dale, you *know* why I've gotta go,' says Bl – says Burn. 'You get it better than anyone.'

And of course, annoyingly enough, he's right. It's one of the storytelling imperatives the devices bring with them; the same reason mentors throughout myth, literature and cinema leave their protégés before they're ready. *Fly, you fools*, they say, or *Your destiny lies along a different path than mine*, or *I have been, and always shall be, your friend* – and then they're gone, leaving the hero no time to mourn before facing his next trial.

It's rarely their fault, of course – generally speaking some bastard kills them. Merlin got off relatively lightly: in his case Nimue, the Lady of the Lake, just stole his magic and imprisoned him in an oak-tree in the enchanted forest of Broceliande. The point is the effect it has on the hero – it's all part of their journey, you see. I imagine Joseph Campbell had a word for it.

'Yeah... I'm not sure that applies this time,' I tell Burn. 'The boss has other mentor figures. Rev, David, Kinsey, Sir Charles. Well, sort of. But even so. You're just a voice in the crowd.'

(I know, I know – but it's pretty obvious his mind's made up. I might as well make it easier for him.)

'Won't miss me then, will he?' Burn says angrily, and it's that as much as anything – him saying that as if he's got one over on me, rather than understanding why I've said it and coming out with something cleverer – that convinces me Merlin really is gone.

'Yeah,' he says after a minute or so. 'You can help if you want. There's this big wooden box, bottom of the wardrobe in the guest room.' (*His* suite comes with a guest room, obviously. Mind you... with him gone, maybe I can persuade them to move me in.) 'Be careful with it.'

I go into the other bedroom and rummage for a bit, before I find the box.

It's not what I was expecting – not the polished teak and mahogany we see around the castle, linseeded to within an inch of its life, holding anything from solid silver cutlery to duelling-pistols. It fits together OK, but it's battered and grainy, the varnish applied unevenly, and obviously not of good-quality wood. It looks, to be frank, like something someone made in a school woodwork class and never threw away.

Too curious to resist, I peek inside. It's lined with green baize that looks like it came off an old snooker table. In it are cups and balls, matchboxes, bits of string, packs of cards. Cheap silk handkerchiefs. A set of linked wire hoops that look to be handmade. The paraphernalia of a street magician.

'You looked, then?' Burn asks shrewdly as I carry it through into the main living room, and I remember that even before he became Merlin's bondsman, he was never slow. 'Yeah, I'm going back to my old life, if it'll have me.' He takes the box, and stows it carefully at the bottom of a second holdall, before stuffing clothes on top. 'I've kept practicing the tricks – Merlin wouldn't let up about it. He knew something like this was coming.'

'Well, he's the one with the gift of prophecy,' I say. 'We're going to miss you, mate.'

'Yeah.' Burn shrugs. 'But what can you do? It's better than getting stuck inside in a bloody tree forever.'

* * *

When Zara returns to the camp from the afternoon *salat* – performed in a clearing a short way off into the woods, with Ahmed and the handful of other Muslims here – she's suddenly all energy. 'We've been sitting around here for long enough,' she tells the first Chapel members she meets. 'We should *do* something. It's what the Green Chapel's for.'

There's a general, though rather cautious, murmur of agreement.

'Do what, though, Za?' asks Janene, once they're all convened. 'We're all agreed we don't want to be HK's secret police no more. But like Rev says, our faces are in all the media. If we go out and do stuff, everyone'll think he told us to.'

'I've been thinking about that,' Zara replies. 'Rev is worried that if we act, others will think we are acting for HK, yes? We have lost our deniability.'

'Aye.' Scar's frowning – Zara doesn't usually talk this way. Or even this much.

'Well, then,' says Zara. 'We must do something that HK *can* deny. Something everyone knows he would never do. That way he can condemn us in the media and be believed, and we will be free to act as we choose in future without it reflecting on him.'

There are frowns all round now as everyone digests this cunning suggestion. Then Ron says, 'I'm torn as to whether that's barking or genius, Za. What kind of undertaking have you got in mind?'

Zara has an article from *The Guardian* all ready on her phone. 'Look,' she says. 'This is starting tomorrow in Southampton. A big international defence industry trade fair. An annual thing. That means a lot of arms traders getting together to talk deals and prices and contracts. These people sell weapons and security systems to dictators, to use on their own people. This shit props up police states and totalitarian regimes. This is the sort of thing we should be stopping.'

Reactions to this, in the growing crowd of Chapel people who are gathering around her, range from enthusiastic to dubious. 'But Za,' says Janene, reading the article over her shoulder, 'these are the guys who make the guns and tanks and helicopters for HK and the Circle. Webley and Westland and British Aerospace and all them lot. I don't know about abroad, but they're propping up his regime here. And we *like* his regime. Right?'

'I'm not saying we'll put them out of business,' says Zara. 'Like you say, the High King needs them. They make the toys he needs for his war games, yes. That's why he lets this sick trade carry on. But selling guns and mines and surveillance systems to states where women mustn't drive and can be stoned for being raped? No just country should allow that. And HK is a just king, which means he must not *want* to allow it. He has to for political reasons, that is all — because the arms trade is important to the economy or whatever bullshit.'

'So what you're asserting is…' says Ron, picking his way through this, 'that this is something HK would want us to do but can't tell us to? And if we do it now, no-one will believe he told us to, 'cause he didn't? And that will free us up to do what we want in future, whether he tells us to or not?'

Zara gives a tight smile. 'Something like that,' she says.

Ron shrugs. 'All right,' he says. 'I'm up for it.'

It sounds as iffy as all hell — but as I've said, the Chapel are getting bored out of their tiny minds sitting on their arses here. This is the first time in nearly two weeks that anyone's suggested doing anything constructive — and fundamentally, nobody here would be here at all if they didn't want to take direct action to make the world better. As Zara says, that's what the Green Chapel's for.

Scar says, 'Aye, me too.' She may be puzzled by her partner's changed behaviour, but she's kind of impressed that she's being so masterful all of a sudden. 'So what's your plan, then, boss woman?'

* * *

Jory travels down personally to Wells — again in the Iceni with Bonnie. As the helicopter approaches the venerable cathedral city, he sees Lake Glastonbury shimmering red in the sunset, the Tor surmounting the island where the town now stands.

The flooding of the Somerset Levels — at least, the area around the basin of the River Brue that now forms Lake Glastonbury — was the final, and most puzzling, act of that most Dadaist of devicial terrorist groups, the Sons of Gore. Notionally a separatist movement for an ancient British kingdom which probably never existed and may in fact have been a misunderstanding of the Celtic concept of the otherworld — and whose location is obscure and contradictory, being somewhere on the Scottish border near South Wales, surrounded by water and with its capital at Bath – the actual aims of the Sons always baffled outsiders and, very possibly, the Sons themselves.

There's no doubt that their intentions, whatever they were, were violent. The targets of their sporadically successful bombing campaigns appeared chosen entirely at random – school parties, nuns, an estate agents' conference, a reunion of the surviving cast members of a dodgy 1980s sitcom – and their incidental victims included a Knight of the Circle, Sir Griflet's bondsman Harold Lenton, who after losing a foot to them spent years trailing a dispirited troupe of men-at-arms around the Borders in an increasingly morose attempt to track them down. Only the clear Arthurian identity they claimed (Gore being the kingdom of Morgan le Fay's husband King Uriens) convinced the Circle that they were device-driven at all, and the assumption that one of them carried either Uriens' device or that of King Bagdemagus, also of Gore – though both were sometime allies of Arthur – remains unconfirmed.

The Sons were the last of the renegade devicial groups to be eliminated after the war, but not before they'd carried out the complex and co-ordinated act of environmental sabotage which led to the Brue bursting its banks and re-establishing the lake which had, far back in Romano-British times, encircled the once and future island of Glastonbury.

Jory and his men eventually tracked them down to a brewery in Bridgwater, only to find that they'd drowned themselves in the fermentation tanks. Identifying the five bodies brought the Circle no nearer to understanding what the hell they thought they'd been up to, or why they'd carried out this weirdly beautiful act of wanton destruction.

It would have been possible to undo the damage and restore the farmland around Glastonbury to its previous, painstakingly drained state, but enough people felt it made for an appropriately haunting symbol of the new reality of Britain under the Pendragon Settlement that – despite the vocal protests of some of the residents, who were eventually bought off with offers of land elsewhere – Lake Glastonbury remains, the largest body of water in the south of England and one of the shallowest. Glastonbury Island has become, even more than it was before, a refuge of hippies and New Age cultists, including at least four new religious movements who worship Jory personally. It's also a popular holiday destination for anglers, especially ones who appreciate a high-quality spliff.

This evening the lake's beauty almost justifies the Sons' vision for it, whatever that may have been: glowing like molten metal in the sun's reflected red, the conical Tor with its nipple-like tower making the whole thing look like some surrealist dessert.

The Iceni sets down in the boarding-school's lacrosse field. Tania Woodville and her squire Jamie come over to help Jory and Bonnie disembark while, from the dormitory windows behind them, hundreds of wide eyes stare and hundreds of mouths gape at this unprecedented visitor.

'Where is she, Woodville?' the High King shouts, as he steps out of the helicopter.

'Head's study, my lord,' Woodville replies. 'If you came to break the news, though, you're too late. It's all over the school. Only thing any of them are talking about.'

'Even so, Tania,' the Pendragon says, lowering his voice a little as they hurry away from the Iceni, 'it's the least she deserves.' Bonnie and Jamie scurry after them. 'I killed the girl's father, for heaven's sake. He was a Knight of the Circle.'

'And a traitor, sir,' Tania reminds him. She has strong feelings about that sort of thing.

'That's hardly her fault,' Jory points out. 'It's the least I can do for the poor kid.'

Tania shows him up to the headmistress's study. At a knock the principal herself comes out and there's a hasty, whispered, blackly farcical conference in which she flat-out refuses to leave her charge unchaperoned, even with the

High King, and they eventually compromise on Bonnie and Tania going in with him.

They find Izzy McCutcheon sitting in a chair that looks too large for her. She's a slight girl, blonde, with a potentially pretty triangular face that's currently red and tear-stained. She has her feet up on the seat, knees under her chin, and is hugging her ankles. Right now she looks more like a girl of eight than thirteen.

Jory sits at the desk in the headmistress' high-backed chair, ignoring the blood and pigeon droppings on his surcoat. Bonnie and Tania move to flank him, but he waves them irritably away and they take seats, rather awkwardly, beside the door.

'Izzy,' he asks the girl. 'Do you know who I am?'

The kid looks at him as if he's mad. 'Of course.'

'Have they told you what happened today?' he asks her gently.

She's silent for a while. Then, 'They tried to stop me finding out,' she says. 'They wouldn't tell me why *she* was here.' She jerks her head at Tania. 'But they couldn't keep it quiet any more when you started fighting my dad in the middle of London.'

'No, I don't suppose they could.' Jory's voice is soft. 'Your dad's dead, Izzy. I'm so sorry.'

'I know that,' Izzy snaps. 'I'm not stupid.' She gives one sharp sob, but that's all. She gets her breathing under control again, then says, 'Is it true what everyone's saying, my – my lord? Did he really try to – hurt you?'

Jory nods, slowly. 'Some people find carrying a device confusing,' he says, picking his words with great care. 'It can be very stressful. Sometimes our devices ask us to act in ways that are... not against our nature, but against our better nature. They can be very persuasive. Not everyone is strong enough to resist them, Izzy, you know?'

Izzy nods a few times herself. It makes her whole body rock backwards and forwards. Then she says, 'I knew that. I knew it was Sir Accolon, not him. We've all read the *Morte*

D'Arthur, it's on the English syllabus. I realised straight away his device must have made him want to fight you.'

Jory nods. He says, 'I'm going to talk to the school bursar. Your fees here will be paid – the Circle will look after you financially now, until you're ready to support yourself. But for the moment I think you should go somewhere else, somewhere safe and familiar. Do you have any other family?'

She shakes her head vigorously. 'No. Dad adopted me. I'm the only family he's got. My mum died – I don't think even she knew who my real dad was. I say *my real dad* because that's what people say, but he never was. My real dad's – was…'

After a few moments she asks, 'Did you have to kill him, though, my dad?'

'He challenged me,' the High King tells her simply.

'You didn't have to take him up on it, though, did you?' The girl sounds less indignant than honestly perplexed. 'You had all those people there. You could have got them to arrest him. You could have taken him to prison, or hospital even. You could have made him better.'

Jory looks stricken. 'The Circle has a code of honour,' he says. 'I'm bound by it as much as any other Knight.'

'That's shit, though.' Izzy looks horrified and claps a hand over her mouth. 'Oh God, I'm sorry, my lord, I didn't mean –'

'Not at all, Izzy,' the Pendragon says. 'You're upset. I understand that. Please go on.'

She looks at him carefully, gauging whether or not he means it, before evidently deciding that he does. 'I mean, my lord, that that seems a bit rubbish, really. You're the High King. If anyone's allowed to break the rules, you can.'

He shakes his head. 'I'm afraid not.' He gauges her in turn, considering – but quickly rejecting – the *You'll understand when you're older* gambit. 'People look to me as a moral example. Apart from popes, I don't think there's ever been a head of state who that's been truer of. If I go round breaking the rules when it suits me, then everyone else will think they can

203

do the same. Or else they'll think there's one rule for the powerful and another for the weak, and that that's tyranny. And they'd be right.'

She looks up at the word *tyranny* – she must have heard, somehow, what her dad said before the fight went down. But all she says is, 'Here they teach us, if another girl tries to start a fight with you, just walk away. They say that's the mature and grown-up thing to do. I like that better than your rule,' she tells the High King stubbornly. 'Yours is stupid.'

Jory's shoulders slump, and he bows his head.

He looks up, swallows, then says, 'I know it is. Izzy, I agree with you completely. I inherited the code of honour, I didn't make it. But it's the code I have to live by now, or any claim I have to rule this country goes out of the window. And then… there'd be another war, at least. And I honestly think that that would destroy us.'

There's a long, long silence. Then Izzy says, in a tiny voice, 'I suppose I understand that. But I loved my dad.'

And, for the second time in seven years, the High King weeps.

* * *

Later that evening, in a de luxe room in an expensive hotel-cum-conference-centre in Southampton, a businessman from Illinois starts to whimper as the woman he met in the bar, and the three people she let into his room when his back was turned, handcuff him to the bed. The fact that the handcuffs are his company's, used to lock his sample case to his wrist during his transit from the States, does nothing to alleviate his terror.

'Oh, don't start that,' the woman says, not unkindly. She's tall, black, beautiful, dressed like a hooker but – he's belatedly realising – definitely not one. 'We were getting on so well, too.' She has one of those regional British accents he can never tell apart from each other – is it Liverpool? Manchester? Scotland? Not London, anyway.

'Listen,' he says, keeping his voice low and, as far as he possibly can, calm. He has a terror that they'll gag him, and that when they kill him he won't be able to pray. 'I have money. About a thousand pounds cash, and I can get more. That has to be worth more than whatever you're doing this for.'

'I don't think so, Mr Schumacher,' replies the second woman – the younger, quieter, infinitely more terrifying one. She's white, but wearing one of those headscarves Muslim women wear, which is why he doesn't think he's going to get out of this alive. She crosses over to the room safe, and bends to peer at it. 'I think that what's in this safe will be more useful to us.'

Like all of them – including the non-hooker, who's shrugging one on over her low-cut blouse – she's wearing a top with a hood, though she's wearing the hood down to show her headscarf. Three of the tops are green, which Schumacher thinks means something factional in British politics – some kind of rebel group, he thinks, from the war seven years back – but he can't recall the details when chained to his bed wearing only his shorts.

The third woman – the older one, the only one wearing a red top – steps up to the bed and leans across him, resting a muscular arm on the headboard. 'Hey, sonny,' she asks him, 'give us the combination, aye? Save us a lot of effort all round.' Slowly, she pulls a crowbar out of the hand-warmer pocket of her hoodie.

Schumacher bites his lip to stop himself whimpering again.

'Picking up girls in bars, eh?' The boy – young man, Schumacher guesses, though he's pretty youthful – sits down on the bed next to him, and pats his thigh companionably. Schumacher's attempt to silence his whimpering fails. 'And you a married man,' the kid adds, nodding at Schumacher's chunky gold wedding-band. His accent definitely is London. 'You naughty boy. Sometimes when a bloke does that, it's 'cause he can't contain his rampaging libidinous heterosexuality. Other times –' the pat becomes a caress '– it's 'cause he wants *something else*, but doesn't want to admit it to himself. Which are you, Mr Schumacher, eh? Or can I call you Chad?'

The tall woman smothers a giggle. 'See, Chaddy,' she says, 'we've got lots of different ways of making you feel uncomfortable. Such as…' She holds up his cellphone, taken from his pants pocket. Schumacher groans. 'I bet your wife's number's on here, isn't it? Hang on a mo – shouldn't take too long to work out how to text her a photo…'

'These two and their games,' the older woman says, rolling her eyes. 'Still, they can have their fun. You're mine afterwards.'

Schumacher squeals, then bites his tongue as the woman clamps a hand over his mouth. His nostrils flare wildly as he gets his panicked breathing under control, then grunts pleadingly. Suspiciously, the woman lifts her hand, but hovers it an inch above his lips, ready to descend.

'I'll tell you,' he squeaks. 'Please, I don't want any trouble. The combination's 10252014, the date of my – my wedding. I'll show you how to open the case, too. It needs my thumbprint, and a code sent from my cellphone. Just… be careful, please. The sample in there's inert, but there are still precautions.'

'Oh, I wouldn't fret yourself,' the tall woman says. 'We've got a friend outside who's dead good with explosives.'

* * *

The High King arrives back at Windsor in a foul mood. He climbs down from the Iceni onto the darkening lawns and stalks back across the crew-cut grass towards the Castle, the loyal Bonnie dogging his footsteps.

At the entrance to the East Terrace, Jason meets them. 'My lord,' he says. 'Congrats on getting that bastard McCutcheon.'

'Thank you, Jason,' says the Pendragon shortly. 'I didn't expect to see you. Have you made contact?'

'Not yet, my lord,' says Jason, 'but we're getting warmer. I've got that Laney up in the big red room. She's been working for Merry the past six years.'

'Laney?' Jory asks. 'Working for Malory? Are you sure?'

Jason purses his lips judiciously. 'Well, she says she has, my lord. She said it right before I arrested her, so that would've been pretty clueless if she wasn't.'

'Clueless either way,' puts in Bonnie. 'Unless she wanted to get arrested.'

'Quite,' the Pendragon agrees. 'What else did she say?'

'Er... that we're never going to find Merry and her kid, my lord,' says Jason. 'That Merry wants us to leave them all alone, her dad too. Some stuff about a woman called Claudine – that's Merry's double, yeah, from the hotel in Leeds? She was working for the Paladins, that's what Laney says anyway. Plus some stuff about one time at this party we were at, right, her and me and Liss and this lad called Waz, and Liss and me got E'd up and we –'

'I think that's sufficient detail, Jason,' Jory observes, and Jason stops wittering. They enter the castle, past the saluting men-at-arms, and climb the Grand Staircase to the state apartments.

'You've done well, Jason,' Jory eventually observes, breaking his silence. 'After today we've more reason to find Malory than ever. Assuming Laney's telling the truth, this must be the nearest we've come in a long time. I realise it can't have been easy for you to arrest her. So thank you.'

They're at the door of the Crimson Drawing-Room now. 'Who's in there with her?' the Pendragon asks.

Jason names half a dozen men-at-arms, and Jory frowns.

'No Knight?' he asks. 'She's carrying the device of Elaine of Corbenic.'

'She can't seduce them all, my lord,' says Jason. 'And she wasn't feeling that sexy when I left her.'

Two men-at-arms slowly swing open the heavy doors, to

207

reveal Laney sitting demurely at a gilt coffee-table in a plush room as big as a medium-sized restaurant. Two more men-at-arms stand beside her, with another stationed at each of the exits.

'Dismissed,' the Pendragon snaps as he tramps in, and the men-at-arms file out. Jason and Bonnie exchange a nervous look, but tacitly agree to assume they're still required.

* * *

The conference centre proper is in a separate part of the hotel complex from the residential rooms, with its own separate security arrangements. Though the Green Chapel haven't been an openly active force in Britain for seven years, at the height of the civil war they instilled their values into enough young British activists that events like this will always be vulnerable to protest and potential sabotage.

The stalls are still being set up ready for the influx of delegates in the morning, and the area is being continually patrolled by an elite private company who provide security for events where every delegate is a security expert. Fashionable trends in crime and law enforcement in Pendragon-era Britain mean that they carry Circle-style swords as well as handguns. Although the upper floors full of smaller meeting-rooms are dark, the ground floor of the circular conference centre is walled with glass, and light pours out across the hotel forecourt.

'It's even environmentally wasteful,' Zara observes primly, from the roof of the residential block next door.

The conference centre doors are naturally equipped with biometric scanners which will allow only authorised personnel to enter. There's no way the Green Chapel could infiltrate the event without raising the alarm – not now, and certainly not tomorrow when the delegates are inside. If they were still working for the High King, then of course strings could be pulled, but as individuals they don't have that kind of clout. With more warning, they might have been able to

208

get someone in as a cleaner, but that won't fly either at this kind of notice.

Which was why Zara came up with the plan to steal the sample of next-generation plastic nano-explosive from the sales rep for Thunderbird International Munitions Inc – still lying cuffed, and gagged now, in a room five floors below. 'How are we doing, Vicks?' she asks.

'Well,' replies the Chapel's go-to woman for bomb-related issues, 'I think I've figured it out. According to the specifications Schumacher had in the case it's harmless without a piezoelectric trigger. All that means is we need to embed a crystalline structure in the plastique and make sure it gets a proper jolt on impact. I nicked a stick of sugar from the dining-room.'

She holds up one of the hypodermic arrows the Chapel use in lieu of tranquilliser guns. The syringe has been filled with the grey putty-like substance, and crystals of sugar glisten at its leading edge.

'Will it work?' asks Zara. There can't be more than ten or twenty grams of explosive there.

Vicks pouts. 'As long as you hit something hard, like a wall. Hit something soft, like a guard, and you just have an angry bloke with an unexploded bomb hanging off of him.' She hands over the arrow. 'You have to be really careful, though. This stuff's high-yield. The last thing we need is you dropping it.'

Zara looks scornful. 'I'm not going to drop it.'

'OK, then.' Vicks holds her hands up. 'I'm just saying.' She takes a few steps backwards anyway.

Zara fingers her powerful compound bow, peering down at the great brick cylinder with its bright glass skirt. She feels Scar's presence next to her. 'So we're really going to do this?' her partner asks softly.

Zara nods, not taking her eyes off the target. She twirls the arrow absently in her right hand, then tightens her grip after a collective gasp from the others. 'This –' she says, indicating the centre, 'this abuse of power and money, enriching people who are already rich at the cost of poor people's lives – *this* is what we fight against. We've kept ourselves out of the struggle for too long, Scar.'

'Maybe.' Scar says. 'And it's your ally telling you that, the Saracen, is it? Is it still Morgan Freeman's voice he's talking in, Za?'

Zara says, 'We will talk about that later. After we've done what's necessary.' She pulls her green hood up over her hijab, so that her face is in shadow.

'Stand back,' she tells the others. None of them ask why she's the one who gets to shoot the arrow. She's not the only brilliant archer here – Lee, for one, is just as good – but this is, after all, her plan. And everyone's deferring to her today, for some reason.

Zara lifts the bow and nocks the volatile arrow. 'Hey!' she shouts at the top of her lungs.

'What the fuck are you doing?' Scar asks. Beneath them in the forecourt, a guard points up at Zara and shouts a warning.

'You people are here to see weapons?' the green-hooded figure yells. 'We can show you weapons!' She lets the missile with its high-yield payload fly.

* * *

'King Dan,' Laney says sweetly. 'Long time no see. How's the galloping pent-up sexual frustration?'

'Laney,' Jory sighs. 'I've missed our chats.' He lowers himself into the chair across from her. He still hasn't had time to change out of his armour. 'Squig says you're working for Merry. Tell me, is that true, or were you bullshitting him? Because I warn you, I'm not in a mood to have my time wasted today.'

'No,' Laney says. 'I've heard all about your day.'

Jory looks questioningly at Jason, who groans. 'Bollocks. Not me, my lord. Must have been one of the men-at-arms.' Laney gives a winning smile.

'Well, then,' the High King says. 'Perhaps you can appreciate why I'm keener than ever to talk to Malory.'

'Yeah, well,' says Laney precisely, 'fuck that. You can stick it up your royal arse, King Dan. Your crawling flunky there may have kidnapped me, but that doesn't mean I'm going to talk to any of you. Certainly not about where Merry is. And if it's all the same to you, I'd like to see my lawyer. He's a friend of my dad's who tried to feel me up when I was fourteen so he's going to be a little bit surprised to hear from me, but he's supposed to be very good.'

The High King's been sitting patiently – or at least uncomplainingly – throughout this show of disrespect. Now all at once he's on his feet, tossing aside the gilded table – and let me tell you, those things are *heavy* – and leaning across Laney's chair, his hands on the armrests, his face in hers. Jason takes an involuntary step forward as the girl cowers and gives a tiny whimper. The table rolls slowly across the carpet.

'I *said*,' the Pendragon tells her, ' that I was *not* in the *mood*.'

'My lord…?' says Bonnie cautiously.

'Yes, Bonnie, thank you,' says the High King without turning round. 'You can go. I'm grateful for your help today. You too, Jason, good work. Good man. Good woman. Good night.'

Bonnie struggles with herself for a moment, but in the end comes down on the side of her strict vows of Knightly obedience. ''Course, my lord, yes. Come on,' she adds, putting a gauntlet on Jason's vambrace to steer him out.

They leave the High King towering over Laney's trembling figure. The men-at-arms heave the doors shut behind them with a solid thud.

* * *

For such a tiny bomb the yield is indeed, as Vicks predicted, pretty damn spectacular. The detonation wakes everyone in the hotel, and probably within a mile's radius.

Zara's aimed for one of the structural pillars between the glass walls of the ground floor, a quarter-circuit of the building away from the main doors. The compression of the sugar crystals as the arrow hits sends out electrical impulses which trigger the nano-explosive instantly. The pillar vanishes in a ball of fire and smoke, as every window in the hotel shatters.

Alarms shriek throughout the complex and from most of the cars in the street as the smoke-cloud expands. Shrill yells emerge from the centre, along with the security guards and the panicked set-up crew. Through the slowly clearing fug it becomes clear that Zara's shot has taken out a large chunk of the ground floor wall – the pillar she aimed at is obliterated, along with the floor of the room above, and those to either side are snapped in two. As the Chapel members watch, the cylindrical building begins to creak, and a crack starts creeping up its side.

Sirens are already approaching down the street, and those guards with sufficient presence of mind in the face of crisis are already running for the hotel lobby. 'Time for stage three,' Zara decides. Her face holds a quite uncharacteristic grin of delight at all the mayhem she's caused.

The Chapel contingent head for the service stairs. Besides Zara, Scar, Janene, Ron and Vicks there are Lee, Ahmed, Shell and four others, all of them armed with crowbars. Beneath them there's a hubbub as the guests, many of whom have recurring nightmares about exactly this kind of terrorist attack, vacate their rooms, either voluntarily or at the behest of the hotel staff. No-one is looking back to see the green-clad figures emerging from the service stairs onto the top floor.

A few guests have left rooms unlocked in their haste; others have to be crowbarred. Again, while many have taken their wallets or purses with them or left them locked in the room safes, others were in too great a hurry – and these people, like Schumacher, have cash to burn. Quite quickly, the Chapel have amassed enough for a very generous anonymous donation to a charity for landmine victims, and they head once again for the service stairs.

Two of the security people who spotted them from the courtyard have nearly reached the top, and Zara throws herself at them with immense enthusiasm. She wrests the first one's sword from his scabbard, then sends him sprawling with a push as she leaps at the second. He barely has time to pull out his own weapon and defend himself before Zara is upon him, blades clashing as she forces him further down the stairwell.

'It's nice to see her enjoying herself,' Janene comments as she checks the first man isn't too badly injured. Scar grunts in annoyance.

'She'll be brachiating off the fucking chandeliers in a minute,' comments Ron.

Five minutes later they're through the car park, where the police and convention security are still attempting to marshal and count the guests, and driving off into the night in a stolen police van. Behind them, a large section of the conference centre falls into the empty courtyard with a crash.

Zara says, 'Those people will be queuing up to buy Mr Schumacher's explosive now. We should have asked him for commission!' She laughs – actually and genuinely laughs, something that even Scar has rarely heard her do before.

Janene says, 'I'll lay odds the trade fair's off. I just hope those buggers never come back.'

'No question about them knowing it was us, anyway,' Ron notes.

'That's good,' says Zara. 'We wanted to make a public statement with this. The country will see it, and they will know that the Green Chapel follows nobody's orders. We're outlaws again! For the first time in seven years, we're free.'

Scar's earlier pride has turned to deep concern. Curtly she says, 'You do talk bollocks, Za.'

'Fluently,' says Zara, and laughs again.

* * *

213

Bonnie and Jason are sufficiently bothered by Jory's behaviour that they come to find me before they go off-duty. We ex-Chapel types in the Pendragon's service have a bit of an unofficial support network going on, and the young ones… well, they sort of look up to me. When Rev's out at the pub, anyway.

It's obvious to us all what's going on, of course. You remember how I mentioned that Sir Accolon was the lover of Morgan le Fay? Well, no-one reckons it's particularly likely that McCutcheon and Malory were actually shagging – they wouldn't even have overlapped at the MRF – but even so, it makes it look pretty likely that it was her who put him up to his spectacular confrontation today. Especially when you consider that, according to some versions of the myth, it was Morgan and not Nimue who imprisoned Merlin in his oak.

My worry – and Squig's and Bonnie's too, of course, they're both good kids – is that his eagerness to track down the woman responsible for today's horrors may have tempted the Pendragon to get a little bit *too* medieval on Laney's shapely arse.

So, when the High King comes out of the Crimson Drawing-Room, I'm waiting for him. He looks at me, then details the men-at-arms to take Laney to one of the wine-cellars and 'make sure she's comfortable' before locking her in.

Then he turns his attention to me. 'No, Dale, you can't see Laney,' he sighs. 'I'm having her held incommunicado.' Is there more blood on his surcoat than there was earlier? It's difficult to tell.

'I wanted to see you, boss,' I tell him. 'A lot's happened today. I thought you might want me to chronicle it for you.'

'Not really,' he says. 'Not now.'

'But while it's fresh in your memory, boss,' I suggest brightly.

He makes a noise between a sigh and a groan. 'Walk with me, then.'

Back in his study, he has the pages disarm and disrobe

him while he talks. The cut in his knee is shallow, but it hasn't been cleaned or dressed since mid-afternoon, so one of them fusses about with a medical kit while the others unstrap his ceramic-polyamide cuirass.

He tells me all about his fruitless visit to the MRF this morning, which isn't really what I was after. His account of the fight is terse and factual, mostly confirming what I saw on TV. The Pendragon's usually a bit more lyrical than that, especially on the rare occasions he sees action. It's obvious he must be utterly exhausted, and who can blame him after choppering halfway round the country and back with a fight to the death in the middle of it?

We'll get to whatever just happened with Laney eventually, I hope. But first he has to tell me about Izzy McCutcheon.

When he gets to the bit where he met her in the study, he goes off at a tangent. 'What a horrific day for the poor girl,' he says. 'Bad enough to learn your father's dead – even worse to learn he's been killed as a criminal – but from the media? As passed on by a school full of gossiping, whispering children? I can't imagine how she must be feeling right now. I can't see how she can stay at that school now, even with the Circle seeing to her fees. With all her peers knowing her dad was a traitor, it'll be unbearable. She needs a fresh start.'

I'm pleased his empathy hasn't completely deserted him, anyway. 'Must have been a right bastard for her,' I say. 'Then after that, you came home…?'

'The awful thing is, she's got no other family,' he carries on, oblivious. 'She was adopted, and McCutcheon was a single father. She had a terrible start in life, and now I've taken away the only stability, the only loving family, she's ever had.'

'Well, perhaps someone else will adopt her,' I say vaguely. 'Boss, it sounds awful, but afterwards –'

Jory looks shrewdly at me, as if I've confirmed something he was rather thinking himself. 'Yes,' he says, nodding. 'Yes, I owe her that, I think. It's not as if I'm going to be having children of my own.' He glances bleakly at his desk drawer, where I know he keeps a copy of that grainy photo.

I'm quite taken aback. 'What, you mean *you?*' I ask, too surprised to be more tactful about it. Would the High King adopting the girl make her a princess, I wonder? Do any of the legends give Arthur daughters? I'd have to check. 'That would be quite a responsibility, boss. Are you sure you've got the time?'

'I'll make the time,' he says. 'You never know, I might be able to make a difference.'

'Well, sleep on it at least, eh?' I suggest nervously. 'I mean, you're knackered, you may not be thinking straight. I'd have a good night's kip, come to it fresh in the morning.'

'I doubt Izzy will be sleeping tonight,' the Pendragon says.

* * *

It's only as I'm experiencing insomnia of my own, lying in bed at two-thirty staring at the ceiling and counting the hundred thousand sheep which Caswallawn son of Beli slaughtered for the first of the Three Immense Feasts of the Island of Britain, that it occurs to me to wonder whether – given how careful Jory's been to avoid fathering any more potential Mordreds, and how good the devices can be at finding loopholes in people's oaths – for him to adopt a kid is necessarily an entirely good idea.

216

12. ROBIN HOOD

The High King may have told me I wasn't allowed to see Laney, but he didn't tell me I couldn't try to talk to her. (Well, technically he did, that being what 'incommunicado' means. But I'm not one to quibble over technicalities.)

I sneak down early next morning to the entrance to the wine cellar – one of the ones that's not in use at the moment, because obviously it would be insane to lock Laney in with the expensive vintage, unless you fancied wading through haphazardly-blended plonk full of glass shards the next morning. As it is, I don't give much for the antique Victorian racks' chances of survival.

The first sign that something's a bit off is that there's no man-at-arms on guard duty. Laney is, of course, supposed to be locked in (and when I check the door is indeed shut fast), so she shouldn't be able to escape anyway... but when you're imprisoning someone it's standard practice to post a guard or at least have some kind of surveillance in case of an escape attempt. It's only polite.

I bang on the door. 'Laney? Laney, it's Dale. Are you in there?'

Silence. Still, it's a thick door, and it's six in the morning. Maybe she's asleep. Maybe there was some wine left in there by mistake – a case or two, say – and she's drunk the lot.

I don't want to shout much louder in case I draw someone

else's attention, so I head off to the guardroom. This time in the morning I'd not expect anyone to be in there, but in fact there are two men-at-arms. One's lying head-down on the table, while the other's lying sprawled out on a bench. I have a tiny panic attack just for a moment, before I realise they're both snoring heavily.

Something's not right here, even so. There are a couple of mugs on the table, with the dregs of some congealed coffee in both. I sniff it, but it just smells of horrible coffee.

This is looking distinctly suspect, but I don't want to wake the blokes just yet. I don't want to get Laney into unnecessary extra trouble if it turns out they just made their coffee with hot vodka for a bet.

As I expected, one of them has the key. This is an old building – few older still standing in the country – and it's a proper clichéd dungeon key, a rusty shaft as long as my hand with a circular grip and square teeth. It's sticking out of the bloke's pocket, which would normally make it tricky to get free without waking him – you tend to notice someone getting frisky in your trousers even when you're spark out – but he just snores through it. It's all very Sleeping Beauty, and it's freaking me out a little.

I tiptoe back to the cellar, and I've pushed the key into its slot before it occurs to me that maybe this is what I'm meant to do. Quite clearly Laney or someone working with her has managed to get some drugs into the guards somehow, but how's that going to help her if no-one lets her out? Either she's relying on me or Squig or Bonnie to check up on her and do exactly what I'm doing now…

…or I could run into whoever's meant to be rescuing her at any minute. Bollocks.

Quickly I pocket the key and nip back to the guardroom, where I retrieve one of the unconscious men-at-arms's Webley 2020s. I don't know how to use it, and wouldn't anyway, but Laney doesn't know that. (Well… she might have forgotten what I'm like, or something.) Anyway. Better have something deadly to wave threateningly at people than not.

Back at the cellar, I fit the key to the lock once again. I try to hold the gun like I know what to do with it, turn the key and kick the door open.

Except that this door, like most of the ones upstairs, is bloody heavy, and I just bang my toes. I drop the Webley and hop around cursing for a minute, then pick it up again and force the door open slowly, putting my back into it.

'Laney?' I shout cautiously. 'It's Dale. Just coming to see how they're treating you. Don't worry, the gun's only a precaution. Just don't try and rush me or anything, and –' The hand I've been fumbling for the light with finally finds the switch, and a string of dull bulbs illuminates the room. '– And bollocks.'

The cellar's big, cavernous even, but all the corners of it are clearly visible. There's a comfy chair, a camp bed, an upended crate with a glass and plate on it bearing the remnants of some water and a sandwich, even an ancient but clearly non-priceless commode dragged down from one of the attics. There are the wine racks, obviously, but those are empty as expected, and I can see right through them. I do a quick circuit just to check – making sure I take the key with me, in case of hilarious pranks – but it's obvious Laney isn't in here.

It's obvious the men-at-arms took their orders to keep the prisoner comfortable seriously, which is what I really wanted to check on, and that's great. It's just that there's no prisoner.

* * *

'I just want us to be real clear on this,' Rev Cantrell tells the Green Chapel severely, a couple of hours later.

The bare fact of the attack on the trade fair got to us before the Pendragon made it to bed last night, but he barely had the stamina to issue a boilerplate statement of sympathy before crashing. We woke him up when I discovered Laney was gone, obviously, and it was barely twenty minutes after that that he saw the police report detailing the Green Chapel's involvement.

Jory was so furious he sent Rev up to the encampment in the Iceni – either a thoughtless or a very canny reminder of his own reliance on the defence industry. The helicopter's idling in a nearby clearing while Cantrell gives Zara and the others – who only got back to the camp a couple of hours before dawn – the bollocking of their lives.

'You blew up a building full of unallied civilians,' Rev says with only slight exaggeration, 'including a bunch of foreign nationals, businessmen and dignitaries. The Saudis won't be sending us any more royal representatives, I can tell you that.'

As it happens everyone in the hotel complex was evacuated safely – even Chad Schumacher, once they found the poor sod – but some of the people in the conference centre sustained minor injuries when Zara's arrow hit, and the guard she fought on the stairs is still in hospital being stitched up. 'You destroyed millions of pounds worth of technology,' Cantrell goes on, 'terrorised the delegates and then stole their money. Some of them have left already, and I can't see the trade fair being held again next year, or any year. You've caused irreparable harm to the UK's standing with other governments, and sabotaged a multi-billion-dollar industry.'

He glares at them – Zara looking relaxed and defiant; Scar stubborn but still with that undercurrent of worry; Ron hurt and indignant; Janene troubled but standing her ground; poor unallied Vicks obviously wishing she was somewhere very far away indeed – until his stern expression cracks into a grin.

'Between ourselves,' he says, 'I'm proud of you guys. Those fuckers were a blight on this fair nation long before HK came to power, and the way we've been tolerating them is a national disgrace. Speaking personally, I *love* what you did. But,' he adds, dropping the grin, 'what you've done is bad for HK's reputation too, and that's not something we can let go by, you hear me? The public's either going to believe the Pendragon ordered this, or that he's lost control of some of his closest allies – which would be true. HK is *most* unhappy about this. It's only because he has a couple of other middling-sized crises to attend to that he's not here telling you this personally.'

Ron finds the courage to speak up. 'But Rev, him getting irascible about it is the clever bit. It means he can disown us again. Everyone will believe he's proper exercised about it, 'cause he really, truly is. And that means –'

'It means what?' It's rare for Cantrell to interrupt. 'You think HK's ever going to trust you guys again? You must be crazy. You think he'll believe you'll do what he tells you to, instead of whatever comes into your goddamn heads? Goddamn it, Ron, what were you even *thinking?*'

Zara says quietly, 'It isn't Ron's fault, Rev. This was my idea. I'm the one HK has a quarrel with, not them.'

'Oh yeah?' Rev glares at all the others. 'And not one of you tried to stop her, am I right?'

There's some embarrassed shuffling of feet. Cantrell sighs. 'Look, Zara, I get it. I've seen a bunch of people transition between allies. HK himself, for one. Janene's done it. So have David and Squig. The change isn't easy, and taking on an ally as powerful as Robin Hood's going to throw anyone out of whack for a while. You didn't have to deal with it alone, though, kid. I would've been here for you. Hell, so would HK, though admittedly he was kind of busy most of yesterday. You should've just *asked.*'

'You make it sound like an illness,' Zara says. 'I feel better than I have for years.'

Rev looks at her – the smile that haunts her lips, the quizzical cock of her head. 'Well, yeah,' he says. 'Yeah, I can see that.'

'It's true, then?' Janene asks. 'I mean, that's what we all reckoned, like. But HK's really lost the Robin ally, then?'

Rev sighs. 'He was standing right by Blaze when the devicial mine went off. Having two allies protected him from the worst of it, I guess. God knows what would have happened if we'd lost King Arthur.'

Janene says, 'That's terrible. I mean, no offence, Za, you'll make a great Robin, but Dan – HK, I mean – being Robin and Arthur was what stopped the war, right? What happens now?'

'Well,' Cantrell says, 'I guess that's kind of up to Zara, isn't it?'

Zara smirks. Scar puts a hand on her shoulder, but she doesn't seem to notice.

'If you're asking me, I don't think the country's gonna split the way it did before,' Rev says. 'The Pendragon's too powerful for that. Sorry, Za, but Arthur's the stronger ally by far – that's why Robin was the one who got banished. Arthur's all about the power, whereas Robin's an underdog from the underclass. Hell, he's an outlaw – being banished is kind of the job description. Yeah, the Chapel and the Circle were evenly matched back in the war, but the Pendragon wasn't around back then. So you can't bring down the High King – but you can sure hurt him if you choose to.'

He and Zara hold each other's gaze for a moment. He says, 'You don't need me to tell you you'll lose me if you do. My support, my friendship, my ally. If the High King's all that's keeping this country together, then I'm with him and so's Friar Tuck.'

'Sticking with the winning side, aye Rev?' asks Scar, but he can tell her heart's not really in it.

'So how about it, Za?' Rev asks. 'What kind of Robin Hood are you going to be? The kind who fights with the King, or against him?'

Zara considers.

* * *

Izzy McCutcheon arrives at Windsor in the afternoon, having taken the train up from Bristol with Tania Woodville and Jamie. Jory could of course have sent the Iceni to pick them up, but he decided in the end that the more normal the girl's journey was, the less overwhelmed she'd feel.

Jory greets her personally, of course. He'd be a complete git not to, however much he's got on his mind. The girl's being brought to live in a royal castle, after all, so a certain amount of overwhelmitude is pretty much inevitable.

The best available theory of how Laney escaped has someone in the Castle drugging the guards, borrowing the key to let her out, then locking up neatly afterwards and putting the key back in the man-at-arms' pocket. It's a weird and stupid risk to have taken for no clear gain (since it would have been obvious something was afoot as soon as the men were discovered unconscious), but it's more plausible than, for instance, the secret passage that other men-at-arms are currently inspecting the cellar for. The drugged men are fine, but they claim to have no memory of what happened – which is peculiar in itself, because the sedative used, while powerful, isn't usually associated with memory loss.

Jory sent the Bentley with his chauffeur to pick up Izzy, Tania and Jamie from the station. The girl's more prepared this time for her meeting with the sovereign, and she attempts a curtsy as she gets out of the car.

'My lord,' she says carefully, 'thank you so much for inviting me here.' Woodville's squire follows with her bags.

'There's no need for that, Izzy,' Jory says gently, and leads her up to his study.

'Ms Woodville's told you why you're here, I assume?' he asks her, once she's made herself comfortable in one of his big armchairs.

Izzy nods.

'Well, then,' says Jory. 'If I adopt you, I certainly won't want you curtseying and calling me your lord. I know that may not happen – nothing's going to happen unless you agree to it, I promise – but we may as well start the way we hope to go on.'

'What should I call you, then, my l– sir?' Izzy asks. 'Do you want me to call you "Dad"? Because –'

Jory winces. 'No, no,' he says. 'It's much too soon for that, I know. Maybe one day, if you want to. I know I'll never replace your dad, and that's not my intention. No, for the moment I'd like it if you could call me Jory. Nobody else will, these days. Even my own mum and dad get nervous doing it.'

'Jory?' Izzy considers this, and nods. 'OK,' she says.

'I've sorted out a room for you,' Jory says. 'It used to be Queen Victoria's when she was a girl, apparently. I'm not sure anyone's lived in it since then. You can furnish and decorate it how you like – just talk to the head housekeeper. I'll introduce you later.'

'Can I get a 1.8 metre ExHD TV with a palm console and gesture recognition?' Izzy asks quickly.

The High King blinks. 'Erm, yes, if you like.' Then he thinks for a moment. 'One with parental control.'

'Oh,' says the girl. 'OK then.'

'In the meantime, though,' the Pendragon says, 'and I'm sorry to bring it up, but… we've got to think about your dad's funeral. The Seneschal's sorting out the details, but he's asked for your input if you want to give it. I thought he should be buried at the Circle cemetery in Winchester, with full honours. He was a brave Knight, and… well, mostly a loyal one. It wasn't his fault he drew the device he did. What do you think, though? It's important that it happens as you'd want it to.'

'I didn't want it to happen at all,' Izzy reminds him, then looks ashamed. 'Sorry my l– Jory. You're being so nice.'

'Not at all,' Jory says. 'That was entirely fair.'

'I guess that all sounds OK,' Izzy says. 'I don't know much about funerals. I was only five when my mum died. Will you be there?' she asks.

'I'd like to be,' says the Pendragon. 'But I'll completely understand if you'd rather I wasn't.'

'Oh,' says Izzy. 'I thought you wouldn't want to because you killed him.'

Jory winces again. 'It won't be very comfortable,' he admits, 'but I'd like to pay my respects.

Izzy stares out of the window for a while. 'OK,' she says. 'Actually, I think I'd like it if you were. If you don't mind.'

She smiles at him.

* * *

Later that week, Sir Marhaus's device-bearer Patrick Sullivan emerges from his disciplinary hearing, to all appearances a chastened man. The witnesses, from Woodville and Mukherjee to the Duchy man-at-arms Woodville recruited at Fort Cador, have given their statements, and the tribunal has considered its verdict.

In the absence of an active Merlin bondsman, the Bishop of Lichfield – the Rt Rev Sally Marvell, who a few years ago inherited the device of Arthur's chaplain, St Dubricius, from the late Fr Hywel Evans – sat on the panel, with the Seneschal and the young director of the Benwick Institute who bears the device of Sir Leondegrance. They hauled him over the coals and back again, then hauled him back onto the coals and dropped him there to watch him wriggle, but in the end they've shown forgiveness. Sullivan's pay is docked, the services of his squire (who is in any case the subject of disciplinary proceedings himself) have been indefinitely revoked, and he has to undertake no fewer than three penitential pilgrimages – but he gets to keep his commission as a Knight, and will return to active duty.

Frankly, he's got off lightly – things are looking even worse for Rudge and Hithers when their courts martial come through. (Stein, of course, was less lucky still.)

Sullivan leaves the Fastness, and takes the tube back to his flat in Kentish Town. He has to travel to Carn March Arthur in Gwynedd, a stone that supposedly bears the hoofmark of King Arthur's mare Llamrei, on foot and in full armour, before returning to London and striking out again in the same manner for Loch Arthur in Dumfriesshire, one of the possible resting-places of Excalibur. After that, Colchester in

Essex, one of the less likely sites for Camelot, will feel like a gentle stroll.

A walking tour of Wales, Scotland and England. The tribunal obviously wanted to drive the point home. There's a dearth of Arthurian sites in Northern Ireland, or Sullivan's pretty sure he'd be heading to the province too.

If so, he'd probably have waited till he was there to do this. As it is, there's no time like the present.

He fishes out the disposable, and almost certainly stolen, mobile phone he bought from a second-hand electrical shop in Camden, and dials a Dublin number he knows by heart.

'It's Sullivan,' he tells the voice that responds. 'I'm reinstated. Month on the road and I'm back in.' He pauses. 'Understood. I'll wait to hear.'

He hangs up, then removes the SIM card and flushes it down the loo. The phone he seals into a plastic bag, crushes underfoot, and slips into his pack to dispose of in a bin somewhere between Watford and Machynlleth.

The bondsman of Sir Marhaus dresses, arms and boots himself, locks up his flat and begins his long walk west.

* * *

McCutcheon's memorial service is an odd affair, not least because the most prominent mourner killed him. I don't suppose the High King intended to upstage Izzy or McCutcheon's friends and colleagues, but when you decide to make yourself royalty you end up kind of prominent wherever you go.

I didn't really know McCutcheon, but I'm there too, in case the Pendragon needs moral support. Things have been weird recently, and the last thing we need is an inappropriate public show of emotion. A bowed head, a manly tear, that's the sort of thing the public expect from their monarch; any more than that looks like a sign of weakness, and would not be helpful in the current climate.

The hymns were chosen by Izzy herself, in consultation

with the High King. She's made some conventional choices – 'Abide with Me' and 'Nearer, My God to Thee', as well as the slightly pointed 'Make Me a Channel of Your Peace' – but she wanted to end with something highlighting her dad's career of patriotic service. I pushed for 'I Vow to Thee, My Country', but Jory insisted on the one he thought the most appropriate – as usual. It's his favourite hymn, and he can't see any good reason why others wouldn't share that view.

Of course, there may be those who don't approve of the update.

'And did those feet in ancient time
walk upon Logres' mountains green?'

…is how it starts now. Jory reckoned we should use the Celtic name for Arthur's realms instead of the traditional *England*, so that the other nations of the UK wouldn't feel too left out. I have to admit it makes me cringe a bit, thinking about it later.

'And was the holy Lamb of God
on Logres' pleasant pastures seen?'

The mourners are crowded into the little chapel attached to the Circle cemetery. Larger Circle funerals use Winchester Cathedral itself, but the manner of Izzy's dad's death, as well as the kid's own feelings, make that inappropriate this time round.

'And did the countenance divine
shine forth upon our clouded hills?'

Sir David's here, of course, and various Knights who knew McCutcheon – among them old Charles Raymond, bellowing his way tone-deafly through the hymn and stumbling over the changed words. The MRF have sent a token delegation led by Freda Tate-Hendricks. Izzy's the only family, as she predicted.

*'And was an Avalon builded here
among these dark satanic mills?'*

…Yeah, there's that bit too.

*'Bring me my bow of burning gold!
Bring me my arrows of desire!
Bring me my spear! O clouds unfold!
Bring me my chariot of fire!'*

Izzy's eyes are damp, as you'd expect them to be – she's being unbelievably brave through all of this, but even so. Jory, too, is looking moved, though for fundamentally different reasons.

*'I will not cease from mental fight,
nor shall my sword sleep in my hand
till we have built an Avalon
in Logres' green and pleasant land!'*

The patriotic hymn goes into the third verse –
– and yes, yes, I know, yes. I cringe even more, and try my utmost not to catch anyone's eye.

*'Yea, in the towers of Camelot,
and in the dale and fen and weald,
King Arthur ruled with wisdom bright,
with justice and with radiant shield.'*

Boss, I said, *you're asking me to paint a hat on the Mona Lisa.* But he insisted. The song – his favourite, remember – should be an inspiration, he said, a rallying-cry, showcasing the continuity between the new order and the old.

*'And so again, in Logres' land,
on moor and tor and fell and down,
we'll build anew our Avalon
beneath Pendragon's shining crown!'*

Looking around the older faces here, it's pretty clear I'm not the only one who's not convinced.

Still, Izzy's only thirteen. She probably doesn't remember that it used to be called 'Jerusalem'.

* * *

It's late at night a few days later, and the university library is almost deserted. Only a few students are still at work here, one of them a blonde woman in her very early twenties. She's dressed in jeans and a blouse which look like ordinary, sensible, perfectly standard studentwear: only a close examination would tell you that they're both designer labels which would cost the average student, even in this city, six month's rent.

She's irritated, because her security detail are being jumpier than usual right now. They wouldn't let her out this morning because of a bomb threat which turned out to be some bored teenager having a laugh. She'd like to flay the little bastard – she should have this essay in the bag by now, but she needed some of the paper books here at the library. She's meant to be out with the girls this evening, at a new club in town that Tilly knows, but she absolutely has to finish this by tomorrow morning.

Her tutor's been complaining about her work ethic, and she knows it's more important than ever that her family be seen as hard-working and conscientious. She's shocked, on the rare occasions when she mixes with students from different social backgrounds, how many think she comes from a lineage of pointless freeloaders. She's sure they're still very popular in some parts of the country, although she can't quite pinpoint where.

She knows who to blame for that, of course. Since the High King came her family looks superfluous, an extra layer of royalty that no-one really needs. The only ways to fix that are for the Pendragon to go away again, or for the family to hitch their fortune to his in some way. Her uncle was working along the right lines there – although his plans for her were unpalatable, and in the end have only made things worse for the rest of them.

The student frowns at the screen of her top-of-the-range tablet, and wonders whether she can leave her essay where it is. It doesn't really come to a conclusion, but then she doesn't really have one. At least she's quoted an awful lot from proper books, and that ought to impress her tutor.

She glances at her watch – a tastefully understated gold Cartier number that brings out the honey tones in her hair. She might have time, if she emails the essay to her tutor now, to join Tilly and the others for a few swift drinks before her curfew.

'When do they make you go to bed, your highness?' a low voice speculates. There's a woman sitting a few bays to her left along the line of desks. The student didn't notice her before, and wonders how long she's been there. 'I imagine they insist on you getting your beauty sleep.'

The woman pushes her chair back to face her properly, and the student sees she's about forty – a tutor certainly, not a student. Her russet-red hair's gathered into a bun, and the eyes behind her metal-rimmed glasses are faintly lined. Her voice is melodious, as if she's used to laughing or singing.

The student tries not to sigh too audibly. The public are always wanting to talk to her – they don't seem to understand she just wants to be treated like any other student. Still, her family are always telling her to be polite and pleasant at all times.

'People don't call me "your highness",' she tells the woman, keeping her voice low out of respect for other library users. 'I'm just a Lady, usually. But then I don't really like titles,' she adds dutifully, remembering the need to appear a woman of the people.

'Your ladyship, then,' smiles the older woman. 'I've been wondering – what are you planning to do when you leave here? The university, I mean,' she adds as the blonde woman glances reflexively at her watch. 'What are your plans in life?'

'Well, I...' the student gets no further than she usually

230

does when asked this question. Her uncle's agenda may be off the table now, but she doesn't suppose that what she ends up with will be much different. She'll get an undemanding job in the media or somewhere, she supposes, to mark the time until she meets an aristocrat or princeling of about her own age whom she doesn't altogether dislike, and in a jiffy she'll be married off and adding entries to the line of succession. If she's lucky her husband will favour equal-opportunity infidelity, but that's about the best she can hope for.

She says, 'I'm rather afraid that's none of your business,' softening it with a smile.

'Ah,' says the redheaded woman. It occurs to the student that she looks a little familiar, as if this – like so many of the people she meets – is somebody she's supposed to have heard of. Some senior academic, possibly? 'The thing is, your ladyship, I'm hoping it might become my business.'

'I don't think so,' the blonde woman says, frostier now, as she gathers up her books and tablet. 'I'm afraid I'm going to have to ask you to leave me alone. I have bodyguards on call, you know.' She looks round nervously, but can't seem to spot any of them just at the moment. They've probably nipped out for a smoke again. She'll have to have a word with them about that.

'Don't worry,' the woman tells her with a reassuring smile. 'I'm really not as frightening as they say. I'm actually here to offer you a job.'

The student frowns in bemusement. 'A job? Me?'

'Yes, your ladyship, you.' Dr Malory Wendiman smiles. 'I'm hoping you might come and work for me. I think you have potential.'

II
AVALON

13. THE GREEN KNIGHT

On a chill and icy afternoon in the last week before Christmas, seven and a half years after the Battle of Tregorlois and the challenge at Piccadilly, Tania Woodville, bondswoman of Sir Tristan and Knight in charge of the Circle's counterintelligence quest against the Children of Oisín, bangs on the door of the flat belonging to Patrick Sullivan, Sir Marhaus' device-bearer and a Knight in good standing with the Circle.

'Sullivan?' she shouts through the door. 'It's Woodville. Are you in?'

There's a thump from inside the flat. It's followed by a muffled swearing noise, the sound of a loo flushing, and annoyed footsteps stomping towards the front door.

It opens with a crash and Sullivan's there, buckling his belt. Nearing fifty now, he's huge still, his short-cropped hair iron grey but his muscles as firm as ever. Tania, still untroubled in her mid-thirties by such bodily disruptions as childbirth, has kept her physique too, although she was always tiny compared to him.

'What is it, Woodville?' Sullivan growls. 'It's my day off.' He see she's in full armour, bearing her sword and her green-and-gold shield. He scowls. 'There some crisis on? Why didn't you call?'

'Can I come in, Patrick?' she asks, stepping smoothly into the hallway. Uncomfortably, he steps aside and follows her through to the messy living-room. He gathers up an unfinished pizza and some empty beer-cans in one arm and dumps them in the open-plan kitchen.

'Tea?' he asks, filling the kettle and setting it off to boil. 'Got some mince pies somewhere. Or are we in too much hurry?'

'A mince pie would be superb,' says Woodville. 'No tea though, thanks.'

He brings the box through, opens it with a finger and offers her the plastic tray. She picks one out, and he takes one for himself. 'What's this about, Woodville?' he repeats.

'We've lost a Fianna spy,' Woodville admits. 'We wanted your help running him down.'

Sullivan grunts in amusement. 'More your area than mine, isn't it?' He inserts his pie into his mouth whole, and chews emphatically as Tania considers her response.

'He's been trying to suborn one of our Knights,' she says. 'I'm not going to tell you who, except that it's someone who doesn't see a lot of action, if you catch my drift. The shifty swine's been working on this Knight for months, trying to build up a rapport he can parlay into something a bit more political. Fortunately, our Knight still had just about enough nous to realise they were being taken for a ride.'

'"Working on them?"' notes Sullivan with his mouth full. 'Shagging them you mean. And you're saying "they", so you don't want me knowing whether it's a woman or a gay bloke. You can both be a hell of a security risk,' he adds with the serene unselfawareness of someone whose gender and sexuality are the assumed default. 'I'll have that cup of tea, if we're not going anywhere,' he adds, getting up and going to the kitchen. 'All right, so where's this bloke now?'

'Well,' Woodville says, 'he didn't show for their scheduled tête-à-tête this afternoon, which means he must have got wind somehow that something was up. We think he's gone to ground. Fortunately, our Knight happened to have a GPS tracker bead knocking about from a previous quest, and when they realised what was up they managed to plant it on the fellow.'

It's an outrageous lie, of course. Poor Nate Busman was too much of an emotional wreck, when he realised that his gentleman friend was pumping him for other things than their mutual pleasure, to do anything so constructive or forward-thinking as plant a tracker, even if he'd had such a thing lying about the place. He could well have ended up doing something tragic, stupid or both, if he hadn't known that the Seneschal also favoured male company and would likely be sympathetic. Things might have gone altogether differently under Charles Raymond.

The point is, Sullivan can't be certain she's bluffing – and ultimately it doesn't matter. Whether it's true or not, the fact that Woodville's bringing it up now, here in his lounge, can only mean she suspects him of harbouring the Fianna spy. If the man isn't here – or, of course, if Sullivan's actually innocent, although he jumped to the conclusion that sex was involved remarkably quickly for someone without prior knowledge of the situation – he need only deny all knowledge and let Tania search his flat. If the spy's in, say, the bathroom… well, that doesn't leave him with a lot of options.

Woodville knows this as well as he does, of course, which is why she lifts her riot-shield as Sullivan turns, and why the kettleful of boiling water splashes across her capering gold lion on its green field, instead of her face beneath its open visor.

Not innocent, then, she thinks briskly. Well, that's useful to know.

She noted as she entered the flat that Sullivan's sword and shield were hanging on the hat-rack by the door… but Sullivan has a well-appointed kitchen, and it's obvious he maintains his kitchenware with a zeal that doesn't extend to the state of his living-room.

He bellows, 'Get your arse in here, MacNeill!', before he charges at Woodville with a carving-knife.

* * *

Poor Busman, thinks Sir David Stafford ruefully, remembering Harding Steele's attempt to blackmail him, years ago now. *He didn't think I even knew he was gay.*

To give the Children of Oisín their due, this seems to be a somewhat more humane honey-trap than Steele's, apparently aimed at turning Nate Busman rather than crudely blackmailing him. Not that that makes much difference to Nate's sense of shame and betrayal, the poor lad. (The 'lad''s in his early thirties, but David's within hailing distance of sixty, and feels quite paternal about the younger men and women.)

As far as Sullivan's concerned, the betrayal Stafford feels takes second place to indignation. The High King himself intervened behind the scenes at the disciplinary hearing, leaning on David to support Bishop Sally against the protests of Sir Leondegrance's man Lambert, and ensuring the rogue Knight was reinstated. The Seneschal still hopes that maybe Woodville's tenuous information will turn out to be incorrect, but if he's honest with himself he should have been expecting something along these lines. It explains certain things about the ex-Duke of Cornwall's abortive rebellion, for a start. Sullivan must have sold out to the Fianna shortly after Stonehenge, and been their agent ever since.

The tablet on his desk chimes, and Sir David sees Theo Harte's phone-icon flashing. Relieved it's not Busman wanting to apologise again, he opens up the connection.

'Sir,' says Harte excitedly (he's pushing forty now, but still as boyish in his sudden enthusiasms), 'we've found Edward Wendiman!'

'Really?' The Seneschal's incredulous. He'd thought Wendiman as effectively hidden from Circle scrutiny as his daughter, who's still evading justice for her infiltration of the MRF after more than a decade. 'I'm amazed he's even still alive.'

Theo says, 'Ah.'

David sighs. 'Just tell me, Theo.'

'A man called Hamish McTaggart died last week in Scotland, sir,' Harte explains. As part of the independence settlement, and in recognition of their reporting directly to the High King who rules both nations, the Circle's remit continues to cover both the Republic of Scotland and the United Kingdom of Southern Britain and Northern Ireland. 'He lived in sheltered housing in Strathclyde. He was ninety-five, or so he'd told the staff there – very elderly, anyway. Went peacefully in bed, apparently, and was found by one of the support staff. He had no relatives living, or so he'd always said, so they've been going through his things.

'Well, that is,' Theo continues, 'they turned out not to be his things. Or rather, he turned out not to be Hamish McTaggart. When they found the name Edward Wendiman, they googled him and realised who he was. They called Chief Superintendent McIntyre in Edinburgh immediately.' Much to Jade Kinsey's frustration, the Scots have rejected the jurisdiction of her force and set up their own Devicial Crimes Unit.

'Very civic-minded of them,' David observes. 'I assume you told them not on any account to throw anything away?' It's hellishly unlikely that Wendiman left anything behind that could lead them to Malory, but you never know.

Theo nods. 'McIntyre's sent people over to box and seal everything.'

'Very good, Harte,' says David. 'I'll need to have a word with the High King about this.' He thinks for a moment longer. 'Have they cremated him yet?'

'They were going to tomorrow, sir,' Theo says. 'Should I ask them to hold off?'

The Seneschal pauses, considering. The High King, sentimental as he is about Malory and her family, may ask for Edward to be buried with appropriate honours – he was a Knight before he carried the Merlin device, after all, the bondsman of Sir Menw son of Teirwaedd – and that could

239

cause no end of complication and controversy. It would be the McCutcheon funeral all over again.

Better to present him with a fait accompli, and let him go and pay his respects later if need be.

'I think not, Harte,' Stafford says. 'Just make sure we've got someone at the funeral who can recognise the younger Dr Wendiman. With backup standing by, just in case. I can't imagine she'll turn up, but… well, best be on the safe side, eh?'

Theo nods. 'Very good, sir.'

The Seneschal reaches out to the table, then stops. 'Oh, and Theo – make sure there's someone guarding the body tonight.' He cuts the connection.

* * *

According to the strict rules of chivalry, Tania Woodville should, at this point, be divesting herself of her armour and shield and selecting a kitchen-knife of her own from Sullivan's knife-block, so as to meet him on equal terms. Fortunately for her, he isn't giving her the opportunity.

His knife glances off her shield in the direction of Woodville's eye, and she has to turn her head quickly so that her helm deflects it. (She can't, of course, lower the visor: that would be increasing her unfair advantage, rather than reluctantly acceding to it because her opponent leaves her no choice.) For a moment she regrets the replacement of wooden or leather shields, in which a knife like that might well have become lodged, with smoother, harder polymer.

Using her sword's edge or point, except to defend herself, is now unfortunately a no-no, which means she's obliged to hit Sullivan a whack across the skull with the flat. There's a resounding thud, but Sullivan's not noticeably affected.

Tania's shield, though, is technically a defensive weapon, which paradoxically means she's justified in using it how the hell she likes. She coils herself behind it now and springs forward, barrelling it into Sullivan's body, catching him off-balance and sending him sprawling backwards towards the breakfast bar. A tall stool breaks his fall and he rights himself at once, lifting the seat and swinging its tubular chrome base at Woodville's head while leaning on the bar to steady himself.

This is where Tania's smaller stature comes in handy. She ducks, and dives towards Sullivan's legs, again leading with the shield. The breakfast bar supports him, though, and she earns herself a rough kick which sends her spinning backwards across the room.

He's had a moment or two to think, though. 'Take it off,' he says as she stands. 'Let me get my sword and shield. You know you have to play by the rules, Woodville.'

She glares at him frostily as she removes her helm. '*Of course* I'll follow the rules, Sullivan. But I'll get the weapons – you're not going near that door. And you tell your friend MacNeill to keep his distance till we're finished. OK?' She nods significantly to the bathroom door, which is hovering slightly ajar.

Sullivan nods. 'Done.'

Keeping him carefully in view, she unbuckles her armour, stripping down to her leggings and T-shirt. (It's lucky it's winter, all things considered – in hot weather she's been known to wear nothing under her armour except knickers and a camisole.) Then she walks down the hall to the door, collects Sullivan's own sword, and his shield with the red lion sporting in a sea of blue and silver waves, and walks back to the living-room, where she picks up her own arms before handing him his.

They face each other again, gripping their weapons, over the coffee-table where the plastic tray with its four remaining mince pies lies abandoned. The bathroom door opens a little more, and Tania glimpses two wide eyes staring at her from the darkened room beyond.

'Tell him,' she says again.

'MacNeill, you keep out of this,' Patrick Sullivan confirms.

'Sure, OK,' replies a gently rolling voice. 'I'm allowed to watch though, right?'

'OK by me,' mutters Woodville, not letting the bastard distract her.

'Well, then,' says Sullivan.

'Well, then,' says Woodville.

Then he lunges at her, and the fight begins in earnest.

* * *

There are more Knights assigned to Windsor Castle these days – fourteen under the command of Bonnie Laing, the device-bearer of Sir Bedivere, plus Sir Gareth's bondsman Jason Smith, who acts as the High King's roving envoy. They patrol the Castle and its grounds, as well as the town of Windsor, on a permanent quest to safeguard the High King's security, and act on his behalf across the two nations as necessary, independent of the Circle's standard command structure.

Oli Montalban knows the Castle well – she was a page here before she undertook her squirehood at the Fastness – and she knows the grounds considerably better than the backs of her new plastic gauntlets. For three weeks now she's been the youngest Knight on record to carry the gold-on-red pentacle of Sir Gawain of Orkney on her riot-shield – and also the first since Jordan Taylor himself. She's acutely aware of the expectations this places on her.

She directs her horse in a gentle trot down the Long Walk from the Castle down to the Park Street gates. If it's a cold day in the capital, it's freezing out here in Berkshire. There's a biting wind, and the Turbine Tower at the south-east corner of the New Quadrangle's whirling in ponderous, uncanny silence. The ground is crisp with frost, and icicles are strung from the leafless trees. The tourists are absent, and even the locals are doing the sensible thing and staying inside. Oli's glad of her thermal underwear, as well as the body-heat rising from the large warm-blooded mammal she's sitting astride.

Oli's the product of a recent trend among upper-class families who, finding the older, tried-and-tested methods of getting their surplus offspring into the Circle no longer as reliable as they once were, are resorting to gaming the system. Those older methods typically involved the son in question attending one of the older universities, followed by a brief and very notional period of pagedom at the Fastness, then squiring for a senior Knight and finally acclamation as a Knight himself – or (if the devices failed to go along with the family's plans, which was a significant danger in the case of the truly talentless) a well-paid secular job in the Circle doing admin, finance or liaison work.

The democratising movement in the Circle that's followed the Pendragon's return and his appointment of David Stafford as Seneschal, has led to the true pages – those who do the actual work of serving the Knights' food, laundering their clothes, maintaining their weapons and the like – being treated on an equal basis with these aristocratic squires-in-waiting. This means that pages recruited from the working classes, like Laing and Smith, now have an equal rather than a minimal chance of becoming Knights.

The obvious response to this, among those families who've traditionally offloaded unwanted sons onto the Circle and see no reason these days why they shouldn't do the same with unwanted daughters, has been to bypass the time-wasting and expensive business of university altogether, and place these children as proper serving pages at school-leaving age instead – trusting that blood will out enough to see them elevated to Knighthood in good time.

It's not an especially reliable gamble, but the cheapness of the initial investment means it pays off enough times to be worth it. In Oli's case, her great-uncle George 'Monty' Montalban, the bondsman of Sir Sagramore, helped the family wangle her a placement at Windsor instead of Southwark – still under the Circle's auspices, but with the hope that direct contact with the High King (and his adopted daughter Isabella Taylor, who's more or less Oli's age) would boost her chances of Knighthood.

It worked, of course. Indeed (worries Oli, feeling on

her arm the weight of the pentacle shield and its attendant expectations), the outcome's been more impressive than they could reasonably have expected.

Oli turns off to the left before she reaches the gates, and canters down the avenue of stark trees that further on becomes Queen Elizabeth Walk, leading to the Thames. From there, she'll take Prince Albert's Walk along the riverbank and back round to the north side of the Castle past the New Quad. It's a standard patrolling route, one which takes half an hour or so at a horse's walking pace. Another Knight will follow her in another half-hour. They'll probably need a head-lamp: the afternoon's darkening already.

The Knights are out in more force than usual today, anticipating the Pendragon's pre-Christmas banquet tonight – but despite the heightened state of alert that's been in place for years now, there's never been a serious threat to the High King here at Windsor. They've all been while he's out and about in the country, meeting the populace. Laing does her best every so often to persuade him to stay here where he's safe, but naturally the Head isn't having any of that.

An attack at the Castle would be unprecedented, though. There hasn't even been a serious security incident since Laney Wardsley went missing from custody seven years ago.

Which is why Oli's shocked to the point of terror when three green-hooded figures, wearing antlers and carrying longbows, step out from the winter-stark trees ahead of her and block her passage.

* * *

After the first few minutes Sullivan's living room and kitchen are pretty much a wreck. The coffee-table's trampled into splinters, crumbs and splatters of mince pie trodden into the faded carpet. The breakfast-bar stools are smashed, the light-bulb and the window shattered by stray sword-blows. The sofa and curtains have great slashes across their fabric, and the tiling is littered with fragments of glasses and crockery.

Sullivan's a powerful man, and his sword has a strength, thrust and sheer mass behind it that could – given Tania's unarmoured state – quite easily end up severing limbs or skewering her torso. Woodville's swordplay, by contrast, is quick, slippery and dextrous, and she presents a relatively small target. She also carries the device of one of the foremost swordsmen of Arthur's court – and while Sullivan's patron Sir Marhaus was also a devastating warrior, the personal champion of Ireland's splendidly-named King Anguish, they both know full well how *that* fight ended up. Tania at least has had it in mind on every occasion she's met Sullivan since that first time in Newquay.

This means that, while Woodville fights with speed and skill and righteous anger, Sullivan's fighting has a desperation to it which makes him a danger – even in this battle, even to her. Although it may seem otherwise at times, especially to the Knights themselves, it's the bearers who are in control, not the devices. Sullivan knows he's meant to lose – and he's not the kind of man to take that lying down.

Their motion as they contest together is like the struggle between unequal binary stars: Woodville orbiting Sullivan's greater mass, the two facing each other always, the constant flurry of their arms and blades joining them like streams of outdrawn plasma.

Neither is unscathed by the fight. Sullivan bears numerous cuts and nicks where he's failed to parry Woodville's blade in time, but none of them are serious. Tania has fewer wounds – one on her upper shield-arm, one on the left side of her torso, a gash above her right eye – but they're deeper, and are bleeding profusely, darkening her T-shirt and leggings.

She needs to change her game. She begins to whirl and spin, taking on an irregular orbit as she darts in and out, using the greater momentum to land harder blows on Sullivan. With every turn her back is vulnerable, so she ducks and crouches as she turns, relying on her speed and facility of movement to foil Sullivan's thrusts. Her blows land low, cutting at Sullivan's shins and thighs. Some of them meet their mark, and cause him greater damage than before.

She's aware of MacNeill, the Fianna spy, hovering at the bathroom doorway, watching intently. She hasn't the leisure to look at his face, but somehow she feels a smirk there, a smile of satisfaction at seeing Knights of the Circle set against each other. *Or perhaps he just likes being fought over?* she wonders, across the instants in the mêlée when her brain has the spare processing power available.

If she gets too vulnerable, she fears the Irishman will interfere, regardless of Sullivan's instructions. She needs to end this soon, and definitively.

This time, instead of whirling and ducking away from Sullivan, she dives towards him, throwing her shield above her head to deflect his ill-prepared blow. She goes barrelling into his feet, which causes barely a wobble in his solid foursquare weight.

It does, however, put her in a prime position to leap to her feet *inside* his shield – ignoring the ignoble temptation of stabbing him in the crotch on her way up – to bring her sword to bear at close range upon his unprotected chest.

At once he has her in a bear-hug, squeezing the breath – and, through the holes he's opened, the blood – out of her. But this puts extra force behind Woodville's own strength as her sword slides in through his shirt and skin to skewer his lungs.

Sullivan coughs, and vomits blood into her hair, but still he holds on grimly to her as he topples back into the crumby, suety shards of table. It's only after thirty seconds of frantic struggling that Tania can free herself from his loosening embrace, and by that time it's clear he's dead already.

She winces at the blood that's trickling from the wound on her abdomen – then realises that there's another gash across her back, a deep one, that she's not registered at all yet. Struggling over to the bloodied sofa, she collapses on its cushions – gasping, dazed, shivering.

The man called MacNeill steps out of the bathroom.

* * *

A whimper escapes from Oli's throat as the central figure comes forward to face her. Fortunately her horse whinnies nervously at the same time, so it's unlikely the green-clad strangers hear it.

Now she's over her immediate panic, she sees that only the middle figure is wearing antlers. They're impressively broad ones, though, with ten tines between them. She can see from the stumps that they're cast-offs, shed by the animal at the onset of winter, rather than being taken from a dead specimen.

The central figure is also the only one of the trio that isn't aiming a bow at Oli. The axe it's carrying isn't any more reassuring, though.

'You're Olivia Montalban,' this person says. It's a woman's voice, with the faintest hint of an accent. All three faces are invisible beneath the interlopers' hoodies, but Oli guesses from their various shapes that all of them are female. This woman's actually the shortest of the three, but the magnificent bone structures strapped to her head more than compensate. 'You are the device-bearer of Sir Gawain.'

'I'm – oh God,' Oli says, not altogether valiantly. 'You're right, that's who I am.'

The woman inclines her antlers gravely. 'You know who we are, then.'

'You're… Zara,' Olivia stammers. She's been told the woman's full name, but it completely eludes her. 'Robin Hood's bondswoman.' And thus, she knows, that of Sir Gawain's elemental antagonist the Green Knight, the two being the same in some archetypal sense which she still doesn't really understand. She was thoroughly briefed on all of this after her acclamation, but she wasn't really listening. 'You lead the Green Chapel.'

The woman Zara nods again. 'And can you guess why I'm here?'

Oli knows, but her mind hunts desperately for an

alternative explanation. The Green Chapel haven't been seen near Windsor for years. Since Zara took on the Robin Hood device they've returned to their old peripatetic outlaw ways – stealing from wealthy corporations, sabotaging their anti-environmental initiatives, kidnapping senior executives for ransom money. Robbing from the rich, in other words, and giving to the poor.

All criminal activities, of course – and they're wanted for them by every regional police force in the UK and Scotland, as well as the Device Squad and the Scottish DCU – but only against commercial targets, never civil or governmental ones. And certainly never against the High King.

Which means... well, it can only mean that this is personal.

'Because I'm Sir Gawain's bondswoman,' she tells Zara huskily, 'and you're the avatar of the Green Knight.'

'That's right,' the woman says. 'And it's midwinter's day. It is time for the contest.'

Behind her her companions, the chunky woman and the tall one, exchange a glance. Whether they can see each other's faces behind their hoods is dubious, but it's a clear indication that they're bothered by this.

'Contest, Za?' the tallest woman says. Oli can't see the colour of her skin – like the others, she's wearing gloves – but she guesses from what she remembers of the briefings that this is the Little John avatar, Long.

'Oh Christ,' the stockier woman groans. Oli assumes she must be Millar, Zara's lover, who these days is believed to embody the Maid Marian device. 'You're no starting *that* shite now, are you? Did you no learn anything from Shaun and Shaf?'

'Quiet,' Zara snaps.

The perennial contest between Sir Gawain and his adversary isn't just a matter for the Circle briefings, of course, but a staple of the modern history Oli learned at school. It's how Jordan Taylor, who himself once held the Gawain device, first got involved with the Green Chapel twenty-four years ago.

'I don't...' she says. 'I don't want to cut your head off.'

'That's fine by me,' says Zara flatly. 'I'll take my turn first. Gawain can send a new ally for me next midwinter.'

'Oh God.' Oli feels sick. She didn't sign up for this. She's always understood, of course, that being a Knight – especially carrying the device she does – could well involve some fighting, possibly even killing somebody at some point. She's done all the combat training, has turned out to be pretty good at it under controlled and contained conditions – which is why she's ended up with a device at all, of course. But striking someone's head off their shoulders in cold blood – even without knowing that that means, at some point, that their successor will be out for your head in recompense – that horrifies her more than any combat situation could.

(Well, she hopes so anyway.)

'Get down off your horse,' Zara commands her. 'Remove your helmet. Unless you want the first blow after all?'

'I...' Oli knows she's being challenged, knows that the honourable thing for her to do as a Knight is to accept. She knows that the *sensible* thing to do is accept and insist on taking the first strike. Behead Zara then jump back on her horse, gallop for the Castle and raise the alarm. Live to fight another day... and, in the meantime, get really, *really* good at dodging axes.

'I...' she says again. 'You can't expect...'

Zara steps forward again, and Oli's horse skitters in alarm at the approach of this bipedal antlered thing. Yanking the reins, Oli turns the animal and spurs her into a gallop. More green-hooded figures (and a red one) stand on the path behind her, but they scatter at the approach of her hard-hoofed steed.

Crushed with shame and terror, Oli thunders off up the tree-lined avenue, leaving her chivalric honour behind her with her nemesis.

* * *

The Irishman comes towards Woodville from the bathroom, holding something in his hands.

She raises her sword-point in her best attempt to be threatening – the best she can manage while sitting down, at least. Her body doesn't feel like it will tolerate another attempt to stand up.

'Keep back,' she tells him, raising her voice painfully. 'In the name of the Circle and its Head, the High King of Britain. I've just killed a brother Knight – don't think I won't do the same to you.'

'You're hurt,' he says, concern infusing his voice. She realises that what he's holding is nothing more threatening than a phone. He's a slight man, boyish, no older than mid-twenties.

'Never mind me,' says Tania, looking at Sullivan's massive corpse sprawled across the floor. 'I have friends coming.' She really wishes this were true. Sir David knows where she is all right, but she refused his offer of backup and he'll respect that wish for quite a while before he checks up on her.

Her sense of honour – or her device's – told her she owed it to Sullivan to confront him alone. Another of the idiocies chivalry inflicts on those who subscribe to it.

'Are your friends trained paramedics?' asks the man, crouching in front of her. His voice is brown and honeyed with Irish vowels. His eyes, too, are brown, like rich fresh earth from which good things might grow. Tania hasn't been to Ireland since a family holiday in Kerry in her teens, but she remembers, with longing now, the lush maternal roundedness of the landscape.

Her sword wavers.

Woodville doesn't do this sort of thing. She's a professional. 'Are you?' she asks curtly, raising the sword again.

'Not really.' MacNeill says. 'But I've got a phone,' he smiles, holding it up.

She watches as he dials three nines. 'No funny business, I promise,' he assures her. 'Yes, hello,' he tells the operator. 'Ambulance, please.' He gives Sullivan's address. 'There's a Knight of the Circle here who's been gravely wounded in the course of her duties. No, really,' he adds, his face all wide-eyed sincerity. 'Why would I be having you on? This is serious, there's a woman hurt here. OK, then.'

He smiles at her, pushes the sword-point gently aside. 'They're on their way.' He moves in closer, tries to take the sword from her hands, gives up at once when she resists him.

'Why are you doing this?' she asks him. 'You're on the run. From me.'

He smiles ruefully. 'Make my escape and leave you to die? I'm not that sort of spy, darling. All this violence and fighting isn't for me. I reckon I wait here for the ambulance to come for you, and then I make my goodbyes and go. Unless you're going to get sneaky about it, I guess.' He gives her a mock-serious frown. 'Give me your word you won't arrest me if I stay?'

Tania considers carefully. Then she looks up into his chocolate-brown eyes. 'I won't arrest you,' she tells him. 'On my honour as a Knight of the Circle.'

He grins. 'I knew you'd say that. You're a good woman, Woodville. I'd hate to see that go to waste.'

'Tania,' says Tania for some reason. 'My name's Tania.'

'Pleased to meet you, Tania,' MacNeill grins. 'I'm Eoin.'

He follows her gaze to Sullivan, and sighs. 'Yeah, what a waste. I only met him today. They gave me his address, told me to come here if I was in trouble. I didn't know he was a Knight. Makes you wonder what I was doing working my wiles on poor old Nate, if they had a fellow in the Circle already. It's a pity you've killed him and all, but he seemed like a bit of an arse.'

'He was. But he was brave, too.' Honour demands Woodville give her fallen enemy his due – though no more than that. 'Brave and treacherous, as it turns out.'

'Yeah, well,' says the Irishman. 'Bravery's a fine quality, but people shouldn't act all surprised when it gets them killed.'

* * *

Sir David Stafford is considering how to announce Edward Wendiman's death within the Circle – there are plenty of Knights left who remember the old man as Merlin's avatar, who'll have ambivalent feelings about the news, so tact is called for – when Theo contacts him again.

'It's, erm, one of Dr Wendiman's neighbours, Sir David,' he says, when the Seneschal answers. 'That is, one of his former neighbours. And of course she knew him as McTaggart. I think she's worked it out, though, sir, or she wouldn't be calling us. She has some... information, sir. I mean, she may be completely dotty of course, it's difficult to tell. But, er, I thought you'd want to hear it straight away, sir.'

'Very well, Harte, put her through,' Stafford says.

'–llo? Hello?' a voice is saying at the other end, apparently not realising that it's been on hold. Though quavery with age, the voice is forceful and extremely Scottish. 'Who's there now? You'll have to speak up, I can't hear a word you're saying.'

'Good afternoon, Mrs Tang,' Sir David says loudly, after glancing at the caller ID. 'You're through to the Seneschal of the Circle. My name's David Stafford. How can I help you?'

'Oh, *you're* the Seneschal?' Eunice Tang says. 'Well, it's about time. I've been asking for you for the past twenty minutes.'

'I'm sorry about that,' the Seneschal tells her calmly. 'We get a lot of calls. My colleague tells me you have some information for us?'

'Well, I've already told him,' the elderly woman replies. 'But I suppose I can repeat myself.'

'I'd be very grateful,' Stafford says.

'Aye, well...' begins Mrs Tang, evidently settling in for a lengthy session of storytelling. 'You people know already,

I'm sure, about that neighbour of mine who passed away. McTaggart, he called himself, and very polite he always was, but I knew something wasn't right about him, even before the police turned up at his flat this morning. I may be ninety-two, laddie, but I've got my wits still.'

'I can tell that's true, Mrs Tang.' He smiles as he says it. 'Yes, we're aware of your neighbour's death. And no, his name wasn't Hamish McTaggart. I'm afraid I can't confirm his real identity at this time.'

'Oh, you English and your secrets,' Mrs Tang sniffs. 'I used to work for IBM, you know, last century – plenty of trade secrets there. You're no so important. Anyway. You and I both know who we're talking about, and that's what matters. My front window overlooks his front door, and, well, I don't really get out these days. Or get up much either, to be perfectly honest with you. I like my chair. So I'm able to tell you that our "Mr McTaggart" didn't get many visitors – no from outside the flats, anyway. Although he was *very friendly* with Miss Gonzales from number sixteen, if you catch my drift. The wee hussy.' She pauses hopefully.

'I sense there's a "but" coming, Mrs Tang,' the Seneschal says, ignoring the innuendo.

'Oh, you're a sharp one, you are,' the old woman tells him. 'Aye right, there's a "but". There *was* one visitor, years ago, soon after I moved here. A young laddie, it was,' she adds, immediately dashing Sir David's hopes that this has all been building up to a sighting of Malory. 'He didn't look like anything much, especially with that beard, but I knew I knew him. My granddaughter passes me her old tablets, you know – I'm calling you on one now. My fingers don't work so well, but I can type if I'm patient about it, and I'm no past googling a face. That's how I worked out who Mr McTaggart was, of course. Well, I knew I knew that young man from somewhere, and it didn't take me long to work it out.'

'All right, Mrs Tang,' Sir David says patiently, wondering exactly how long Eunice Tang has known Hamish McTaggart's real identity. 'You've certainly got me interested. Who was this young visitor?'

'I moved here, to this flat,' Mrs Tang says, not to be deflected, 'eight years ago. And this would have been the spring after that. So he was still quite young, though no as young as when I'd seen his pictures before, you know. He was someone you'd have once been *very* interested in, Mr Stafford. Your opposite number, as it were.'

Sir David tries to work this out – noting that Eunice Tang has obviously been googling him as well. 'I'm sorry, Mrs Tang, I'm being obtuse. You'll have to spell it out for me.'

Mrs Tang sighs loudly. 'The other false Pendragon claimant, you ninny! Wee Jason Smith! He came to see Mr McTaggart here seven years ago. Well, I thought you'd want to know – because he's a Knight now, isn't he? So Wikipedia says. One of your lot. But I bet he didn't tell you he'd found Edward Wendiman, did he? Or you'd have been all over this place like a dose of the clap.'

Stafford frowns. 'That's... very interesting, Mrs Tang,' he says. 'Thank you. I'll have my adjutant come up and take a statement to that effect, if that's all right with you?'

'Oh, it's fine by me, laddie,' Eunice Tang replies. 'I don't get so much company these days. No like I used to.'

He extricates himself with difficulty from the elderly lady's conversation, and is eventually allowed to cut the connection. He sits back and starts brooding about what she's told him.

He gets all of eight seconds of that before the call comes through about Tania.

* * *

MacNeill gets Tania some painkillers from the bathroom cupboard, and a glass of water. She accepts them gratefully. If he wanted to kill her, he has less elaborate ways available than poisoning her.

254

Fourteen years of proper funding for the NHS, and the High King's ban on profit-driven private companies running vital public services, mean it takes only five minutes for the ambulance to arrive – but staying conscious even for that long is a phenomenal effort. Upfront and genuine though MacNeill seems, she can't afford to slip away while they're alone, and let him slip away in turn.

With the paramedics comes Stephen Mukherjee, as Tania had known he – or one of her fellow Knights – would. It's standard practice for the emergency services to notify the Fastness whenever they get a call involving a Knight of the Circle, and given the address of the incident – and the information that the wounded Knight's a woman – the Seneschal will already have a pretty clear picture. That the nearest Knight was Mukherjee, who Woodville knows and trusts, was just a lucky coincidence.

'Woodville, are you all right?' asks Stephen. He eyes MacNeill dubiously. 'Is this the chap who called it in? Is he –'

'It's Rochester, my dear fellow, John Rochester,' says MacNeill with a charming grin and an English accent which would have been impeccable in the 1930s, shaking Stephen's hand. 'I was just passing by on the street when I saw the broken window, and heard this lady crying out in distress. I'm afraid she's been stabbed,' he adds to the paramedics, a note of real anxiety creeping into his assumed voice. 'There's a nasty wound in her side, and one in her back. Other places too, but those are the worst.' He stops. 'I'm awfully sorry, I'm telling you your job, aren't I?'

'It's OK sir,' says the woman, 'we can take it from here.' She looks at Sullivan's body in the wrecked furniture, and sighs heavily. 'Christ, you Knights,' she says, but she doesn't elaborate.

'Well, now you're all here,' MacNeill says, 'I'll be going. I can see she's in safe hands.'

'Mukherjee,' says Tania, as Stephen looks to her for confirmation. 'He's…' She winces as the paramedic briskly slaps a dressing onto her side, then takes a deep breath and

255

looks away from the spy. 'His name's Eoin MacNeill. He's with the Children of Oisín. He's the one I was here looking for.'

MacNeill looks crestfallen. 'Oh, that's a nice way to return a favour, I must say,' he replies bitterly, Irish again. 'I thought you Knights of the Circle kept your promises?'

Feeling like a complete bastard, Woodville forces herself to look him in the eye again – both his lovely, deep, dark eyes – and says, 'I promised *I* wouldn't arrest you, yes. I'm sorry, MacNeill,' she adds. 'We keep our word, but we're not always fair about it.'

'I'll do the honours, then,' says Stephen cheerily. 'Eoin MacNeill, I'm taking you into custody, in the name of the Circle and its Head, High King Jordan of Britain.'

MacNeill smiles weakly, and presents his wrists as if for cuffing. 'It's a fair cop, guv'nah,' he says in excruciating mockney.

'Take him back to the Fastness,' Woodville says. 'I'll join you when I can.'

'That's not going to be for a while, miss,' the paramedic tells her severely.

'As soon as I can,' Tania repeats, unsure now whether it's Stephen or Eoin MacNeill she's promising this.

As they leave, she allows herself to slide into unconsciousness at last.

* * *

The Green Chapel disperse through the naked trees, blending into the bleakness less by dint of their green attire today than through the perception-fuddling effect of what Malory Wendiman used to call the 'Sherwood distributed devicial emanation'. It helps that Olivia Montalban doesn't seem in any hurry to raise the alarm.

They meet again, as arranged, beside an oak tree in the Home Park, a little to the north of Frogmore House. Built in the seventeenth century, the vacant stately home is used occasionally for state events – though fortunately not the banquet tonight, or the area would be crawling with catering and cleaning staff. At present it seems deserted.

'What the fuck was that about, Zara?' demands Scar angrily. Though she hasn't worn her scarlet hoodie for years, she's kept the nickname: the coincidence between Maid Marian's name and her own, which is Marianne, is too close for comfort. 'You said we'd ask her about security for tonight. Let's pick the youngest, you said, she'll be easy to scare. You bloody knew, didn't you? You knew which one she was.'

'Aye,' interposes Janene, equally indignant. 'I thought this was about snatching that Scottish billionaire. You know, the petrochemical bloke? That's what you *said*, Za.' Her tight-wound hair is greying round the edges, while Scar's developing deep smokers' creases across her cheeks.

Some of the others nod. The Chapel isn't here in full force – that would be too difficult to hide – but Ahmed's here, and Lee, and Will Scarlet's ally of six years' standing, a burly bloke called Chaz, as well as those of Much the Miller's Son and the Saracen.

'That's still our plan,' says Zara calmly. 'We'll get rid of his driver, put one of us in his uniform, and divert the man on his way to the motorway. We create the minimum disruption for HK's party, we get a good ransom from the billionaire's family on condition that they say nothing to anyone, and we use it to pay the legal costs of those protestors. Nothing has changed.'

'Except you lied to us,' says Janene. 'If we don't need to find holes in their security, then what the bugger was all that back there all about?'

'I had business with her,' Zara says implacably. 'Business she bottled out of. She isn't a good bearer of the Sir Gawain device, that's for sure. Dan was better.'

'You could have got your fucking head cut off, you daft bitch!' Scar roars.

'Quiet, Scar,' comes another voice, a man's this time. 'Or a passing Knight's going to discern us. That wouldn't

257

be expedient, would it?' Calm and authoritative, it's coming from the tree above them.

'My God,' says Ahmed, looking up. 'Man, you almost gave me a heart attack.'

The oak is bare, like all the others at this time of year, but in the gloaming dusk its thick branches are enough to break up the outline of the shadowy figure sitting there.

'Oh, so that's where you got to, then, is it?' Janene asks. 'You communing with nature, like?' Her tone is distinctly sceptical.

'This is a consecrated oak, Janene,' the man says quietly. 'A one-tree nemeton.'

No-one knows what a nemeton is. A couple of the Green Chapel people glance at one another and shrug.

'Zara,' the man in the tree explains to them, 'has understood – as apparently escapes yourselves, Scar, Janene – that maintaining these fabular paradigms of ours entails an outlay. We can't accept their assistance gratis. Rather, they merit our reverence. They have to be propitiated with ritual. With blood. Sometimes – when needful – with severed heads.'

'The ritual didn't do Shaun much fucking good,' Scar mutters. 'Shafiq neither.'

'And yet the individual who took Shaun's head, and others too, is now the High King over us all,' says Ron, as he drops from the tree and lands lightly on his heels. His speech has always been peppered with grandiloquence, deployed with haphazard accuracy; these days, it's as if they've metastasised. 'He is, in fact – allegorically and administratively – *the* Head.' Despite this thespian sesquipedalianism, his cockney accent's just as strong as when he was fourteen.

'A consecrated oak? Really?' Janene asks. 'Looks like any other bloody tree to me.'

'Bloody is right, in more than idiomatic terms,' says Ron. He's wearing antlers of his own – great sweeping sixteen-pointers, cast by a monarch among stags. He's lucky he didn't get them caught on his way down... but Ron seems to get lucky a lot these days. His hoodie is the brown of the wintry bark. 'This oak was planted in 1906, amidst the long-biodegraded compost of a precursor. An earlier specimen whose historic distinction made it quite notorious in its own day. I should have come here before,' he adds, as if in an aside. 'I've been lax in my own propitiation.

'We stand, friends,' he declaims, 'on the very site where once a gamekeeper in this park swung, capitally, in penalty for some malfeasance lost to record, and which thereafter he was said, by Shakespeare among other narrative peddlers, to haunt. This tree is known, by right of succession if not of germinal identity, as Herne's Oak.'

When that doesn't get a reaction, he sighs theatrically. 'Herne as in "the Hunter",' he reminds them. 'My illustrious ally, yeah?'

'Herne the Hunter,' Janene agrees patiently. 'Aye. Right. So?'

14. SIR GAWAIN

The New Quadrangle of Windsor Castle is exactly the kind of late addition to an ancient building which would have the ex-Duke of Cornwall choking on his toast soldiers – ignoring, of course, that by the time his great-grandfather took the castle's name it had already been thoroughly rebuilt by his nineteenth-century forebears based on their own ideas of what a castle should look like.

Accordingly, the New Quad's a twenty-first-century Sustainablist take on the whole 'castle' concept, built from a patchwork of reclaimed stone and recycled glass. Its battlements protect solar-panelled roofs whose organically bulging surfaces optimise their daily exposure to sunlight, dotted with light wells and rainwater collectors that reduce dependency on external electricity and water supplies. Its walls are striped with vertical gardens recycling and purifying waste water. At the north-east corner the Pendragon flag flies from a stubby egg-shaped tower housing the High King's private chambers, while to the south-east a conical tower with reception rooms at its base forms the base of the massive wind turbine supplying the rest of the Castle's energy needs. The whole thing makes the Castle look a little like a sketch begun by an fustily unimaginative Victorian architect, lost for a century then finished in the 1970s by a mildly stoned science-fiction paperback cover artist.

Traditionalists naturally loathe New Quad, and the Turbine Tower especially, but the High King remains a fan, and it's won a number of awards. It's about as far from the Disneyfied fairytale conception of Camelot as the architects could get, which was an important consideration. And it's a hell of a lot more tasteful than Brighton Pavilion or the Albert Memorial, to name only structures commissioned by the ex-Duke's family.

The New Hall occupies the entire third floor of the Quad's eastern side, with dining-tables at one end and a space for social mingling at the other. Everyone's preconceptions about Arthurian banquets – because, while everyone knows about the Round Table, most people imagine it being used for councils of war rather than formal dining – ensure that there's a high table up on a platform where the High King and his most trusted advisors will sit, with the rank and file at lower tables filling up the northern end of the hall.

For now, though, before the High King's pre-Christmas banquet begins in earnest, everyone's milling around at the south end, enjoying their aperitifs and canapés, and trying to work out who they're going to be stuck sitting next to for the next couple of hours.

'It looks like we'll always have a climate in common,' the High King suggests to assorted dignitaries from the Republic of Scotland and the UK, gesturing outside. The New Hall has glass walls and a retractable glass roof – retractable in summer, anyway, and triple-glazed to retain all possible heat at this time of year. Eastward from the Castle, the darkening panoramic view is across the snow-painted Home Park, down to the chilly Thames and the lights of Datchet village huddling beyond. On the other side the guests can view the Quad itself, the topiary shrubs and decorative sculpture-on-pedestals of the now-enclosed East Terrace, lit by solar floodlights and looking particularly picturesque under a shrouding of snow. The vertical gardens are still mostly green, though the Head Eco-Gardener tells me some of the less hardy plants are quailing at the frost.

'Och, this is just a light dusting, my lord,' the Scottish President replies. Her smile betrays no impatience with her liege lord's platitudes. 'We get far worse than this at Balmoral,' she adds, with a sly glance at the late Queen's grandson.

'Yeah, I remember,' the balding Prince laughs, not rising to the bait. His family have to show a lot of restraint these days, although their supporters – already furious with the Pendragon after losing Scotland from the Union – are becoming ever more indignant and vocal. The same Act of Parliament that stripped this man's father of his dukedom barred the disgraced heir from succeeding to the throne, and his son has loyally refused to accept it out of turn. Accordingly the monarchy has been in abeyance since the late Queen's death two years ago, much to the rage of the Crown loyalists in the UK and around the globe. Mind you, thanks to the ex-Duke's unavailability (having spent the seven years since his trial for treason under house arrest at Corineus House) and his increasing eccentricity (he now claims to embody the device of Britain's founder, Brutus himself), republican movements across the Commonwealth are also growing apace.

'At least your architects have cut down on your heating bills, my lord,' the UK's Prime Minister observes. 'I'll bet Balmoral costs even more to heat than Chequers at this time of year.' The hope at Pankhurst House – the new, purpose-designed Parliament facility built on the former site of Victoria Tower Gardens – is that that the High King will at least outlive the ex-Duke, meaning that the succession can eventually pass to this more docile Prince. Or, better still, that the Pendragon will appoint a successor as High King before his death, thus maintaining the final constitutional link between Scotland and the UK.

(The President is presumably hoping this doesn't happen. Meanwhile, a sizeable faction of Scots continue to agitate for true independence – many rallying to the banner of a politician professing to bear the homegrown device of

Robert the Bruce, a claim the Circle's analysts remain dubious about.)

Nearby, the hostess for the evening, the High King's daughter Izzy Taylor, is welcoming the lead singer of Boy To Let. She find their music kind of embarrassing these days, but her dad still insists on inviting them to these things for her sake. It's sort of sweet on the whole, but it could well have got quite awkward if two of them weren't secretly gay, one secretly married, one very publicly engaged to a *Blue Peter* presenter, and one, the drummer, a virtual construct run by AI software derived from the games industry. (He never turns up to these events, for obvious reasons.) As it is, she knows the singer well enough by now to ask after his nan's sciatica.

From where she's standing Izzy can see the youthful lead from the BBC's new *Prince Valiant* series, who she would actually quite like to talk to, but he's being monopolised by the Artistic Director of the RSC, who seems rather taken with him.

Izzy is twenty now and beautiful, still putting off her studies in favour of staying with her dad and helping out at this sort of thing. She wears a cloth-of-gold brocade jacket with flared sleeves over a traditional black cocktail dress. (The faux-medieval look went out of vogue after the first novelty of Jory's reign, but that's long enough ago for a nostalgic revival. Some of the models at the last London Fashion Week were wearing wimples.) She's naturally considered one of the most eligible young women in the Pendragon's realm, but men who attempt to press their suits at these events tend – whether at Izzy's behest or her father's – not to get asked back.

She smiles charmingly and moves on to one man who's never shown any sign of misbehaving in her presence: Paul Parsons, looking typically ill-at-ease in black tie and dinner jacket, with a silver shield lapel-pin bearing the three red stripes of Sir Lancelot. The skin of his artificial hand perfectly matches his own, and he's as adept at juggling his wine-glass and canapés as anyone else here, but he's visibly bored and a little annoyed by the whole thing.

During the years of the Pendragon's reign it's been abundantly clear that Sir Lancelot's bondsman is the one Knight everyone wants to meet, and there are only so many times he can make his excuses and boycott this kind of event. Despite all that, and despite the awkwardness that persists between Parsons and his High King, he and Izzy have always got on rather well.

'Good evening, Paul,' Izzy beams. 'You're looking very dashing.'

He gives her his usual reserved smile. 'I'm glad to be here, Izzy.'

'Oh, don't give me that,' she smirks. 'We all know you'd far rather be off hunting the Green Chapel with Chief Superintendent Kinsey.' Parsons has been seconded to the Device Squad for six months now, spearheading a so far fruitless attempt to clamp down on the recent upsurge in Chapel activism.

He frowns. 'You know I can't talk about that.' She's lost count of the number of times he's said that.

She says, 'Well, if you don't want to talk shop, the editor of *Manspread*'s over there. You can talk to him about shaving equipment, or cars, or different sizes of balls. Come on!' Smiling still, she propels the reluctant Knight in the direction of the journalist.

There are other Knights here tonight, of course. About half are in armour, stationed by the doors or keeping watch on particularly important guests. Most wear the latest augmented reality specs, feeding them visual data on the attendees. Bonnie Laing's red gonfanon shield is never far from the High King's side; among the others are the gold-and-green tiling of Sir Safir; the silver armoured arm of Sir Brastias; the seven red fleurs-de-lys, each nestling in a silver circle, of Sir Mador de la Porte.

The rest are off-duty. Adorning lapel-pins rather than full-size riot-shields are Sir Gareth's red-barred gold eagle, Sir

Percival's gold crosslets on purple and Sir Sagramore's four-coloured square-and-stars motif, while a shield brooch pinned to the bodice of Oli Montalban's blue silk dress displays the pentacle of Sir Gawain. The High King himself follows the custom: although his gold circlet is a less subtle symbol of what he represents, a gold dragon's head on a blue shield skewers his own lapel. When he gets a moment to match it with the red cross of Sir Galahad, he tells Sir David, 'I was sorry to hear about Sullivan. How's Tania?'

Sir David frowns slightly, unsure as to whether his boss is sorry that Sullivan was a traitor, or that he's dead, or both. 'She's doing well, my lord,' he answers. 'She'd do better still if she'd co-operate with the doctors rather than trying to discharge herself. I had to order her personally to stay put.'

'I suppose she's keen to question the Fianna spy,' the Pendragon notes, possibly slightly reproachfully.

David nods. 'Mukherjee's been trying, but the chap says he'll only talk to her. She must have made an impression. I won't have her endangering her health, though.'

'Well, it's your call,' the High King concedes. 'Let me know when you start finding things out. How's Busman holding up?'

Stafford shrugs. 'He blames himself, my lord. As he should do. I don't think we need to take it any further than that. It'll be a salutary lesson to him, I'm sure.'

The Pendragon nods. 'I was grateful for his help once,' he recalls. Nate Busman's the bondsman of Sir Kahedins, one of the two who helped subdue the Malory lookalike in the Leeds hotel fourteen years ago. 'So, tell me about Montalban,' he suggests. 'Olivia I mean, not Monty.' Oli's great-uncle, the largely retired device-bearer of Sir Sagramore, is over by the canapés just now, chatting up a pair of waitresses whose combined age is probably half of his. 'I mostly know her as a friend of my daughter's – I'd be interested to know what you make of her as a Knight.' Oli herself is talking awkwardly to Bishop Sally Marvell, whose lapel pin bears the twin croziers of St Dubricius.

The Seneschal considers. 'She's a capable woman,' he begins. 'At least, I'd say so. She's not been tested in any kind of combat situation, though. And she's very young. A little nervous, possibly.'

'What do you think she'd be like as a negotiator?' the Pendragon asks.

Stafford is surprised by this. 'Well, she's twenty-one. I don't suppose she's had a lot of experience…'

'She'd have support, obviously,' says the High King. 'From senior civil servants and diplomats. But I need to send a personal representative, you see. As head of state.'

'I see, my lord,' says David. 'You mean for the NATO talks in The Hague.'

Britain hasn't been trusted with NATO membership since the social upheaval of the War of the Devices, and the political changes brought about by the Pendragon's presence have been causing recent palpitations among the remaining members. In the United States especially, concern about the situation in western Europe now extends far beyond the Founding Frontiersmen. Scotland's independence and the High King's polite claim to sovereignty over the territories west of the Irish Sea have been destabilising enough, but many Americans see the rise of the devices – both in Britain and, in defensive response, in other European countries – as something insidious, even satanic. The recent referendum vote by Brittany to secede from France and join the Pendragonist realms (a demand which is still being puzzled over by the French legislature) had President Gomez out on the White House lawn comparing the region to the Middle East. It's not difficult to work out what she might mean by that.

Fortunately, NATO's European contingent don't very much want a war on their front lawn, so they've been holding the USA back like a belligerent Geordie's slightly less drunk friends in a Magaluf bar. It wouldn't take much of a pretext, though, for that fragile détente to go tits-up, and the talks in The Hague are rather optimistically aimed at averting such an eventuality.

'It has to be someone with a device,' the Pendragon explains. 'It would look like an insult otherwise. Well, sending Izzy would probably be acceptable, but she's never wanted any official status and I respect that. The Circle need you here, I've another quest in mind for Jason, Paul's... well, not a natural diplomat, and Rev's a bit erratic at the best of times. Montalban is carrying my old device, though – that's a personal connection. And Sir Gawain's canny enough when it comes to talk of war,' he thinks to add.

While they've been talking, Oli and Bishop Sally have been sucked into a conversation between Rev Cantrell and the directors of a couple of human rights charities. 'You surely see that we have to investigate this, though,' the Chair of Amnesty UK is telling them all. 'Journalists blacklisted, royalist activists disappearing... those aren't the sort of rumours the international community can ignore.'

Rev's widely known as the only Green Chapel member still loyal to the High King, though like me (and people generally forget about me) he's strictly ex-Chapel these days. For those of a progressive bent, this makes him the most obvious of the High King's advisors to approach about stuff like this.

'Sure, I can see that,' sighs Rev, who respects the woman's concerns but would really prefer to be getting drunk. 'Even if everyone in the *national* community knows they're a pile of horseshit. It's your sections abroad who are pushing for this, right?' The old man flatly refuses to wear black tie, instead donning a too-large tux over faded grey slimline jeans, Doc Marten boots and a Grateful Dead T-shirt with dog-collar. He's well into his seventies now, and nobody quite feels it's worth arguing with him about dress code.

The Chair shrugs. 'They'd say we can't be objective about it, and they'd be right. By definition it's impossible for anyone British to be dispassionate about the Pendragon device.'

'Makes investigating him kind of a drag,' Rev observes. 'I guess you're getting foreign investigators in. I just hope you're vetting them properly.'

'Where are these rumours coming from, though?' Oli asks, fascinated.

Cantrell shrugs. 'Hurts me to say it, kid, but most likely it's my ex-countrymen. Propaganda's something the Founding Frontiersmen excel at.'

'It isn't completely untrue, though, is it?' the Director of Liberty asks. 'The Pendragon's human rights record isn't exactly spotless. The Benwick Institute holds people indefinitely, for the crime of having the wrong device. People like Sharon Brain, Mark Addis, Bretwalda Ward...'

'Those are rogue devices,' Oli protests. 'They're dangerous.'

'So the Circle would have us believe,' the Director agrees. 'Although nobody thought Sandy Hithers or Ken Rudge were dangerous before they turned against the High King.'

'Hey.' Rev holds up a placatory hand. (Oli, for some reason, flinches visibly.) 'I hear what you're saying, but I just live here, I don't make the rules. HK's just over there, why not take it up with him? While I find myself a large drink, maybe?'

As he says this, though, the High King's drawing Jason Smith away from the press of the crowd into the dining area. Silver service gleams all about them, like exotic weapons protecting the entrées from the depredations of the marauding floral centrepieces. Several hundred red linen swans sit poised to take flight into the winter skies, if only someone would open the roof for them.

Laing stands nearby, glowering at anyone who looks like approaching, as the Penragon checks for listening ears, then tells his envoy, 'I had Bonnie check Herne's Oak earlier. There are footprints.'

'My lord?' asks Jason, mystified. The Head's been getting a bit elliptical recently, but he usually explains stuff like this if you ask.

'Sorry,' says the High King, backtracking. 'I realised earlier, when I saw the sun setting at about four o'clock, that

268

this must be the first Midwinter's Day in donkey's years that the Sir Gawain device has had a bearer.'

'OK,' says Jason, certain there must be more coming.

'Our intelligence suggests that the Green Chapel have succeeded in invoking the device of Herne the Hunter,' the Pendragon elaborates. Seeing Jason's expression, he explains, 'A woodland spirit, possibly once a god, associated with the grounds here. So I had Bonnie go and scope out the tree they call Herne's Oak, and she found footprints. Lots of them.'

Jason twigs. 'And you reckon they're here after Oli?' He glances round to where the young woman's extricated herself from the charitable huddle and is grabbing herself another drink. She's clutching it perhaps a little too fervently. 'Like that time with you and Shaun?' Squig was too young to have been there for Jory's first encounter with the Green Knight device – he hadn't even joined the Chapel at the time – but he heard the story told many times around the camp fires in his teenage years.

'I'd have made sure Montalban was on indoor patrol if I'd realised earlier,' the sovereign admits. 'She assures Bonnie she's seen nothing untoward today, but yes, I'm pretty sure they were looking for her. I don't think she's ready to face them, yet. I wasn't at her age. I'm sending her back to London with the Seneschal tonight, and then on a diplomatic mission to The Hague.'

'OK,' says Jason again, glossing over his surprise at that last bit. 'Thing is, though, you sure it was them that was here? If this tree's got this magic rep, couldn't it be… I don't know, hippies or druids or something, celebrating the solstice?'

'If so, it's the first time they've done it.' The Pendragon shakes his head. 'And nobody saw a thing. There were at least half a dozen sets of footprints, and eight Knights on patrol. For them to stay out of sight even so… that sounds like our Sherwood friends.'

Jason turns this over in his head. 'All right,' he says. 'So what do you need me to do?'

'Find the Chapel,' the High King says. 'Not like Kinsey

and Parsons, not as an official investigator, but through the back channels. Try everything you remember from the old days – dead-letter drops, newsagents' windows, all the forums. Contact anyone whose details you still have. See if you can get any clue as to where their encampment might be now. Then go and – what is it, sweetheart?' he asks, as Izzy approaches and Bonnie stands aside.

'You said to let you know when the Norwegian Ambassador arrived,' his daughter says. 'She's talking to the Foreign Secretary now.'

'Ah, right,' the High King says. 'I'll get to her shortly.'

He watches her return to the fray with a smile. 'Fatherhood's an odd thing,' he tells Jason quietly. 'You know, I never expected to feel… Well, it's odd, that's all. When's yours due now?'

Jason grins and blushes. 'Still March, my lord. Plenty of time to get at the Chapel before my paternity leave. Debbie sends apologies and that, but she was feeling too pregnant to come.'

'Do give her my best,' the Pendragon says absently. 'So, anyway… I need you to find them, and find out what the hell they think they're up to. And then, you know, tell them to stop it, from me. When they come after someone under my protection, it's personal.'

'All right, my lord,' says Jason, leaving unexpressed his private reservations about how effective this course of action's likely to be.

'Best not mention this to Paul,' adds the High King as an afterthought. 'He'd be annoyed at me going behind his back. And Jade would be *furious*.' He heads back towards the sociable end of the room, Bonnie at his side. Jason peers around the vast glass hall – at the press of photographers and philanthropists, clerics and comedians, ministers and millionaires – before eventually locating Parsons so he can be sure of not accidentally telling him.

Paul has, in fact, become attached to a group of policy wonks and business types, including an irritating man from

Aberdeen who's insisted on explaining to Paul exactly how much money whatever oil-related thing it is his company does makes for him. Now that's over with, they've got to talking about the Breton situation.

'The vote's not binding,' an English civil servant's saying authoritatively, 'and France isn't even federal. There's no provision to just carve off a chunk of it. Brittany's an administrative region, not a state – it doesn't even cover all of the historical Brittany.'

'It seems to be what the Bretons want, though,' a softly-spoken MP suggests. 'Shouldn't France accommodate that?'

'What, just sign over five million of their people to the High King?' the Aberdonian magnate scoffs. 'What about the Bretons who don't want it?' There's still a significant minority in Scotland who resent this whole independence lark and would quite like everything back the way it used to be. 'It'd be like asking for home rule for Kent.'

'It could have worked for Cornwall,' the MP murmurs, and Paul springs into action.

'With respect, Dr Chisholm,' he says, 'no, it couldn't.' He favours the company with a superior smile. 'Only a handful of Cornish-speaking yokels cared about independence before the ex-Duke started stirring things up. Even he only got as far as he did because of the Duchy's special status. And *he* wanted Cornwall to leave the High King's realms, not join them.'

'Well, he never got far enough for us to be sure of that,' Dr Chisholm points out quietly. 'So what would be your preferred solution, Mr Parsons?'

Parsons frowns. 'Well, if the Bretons really want the High King's protection… well, perhaps we should be extending it to them, never mind what the French think.'

'Let's not be hasty,' the civil servant puts in hurriedly.

'Oh, wouldn't that be fun, though?' the MP says. 'It's ages since we last invaded anyone. And I'm sure you'd be keen to lead the charge.'

Paul looks hurt. 'If I was ordered to, of course. I'm a Knight of the Circle, I serve at the Head's command.'

'You're very loyal.' Dr Chisholm's gentle voice is mocking now. 'The High King's lucky to have you. And, of course, you're both lucky he doesn't have a wife.' Smiling, she walks away, leaving Paul looking thunderous.

The MP circles past an eminent physicist and his teenage wife, dodges the expansive hand-gesture of a Premier League footballer who's drunk far too much already, apologises as she briefly separates two literary critics about to come to blows about the recent mainstreaming of the fantasy genre, and almost collides with Izzy Taylor, who's leading Oli Montalban to an audience with the Pendragon. Dr Chisholm apologises again, and makes for the nearest conversation about fishing quotas.

'Chills, Olz,' Izzy's insisting, trying to reassure the young Knight. 'You've talked to my Dad loads of times.'

'Yeah, I know.' Oli's panicking slightly. 'He's my commanding officer now, though, yeah? That's kind of… pressuring.'

'Well, he's always been High King,' Izzy reminds her pragmatically. 'I mean, not always, but as long as you and I can remember, pretty much. Isn't a High King scarier than a commanding officer?'

'Thanks, Iz. Not helping much,' Montalban groans.

Izzy stops suddenly, grabs her friend's shoulders and talks earnestly. 'Listen, damz. We've talked about this, OK? He's got a quest for you. That's *good*. This was the career plan, remember? You can make something of this. Wasn't that what you wanted, Olivia Nigella Montalban?'

'Yeah, well, put it like that,' Oli grumbles. 'I mean yeah, that's why I wanted to be a Knight, isn't it?'

'You bet your pert bottom it is,' says Izzy, and kisses her friend's forehead. 'Now go and knock him dead. Not literally, obz, they'd arrest you for high treason and I wouldn't have a dad. Again. Just, you know, impress him instead.'

I watch them as she steers Oli gently in the direction

of the High King, makes some kind of joke to break the ice between them, kisses her dad on the cheek and heads towards the door to welcome the Lord Mayor of Manchester and his husband, with only the briefest of wistful glances at Prince Valiant as she passes.

...Me? Well, yeah, I'm over here by the drinks. Where else would I be? Of course I can't overhear all these conversations – I'm relying on other people to tell me those later – but I've been watching the currents and tides and eddies of people round the room, the faces glib and sincere, the tentative alliances and the hidden skirmishes. Later I'll give the High King my account of what I saw, and he'll thank me. It's one of the reasons he keeps me around, after all.

The other's my actual job, of course. Later on I'll be treating the assembled company to a rousing rendition of the romance of Sir Breunor and his Badly-Fitting Coat... and yeah, I know. All the more obvious Arthurian stories have been done to death over the past fourteen years, and for some unfathomable reason Robin Hood tales are bang out of fashion just now.

'Smashing, isn't she?' Bob Thackett says, joining me at the glass wall by the Quad. Bob took early retirement a few months back – his job's been getting steadily more redundant in any case, with Bonnie effectively acting as the High King's personal bodyguard – and for the first time he's attending the annual shindig as a guest. He's been fond of Izzy since she first arrived here, and he's obviously noticed the direction I've been looking in.

'Izzy? She's a good kid,' I reply. 'She's been good for the boss, I think.'

'You reckon?' Bob says. Years ago he arrested me at a leisure centre as a member of the Green Chapel – then, as now, considered a dangerous terrorist organisation – but we got over that little hiccup. I'd known him for years anyway, in my capacity as an occasional entertainer at Circle events. I used to have these ideals about bardic neutrality, before the

War. 'I reckon he's moodier these days,' Bob says. 'Distracted, too.'

'Yeah, well,' I say. 'We don't know what he'd be like without her, do we? I think she's given him an outlet for all that. Family's good for people, you know that better than I do.' Bob's youngest is just finishing college, after training to be a dental nurse.

'Yeah, I know.' Bob seems troubled. 'Mate, you're the only bloke I'd say this to, but... well, some people reckon... I mean, I've heard them say... they think he might be a bit *too* into her. You know, kind of unhealthy like. You don't reckon any of that, do you?'

I can see what they mean, certainly. The way he looks at her sometimes, it's... kind of intense. Appraising. Like he's considering his options carefully. Izzy's never had a boyfriend, that I know of anyway – no girlfriend either, though plenty of girl friends like Oli – and a lot of people think that's because he keeps eligible young people carefully away from her.

Maybe that's not it at all; maybe she's just not interested. But maybe that's not healthy either. I don't know.

Honestly – and I'm saying this as one of the best friends the High King's got left – the jury's out. 'Definitely not, Bob,' I say with a smile. 'He loves his daughter, that's all. He thinks she's great, yeah, but that's because she is. Isn't she?'

'Yeah,' Bob says, smiling, reassured. 'She is that.'

Across the room where Izzy came from, beneath the removable solar chandeliers that have been hanging charging all day from the glass roof and are now favouring us all with the sunlight they've collected, the Pendragon's giving Oli a pep-talk.

'You'll get a full briefing at the Fastness,' he's saying, 'so don't worry. And then another at the Foreign Office, of course. You'll be heading the delegation, but we've got trained negotiators to do most of the actual talking. You get final sign-off on any agreement, but mostly what you'll be doing is social functions like this one. Well, a bit less lavish, probbaly. That's where you need to be on the lookout, though. Supposedly the NATO negotiators will all be secular, but they'll definitely have device-bearers accompanying them – and I wouldn't put it past them to sneak a couple into the negotiations, either. I've just been talking to the Norwegian Ambassador, and we can trust the Ragnars Synir unless things go completely to pot. You don't need me to tell you that the Paladins and Children of Oisín are bad news for us. I doubt the Nibelungentreue will involve themselves, but if they do it means things aren't going our way. The ones you really need to watch out for are the Founding Frontiersmen…'

To her credit, Montalban's nodding and 'Mmm'ing intelligently in exactly the right places, with only her eyes looking like those of a small mammal gazing at something larger and toothier that thinks it's lunchtime. At one point, feeling the need to make a more substantial contribution, she offers, 'I'm honoured by your trust in me, sir.'

'I'll be honest, Montalban,' says the Pendragon. 'In matters where you have experience, I trust you, but I know how new this is to you. With the professionals to advise and guide you, though – and Sir Gawain, of course – I doubt you'll go wrong.'

'That's fair, sir,' Oli says, and nobody's looking at her eyes then, to see the wave of misery and self-loathing that surges across them.

Nobody's looking, either – and certainly not the attendant she bribed earlier – when Izzy, with the confidence of someone who lives here and is *obviously* allowed to go anywhere she likes, strolls into the otherwise empty gentlemen's cloakroom just as Paul Parsons is washing his hands, and tells him, 'If you're serious about finding the Green Chapel, and not just messing about, you need to put a tail on Jason Smith. Tonight, if possible.'

At least five different responses collide in Paul's mind, and he's left spluttering as Izzy continues sweetly. 'You knew he started off with the Chapel, didn't you Paul? Started off and… well, some loyalties die harder than others. I wish I could tell my dad, but Jason's been his right-hand man for years. If you bring him proof, though, he can hardly argue with that.'

She kisses Parsons lightly on the cheek and trips out, back to the party where even now the guests are beginning to sit down to eat, and takes her place at her father's side.

15. SIR PALAMEDES

'Don't get me wrong, Steve,' says Eoin MacNeill. 'I think you're a fine handsome fellow, even if you're a spot too fond of the old handcuffs. I just don't think of you that way.'

'Yes old boy, jolly amusing,' sighs Stephen Mukherjee patiently. 'Fact of the matter is, though, it's me you have to deal with. So shall we go through it all again?'

The interview room is in the curtain wall of the Fastness. It's the very one where, nearly fifteen years ago and freshly released from hospital after the gunshot wound that nearly killed him, Stephen interrogated a biker named Mark 'Adze' Addis, who had tried to start the Battle of Camlann at the Stonehenge Summit.

It was the culmination of a quest which had occupied Stephen for a year – the hunt for the Questing Beast, a fabulous creature which Sir Palamedes himself spent many years fruitlessly pursuing, and whose device had for most of that time been manifesting itself in Adze's mind. With an obsession emanating ultimately from Palamedes, Stephen had single-mindedly hounded Addis, with no care for his other duties, his honour, the reputation of the Circle, or, in the end, his own health.

In the end in fact, his fixation very nearly killed him.

'No, I think that would just get us both riled up,' MacNeill replies now, leaning back lazily in his chair. 'You know how it goes. You ask what I've been doing here in England, I say *Why, your colleague Nate*, you ask who I'm working for, I say *Listen to the feckin' accent and take a guess, you big eejit*, then you ask what they sent me here to find out, I say *I'm not telling you but I'll tell your pal Tania*, and we have to go back and forth till we're all shagged out. Hardly seems worth the bother, does it, when your Ms Woodville comes back to work tomorrow?'

Expertly, Stephen hides his irritation. 'Who told you that?'

'Oh, just one of your lady men-at-arms,' MacNeill grins. 'I think she feels sorry for me. Protective, you could say.'

Stephen can see he's not getting anywhere with this chap today. He sighs. 'Righto. Back to the cells for you, then.'

The thing is, he thinks as he escorts MacNeill back down the stairs to the underground holding area, under other circumstances he might get on rather well with their prisoner. There's something awfully engaging about the lad. Stephen's done volunteer work with teenage boys for ages now – he's a leading light in the Youth Page movement, the Circle's equivalent of the Scouts – and Eoin MacNeill, though obviously older, strikes him as much the same as many of those kids. Wayward, but good-hearted. Needing a reliable friend, who'll give it to him straight, man to man, and keep a firm hand on his... his tiller.

He's old enough to make his own decisions, of course, unlike the kids – but...

'Steve,' says MacNeill, when Mukherjee's locked up and is about to leave him. He stops, and raises an eyebrow. 'I'm a joker, I know,' the young man says, fixing him with sorrowful brown eyes. 'And you're a very patient fellow. When our mutual pal comes back I'm guessing we won't see so much of each other, so I wanted to say thank you. I haven't been what you'd call a model prisoner, but you haven't had your lads beat me up or strip or starve or waterboard me, or any of that. I guess all that honour business means something to you, after all. And, you know, Steve, you're all right by me.'

He holds Stephen's gaze, heliographing his sincerity, then

278

drops his eyes. For the first time Stephen notices his long, dark, girlish eyelashes.

'That's – quite all right, old fellow,' he says, and walks away stiffly.

Stephen's in his forties now, and has never had much time for romance. He had a girlfriend once, when he was up at Oxford, a nice enough girl called Jocasta, but he didn't get much out of the experience. Since he became a Knight, he's never really bothered. A lot of the fellows have private lives, of course – the ladies too, and good luck to them – but as Busman's discovered, it's a liability. The way Stephen sees it, he's married to the job. He hasn't felt the lack of... companionship... in a good many years.

He's also definitely, emphatically, nothing-wrong-with-it-obviously but without the slightest shadow of a doubt, not gay. No question about that.

So. That's all all right, then.

* * *

'And what's our little friend been up to today?' Paul asks, as he stops by Chief Superintendent Kinsey's office.

Popular anti-Scots sentiment following the breakup of the Union has led to New Scotland Yard being renamed Metropolitan Yard, but it's as rife with petty factionalism and power-struggles as ever. Paul's temporary office is two floors down from Kinsey's doman, so that he has to climb the stairs to visit the Device Squad's Green Chapel taskforce, reminding him constantly that he's here for their convenience, not vice versa.

Naturally a Knight of the Circle should be able to rise serenely above this kind of petty tribal politicking. Paul, who nature never designed for serenity, does his best.

'Liverpool,' Kinsey replies shortly. 'Talking to people at the docks.'

Over the week since the High King's banquet – aside from Christmas Day spent at home with his girlfriend Deborah

Charner – Jason Smith hasn't stopped moving. He's been in Durham and Plymouth, Newport and Glasgow, Sheffield and Manchester and briefly the Isle of Wight, generally getting about by train so he can use the wi-fi as he goes. (Annoyingly, the Circle encryption on his tablet means that even the Device Squad's techies aren't able to find out what he's been looking at. Theoretically one of the plainclothes officers Kinsey has following him could look at the screen over his shoulder, but that wouldn't exactly be subtle, and the last thing they want to do is tip Smith off.)

'People?' Parsons asks.

'Sailors,' says Kinsey. 'Dock hands, bar staff, prozzies. The people you find round a working docks in the middle of fucking winter. A couple of known Chapel sympathisers, but mostly they weren't on our radar before. Of course the bastard could be trying to throw us off the scent.'

Paul frowns. 'That would mean he knew we were onto him. Have any of your people been sloppy, Kinsey?'

Kinsey tuts. 'They're trained in covert surveillance,' she says. 'I'm keeping anyone Smith knows well clear of the tail. But he's got a device. It's only a matter of time.'

'Well, just keep at it,' Parsons says. 'He'll lead us to the Chapel eventually.'

Kinsey says, 'I bloody hope so. If your informant turns out to be winding you up, we could all end up looking incredibly fucking stupid here.'

'My source is sound,' Paul insists. He's been making casual enquiries at the Circle, being careful not to alarm anybody. *How's old Jason Smith these days? We hardly see the bloke any more. Any idea what the High King has him doing now?* No-one apparently does, but in an unguarded moment Theo Harte let slip that he'd heard something odd about Smith just recently. An impromptu trip to the pub and several pints later, he confided in Parsons that he'd come across a rumour that Smith had known where Edward Wendiman was hiding for ages, had in fact visited him there years ago.

('But it's probably all nonsense,' he added. 'We only have

some old lady's word for it, although she seemed a sharp enough old bird.')

As far as Paul's concerned, this confirms that there's something fishy about Smith. Certainly the Circle's top brass didn't know Wendiman's whereabouts until his death, which means Smith either kept the whole thing to himself, or – well, the alternative would be that he'd told the *High King* and the High King had taken no action on the matter, which hardly seems likely.

What Harte told him was a confidence between brother Knights, though, and Paul wouldn't dream of sharing it with Kinsey, any more than he'd drag Izzy's name into this. He says, 'Smith's trying to re-establish contact after a long time away. With the Chapel in hiding that's going to take him a while.'

'What the hell does the High King think he's doing, though?' Kinsey wondered. 'Smith answers to him. He can't just charge up and down the fucking country without giving him some kind of reason.'

Paul wishes he could just ask the Pendragon this – it would certainly make things simpler if they knew. But with the distance there is between him and Jory, he can't think of a way to ask and make it sound natural, and he certainly doesn't want to go into detail about his suspicions without proof.

He says, 'I suppose he's combining it with some other quest. Perhaps that's why only some of this stuff seems to relate to the Chapel. Perhaps he's...' His imagination fails him. 'Perhaps these people are important to the High King for some other reason,' he finishes lamely.

Kinsey grunts. 'That means we'll be in even more trouble if he makes one of my officers. Surveilling a Knight of the Circle's way outside my remit, but spying on the High King's envoy doing the High King's business... If we get shopped, I'm bloody blaming you, OK?'

'Understood,' snaps Paul. 'But Smith won't report it. He'd have to explain to the High King what we suspect, and he won't do that. He'll keep it quiet and try harder to lose us, that's all.'

'Only if you're right about him being guilty,' says Kinsey. 'If it turns out he's legit, a tankerload of shit hits the fucking Windsor Turbine Tower and we all end up buried six feet deep. I don't like relying on anonymous informants.'

'The source is fine,' Parsons repeats stubbornly. 'It's someone we can trust, yeah?'

And surely that's true. After all, what reason would Izzy have to lie to him?

* * *

At this dead time between Christmas and New Year, the university and all its adjuncts are closed down. Large parts of the town are mothballed, like the set of a TV soap on hiatus, with only the largest department stores attracting shoppers to their winter sales. At this time of year there are no tourists, barely any students, and most of the lecturers are grateful for the time away from the constant demands of tutees and research projects, grant applications and unfathomably pressing requirements for evidence-based costing data.

Freda Tate-Hendricks would be enjoying just such a respite if she had any say in the matter, but she hasn't been given the opportunity. At the High King's express order, the expanded personnel of the Excalibur Programme have been working through the holiday to complete the Pendragon's devicial weapon.

Ernst Schmidt no longer has any life or interests outside work – if he ever had them, even in Dusseldorf – and the Director suspects he would have been down in the basement on Christmas Day anyway, for want of anything better to do. His colleagues – recruited internationally, in response to the High King's increasingly urgent insistence on results, to staff the equally secure laboratories excavated beyond Schmidt's own – haven't been as happy.

Dr Kawasima, who bears the *kamon* of the legendary

katana-maker Muramasa (and whose costly headhunting has made the High King a whole new set of enemies in the Yamato No Senshi), wouldn't normally have paid much attention to Christmas either, but has strong views about being expected to work on New Year's Day, which he's expressed with counter-stereotypical forthrightness. Benjamin Ben-Ari, imbued with the *ruach* of Tubal-Cain (the original 'instructor of every artificer in brass and iron', according to the Book of Genesis) had similar objections to being on duty over Hanukkah. And Cécile, the Haitian scholarship student who serves as the *mambo* of the *loa* Ogoun Ferraille, was so incensed at being asked to forego the *Noël* festivities that she organised a walkout among the men-at-arms of the MRF's Circle security detail, which their commander, Johnny Quayle, was only able to stave off with the promise of double pay during the holidays.

(Since Tate-Hendricks's other deviced researcher – Thora Yrsasdottir, runeholder of the Norse inventor-hero Ref the Sly – is here on secondment from the Ragnars Synir, compelling her to work over the holidays wouldn't have been diplomatic. She opted to show solidarity with her colleagues rather than flying back to Iceland for Yule, but it hasn't helped her mood.)

It's been a human resources nightmare, to say the least. And that's without the everyday friction of forcing such disparate devices into close proximity – the constant cultural misalignments which complicate the integration of stories which were never intended to be read in conjunction. Stopping Kawasima from jealously comparing his work with everyone else's, for instance, or Thora from playing elaborately-constructed practical jokes on the others. Reminding Cécile she should live on something other than rum, and restraining Schmidt from trying to serve it to her in the skulls of her various pets. It makes Tate-Hendricks thankful that at least she doesn't have a device of her own to complicate things further.

And now she's about to get a call from the High King,

who she's finding increasingly difficult to deal with these days. Well, she at least has good news for him.

Although she's expecting it, she still jumps when her tablet chimes. She props it up, takes a deep breath and accepts the connection. 'My lord,' she says. 'Hello.'

'What news, Freda?' the Pendragon asks abruptly. He's been getting less patient and less polite with her as the project's neared completion.

'Well,' the Director says. 'Barring disaster and all that kind of stuff... we think in a couple of weeks we should have a working prototype.'

* * *

'Listen, MacNeill,' says Woodville sternly, 'we've had enough of these games.'

'Oh, MacNeill, is it?' the prisoner says, mock-indignantly. 'I thought we were on first-name terms, Tania. I know I'm your prisoner and all, but still – we had a moment there, back in the flat. Didn't we? Didn't we have a moment?'

He's feigning upset, of course, but there's some real hurt lurking there in his dark eyes. Tania sighs, and steels herself to ignore it. 'There was no "moment", Eoin. I'm glad of your quick thinking, and that you called that ambulance. I'll make sure it gets taken into account. But I don't think you get how much trouble you're in. High King Jordan takes a dim view of spying, and of blackmail.'

'Ah well, I've said all along I'll co-operate,' says MacNeill easily, all smiles again. 'It's just yourself I'll be co-operating with, that's all.' His moods are as mercurial as ever.

Woodville tries to forget the proximity of this strangely appealing young man with his endearing crush on her, and marshals her thoughts.

She thinks she's pieced it all together now, with a bit of help from the Seneschal. It's not clear when Patrick Sullivan first turned against the Head of the Circle, but it was perhaps as early as Jory Taylor's accession as High King. Even back then, in that first overwhelming effulgence of the most powerful device Britain had seen since the original Arthur, there were those like Craig McCutcheon who responded with repulsion rather than devotion. That, too, was part of the myth – Taylor, like his archetype, needed to prove his legitimacy by subduing his enemies and uniting the country, and that couldn't happen if the entire populace were behind him from the outset.

Whether Sullivan's rebellious impulses came then or later, though, it suited him to stay at Tregorlois in the unofficial service of the then Duke of Cornwall, exploiting his employer's eccentricities to build up a Circle splinter group with its own loyalties, and all the while secretly negotiating with the Children of Oisín. And all the signs suggest that his first task for his Dublin paymasters was to drive a wedge between the Pendragon and the Crown loyalists, by setting the heir to the throne against the High King.

The reason why all the Duke's machinations – using Roberto Schultz against the Chapel, recruiting Valentine Brewster as his catspaw, attempting to turn Woodville herself – failed so signally to co-ordinate with one another was that there was no greater plan behind them. Instead – as the High King speculated to Blaze at the time – they were intended purely to annoy him.

...Or perhaps not quite. Because – doubtless with detailed advice from Dublin – Sullivan managed to engineer a particular kind of crisis which would allow him to save the Pendragon's life, emerging from potential disgrace with the High King himself in his debt. (It never was quite clear how Sullivan, after so long in the Duke's service, had managed to stay ignorant of the mining of the Quintrell Downs road bridge.)

What's plain is that someone in Dublin has been playing a long game, with Sullivan, the ex-Duke, Busman, MacNeill and Tania herself among the pieces. Tania can only imagine that it's Henry O'Leary, the mac Cumhail himself – the elderly director of the Children of Oisín and the *aithgin* of the original Fionn mac Cumhail, whose devicial attributes include the gift of knowledge. (It's a long legend – suffice it to say there's a fish involved.) It's not clear, though, what his ultimate goal's been, and that's what this interview can hopefully cast some light on.

'So, Eoin,' Woodville begins again, 'what did your bosses tell you about Patrick Sullivan?'

'Only his name and address.' The young man shakes his head, in apparent regret. 'They don't tell me stuff. Like I told you, till I turned up at his flat I didn't even know he was a Knight. I was pissed off to find it out, too. Like I said before, if they already had a man in the Circle, why'd they be needing me to seduce poor old Nate?'

Tania isn't going to say so, but she doesn't share her beguilingly tousled prisoner's puzzlement on this point. Two years ago Nate Busman was appointed the Fastness' Warden, responsible for the building's security: conflict of interest means he's had to hand his duties over to a deputy for the duration of Eoin's stay in the cells. As such he'd certainly have made the Fianna a more valuable asset than Sullivan… but hardly one worth the risk of exposing Sullivan himself for.

'Did he say anything to you when you were at his flat?' she suggests. 'About how long he'd been working for the Children of Oisín, or what his quest for them was?'

MacNeill pouts. 'I'm beginning to think you're only interested in me for my mind. No, we didn't talk much, not after I told him what I'd been up to. I think he wasn't so keen on the whole men-shagging-each-other business, you know?'

Tania nods thoughtfully. She opens her mouth for a follow-up question, but what comes out is, '*Are* you gay, Eoin?'

She winces, surprised at herself. Not only is the question irrelevant, it's something the modern Circle's equalities policy explicitly forbids her to ask. *Did you have sexual intercourse with [insert name here]?* is fine if necessary, but *What's your self-identified sexual orientation?* is an infringement of personal privacy, or something. She's going to get a disappointed look at the very least when the Seneschal reviews the interview file.

Eoin doesn't seem to take it amiss, though. 'Darling, in this job I'm whatever they want me to be. Since you ask me nicely, though, I'm happy to swing either way.'

Tania converts her smile into a stern grimace. 'So Sullivan told you nothing? Really?'

MacNeill shakes his head. 'He wanted me out of there, as soon as he could organise the necessary. Said I was a dangerous man to know.'

Which turned out to be perfectly true, of course. Even if Sullivan had fulfilled the Fianna's initial purpose for him, in sowing dissent between the UK's complex royal factions, he remained their man – she *hopes* their only man – inside the Circle. Why would they risk that by using his flat as a safe house? They could surely have found someone else who'd do as much for MacNeill. Even with the current tensions going on, there are tens of thousands of Irish people living in London.

'So you don't know anything about his quest here?' she repeats, resigned.

MacNeill sighs. 'I know it's not what you want to hear, but I'm blowed if I do,' he says.

Woodville returns his sigh, shakes her head, and allows herself a heartfelt 'Bugger.'

MacNeill's right. It really isn't what she wants to hear. Sullivan must have spent the past seven years doing *something*. Best-case scenario is that he was just passing intelligence back to the mac Cumhail, who collects information like a spider collects desiccated flies. The Circle must assume that such details as its troops and armament strengths, personnel information and who knows what other intelligence may be compromised.

But what if there was more to it than that? What if Sullivan wasn't passively observing, but was here on a specific quest from the mac Cumhail?

'Eoin,' she says. 'I'll need you to go through the whole thing again, from the very beginning.'

'For you my darling, anything,' MacNeill replies, hand on his heart.

He grins infectiously. Smothering another smile, Woodville rolls her eyes.

* * *

'Smith's gone off-grid.' Kinsey's voice is clipped. 'Get up here now.'

If Paul had been in any doubt about the urgency of the Chief Superintendent's demand, the lack of decorative four-letter words would have alerted him. He leaves his makeshift office and takes the stairs at a run.

He finds Kinsey's ops room in a buzzing panic, with police talking urgently on phones and poring over screens showing maps and data visualisations. 'You've *lost* him?' he asks.

'The bastard vanished,' Kinsey says shortly. 'Five minutes ago in Ipswich. One minute he's ordering coffee from a stall, the next the fucker's gone. Ticia got distracted by a robbery in progress, and when she looked back there's a red van leaving the scene at speed and no fucking Jason fucking Smith.' She reels off a registration number. 'We've got the local force out trying to spot them, but chances are they'll have ditched it already.'

'Roadblocks?' says Paul.

'Not an option,' snaps the Chief Superintendent. Roadblocks are something the Device Squad would certainly have to justify, to the Suffolk Constabulary at least, and unless Kinsey can come up with a plausible excuse not involving Knights of the Circle it's bound to reach the ears of the Seneschal, and thence the High King.

'Do it anyway,' he decides.

Kinsey cocks her head, but before she can forcibly

288

remind him of exactly who's in charge of this operation, she's interrupted.

'Ma'am,' a constable says, 'Suffolk have found the van abandoned in a traffic camera blind spot. They're trying to correlate with other vehicles in the area, but...'

The Chief Superintendent swears copiously and with much feeling.

Sergeant Barry Jenkins scurries across with a map. 'There are three significant-sized woodlands near there,' he says. 'The nearest is Rendlesham Forest. If he's heading for a Green Chapel encampment, the chances are...'

'No,' Parsons says. Kinsey glares at him, but she lets him speak. 'No, that's too obvious. Smith had help eluding us, so the Chapel must have guessed we might be following him, even if he hasn't. They wouldn't be so dense as to just take him to the nearest forest. Either he's in for a long ride in whatever vehicle they've transferred to, or the meetup's somewhere in town, not at their camp.'

'So what do you suggest?' asks Kinsey. 'We just give up? Fuck that with bells on.'

'The Circle has access to surveillance satellites,' Paul says calmly.

She stares at him for a moment. 'So why the *shitting hell*,' she asks eventually, 'didn't you say so?'

Paul says, 'We're sworn to use them only when there's an immediate identifiable danger to life. You know – privacy, human rights, all that? They're not normally much use against the Green Chapel, either – they're pretty good at hiding even from orbital surveillance – but driving a vehicle and carrying a guest? I'd say there was a fair chance.'

Kinsey's eyes narrow, like a ferret about to go for something's jugular. 'And you can get us access to the imagery?' she asks.

Paul takes a deep breath. 'I think we could spin this as an immediate danger to Smith's life, yeah. The Chapel snatching a Knight of the Circle off the street? Yes, I rather think that will play. But it's the Seneschal we'll have to convince. We can't access the satellites without his say-so.'

She thinks about it, grudgingly, for about half a second. Then she groans. 'All right, then. Tell the fucker.'

* * *

Jason tries to keep breathing – instead of, say, flailing about in screeching panic – as his body's jogged up and down on the landscape-broad shoulders of someone who surely has to be Twink. The light and shadow falling through the rough cloth bag they've stuck over his head isn't giving him any clues as to his whereabouts.

Still, they've at least picked one with a loose weave, so breathing's still an option open to him. It's good they're not trying to kill him, yet… but it's not exactly the welcome he'd hoped for from his old mates. The sack, the manhandling into the van, the hurtling ride pinioned between two large strong bodies, the second round of bundling followed by the leisurely drive here in the boot of a car, and now the being jolted about as someone carries him, he guesses, up and down a pair of tallish ladders, don't strike him as exactly friendly.

He didn't even realise he was getting warm in his quest: so far everyone he's talked to has given him the brush-off, a conspiracy of silence as solid as a stone wall. Still, someone must have tipped off someone else, who's passed it along the chain, so now it's got back to the Green Chapel that their old mucker Squig is looking for them.

And now they're helping him with that. Sir Gareth must have been napping on the job, although that Sherwood emanation thingy's fooled better Knights than him. Jason's in his civvies, of course – he'd have got an even frostier reception clanking around Ipswich in armour with his double-headed eagle shield and asking whether anyone's seen the Green Chapel – and his concealed scabbard was the first thing they took off him when they grabbed him.

He's lifted high into the air, and dumped onto the freezing

ground. His scrabbling fingers find iron-hard mud and frost-crisped waste-paper, before the bag's yanked off his head and he sees they're in a tiny patch of urban scrubland.

It's the sort of place where there'll have been a factory or warehouse or something, demolished years ago – perhaps even blown up during the war – and where one day, city planning permitting, there'll be something else. For now though, there's mostly nettles, windblown litter and a couple of stunted trees. As he's heaved to his feet he sees that buildings – the breezeblock structures of an industrial quarter – stand to right and left, while ahead of him's a railway embankment, fenced off with tall metal pilings.

Between him and the railway line stand a huddle of figures in their Chapel hoodies. Those look old-fashioned these days, a fusty relic of a past war. Kind of Napoleonic. It's ages since Jason last saw any of the Chapel, at a reunion during those seven years of reconciliation between Camelot and Sherwood, but though their faces are hidden he recognises their outlines. Zara's at the forefront, of course, her fiddly steampunk-looking compound bow clung across her shoulder. There's a chunky-looking one in red – there always is – but he reckons Scar's the one in green standing next to Zara. Janene's the tall one, obviously, and one of the others must be the new Saracen, and then...

...then there's the bloke in brown with the antlers. The only one with his face uncovered. The one who – though he's standing well to one side of the rest of them – still ends up as the focus of everyone else's body-language.

That Ron. His successor. Squig's never liked the bloke.

He does his best to pull himself up straight, aware of Twink's bulk behind him, on the lookout for the slightest threatening move.

'All right,' he says nonchalantly. 'Been meaning to get in touch with you lot. How's things?'

* * *

'So let's get this straight,' Tania says. 'The mac Cumhail sent you here specifically to seduce our boy Nate Busman, is that it?'

'The mac Cumhail?' Eoin snorts. 'Like I'd get to see him. No, it was your man Dermot Healey, Conán mac Morna's *aithgina*.'

Tania's been in charge of counterintelligence against the Children for a few years now, and she's spent a fair chunk of that genning up on the Fenian cycle of Irish legend – in translation, obviously, but with some glosses which refer back to the originals. From what she recalls, the Old Irish word *aithgin* – routinely used by the Fianna for a device-bearer – can mean 'replacement' or even 'recompense', but one of its oldest meanings is 'rebirth'. There's a legend about the historical chieftain Mongán mac Fiachnai in which he's recognised by Fionn mac Cumhail's elderly nephew Caílte mac Rónáin as the *aithgin* of Fionn himself, strongly suggesting that Mongán was Henry O'Leary's seventh-century precursor.

Though Fionn was supposedly in charge of a war-band some four thousand strong, fewer than a hundred of those men are named in the myths. So although they're more numerous than the Green Chapel, the Children of Oisín can't compete in strength with the Circle, who at times of dire need – like the late civil war – can call on the devices of hundreds of named Knights of the Round Table. They're also disastrously prone to internal division (though, to be fair, the Round Table has its issues with that as well).

Some *aithgin* have powerful attributes. Fionn himself has the whole Salmon of Knowledge thing going for him, and can also cure any wound by letting the patient drink water from his cupped hands. Other legends ascribe him gigantic stature. For the modern mac Cumhail that generally equates to physical strength, outstanding research skills and a heartening bedside manner, but others of the Fianna have other gifts.

There's one in particular who… but no. Woodville can rule that out, thank God. Whatever it is she feels for Eoin (and she has to admit to herself that she really enjoys his company, in a way which goes well beyond simply fancying the pants off him, which she also does), it's not down to the influence of a device.

Well, certainly not *that* device.

'So what did Healey say to you?' she asks.

Eoin grimaces. 'He said they'd found out the Warden of the Fastness was partial to the fellows, like, but that he didn't get out much. He said "There's an opening for you there, lad." And then he laughed a lot.'

Tania feels they might be getting nearer the crux of the matter. 'And why did they pick you for this mission?'

'Ah well, what can I say?' Eoin smiles self-deprecatingly. 'I'm a popular guy. People like me. Men, women, dogs... Jesus, you should have seen some of my friends' mothers when I was growing up, it was embarrassing for everyone concerned. I've never had any trouble getting people to take an interest.'

Woodville's amused. 'You're pretty sure of yourself. Are you an *aithgin*, Eoin?' The Circle's standard intake tests didn't pick up any device when MacNeill was arrested, but as far as Tania knows no-one in the Circle's ever had the opportunity to carry out psychometric tests on a Child of Oisín.

'An *aithgin*? Me?' Eoin laughs again. 'Not everyone who works for the mac Cumhail's got an imaginary pal, Tania my darling.'

Woodville believes him. The fact is, the Dublin offices of the English and Scottish secular intelligence agencies share the task of keeping track of the most prominent Children of Oisín, and she gets to see the reports. All the most powerful Fianna are currently accounted for: those bearing the *aithgina* of Caílte mac Rónáin, with his speed and affinity for animals; of Diorruing mac Doba the seer; of Lughaidh Stronghand the sorcerer – and of Diarmuid Ua Duibhne, aka Diarmuid of the Love Spot, whose particular talent (and it causes less trouble than you might expect, given that the Fianna lived largely in the forest and tended to interact mostly with other warrior-bands) was that no woman could look long on him and not fall in love with him.

Diarmuid's current *aithgin* is a handsome silver fox of fifty-eight, one Eamonn Costello, seen alive and well in Cork over Christmas. Eoin started screwing with Nate Busman, in both senses, around the beginning of December.

'It's not like I'm boasting,' MacNeill adds now. 'I know my limits. I can't hold my drink, I'm dreadful in a fight, and I'm not much of a strategic thinker. There's only two things I can do well, and I wouldn't much care for a career making shadow-puppets.' He waggles his fingers in a rabbit shape. 'You've got to go with what you're good at, right?'

She smiles. *Your charm might just get you out of this*, she thinks. It's true that espionage is taken very seriously these days, but in the end Eoin's harmed nobody but Busman... and Sullivan, of course, but that eliminated a significant threat to the Circle's security. She doubts Busman, or the Seneschal for that matter, will be much wanting everything to come out in a trial, and the diplomatic consequences of clapping a foreign national in the Benwick would be grave. She'd put money on Eoin ending this a free man, thank God.

Because everything in Tania – not just those baser instincts of hers, though their allure is quite insistent, but her understanding of character, her experience of people – is telling her that Eoin's a kind, good, generous and considerate man, quite apart from being charming as all hell. Even the Tristan device, which you might expect to have more suspicious instincts, is taking a keen interest in him.

(You may have spotted the potential problem with this. As I believe I've said before now, that story-blindness can be a killer.)

16. SIR TRISTAN

You wouldn't – if indeed you have been – be the only one troubled by this extraordinary charisma on the part of the Fianna spy. Stephen Mukherjee has been conscientiously torturing himself about it since their last meeting, and has been forced to concede that yes, tedious though it may be – not to mention wildly uncharacteristic of him – he has somehow acquired a passion for the lad.

Stephen's older than Tania, though, and his experience encompasses the War of the Devices, when all kinds of peculiar things went down. He has, in particular, experience of having his life hijacked by a devicial obsession... and what Stephen realises now in retrospect is that his mania for hunting Mark Addis had something stalkerish about it – that it felt strangely similar, in fact, to his infatuation with MacNeill.

Fortunately for him, Mukherjee is the product of an enlightened era. It's true that the boarding-school he went to was hardly a bastion of liberalism, and he grew up, like many of its alumni, expressing an unthinking revulsion for 'queers', while placing the various activities aimed at relieving sexual frustration in the communal dorms after lights out in an entirely different mental category. At university, though, he quickly found that homophobic sentiments were wildly unpopular, and, as he met and befriended some actual gay people at his college and on his course, he came to realise – even as he subsumed the remembered sensation of those frantic nocturnal gropings and mouthings into his newly-manufactured interest in girls, or at least in Jocasta – that his prior intolerance had been entirely beyond the pale.

Before he met Eoin, Stephen had never, for more than a fleeting moment, considered that he might himself be homosexual. His family's never been prone to recreational buggery, and nor, on the whole, are the Knights of the Circle. It's simply not something he's ever felt inclined to consider – and, truth be told, the fact that no-one's making him is something he's always been faintly thankful for.

But he's a Knight. A man – or woman these days, though not in Stephen's case obviously – of honour, integrity and courage. He's sworn himself to uphold the truth, and that applies in his private life just as much as in the public sphere. He also knows that, under Sir David, the Circle's far more accepting and tolerant than it ever was in Sir Charles' time.

So now, when Stephen finally, in his forties, confronts this long-camouflaged part of himself, he brings to it all the bravery, honesty and dignity he would to any other confrontation.

He acknowledges that his one foray into heterosexuality, with poor patient Jocasta, was never characterised by anything so straightforward as lust. He realises that not all of his friendships with his brother Knights have been, on the inside of his head at least, quite as platonic as he might have might have pretended. And he allows himself, at last, to recall with nostalgia, and a deep regret for all the years he's lost, the soft bed and the hard young body of his dorm-mate Foley Minor during those sweet, illicit schoolboy nights.

If that was the end of it, that would, of course, be cause for celebration. A small step forward for the Circle's diversity, as well as a huge one for Stephen's personal growth.

It isn't, though – the end, I mean.

As I've said, Stephen's been given the runaround by his device before. Admitting that he might be susceptible to the charms of dark-eyed, long-lashed, honey-tongued young Irishmen is only the start of the self-awareness required of him here. Apart from anything else, he's seen how Tania Woodville looks when she come away from her sessions with the prisoner. He can see he and Nate Busman aren't the only people at the Fastness who've been left vulnerable by the lonely calling of a Knight.

He's only ever studied the myths of the Fianna – back then still allies of the Circle – quite cursorily, when he was assigned to escort Conán mac Morna's aithgin Dermot Healey, along with the Paladin Marie-Odile Laclos, around the apocalyptic London of the early war. He read the list of Fionn's best-known warriors then, though, and some of the entries have lodged in his mind. It doesn't take him long to recall the story of Diarmuid of the Love Spot and – unlike Tania, who must have stared at it a dozen times over the past few years – he rereads it now with a fresh and open mind.

Diarmuid was, as I've said, Fionn's trusted friend and comrade. He was – chronology in these stories being elastic when plot demands it – still a young and handsome man when his long-term brother-in-arms was old. And he was, as I've mentioned, inconveniently irresistible to women.

You might think, under these circumstances, that when the widowed Fionn became betrothed for a second time to the intended bride of his old age – Grainne, the young and beautiful daughter of the High King Cormac mac Airt – he might have had the good sense not to invite Diarmuid to their engagement party.

If so then you have, it possibly won't surprise you to hear, a great deal more common sense than the all-wise, all-knowing leader of warriors Fionn mac Cumhail.

Young Grainne fell for her intended's handsome comrade, as hard as a sponsored skydiver with a faulty parachute. Diarmuid was more cautious, refusing – even after Grainne sneakily dosed every other guest at the event with a sleeping-potion – to betray his leader in such a base way as to elope with his fiancée. Grainne, however, laid a *geas* on Diarmuid (it's a bit difficult to explain, but basically it's a Fianna thing) and he was obliged to run off with her or face dire consequences. Fionn pursued them angrily and relentlessly, until eventually persuaded by the intervention of Diarmuid's foster-father, the faerie Aengus Og, to forgive and forget.

Years later, though, when Diarmuid was gored by a wild boar – because he had no more sense than his boss, and was perfectly relaxed about going on a boar-hunt despite a prophecy that he'd die in precisely this way – Fionn had the chance to heal him with water from his hands, and instead, out of this old vindictiveness, allowed his friend to die.

These things rarely end well, in myths at least.

As Stephen reads this legend in the Fastness library (whose World Mythology section is growing almost daily as the High King makes new and more exotic enemies), it feels familiar to him. As if, although he's certainly never read the full version before, it somehow feels like a story that he knows very well indeed.

Then, because the paperback he's reading is a recent Penguin Classics translation of a collection of Old Irish legends, he flicks to the introduction, where the editor explains some of the reasons why these Celtic heroic epics might be of particular interest to British readers in the New Arthurian Age.

The library's in the basement of the keep. The Seneschal's office is on the ninth floor. It takes Stephen a surprisingly short time to cover the distance between them.

* * *

Paul and Kinsey arrive in Ipswich less than an hour later, in one of Metropolitan Yard's marked helicopters. On the way, Parsons has phoned Sir David Stafford to explain to him what's going on – up to a point. As a man of honour and a Knight, he still feels duty-bound to keep Izzy's name out of the equation, and similar considerations (as well as an ill-defined unease about the Seneschal's own past dealings with the Chapel) persuaded him to omit any mention of Smith's treachery. He had to handwave the question of how the Device Squad happened to find out about the abduction, too. Even so, Stafford arranged for the satellite linkup, strictly one-shot and for Parsons's use only. Having to operate the system interface himself via his tablet isn't improving Paul's mood.

The chopper comes in to land in the car park of a factory which Kinsey's phoned ahead and had evacuated. The Suffolk Constabulary are awaiting them in force.

'This way,' cries Paul, who pinned down the location on a map on their approach. On the helicopter, between bouts of wrestling with the satellite network's operating system, he's climbed into his armour. There was no room for his squire in the aircraft, and despite his years of familiarity with his artificial hand, he still finds the process annoyingly awkward.

He leaps from the still-windmilling helicopter and strides off in the appropriate direction, bellowing, 'This quest's under Circle control now.'

'Is it fuck!' yells Kinsey. 'Ignore him. This is a Device Squad operation,' she adds to the locals before dashing after him. The local SWAT team shelve their perfectly justifiable complaints about chains of command, and follow at a run.

They find the place: a narrow alley between buildings giving on to a larger space behind, cut off by a chain link fence. Momentarily baffled, Paul weighs up the wisdom of blunting his sword on the links until a local constable runs up with wirecutters.

They stride in – Parsons and Kinsey jockeying for pole position, despite the fact that he's both armed and armoured, while she carries nothing more deadly than her riot baton – to find a scrap of wasteland, partly claimed by vegetation.

The Chapel are long gone, of course. But they've left a message.

'Man down!' yells Paul, and at the same time Kinsey cries out, 'Medic!'

To one of the withered trees a nude, bloody figure has been tied. At first it appears headless, but as they run towards it, it becomes obvious that it's been positioned upside-down. Nearby, a pile of clothes lies; on top of it a Circle-issue scabbard and sword.

They rush to Smith's body. Paul holds him while Kinsey cuts him down, and they lay him naked in the muddy undergrowth.

'He's breathing,' Kinsey reports, ear to Jason's chest, while Parsons struggles to undo his own helmet. 'Wake up, Smith,' the Chief Superintendent says, gently for her. 'Can you hear me, Smith? It's Chief Superintendent Kinsey.' She pulls off her jacket and places it across his torso.

Jason coughs feebly, bringing up a little blood. He rolls his head over to one side and vomits over Parsons' armoured boots.

Paul tries not to look disgusted as he shakes the sick off his feet. 'Smith,' he asks, 'who did this to you? Was it the Chapel?'

Smith's eyelids flutter, but he doesn't open them. 'Is he going to be all right?' Parsons asks Kinsey, wresting off his helmet at last. She shrugs, and shouts 'Medic!' again.

'P-P-P-Parsons?' Jason groans, shivering violently. 'P-Paul mate, is that you?'

Parsons squats down beside him. 'Yes, Jason,' he says. 'Yes, it's me. I'm here.'

'Paul,' Smith says again, his voice little more than a whisper.

'What is it, chap?' asks Parsons kindly. 'Was there something you wanted to get off your chest?'

Jason coughs again, long and protractedly.

Then he says, 'Mate, you've laid me arse right on a n-n-n-nettle. Can you p-p-pull it out for me?'

Parsons scowls, and Kinsey permits herself a rare smile, as the police medics rush in with blankets and a stretcher.

* * *

'I appreciate you coming to me with this, Stephen,' Sir David Stafford says. 'Particularly given what you've told me. It can't be an easy thing, to come to that kind of understanding about yourself at your age. I want you to know I'll support you in any way I can.

'But,' he goes on, 'MacNeill can't be carrying the device of Diarmuid Ua Duibhne. Not unless the Children of Oisín have been feeding us false information for decades. Eamonn Costello's my age – he's been with the Children since the 1990s. And we were on friendly terms with the Fianna back then, as far as our mythologies allowed. I suppose the device could have moved on to another bearer,' he adds dubiously, 'but our people have seen no signs of that. Costello's still in the same standing with the Children. And as much of a Casanova as ever, by all accounts.'

'I'm sorry, sir,' says Stephen, still slightly breathless from his climb, 'but that isn't what I'm suggesting. Look.'

He opens up the Penguin Classics paperback – which has got slightly creased during their his headlong rush up the stairs, and which he shouldn't in any case have taken out of the Fastness library without checking it out first – and smooths it down on Stafford's desk. David bends to take a look.

I've said that Stephen has experience of freak devicial occurrences during the war. It was a time of extreme mythopolitical tension, with archetypes warping and stretching under pressure. When Stephen finally caught up with Mark Addis, his Questing Beast, it was at the Stonehenge Summit, where Adze had infiltrated the Circle army intending to cause trouble and prolong the conflict.

The Beast's description in the *Morte D'Arthur* is a typical assortment from a medieval bestiary: leopard's forequarters, lion's haunches, a hart's hooves and the head of a serpent. The biker gang led by Adze, the British Beasts, painted representations of their totem animals on their motorbikes, but those were mundane species: boars, wolves, wildcats. Adze's paint job was so complicated it extended to the rider.

His bike was a patchwork of spots, sandy fur and dappled hide, but his helmet and leathers were painted with the scales and head of a snake.

And it was as a snake that he struck at Stonehenge: away from his machine, his device mutated to become the viper that broke the peace between the reconciling armies of Arthur and Mordred at Camlann, and triggered their final, fateful battle. Mark Addis had entered Stephen's life in one devicial capacity, but it was in quite another that he nearly killed him. Stephen's familiar now with the ways in which the devices can twist and slither in your hands, becoming things you never imagined they could be.

'Look, sir,' he says again, pointing at one particular paragraph of the introduction.

> *The Pursuit of Diarmuid and Grainne depicts a familiar love triangle: an older husband, a reluctant bride, a handsome lover. Its influence, and its influences, extend to accounts of doomed love affairs from Deirdre and Naoise to Lancelot and Guinevere. But there is one romance which it resembles more closely than others — in detail as well as overall outline. The drug at the betrothal (though here it is a sleeping draught rather than a love potion, and everybody but the lovers is affected rather than the couple alone), the sword that separates the sleeping pair, the peaceful interlude in the forest, even Grainne's taunt that the water wetting her thigh is bolder than her reluctant paramour; all recur in the popular Arthurian legend of Tristan and Iseult.*

As I've said, foreign devices often have trouble interacting with British ones. (Not because the British ones are special, of course — it applies across any boundary between cultures, although less so the more they have in common.) They try to mesh, to make their stories work in one another's context, but there are glitches and friction and occasional drastic misalignments. The legends of Tristan and Iseult and of Diarmuid and Grainne, though — they line up fairly readily.

Admittedly Sir Tristan doesn't have Diarmuid's way with the ladies, King Mark's more of a villain than Fionn, and Grainne's a lot less innocent than Iseult... but once the affair gets going, the whole romance follows a closely parallel arc.

'I don't think MacNeill's Diarmuid,' Stephen repeats. 'I think he's Grainne. Which, in our terms – I mean in Woodville's especially, and in Tristan's – would make him La Belle Iseult.'

* * *

Jason gives his first account of his ordeal in the ambulance to the hospital, Paul and Kinsey pressing him for details as the vehicle rattles around corners. The paramedics in attendance are grumpily tolerating their authority for now, but they have limited time before they get to A&E.

'That lot weren't pleased to see me at all,' Smith tells them bitterly. 'We go back ages, them and me. I know I'm Circle now, but I never thought they'd be like that about it. It was like we were right back in the War of the Devices.'

'They haven't threatened a Knight since then,' says Paul, who like the rest of us knows nothing of Oli Montalban's experiences in the Home Park.

'Yeah,' groans Smith, 'they're coming right off the Christmas card list. Bloody hell, it's a joke,' he adds, as Parsons and Kinsey stare accusingly at him. '"Course I haven't got their bloody *addresses*. God, why're you both looking so serious?'

'This *is* serious, Smith,' Paul reminds him. 'It amounts to a declaration of war.'

'No, bollocks to that,' says Smith with feeling, then has to have another coughing fit.

'Nobody wants to go back to all that,' he groans eventually. 'They were just being arseholes, was all. Mostly it was that Ron. He was all for killing me – talked about the threefold death, hanging and stabbing and drowning, and how my blood would fecundate the land and stuff. You ask me, he's gone completely *Wicker Man*. Scar and Zara wanted to strip me and let me go – warning to the Circle, kind of thing – but Ron said if they did that I'd hang around and follow them. Like I'd be doing *that* with me tackle out. Then he said they'd better tie me to the tree, and when they did he started hitting me with a bloody great stick. They had to pull him off of me. Then Janene heard your chopper coming, and the lot of them scarpered.'

The local force are searching the area thoroughly, of course, but have turned up no sign of the Chapel people so far. This surprises nobody – the Green Chapel are adept enough to hide from deviced Knights, so unallied police without even the Device Squad's secular expertise will naturally be a pushover. Sergeant Jenkins is on his way here with more of Kinsey's people, but they'll be too late to do more than bag the evidence.

'Enough now,' insists the senior paramedic, as they pull in at the hospital. 'He needs to rest.'

'We're staying with him,' Kinsey says. So far, she and Paul haven't had a chance to ask Smith whether he discussed anything else with the Chapel before they started laying into him, or even what he was doing there in the first place. (On the plus side, Jason's still too dazed to have thought to ask them how they came to rescue him, so they're about even there.)

'Is he under arrest?' the paramedic insists on knowing.

Paul and Kinsey frown at each other for a moment, then Paul says curtly, 'No. No, Mr Smith's a Knight of the Circle, injured in the line of duty.'

'Then you can see him later,' snaps the paramedic. 'The doctors will look after him now.'

They wheel their patient away into the back entrance of A&E, leaving Paul and Kinsey hanging around in the freezing car park and suddenly at a bit of a loose end.

'You reckon he's lying?' The Chief Superintendent sounds as sceptical as ever.

'Not as such,' Parsons replies. 'Someone tied him to a tree

and beat him, obviously. But he's not telling us everything, I'm sure.'

'You still think he's loyal to those bastards?' Kinsey scoffs. 'No, your informant got the wrong end of the stick. OK, so he's been trying to contact them, but they're no friends of his.'

'Unless that's what they want us to think,' Parsons muses.

'You think he got himself beaten up just to cover his tracks?' Kinsey sounds almost impressed. 'That's some fucking impressive paranoia you've got going, Parsons.'

'I don't know what his agenda is,' Paul insists. 'None of us do. But I'm damn well going to find out.'

And his first step towards that, he thinks, will have be to another word with Ms Isabella Taylor.

* * *

'La Belle Iseult?' Tania Woodville stares at her Seneschal, aghast. 'How can he be Iseult, sir?'

Sir David sighs. 'He isn't, quite,' he says awkwardly. 'We think he's Iseult's Irish analogue, Grainne. But the legends are similar enough that it amounts to much the same thing.'

'I'm so sorry, Woodville,' says Mukherjee, who's been standing behind the Seneschal's chair throughout his revelation, 'but it all hangs together. Iseult's the daughter of the Irish king; MacNeill's an Irish agent. She heals him after he's injured fighting the Morholt; he called the ambulance after you killed Sullivan. You brought him back here to the Fastness, just as Tristan brings Iseult to Cornwall to marry Mark. And... well, there are your feelings for him, obviously.'

'And what the hell,' Tania asks, furious at Stephen's intervention in her personal life, 'would you know about my *feelings* for him, Mukherjee?'

Mukherjee's face darkens, and he drops his gaze to the floor. 'More than you might think,' he says quietly. 'That's what made me realise. You may remember, Sir Palamedes was in love with Iseult too, although in his case it was a hopeless infatuation.'

Woodville gapes for a moment, then gets a grip. 'Shit, Stephen, I'm sorry,' she says, sincerely. 'But... look, you've got things all mixed up. You're hanging too much on this. I wasn't Eoin's – MacNeill's target, remember. Busman was.' She wonders fleetingly whether there are any male Knights in the building who *aren't* gay, before remembering the twenty or so who've tried – thoroughly honourably, of course – to hit on her at one time or another. At least Mukherjee's never done that.

'Well, as to that,' Sir David points out, embarrassed, 'Sir Kahedins *also* fell in love with Iseult, according to some sources anyway. She was a popular young lady. From MacNeill's point of view, though, the whole Busman business was probably a ploy to bring himself to your attention. O'Leary sent him to Sir Marhaus's bondsman – that's why he was willing to sacrifice him. He was trying to trigger the start of the legend. You were his target all along.'

'O'Leary recruited Sullivan *years* ago,' Woodville protests. 'I wasn't even on our Fianna quest back then.'

'No,' Sir David concedes, 'but there was every likelihood I'd assign you to it. Given Sir Tristan's traditional enmity with Ireland, you were the obvious choice. Maybe that was even why they tried to lure you down to Cornwall with the Duke's Corineus story. Now, whether they've been waiting all this time for the Grainne device to manifest herself, or whether they've developed a technique to summon her, I don't know. They'd have had to be sure she'd bond with a man, after all, given your own preferences.'

'Too right,' mutters Tania. 'But no... I can't credit this, sir. MacNeill's just an ordinary chap who got in over his head. He told me himself he's not an *aithgin*.' She tries to remember, as she says it, just how categorical his denial was.

'He might not be lying,' Stephen suggests gently. 'He might not realise it himself. But Woodville, why did you suspect Sullivan in the first place? An anonymous tip-off, wasn't it – a voice-only call, if I recall? I'm sure we'll have a recording on file. MacNeill had a phone with him at Sullivan's flat. He's a dab hand at voices, but if we analyse it I'm sure…'

'Oh fuck.' Tania cuts across him, suddenly remembering. 'MacNeill gave me painkillers at the flat. A… drug, I suppose. But… it was just ibuprofen. It didn't do anything to me. There's no such thing as a love potion.'

Sir David clicks his tongue. 'Not pharmaceutically, no. But devicially… giving you *any* drug may have been enough to cement the progress of the narrative. Tania, I'm so sorry. Stephen… I think perhaps you'd better leave us now. You've done good work. We'll talk later.'

Mukherjee nods sombrely, and leaves.

'I'll take over the interviews with the prisoner,' the Seneschal tells Tania. 'It's best if we cut off all his contact with you. Mukherjee too. We can't risk either of you being compromised.'

'But he'll –' Tania begins, then stops.

He'll be so cut up if he can't see me any more. He won't understand.

She shakes her head briskly. *Christ almighty, Woodville, get a grip.* 'Of course, sir,' she tells Stafford. She pauses, then: 'Sir, I'm a Knight. My loyalties lie with the Circle, always. And its Head.'

Woodville's no Patrick Sullivan, no Craig McCutcheon. No Nate Busman, for that matter. She won't let the High King down the way they did.

Sir David nods. 'That's understood, Woodville. I realise this can't be easy for you. I have some… experience with f-forbidden love, so I know how unfair this is. If you ever want to talk…'

'Of course, sir,' she says. 'Thank you.'

Inside her, Sir Tristan rages with frustrated yearning.

* * *

'I told them what you said, my lord,' Jason tells the High

307

King over their secure phone link. 'But they weren't having none of it.' His face on the tablet screen is patched, purple and swollen, with stitches in his lip and above one eye. 'They reckon they're done with all of that. Sorry, my lord.'

Jory shakes his head. 'No, Jason, I should be sorry. I should have realised I was sending you into danger. I hadn't realised they'd turned so hostile.'

'It's that Ron,' Squig says. 'That Herne bloke you mentioned, the one with the oak? Does he have great big fuck-off deer's horns?'

'Antlers. Yes,' the Pendragon agrees. 'No-one seems quite sure why.'

'That's him, then,' Jason says. 'It's Ron. It was him beat me up, that bastard. He's got some sort of hold over the others. Not completely, though. He wanted to kill me, but the others stopped him.'

'Oh good God,' the High King says softly. 'Jason, again, I'm sorry. If I'd realised I never would have sent you there.'

'Not a problem, my lord,' Jason replies, with a surprisingly convincing stab at cheeriness. 'We live to serve.'

Jory cuts the call, and turns to me and Rev. We've been sitting there all the while he's been talking, giving each other increasingly grave looks as Jason describes his difficulties.

The new study's in the Pendragon Tower, the egg-shaped one with the vertical gardens, known to some of the less reverent men-at-arms as 'the Tombliboo House'. It's a nice enough room with severe-looking but perfectly comfortable stripped-pine-and-canvas armchairs, a giant glass-topped desk, a connecting door to the High King's private bedroom as well as one to the corridor outside, and walls which curve and taper noticeably toward the ceiling. It looks more like a trendy dentist's waiting-room than a chamber in a royal palace.

Cantrell shakes his head now, wearily. 'Those stupid bastards.'

'What are they playing at?' the High King asks, not for the first time. 'I'd never have thought it of them.' He sounds

308

like a school principal, profoundly disappointed by the latest crop of condoms and fag-ends collected from behind the gym. 'Scar and Zara have known Squig for years. Janene and Ron are after his time, of course, but they're good people. This isn't the sort of thing the Chapel does.'

'Stripping a knight and leaving him tied up for someone to find?' I say. 'Happens all the time in the Robin Hood stories. Normally they'd tie him to his horse, but Jason didn't have one with him. You're right, though, this is different. It's Herne the Hunter's influence – has to be. They've summoned up an ally too powerful to control.'

'Yeah,' agrees Rev. His voice is permanently hoarse these days, and sometimes, when he doesn't think the rest of us are looking, he allows his hands to shake. 'They thought this Herne would be their holy man. They wanted him to replace me.'

'They wanted the cuddly spirit guide from *Robin of Sherwood*,' I elaborate. 'Friendly old shaman bloke, lives in the woods, gives them jobs to do, hands out prophecies when something big's going to happen. Played by John Abineri. Instead they've got... Christ, I don't know. Something a lot older, though, I reckon. The leader of the Wild Hunt, maybe.'

I've been looking into this stuff since midwinter, at the High King's request. The Wild Hunt's a Germanic legend that probably came to Britain with the Anglo-Saxons: a spectral hunting-party said to ride through the sky at midwinter, or at times of crisis, or every seven years, depending who you talk to. It's bad luck to see them, not least because they have a habit of making any mortals they meet into the object of their hunt. 'Their leader's sometimes Herne,' I elaborate, 'although he's just one of lots of possibilities, and it's sometimes difficult to tell whether they're the huntmaster or the quarry. King Arthur's another, though. Or Woden, or Gwydion the Welsh magician. Or the Devil, of course.'

Rev grunts at that. 'You know I'm an easy-going soul,' he tells us, like we might have forgotten. 'But when folk start calling up spirits with horns and putting their spiritual guidance in their hands, my priestly reflexes start getting kind of twitchy. I should have taken those folks in hand a long way back.'

Jory sighs. 'So what happens now?' he wonders aloud. 'Another war, after all this time?'

The old man shakes his head with vehemence. 'Not on my watch. Jesus, not on my watch,' he says fiercely.

* * *

'You bastard,' Tania Woodville's voice hisses in the darkness. 'You little *shit*.'

Eoin MacNeill jerks awake, and fumbles for the light-switch in his cell. 'Tania?' he grumbles blearily. 'God, is that you?'

She snarls, 'Of course it's me. How many people in this place have you tried to seduce?'

Eoin sits upright. 'Well,' he says, his smile returning, 'there's Steve, of course. There's the page who brings me my breakfast in the mornings. She always brings me an extra rasher...' He trails off as he sees her face. 'Hey, what's the matter? Are you pissed off with me now?'

His face seems hurt and apprehensive, but quite sincere.

She says, 'Don't give me that, O'Neill. I know who you are. I know why you were at Sullivan's. You *drugged* me, you bastard, or as good as. And you've been playing me ever since. It was me they sent you here for, not bloody Busman. They wanted you to turn me, didn't they? Well, you people picked the wrong woman.'

'Ah,' sighs MacNeill. 'Ah, shite. I'm sorry, Tania.' He slumps back on the bed.

She glares at him in silence, daring him to say more.

At length he looks into her eyes again. 'They tricked me too,' he says. 'The mac Cumhail's a cunning bastard, you have no idea. They told me I could be an *aithgin*, fight for my country. Well, like I told you, I've never been any good at fighting. I thought we were looking at some kind of *Captain*

310

America deal – you know, how the little nerdy bloke becomes an instant super-soldier? I loved those films when I was a boy.

'So they do their business with all the drugs and the hypnosis and the other mumbo-jumbo, and at the end of it all they tell me they've turned me into a princess instead.' He laughs bitterly. 'Don't get me wrong, I'm all for challenging the old gender stereotypes, but Jesus, there's a time and a place, you know? And then they tell me it's all so I can go to England and seduce this woman I've never heard of, this Knight in armour who kills giants with a great big sword, and I'm terrified. Terrified and just a little bit turned on, if I'm honest. But mostly really fecking scared of meeting you, never mind trying to pull the wool over your eyes.

'And then I met you at the flat, and it was like...' He stops, and takes a deep breath. 'I knew we were supposed to be compatible, my *aithgin* and your device, but I hadn't expected...'

Another pause. Woodville stands impassive, waiting for the rest of the story.

'Tania, my darling,' he says. 'The legend only works if your Iseult loves your Tristan – really, truly loves him, with a love that outlasts any stupid bloody potion. And Grainne – sure, she's as shallow as a spilled pint, but she loved Diarmuid first. Perhaps if they'd let me near old Eamonn Costello, I'd have fallen for him instead, not that he'd be interested in me by all accounts. But O'Leary's a cunning old goat who'd never slip up like that. Even if the original Fionn would and did.'

Eoin smiles, a little sadly. 'As it was, I saw *you*. And I loved you straight away, without any fecking potion or love spot. I gave you the painkillers, sure, but I never thought that would work. It sounded stupid. And you were in actual pain. I couldn't see you like that without trying to help.'

He looks at her face. 'I know I could have told you,' he says. '*Should* have told you. I should've been honest before now. But Tania, I couldn't stand to see that look on your face – that look you've got now. That look of hating me, for what

I am and what I came here to do. I knew you'd find out soon enough – I couldn't stand to hurry that along.'

He spreads his hands as if to juggle. 'So – you can do your worst, my darling. There's nothing you can do to me that's half as bad as knowing how you feel about me now.'

* * *

In the morning, Sir David Stafford details Christopher Timms – whose device, Sir Aglavale, has no connection with the legend of Tristan and Iseult, and who has proved himself over the years to be consistently, indeed assiduously, heterosexual – to collect the prisoner and bring him to the interview room.

The Senschal's sitting there five minutes later, looking through the transcripts of MacNeill's conversations with Woodville and Mukherjee on his tablet, when Timms comes back, his face pale.

'He's gone, sir,' Timms says in a panic. 'He was signed out of the cells during the night, and never came back. I've asked for the CCTV records – all of them – the exit logs, too. Sir David?' he adds, concerned.

The Seneschal lifts his left hand from his eyes, which it's been covering ever since Timms entered the room alone. 'Thank you, Timms,' he says quietly. 'That's very resourceful. We must do that, of course.'

He tilts the tablet forward, and dials an internal Fastness number. 'Mukherjee?' he asks when it's answered. 'Good man. Just checking.' He thumbs the 'off' button, then stares into space for a long, long moment.

Then he stands. 'The exit logs,' he says. 'Yes. They'll tell you a Knight left with a guest in the early hours of the morning. The exit code will be Tania Woodville's.'

Timms looks, if anything, even more alarmed. 'What, sir?'

'I should have sent her away,' Stafford adds bitterly. 'I should have assigned her to the Arthur's Seat Fastness,

312

effective immediately. Mukherjee too. I should have had them both escorted to King's Cross and put on the fast train to Edinburgh. I'm getting old.'

He shakes his head. 'We've got a legend of love and betrayal on our hands, Chris – one involving a Knight of the Circle. And that's the most dangerous narrative of all. The High King is *not* going to be pleased.'

* * *

The High King is already displeased. This morning the Castle staff have found Rev Cantrell equally absent – without a word to anyone, apparently unseen by anyone since our conversation yesterday, he's packed a bag and locked up his rooms and gone. An open window on the ground floor suggests the daft old goat didn't even leave by any of the doors, for fear the guards would tell the High King before he was well away.

Rev's had no dealings with the Green Chapel since the grand falling-out which followed Zara's attack on the arms fair, but still his contacts are more recent than Jason Smith's. The Chapel may be closed to visitors right now, but if anyone can find a side-door left unlocked, it's Rev Cantrell.

The life we live at this royal palace is a fine one, of course. Good food, exquisite booze, great company: all the things a man of Rev's – or Friar Tuck's – predilections really wants from life.

But enjoyment isn't everything. For bondsmen and allies, mendicant monks and lapsed Episcopalian priests, there's still such a thing as a calling.

And after all, what use is a holy man if he isn't there when his people need him?

17. LA BELLE ISEULT

'They tell me your Sir Tristan's gone AWOL, m'lord,' Sir Charles Raymond notes gruffly. 'Flighty customers, the lot of them. Had one years ago who ran off with a shop-girl from Dulwich. Wasn't even Iseult's bondswoman, as it turned out – fellow was just a fool for a pretty face. Damned good man in a fight, though. Of course yours is a woman, isn't she?' he adds, as if that was a sequitur in some way.

Behind the old Knight on the screen, an electric heater's visible, a single orange bar warming the living-room of the retirement cottage. The walls are hung with framed photographs and press clippings from his twenty-something years as Seneschal of the Circle.

'Charles.' Jory greets the ex-Seneschal with a marked lack of enthusiasm. He'd only stepped into his study en route to his bedroom for a shave, when the call came through to his desk. 'It's always good to hear from you, but I'm afraid –'

'Trick is,' says Raymond from the inlaid desk-screen, oblivious, 'they always come back if you forgive them. Tristan device is a silly romantic bugger, always mooning after some filly, but duty's his bread and butter. Duty and guilt. Give your man – woman, I should say – a while to get it out of her system, so to speak. Totty break, we used to call it. Then send her a message saying you forgive her and you'll take her back.

If I know anything she'll come trotting home like a runaway hound.'

'Thank you for the benefit of your experience,' the High King says carefully, staring up at where the rounded walls meet the smaller ceiling. 'But this Tristan hasn't just gone AWOL, she's helped a prisoner to escape, a spy for the Children of Oisín in fact. So I don't think forgiveness is going to come quite that easily.'

'Well, once she's back you can punish her to your heart's content,' says Sir Charles sagely. 'She'll lap it up. As I say – guilt and duty, duty and guilt. Irishman's a different matter, of course. Johnny Fianna's always resented us – something to do with William of Orange and the Cú Chulainn device, never understood the details. Politics. Did I hear that Cantrell fellow's gone missing too?'

The former Seneschal was never the brightest key in the bunch, but these days, without the distractions of an actual Circle to run, he has his finger far more closely on the pulse than before. Never overendowed with marbles, he nonetheless keeps them well-polished in his old age.

'I'm afraid that's confidential,' the Pendragon says – hoping to refresh Raymond's memory about no longer holding any official position, which is one fact that does regularly escape him.

Sir Charles, of course, takes this as confirmation. 'Never did like the fellow. Sneaky. Shifty face on him.' He and Rev Cantrell have history, which starts about seventeen years ago with the ex-priest posing as a country vicar to whisk away Edward Wendiman from under, if not the Seneschal's nose, at least those of his underlings. 'Chap's a Yank, too. And a poofter, although I know we're not supposed to say that these days. How is young Stafford, by the way?'

'Sir David's very well thank you, Sir Charles,' Jory says tartly. 'Although if you have to comment on his sexuality I'd imagine he'd rather you called him gay.'

Raymond snorts. 'See what I mean? Can't use perfectly

descriptive words any more. When I was a boy, flowers and music were gay. Queer just meant peculiar.'

Jory sincerely doubts this. The ex-Seneschal's certainly getting on, but he was a teenager in the 1960s, not the 1860s. 'Was there a particular reason you were calling, Charles?' he asks through gritted teeth. 'Because I'm actually in the middle of co-ordinating a complicated national quest to find these fugitives, so if there's nothing really pressing I probably should be getting back to that.'

Sir Charles looks slightly hurt. It's not an expression Jory's used to seeing on his face, so at first he mistakes it for some kind of grotesque facial tic.

'Thought they'd have told you,' the old man says. 'Got my op this afternoon.' Raymond has been waiting for a hip replacement for a while now, since a bad break from an awkward fall in the summer. 'Thought I'd check in before I went. Don't know how long I'll be in for. Wanted to make sure I was up to date with things.'

'Of course.' Jory softens his voice a bit. It takes some effort, but it's the High Kingly thing to do. 'I hope it all goes well. I'm sure you'll be fighting fit in no time.'

Raymond scowls. 'I'm eighty-four, m'lord. Be a miracle if I can climb the stairs again, quite frankly. Still, doctors know best, eh?' There's a genuine uncertainty to his tone which is quite unfamiliar to the Pendragon.

'I'm sure they do, Charles,' the High King reassures him. 'Now, if you'll excuse me –'

'Yes, yes of course,' the former Seneschal says briskly. 'You've got important work to do. Can't sit around all morning chatting to some old buffer. Hope you find the fellow, m'lord. Talk again soon.'

The old man reaches out to his own tablet and cuts the connection first – rather to Jory's surprise, as he's always assumed he didn't know how.

* * *

The manhunt from which Sir Charles has been keeping his liege lord is the nations' biggest since the search for Craig McCutcheon seven and a half years ago. Thus far, it hasn't been resolved by Woodville or MacNeill climbing a landmark in either capital and proclaiming their defiance to the world.

At Metropolitan Yard in London and St Leonard's in Edinburgh, Chief Superintendent Kinsey and her counterpart, Chief Superintendent McIntyre of the Devicial Crimes Unit, are co-ordinating local forces across both countries to check every transit facility – railway stations, hotels, roadside pubs, service stations, transport cafés – for evidence of the couple passing through. The descriptions circulated with the photographs emphasise that the couple might have disguised themselves, and there've been any number of false positives sparked by random sightings of handsome men in their mid-twenties accompanying muscular women in their mid-thirties.

At the Fastness, Sir David's fielding calls from the Chief Superintendents, the High King and any number of heads of intelligence, armed forces, border control and coastguard. In between times, he and Theo Harte pore over maps and satellite imagery, considering potential boltholes and escape routes. Ned Busman is shoring up the Fastness against the possibility of anyone using this as an opportunity for an attack, and doing remarkably well at resisting the temptation to tell everyone he speaks to that this whole mess is entirely his fault and he's so very sorry.

Paul, back from Ipswich, is liaising with intelligence agents on the ground in Dublin and other foreign capitals, checking for any indication that the pair have already arrived abroad. Jason's been moved to Tud House, the Circle's recuperative facility in Norfolk, where the doctors have had to order him to stay put. He's asked to be copied in to the regular Fastness updates even so, in case there's anything he can contribute.

Oli Montalban, recalled for an interim debriefing at the Foreign Office during a day's adjournment at The Hague, is relieved instead to have a chance to volunteer for surveillance

317

duty at St Pancras station's Eurostar terminal. Sir Safir's bondswoman Amal, thrilled to be adopted as the High King's personal envoy while Jason is indisposed, is standing by to negotiate on his behalf with the Children of Oisín, the Paladins de la République or any other devicial group should this become necessary.

Stephen's the other side of the interview table as Freddie Obote, the elderly bondsman of Sir Ywain the Bastard, quizzes him on any clue Eoin might have let slip to his whereabouts.

At Windsor, the Pendragon himself is doing his best to keep on top of every aspect of the search. It's noticeable that the heads of various services who he keeps phoning are becoming ever more scrupulously polite as time progresses. Bonnie's sticking as close to him as ever, while Izzy brings him occasional cups of tea and kisses on the cheek. The task of tracing Rev's movements since he left has fallen so far down the priority list it's been delegated down to a couple of squires from the garrison.

* * *

Meanwhile I've been tasked with researching all the variants I can find of either the Tristan-Iseult or the Diarmuid-Grainne legends, and working out their implications for this whole miserable mess. It turns out that – what with Malory long gone, the Merlin device in abeyance, Rev wherever-the-hell-he-is and the nations' academic mythopoliticists mostly tied up with Freda Tate-Hendricks' projects – I'm the closest thing the High King has to an expert on the devices which are undermining our fragile peace even as we speak.

This scares me like nothing since the War of the Devices – except perhaps that time I found Blaze and Jory reeling in the study in the aftermath of McCutcheon's devicial mine.

So far the most useful advice I've come up with is to keep certain Knights clear of the quest, because of their patrons' relationship to the Tristan and Iseult myth: specifically the bondsmen of Sirs Dinadan and Sagramore, both close friends of Tristan's. Their devices have each had the same bearer for decades – Sir Sagramore's is, in fact, Oli Montalban's great-uncle Monty. Neither of them know Woodville particularly well, but Stafford has them put under house arrest just in case. Monty at least is highly miffed.

Aside from Tristan, Palamedes and Kahedins – as if they haven't done enough damage – the only other knight with a recorded crush on La Belle Iseult is Sir Andret. With Sandy Hithers in the Benwick for the past seven years, there's probably not a lot of danger from that quarter.

I've also pointed out that Tristan is, by the standards of the Round Table at least, a master of disguise. As well as going incognito in Ireland under the cunningly impenetrable pseudonym of 'Tantris', the myths have him turning up in the guises of a fool, a monk, a leprosy sufferer and just some anonymous knight who definitely isn't Sir Tristan. (To be fair, most of the knights could probably have managed that last one.) I don't have access to Woodville's personnel files, so I don't know how far she's been trained for undercover work, but on this basis, I suggest, the Circle probably needn't assume she looks like herself right now.

This information is widely considered to be rather less helpful.

As far as potential destinations go, I've advised them to look along the Welsh coast, where Tristan first put ashore when bringing Iseult home as a bride for Mark (and which would make an ideal striking-out point for the journey back to Ireland, if that's where Woodville and MacNeill are headed), in facilities for patients with disfiguring or highly contagious conditions (because of the aforementioned leprosy connection), and generally in forests (which are where both the British and the Irish lovers find their longest interludes of peace). I've also pointed out the plethora of non-Knight characters who appear in the romance, from Tristan's tutor Governal through Iseult's nurse Brangain to their dog Husdent – any of whom could have manifested in

Pendragon-era Britain without triggering the Circle's radar, and might potentially be helping the fugitives.

(At this point, I go up a bit of a blind alley thinking about the doubling of names and characters. Tristan and Iseult – or, as they appear in various versions, Tristram, Drystan, Isolde, Ysod and so on – aren't the only people in the legend with those names. Our girl's generally known in French style as La Belle Iseult, but her mother's an Iseult too, and after the lovers are separated Tristan goes and marries a Breton princess, Kahedins' sister in fact, called Iseult of the White Hands. At one point, according to some Scandinavian sagas, Sir Tristan makes an alliance with a giant, known with uproarious Nordic irony as Tristan the Dwarf. In some of the variants where the couple end up together, they have a son and daughter whom they christen... well, I suspect you can guess.

This actually isn't all that rare in the Arthurian myths: I've mentioned that Lancelot has a particular penchant for women called Elaine, and one of those wacky Welsh *Triads* reckons Arthur was married to three separate Gwenhwyfars. At least in the Irish legend there's only one Grainne. Quite what this tells us in the current context, I'm not so sure, except that devicial identity can be shifting and deceptive, which we knew. So in the end I keep it to myself.)

Another point I don't share with the Circle, but which I make a mental note of because it's worrying me, is that in the legends, Arthur has no interest in hunting Tristan and his girlfriend down. That role falls to Tristan's betrayed lord and Iseult's cuckolded hubby, King Mark. Though the Mark device is presumed still safely contained inside the ex-Duke of Cornwall's head, the ex-Duke himself's been rather plaintively insisting recently that he instead carries the device of Brutus, Britain's first king. In playing Mark's narrative role the Pendragon could easily, unless he's careful, end up taking on some of his less admirable characteristics.

Admittedly, because the myth's generally a tragic one,

Mark usually wins Iseult back, but he often acts despicably along the way.

When I mention this tentatively to Jory, he just says 'We should count ourselves lucky they're not Lancelot and Guinevere,' and refuses to be drawn any further on the matter.

* * *

By the next morning, the Circle have a solid lead.

The breakthrough comes from a product of the MRF's research: that algorithm for identifying device-driven body-language, still in beta-testing and lacking sufficient data on foreign devices, but able to pick out Woodville from the previous morning rush hour's surveillance camera footage at London Paddington station. Once pointed out – she's dyed her hair black and is wearing a business suit, but the figure and face are hers – she can be clearly seen queuing at the ticket counter. A cross-reference with ticket sales shows that she bought a single ticket – single as in one-way, but also for one person only – to Didcot in Oxfordshire. Manual inspection of the footage from the relevant platform shows that the software missed MacNeill boarding an Oxford-bound train an hour later. His fellow-passengers are tracked down and questioned by the Device Squad, and several of them remember the charming, recklessly chatty Irishman with his deep brown eyes.

Didcot station's cameras show McNeill leaving on a bicycle, either stolen or left there ready for him. Stafford sets Timms and others to trace Woodville's movements after Paddington, but it looks highly likely that the plan was for them to meet up somewhere near Didcot.

Given this starting-point, and my suggestion to check out possible sanctuaries in forests, the obvious avenue of investigation is the Woodville family's heavily-wooded estate in Oxfordshire.

It's considered wisest not to involve Tania's parents, as however disappointed they may be by their daughter's dereliction of duty, she's still their daughter. Instead Kinsey manages to track down a former groundsman who remembers five-year-old Tania and her brothers playing in a derelict hunting-lodge at the western edge of the estate. By his account the structure, though dating back to the eighteenth century, is an unlovely stone box holding two rooms on a single floor, abandoned for generations except by the children of the Woodville family, of whom there are – according to Debrett's *Peerage*, at least – currently none. It's hardly luxurious: no running water, no electricity, no mobile signal even – but it's pretty close to what you might imagine Tristan and Iseult might have built for themselves in a moorland valley beyond the Tamar, or Diarmuid and Grainne in the Forest of Dooros in Sligo.

As Windsor's en route between London and the Woodville estate, the Pendragon offers the Castle as a staging-post for the Circle's taskforce. Out of politeness Sir David accepts, although he plans to requisition the Woodville Arms pub next to the estate as his HQ proper. The High King did suggest at first that he should lead his troops personally, as he did at Tregorlois, but David and I managed to persuade him otherwise. Not only would it be disproportionate to deploy the Pendragon device against a single Knight and her non-combat-trained accomplice, but it risks reinforcing the dangerous parallels between the High King and King Mark.

As the Knights, squires and men-at-arms assemble, painfully early, for their briefing in the Castle's Upper Ward, Paul Parsons snatches the opportunity for a brief word with the High King's daughter.

'They beat Smith and tied him to a tree, yeah?' he tells her, omitting the indecorous detail of Jason's nakedness. 'He tells me they're not on friendly terms any more.'

Izzy purses her lips quizzically. 'That does sound weird. Could they have guessed that you were following him?'

This is exactly what Parsons himself has been wondering. He says, 'They certainly did their best to lose anyone who was. It could have been a ruse, yes. I wouldn't have liked to be in Smith's shoes if it was, though.'

'From what I heard, he wasn't wearing *shoes*.' Izzy's mouth twitches in just the tiniest smirk. 'But Paul, this is pretty familiar, isn't it? Didn't Patrick Sullivan set up a fight where he could save my Dad, just to convince the Seneschal he was loyal? Why couldn't Jason be another Trojan horse like Sullivan, but this time for the Chapel?'

Paul puffs out air through his lips.

'He always used to be, you know,' Izzy goes on. 'Sir David's forgiven it all, but Jason was a Chapel agent long before he was a Knight. It was Jason who warned the Chapel you were going to raid them at the Nutwood Festival.' All that was sixteen years ago now, when Izzy can't have been more than four. 'You planned that raid, didn't you Paul? If they hadn't been warned, you might have arrested them all then and there.'

Paul is amazed. 'Smith did that?'

'So my Dad says.' Izzy shrugs. 'Things would have been very different then, of course. Apart from anything else, my Dad was with the Green Chapel party that day. If you'd arrested him, I doubt Britain would have a High King now.'

Paul looks thoughtful. He's loyal to his sovereign, obviously – and to the Circle's Head, the Pendragon device of King Arthur. Still, he was Jory Taylor's squire once, and it wasn't a pleasant experience when his Knight turned traitor.

Izzy says, 'How that ties in with Jason leading the Circle during the war, I don't know. Maybe he was holding you back all along. Maybe you would have won without him. Of course it worked out for the best in the end, putting my Dad in charge,' she adds.

Paul's frowning now. Ideas are lining up in his mind like the vans and horse-boxes out on the tarmac in front of the Castle, and he doesn't like the direction they're facing. Slowly, he says, 'If Smith's beating was staged, then I suppose the Chapel still haven't acted against the Circle since the war.'

'Not successfully,' says Izzy. 'But they wanted to kill Oli

Montalban. You know, the old *Sir Gawain and the Green Knight* thing? We think Zara was here with her cronies the night of the pre-Christmas banquet, to try to take poor Oli's head. It's why my Dad sent Olz away to The Hague until midwinter was over.'

'Those swines,' Paul seethes. He doesn't know Oli well, but she seems a pleasant enough kid. 'That's an act of war. If that's true any Knight working with them's a traitor, pure and simple.'

'Too right,' says Izzy tartly. 'Olz happens to be a friend of mine. When people try to behead my friends, I take it personally.'

* * *

Oli Montalban isn't with the Circle's quest team in Windsor. Instead, she's back in London, and still on surveillance duty. In view of the current crisis and its possible international repercussions, the Foreign Office has requested a further day's adjournment at The Hague.

Having spent yesterday standing around St Pancras bored out of her skull, Montalban asked today to be assigned to watching the Irish Embassy at Grosvenor Place, on the loose pretext that her recent contact with the Republic's negotiating team in The Hague might give her additional insight. In actuality her request has just as much to do with the fact that her family's Belgravia townhouse is just a couple of minutes away, so she can pop home for occasional cups of tea.

The Circle's high-tech surveillance vans are in the process of being superseded by the new AR spectacles: while the one Oli's sitting in is still equipped with one of the huge picture-window screens, it's not even switched on. Instead, she and Josh Mahama – a Knight as wet behind the ears as she is, bearing the device of Sir Agravaine, Sir Gawain's less noble, less bright younger brother – wear specs which show them a clear view of the street outside, the augmented reality acting

324

very like those imaginary X-ray glasses that adverts in comics used to try and sell us when I was a kid.

Both Knights are in civvies, the better to nip out for snacks or a comfort break, but their armour and shields are neatly stacked on the van's seats. Like Sir Gawain's pentacle, Agravaine's emblem eschews the Orkney family's gold-on-purple double-headed eagle motif, in his case for a set of three red lions on white which make him look like he's cheering on the England football team.

Shortly after office hours begin – at about the time the Seneschal, his Knights, men-at-arms and horses are in transit from Windsor to the Woodville estate, the Pendragon following with me and Bonnie in the Bentley – Oli blinks to zoom in and stares eagerly at the image in her specs.

She stares for a moment, then jabs a finger. (Fortunately the Knights' specs are set up to allow them to see each other.) 'It's them,' she says.

Although the Embassy's address is on Grosvenor Place, its main entrance is round the corner on Chapel Street, and the van is parked opposite and a little way up the road. In the Knights' field of vision, a muscular blonde in her mid-thirties and a handsome, dark-haired man in his mid-twenties are walking together down the latter street towards the former.

'What, Woodville?' Mahama sounds doubtful. 'Isn't she in Oxfordshire? That's where the Seneschal's gone looking for her.'

'It's a decoy,' Oli asserts with utter confidence. 'Has to be. That's her, look!'

Josh frowns at the image. He says, 'How well d'you know her, Olz?'

'I've met her,' Oli says. 'It's her.' Her voice is only marginally less adamant.

After a false start or two, Josh has brought up MacNeill and Woodville's ID photos from a subsidiary pane. He says, 'She's changed her hair then. And done something to her eyebrows.'

'Tristan's good at disguises, varl,' Oli sighs. ('Varl', like

325

'damz', is from the unholy hybrid of urban slang and cod-medievalism they call Churlish, in which all the streetwise youth are apparently rapping these days.) 'Didn't you *read* the briefing?'

'Him too?' asks Josh, waving a hand at the male half of the couple.

Oli shrugs. 'If you can disguise yourself, you can disguise someone else. Troth.' She compares the moving image with the static one of MacNeill. 'Look, he's got the same nose. Different eyes, yeah, but hello? Contacts exist. It's bloody *them*.'

'Shit,' says Mahama. 'OK, what do we do?'

'We call it in,' says Oli. She knows there are whole squadrons of men-at-arms on standby at the Fastness, itching to jump into vans and screech through the streets like amphetamine-crazed Jeremy Clarksons to wherever they're needed.

''Scuse me, ma'am,' the man-at-arms in her van observes politely, 'but it looks like they're going in.'

The couple have indeed turned at the Embassy doorway, and are climbing up the steps beneath the green, white and orange tricolour.

'Christ, stop them!' Oli yells. Josh flaps for a moment, then throws open the doors of the van, and the Knights rush out in time to see the Embassy doors closing behind the couple's backs.

A passer-by or two looks at them oddly, but most continue on their way.

'So, now we call it in?' says Josh.

'Yes,' snaps Oli. 'No. Fuck it, we're Knights of the Circle.' A surge of excitement runs through her, but she forces herself to consider for a moment.

Then she says, 'D'you think there are actually any Fianna in that building?'

* * *

Meanwhile, Sir David's quest taskforce approaches the hunting-lodge on the Woodville estate. The Pendragon's back in the saloon bar of the Woodville arms, brooding, with Bonnie and me there to watch and – in my case, I shouldn't imagine in hers – hope that the landlord can be induced to start pulling pints soon.

A few miles away, Stafford's troops are deploying themselves across the icy woods as silently as heavily-armoured men, women and horses can, acutely aware that this frozen forest isn't their natural habitat. The hunting on the Woodville estate is limited to game-birds and rabbits these days – it's the main reason the grownups abandoned the lodge – but the mounted Knights still manage to startle a good many of those.

The Circle belongs to the human-made world, you see: the world of straight roads, solid walls and structured communities. They're the root of Arthur's authority, after all. Many Arthurian romances start with the predictable security of Camelot being breached by some uncontrollable force from the outside: Arthur's feasts interrupted by the irruption of a stag pursued by a pack of hunting-dogs, a vision of the Holy Grail, the Green Knight. While technically of course the whole land is Arthur's domain – to the extent that it's sometimes said the land and the king are one – his practical dominion over the natural world is negotiable at best, and its organic unpredictability makes it an uncomfortable environment for his knights. Their horses' hooves may tramp the soil down – in summer, at least, when it's not frozen solid – but new life will spring from it not long after they've passed.

The Green Chapel, on the other hand… the natural world's where their allies are most at home, and green places are their native element, from cultivated timber-forests to scraps of urban wilderness.

For now, though, here, the Circle's Knights have the lodge surrounded, and are closing in. There's clear evidence of occupation: someone's cleared piles of brambles and creeper from the walls, nailed scraps of wood over the empty window frames and even hung a few dead rabbits on a nail outside, ready to be cooked on the camp fire whose remnants are gently smouldering in front of the hut.

The Knights are in position now, backed up by squires and footsoldiers. The Seneschal sits astride his mount facing the door, sword and red-crossed shield in hand, flanked by Parsons and Busman, both of whom insisted – for different reasons – on being here.

It's difficult to imagine the Circle party haven't been noticed by now, but maybe the lovebirds are fast asleep and ready to be surprised. Certainly none of David's people have noticed any attempt to escape or surrender.

The Knights dismount. There's a certain amount of macho hand-signalling of the kind you see soldiers doing in the movies (though it's not so easy with gauntlets on), and then they're moving forward. At his age Stafford doesn't give much for his chances against the device of Sir Tristan, Galahad's bondsman or no, so he sends Paul ahead on the basis that the Lancelot device, if any, will be its match.

Parsons strides forward, halting a couple of metres from the door. There's an etiquette to be followed here, of course, a code of honour. There always is.

'Woodville!' he shouts. 'It's Paul Parsons, with the Knights of the Circle! Come out and face us! Surrender honourably, or face me in combat, it's up to you!'

A stony silence answers him. The Knights' faces are invisible behind their visors, but a number of the men-at-arms are starting to exchange amused looks.

'Woodville, I'm coming in!' At the Seneschal's nod, Parsons kicks the door in. It's newish, fairly sturdy, apparently scavenged from a skip, but the frame its hinges are screwed to is old and crumbling, and it fairly flies inside as his boot strikes it. He marches in, yelling, and a short time later marches out again, visor up, looking furious.

'They've gone,' he says.

Nobody asks if he's sure. It isn't a big building.

Paul's sheathed his sword, but in his prosthetic hand he

carries something else. A weapon, but one made of wood rather than metal. 'I found this,' he spits, 'the other side of the door. Someone had shot it there. Shot it or pinned it.'

The Seneschal takes the arrow. It's a home-made one, the kind the Chapel favour when they're camping away from civilisation, rather than the modern carbon-fibre hunting arrows they use in urban conditions.

He looks at Paul. 'What else?' he asks.

Wordlessly, Paul hands him the paper that he found skewered to the door. Removing his gauntlets, Sir David uncrumples it carefully.

It's a playbill for a pantomime, or at least it's been photoshopped from one. The actors' faces have been crudely replaced with photos of other people, some of them many years out of date.

The text has been tampered with too. Whoever did it didn't considering accurate spelling or grammar to be among their highest priorities, and didn't even take a stab at Zara's surname. It reads:

GREEN CHAPEL PRODUCTIONS PRESENT

TANIA WOODVILL
EWAN MCNEIL
IN
'BABES IN THE WOOD'
WITH
ZARA ZARA AS 'ROBIN HOOD'
SCAR MILLAR AS 'MAID MARION'
JANENE LONG AS 'LITTLE JOHN'
AND INTRODUCING
RON BYRON AS 'THE HUNTSMAN'
'YOU WON'T FIND A BETTER PANTO THIS
WINTER. AND YOU WON'T FIND THIS ONE
NEITHER!'

– WOODLAND TIMES

Sir David very rarely swears, and never in front of his subordinates. '*Bother,*' he says, with feeling.

'Well,' he adds a moment later, 'they haven't lost their sense of humour. That's something, I suppose.'

* * *

It only took the one confrontation with Zara for Olivia Montalban to learn that, as a Knight, physical courage really isn't her forte. It's only now that she's coming to understand what that is – and it has nothing to do with the Gawain device.

She bottled out in the end and tried to put a call through to Sir David, only to be told by his voicemail that he was busy on a quest and to leave a message. In desperation (though pettishly ignoring the fact that Freddie Obote and Stephen Mukherjee, for two, were still at the Fastness and available to advise a young Knight in a fix) she tried the High King directly, but found his tablet rejecting incoming calls.

(In fact he's set it to only accept requests from David for the duration: this was after taking a call from Kinsey, furious as ever that the Device Squad's been cut out of the final coup de grace when they did so much of the legwork. He smoothed it over with his habitual diplomacy, but his distraction was obvious.)

At this point Oli gave in to the inevitable. Insisting to Josh that Woodville was in the Irish Embassy at that very moment, spilling all the Circle's operational secrets over the phone to the mac Cumhail, she psyched herself into phoning the Fastness again, exercising her Knightly authority, and summoning four vanloads of men-at-arms to the junction of Grosvenor Place and Chapel Street immediately. While they arrived, Montalban and Mahama suited up.

It was once they got inside that everything went horrifically wrong. The Embassy's security staff were surprisingly – or perhaps not, given relations between their home and host nations for these past fourteen years – well-prepared, and unwilling to cede control of their reception area without a fight. They hadn't missed the buildup of anonymous-looking vans on the street outside, and when Oli sent Mahama in with the first wave of men-at-arms, they were ready and waiting.

Technically Oli should – for a meaning of 'should' that allows attacking a foreign embassy in the first place to be in any way OK – have led the men-at-arms in herself. Instead she held back until it became clear that taking control of reception wasn't going to be the walkover she'd hoped for.

She hopes the Irish were the first to open fire – certainly the men-at-arms have been trained not to be – but at this stage it scarcely makes a difference. Just at the moment, gunfire's bellowing and bullets screaming around the Embassy lobby as the Circle troops and the Embassy security try to shoot the hell out of each other.

The staff have the benefit of the reception desk as shelter, so the men-at-arms are exposed, strung out across the lobby's entrance. The Irish are making a strategic withdrawal through a security door which gives onto the rest of the embassy. Oli told the men-at-arms to cover all the possible exits from the premises, and for now can only hope they got that right.

Panicking ever more strenuously now, Oli prepares to make a run for the door when the last of the security staff is through, before it can swing closed. That plan takes an abrupt about-turn, though, as someone else strides through it and stands, firmly blocking access, as the last of them make their escape.

It's a Fiann, a device-bearing agent of the Children of Oisín. He wears modern armour of an unfamiliar design, and is wielding a ceramic-tipped ergonomic-handled spear and a round tactical shield with a ring of bulletproof glass.

This answers Oli's question of earlier, of course.

The Irishman gives vent to a deep, droning bellow (which Oli has neither the knowledge nor the leisure to recognise as the ancient Celtic battle-cry, the Dord Fiann), and charges in the direction of the nearest device-bearer, the luckless Josh. Montalban nudges the sergeant-at-arms and flaps a hand at the rapidly-closing security door, before turning her attention to the battle.

It's clear the Fiann knows his enemy: his first spear-thrust finds the vulnerable point in the left shoulder of Mahama's armour, eliciting an impressive spurt of blood. Josh swipes desperately at the man, but the Fiann's spear is longer than a Knight's sword, and he only succeeds in clattering the point against the man's shield.

He rallies quickly. Sir Agravaine may not have been the brightest spark in the Orkney family tinder-box, but fighting was one thing he did know how to do. As the Child of Oisín withdraws his spear for another jab, Mahama dives in under it and slices at the man's right legs. Unfortunately he's assuming that the Fianna armour has the same vulnerabilities as the Knights', and his blade slides harmlessly off the protective knee-plate.

Montalban watches carefully, excused from fighting for the moment by her honourable obligation to respect the boundaries of single combat. This contest between the men who must be considered for present purposes the champions of Britain and Ireland is giving her the opportunity to watch the Fiann in action, and to diagnose exactly where his armour's weak spots may be.

Meanwhile, the Circle troops have wedged the door open and will be spreading out into the ground floor of the Embassy, hopefully encountering less resistance. Those admin and clerical staff who successfully evacuated through the rear and into neighbouring premises have already – she hopes – been rounded up by the remaining men-at-arms.

Oli knows she doesn't have long to bring this to a conclusion. It won't be long before the more experienced Knights still at the Fastness arrive on the heels of the men-at-arms, and take charge of the situation. Josh is bleeding from several of his joints now, and from a graze to his neck. He's struggling on like the trouper Agravaine is, but he's evidently flagging.

Moving carefully so as not to draw the Fiann's attention,

Montalban lifts a Webley 2020 from a fallen man-at-arms. As the Irishman makes another stab at poor Mahama – this time his sword-arm – she steps up carefully behind the Fiann, places the barrel on his neck directly beneath the occiput, and pulls the trigger.

The sub-machine gun shudders and the man groans and collapses, leaking red fluid from his helmet, twitching violently. Before him, Josh Mahama's clutching at the right elbow of his armour, which is all that's holding his arm together after the Irishman's last spear-thrust.

Oli Montalban takes a shuddering sigh, pushes her visor up and surveys the wreckage.

* * *

With the Seneschal and the High King incommunicado except to one another, the staff at Windsor have to call my mobile and ask me to put the Pendragon on. I resist strenuously, of course, until they tell me what's happened. Which is how, when the Seneschal and his troops arrive back at the Woodville Arms, they learn that the long-feared war with NATO has suddenly become all but inevitable.

'I c-can only apologise, my lord,' says Sir David. His face is ashen. 'Montalban was under my c-command. You'll have my resignation as soon as I return to the Fastness.'

The Foreign Office must have briefed Montalban pretty thoroughly for her part in the Hague summit, but they obviously didn't have time to mention in passing that an attack against a foreign embassy in one's own country is traditionally considered, if not necessarily an act of war, then at the very least a warmly-worded invitation to one. With the Irish people naturally incensed at this crime against their civilians, the Taoiseach and the Dáil are no longer in a position to stand in the way of President Gomez and her hawks in the USA – and with Ireland's objections swept away, our Scandinavian allies are unlikely to prevent the rest of NATO from following.

'Nonsense,' Jory snaps. 'How is this your fault? And you resigning might satisfy the Irish, but it's hardly going to placate Gomez. I'm going to need you more than ever now.'

It appears Oli realises what she's done, at least – she fled the moment the Embassy was secure, giving a surprised sergeant-at-arms command of the quest for the few minutes it took Mukherjee and Obote to arrive at the scene.

'I don't understand how Montalban can have been so stupid,' David says now. 'The Gawain device can be headstrong, but…'

In total, seven men-at-arms and four Embassy staff are dead, including the Fiann, Eugene Molloy. It will later transpire that Molloy was the *aithgin* of Fianchad, a minor Fianna, one of Fionn mac Cumhail's six doorkeepers. Assigned to the Embassy's security team some years ago, he slipped under the Circle's radar because of Fianchad's relative obscurity – but Molloy himself trained at Little Creek, Virginia with the US Navy Seals, as part of a 'cultural exchange' between the Children of Oisín and the Founding Frontiersmen. Montalban and Mahama may have been Knights of the Circle, but their inexperience meant Molloy had them hopelessly outclassed. Only Oli's use of a projectile weapon against an otherwise occupied enemy allowed her to defeat him at all – a level of treachery and dishonour that, for the bearer of the Gawain device, is so out of character as to be virtually a contradiction in terms.

'Not this headstrong,' Jory replies. 'This can't have been Gawain. This was Montalban's own decision. We need to find and arrest her urgently, just like Woodville. Oh God,' he wonders in sudden realisation, 'how am I going to tell Izzy her best friend's started a war?'

Among the survivors at the Embassy are a tourist couple from Limerick. The man, dark-haired and about ten years younger than his blonde girlfriend, claims he lost his passport in a mugging last night, and that she persuaded him to visit the Embassy this morning. Obote, Mukherjee and others who've met them confirm that the pair bear only a fleeting resemblance to Woodville and MacNeill.

'For Christ's sake,' the High King groans now, as news of Ireland's and her allies' outraged reactions begin to reach us. 'This is exactly what I've spent the past sixteen years trying to avoid.'

Personally I wonder whether he couldn't have avoided it better by not pissing off the neighbours in the first place, but – as usual these days – I don't say so.

Amidst all the stress and excitement and alarm, nobody really has much attention to spare when the news comes through, from a hospital in Worcestershire, that Sir Charles Raymond died on the operating table following an adverse reaction to his anaesthetic. With all the diplomacy and brinkmanship, the hurried defensive planning and the hasty drafting of the High King's address informing the nation that we're at war, there's too much else going on for any of us to care.

18. FRIAR TUCK

It's getting on for noon by the time Tania and Eoin emerge from the tent they've been loaned at the Green Chapel camp. Both have that glow of serene smugness that you only ever see surrounding teenage missionaries and newly-in-love couples who've just engaged in a protracted and strenuous session of intimate relations.

'Nice of you to join us.' Janene Long's voice greets them from above. 'Much longer and we'd've sent a search party in.' Little John's ally is sitting on a branch of a tree, her green hood down across her shoulders, her bow lying casually across her knees.

Eoin looks up and blushes prettily, but Tania retains her cool. 'Something we can help you with, Long?' She softens the sally with a smile. They really do owe these people, after all, and it's not as if she doesn't have smiles to spare right now. Interruptions aside, for the past day she and Eoin have been getting to know one another as never before, and the passion which germinated in that Fastness interview room has deepened and spread like the roots of the trees surrounding them.

'Summat you should see,' Janene says as she drops to the icy ground.

She leads the way from the couple's love-nest – which has been pitched a tactful distance from the main encampment, to minimise disturbance from nocturnal shrieks and moans – to the main collection of tents and its central ring of frost-crisped grass.

The core members of the Green Chapel are already there – the same group who turned up at the Woodville estate's hunting-lodge in the small hours of the morning, warned Tania and Eoin that the Circle were closing in on them, and spirited them away to their pre-prepared accommodation here. Some of them Tania knows of from her Circle briefings; others she's only learned about today. Of the major devices from the Robin Hood mythos, only Alan a'Dale and Friar Tuck are, for obvious reasons, absent.

As quite often happens, they're arguing.

'What I'm saying – it changes things, is all,' says Jo (no surname given), the woman pointed out to Woodville as the Saracen's ally. She's white, sounds British and doesn't dress like a Muslim: Tania's working guess is that she may be Romany.

'Well, *I* can't see what it changes,' replies HazMat (full name Hannah Matthews), the young Welsh ally of Much the Miller's Son. 'What's it matter to us if Taylor and the Circle get their arses kicked? That's what we've been waiting for, innit?'

'It don't change owt,' says Chaz (no surname given; born Geraldine Coates if Tania recalls the briefings correctly, but everyone's quite clear that he's a he now). His identity as Will Scarlet's ally is plain from his crimson hoodie. 'The Circle and the Fianna are as bad as each other, far as we're concerned.'

'Maybe,' puts in Marianne 'Scar' Millar, Maid Marian's avatar. 'But who's our enemy and who's the enemy of our fucking enemy, eh?'

She scowls at the couple in greeting. 'Morning all,' says Eoin cheerily.

'Hello, you two.' It's Ron Byron, the wildcard. He wears a hoodie like the others, brown in his case. His antlers are discarded on a low camping-table nearby, where they branch like an unhung trophy. 'We're determining in with which party we should throw our lot, for the duration of the coming hostilities.'

'Morning,' says Tania. 'What hostilities would these be, then?'

'You haven't heard?' That's the Robin Hood ally herself, Zara. Last night she was full of merry quips; this morning she seems uncharacteristically sour. 'Of course. You've been too busy.' She smiles wryly at that, at least. 'Well, make the most of it, children. While you've been in bed, the rest of the world has got a bit less *Romeo and Juliet* and a lot more *Troilus and Cressida.*'

Several faces frown, or stare blankly at her. Zara tuts. 'For pity's sake, it's Shakespeare. You people are so ignorant of your own culture. Romeo and Juliet came from opposite sides of a feud. Troilus and Cressida were on opposite sides during a *war.*'

'Yeah?' Eoin asks. 'So who's the Greek and who's the Trojan?' Tania looks at him in surprise, and he says, 'Hey darling, I'm not just a devilishly handsome face.'

'Of course you're not,' she says with a wink. Then, 'Wait though. The Circle and the Fianna are at *war?* Over *us?*' She glances at the tablet lying on Ron's lap, thinking that she's going to need some pretty definitive proof of this. Kind though their hosts have been so far, there's always a possibility that *rescuers* might prove to be a euphemism for *captors.*

'If anything,' says Ron, seizing his chance to reoccupy the centre of attention, 'that understates the case. Though you two aren't precisely the *casus belli.* While you played your part in the causative cascade, the most proximate provocation was one of your erstwhile comrades-in-arms storming the Irish Embassy and killing some Fiann or other.'

'The *Embassy?*' Eoin looks shocked. 'Jesus. I knew the Circle could be bastards enough when they tried. I never thought they'd do a thing like that.'

Zara says, 'We don't think the Circle authorised it. In fact, we met the young Knight who did it a fortnight ago. I didn't think she was very stable then. But your people are taking it as a deliberate act.'

Noticing Tania's preoccupation with the tablet, Ron passes it to her. 'Be my guest,' he says.

She quickly goes to the BBC website and opens up a few links.

The Taoiseach has described the incident as a 'brutal and unprovoked' attack...

President Gomez has spoken out against the 'illegitimate and oppressive Pendragonist regime'...

A spokesman for the ex-Duke of Cornwall has condemned...

After the High King's message to the nation, the Republic of Scotland has moved to distance itself...

NATO General Alec Kreiss, a veteran member of the Founding Frontiersmen, said, 'We owe it to the British people...'

'Oh my fuck,' she says slowly. 'This is the real deal. It'll be like the War of the Devices with the whole world piling in. This could destroy everything the High King's achieved.'

There's an uncomfortable silence. Then Ron drawls, 'A delectable enough prospect, from our coign of vantage. This country's squirmed under the sabatons of that devicial despot for too long already. This is our opportunity to fuck our lord and monster over, not just royally but *imperially*.'

Tania notices Janene looking uneasy, and Scar's scowl deepens slightly. Everyone else, Eoin included, seems to be hanging on Ron's words.

'So we sign up where?' asks Jo.

'Sounds good to me,' says HazMat. 'Well, if you're saying what I think you're saying, I can never bloody tell.'

(If anyone here was able to consult Malory, she'd have told them that Ron's polysyllabic prolixity is a symptom of a serious devicial psychosis. But nobody in the Chapel's had direct contact with Malory in years.)

'What *are* you saying, Ron?' Janene asks cautiously. 'That we should help the Irish soldiers, like? That doesn't sound like what we should be about at all.'

'Janene,' says Ron. He stands. 'Janene, Janene, Janene, Janene, to misquote the divine Dolly.' He reaches for his antlers. Rather than putting them on, though, he twirls them gently in his hands. 'I refer you to the British authorities' lamentable history with our Irish neighbours.' He acknowledges Eoin with a nod. 'It would, I reckon, be risible in the extreme to designate any retaliatory belligerence under such circumstances an act of *aggression*. On the contrary, we should consider it a campaign of liberation, from the colonial menace of British suzerainty that's pervaded the Pendragon's reign no less than those of his insalubrious predecessors, Oliver Cromwell and William of Orange.'

'Oh aye,' says Scar, once she's sure he's finished. 'Aye, the Irish have got a legitimate grievance. Maybe the French too, though I don't think people in Brittany'd say so. But how about the others, eh? How about the Germans and Spanish and Luxemburgers? How about the fucking Yanks? You help NATO kick HK out, you're asking the Frontiersmen to come marching in and take over the country. You fancy living in the fifty-fucking-first state, Ron? 'Cause I don't think the American Dream applies to us anarchist freedom fighters.'

Ron glares at her. He reaches out for his antlers, lifts and places them on top of his head. 'We fight,' he declaims, visibly containing the urge to excess verbiage, 'against the Pendragon. We fight kings. Just like we've always done, just as we always will. We topple Jordan Taylor from his place of unearned, unwarranted authority – and if the Americans set up a fresh tyrant in his stead, we topple them too. If President

Gomez relocates to Buckingham Palace, then we topple her, and all. I say bring them on.'

'Yeah, sure,' a new voice says. 'And if Jesus Christ himself turns up draped in Old Glory and toting an M16, you'll go buy some wood and nails. You're full of shit, Ron.'

Tania turns in shock (as, she half-notices, do Zara, Scar, Janene and Ron) to see that the only major Merry Man now missing from the assembly is – well, me.

* * *

'You were entrusted to safeguard our perimeter!' Ron snarls at Lee and Ahmed, who've emerged, shamefaced, behind the new arrival. 'What were you doing, reading Proust?'

'Yeah, Ron,' says Lee, presumably not to that last bit. 'But it's *Rev*.'

Zara snaps, 'Is anyone else with him?' The pair's eyes widen and they scurry off back into the trees. 'Idiots,' she mutters.

'I came alone,' sighs Rev Cantrell. 'As gay men my age so often have to. Za, if you really think I'd sell you out, you don't know me like you did.' He's wearing faded jeans and an old leather jacket, with a fluffy khaki angora scarf against the cold. An unlit cigarette dangles from his lip.

'So what the coitus are you doing here?' Ron wants to know.

'Wanted a word with you all,' Rev says. 'About that little incident with Squig, at first, but events kind of overtook me en route. Did I hear you trying to persuade these good people to throw their weight behind an army of occupation, Ron?'

'Who is this get?' asks Chaz aggressively.

'This is Rev,' says Janene. 'He's one of us. Rev, this is Chaz. And Jo, and HazMat,' she adds, gesturing. 'And Eoin. Reckon you already know Tania, right?'

'Tania,' says Rev, with a friendly nod. 'I'm glad you guys are safe.' He sounds perfectly sincere.

'Don't get too friendly,' Zara says coldly. 'Rev was one

341

of us once, Janene. Not any more. These days he's the King's man, aren't you Rev?'

'Well, that's a way of looking at it, sure,' Rev says. 'Another's this: ten years ago we were all King's men. Yeah, your allies too,' he adds, forestalling the objections of Jo, Chaz and HazMat. 'It's not me that's changed. And it's not me,' he adds, more emphatically, 'who's talking about backing Uncle Sam against the British people now. Are you out of your mind, Ron?'

'It's worth it if it brings about the demise of that autocrat,' Ron insists again.

'Yeah?' Cantrell snorts. 'Tell that to people in Iraq and Afghanistan.'

Ron says, 'Whatever eventuates later, we can tackle later.'

'Why *are* you here, Rev?' Scar asks. 'Did you come to tell us what HK wants us to do? That's not gonna win you back any friends.'

'He doesn't even know I'm here,' says Rev easily. 'Well… I guess he may have realised by now, if he doesn't have other things on his mind. I came for us, though, not him.'

'So what do *you* think we should do, Rev?' Janene asks.

'Oh that's right, ask a priest,' sneers Ron. 'He's as moribund and insubstantial as his dogmas.'

'Good question, kid,' Cantrell tells Janene, ignoring Ron. 'Thing is, this isn't about the Chapel and the Circle any more. It's not even about the Circle and the Children of Oisín. This is about defending the allies and devices of Britain from an invasion.

'Listen,' he says, raising his voice. 'Most of you know I'm not from around these parts, and if you don't you'll have guessed. But I've lived in Britain longer than a lot of you have been alive, and let me tell you I *love* this country. Don't get me wrong, the USA's fine, but I don't feel any need to go back there. I'm proud to call this my country now, whoever it's run by. I wouldn't try to speak for Zara, but I'm guessing she feels similarly, huh Za?'

Zara nods curtly.

342

Rev says, 'The Circle... they can be domineering fucks at times, but they're *our* domineering fucks. The Pendragon may be a high-handed bastard, but he's *our* high-handed bastard. The same land, the same people, who produced King Arthur and Sir Lancelot and Sir Gawain and all those others, also produced Robin Hood and Maid Marian and Friar Tuck and Little John. Whatever the allies use instead of flesh and blood, we share it with the Circle. We're *family*.

'That doesn't mean I've got anything against the Irish,' he goes on, with a wink at Eoin. 'Sweet guys, a lot of them, if you can get past that Catholic guilt – and in my day I almost always could. They're family too, kind of – if that doesn't sound too incestuous to you guys,' he adds, to Tania's discomfiture. 'Whatever it was possessed Oli Montalban to kill those poor bastards at the Embassy – and believe me, she wasn't working for HK or the Circle – they've got a right to be pissed about it.

'But NATO?' he asks. 'The Frontiersmen? General Alec fucking Kreiss? They've been gunning for the Pendragon for *years*. They're not interested in Irish lives – they care that the King Arthur device has turned Britain into something they can't control. They want to occupy this land and subjugate it, process and sanitise our myth like Hollywood's always done. Before you know our folklore will be all cute dragons and talking unicorns, and there'll be no going back from that.'

'He's spouting drivel,' Ron insists loudly. 'Out of his fundament, no less. All this prognostication disregards our current predicament. All right, perchance we'll be compelled eventually to shore up the polity against these occupiers – but let's use them to our furtherance first. Let them break the Pendragon's back for us. We can take charge of the resultant demotic uprising, and drive them from these isles. But let's not transpose the two priorities, eh?'

Cantrell's shaking his head. 'Jesus, Ron,' he says sadly. 'I don't know what these guys put in your head, but I sure as hell hope we can get it out.

'Listen,' he says again. 'You people don't know the

343

Frontiersmen. OK, that's not so surprising – they're a secretive bunch. This Kreiss has outed himself as one of them, but that's to boost morale among his NATO troops. You're going up against myths, it's good to know you've got a legend leading your side, even if it's only a really big lumberjack.

'But guys,' he says, 'I know the Frontiersmen. And the reality's not pretty. In all the time you've known me, have I told any of you why I left the States?'

It's something I've often wondered, as it happens, but of course I'm not there to hear it.

* * *

It seems Franklin Cantrell was born in San Francisco in 1958, to a young couple called Tom and Martha Cantrell. Tom Cantrell was an aspiring jazz saxophonist, while Martha was a poet in the beat scene. When the hippie movement started blossoming across the city in the mid-60s, both Cantrells embraced it with their arms wide – and they carried their son right along with them. By the age of ten, young Frankie had attended some early Grateful Dead and Jefferson Airplane concerts, met his mother's idol Allen Ginsberg, and watched with wary fascination as his parents freed themselves of their bourgeois inhibitions through the liberal application of cannabis and lysergic acid diethylamide.

(It's not entirely surprising, really, that he'd turn to the Episcopal Church in his teens and twenties, or that he'd return in later life to a freer, more anarchic lifestyle. But all that came later.)

Before Frankie reached puberty – though well after he realised that, like a number of his parents' friends, his interest in the opposite sex would always remain strictly platonic – his family had been pulled into the orbit of Eulalie Goldenchild, the so-called 'Black Queen of the Upper Haight'. Though there were certainly hippies of colour, it was rare for an African-American woman to be so prominent in the scene

344

as Eulalie: tall, charismatic, a friend at different times to Malcolm X and Martin Luther King (although she showed little deference to either of their faiths), she preached not only the staples of free love and psychedelically-enhanced mysticism, but a racial equality and a fierce feminism which contemptuously dismissed the idea that different kinds of people might have separate roles or skill-sets. Her followers not only attended concerts and love-ins, but regularly bussed eastward to joint marches and demos in the Jim Crow states.

In the Haight-Ashbury house bequeathed to her by a rich supporter and sometime lover, Eulalie assembled a coterie of poets, musicians, revolutionaries and psychonauts who reminded one underground newspaper of a medieval court, earning her that regal nickname. Many of them were black, a few Asian or Native American, but many too were white – and among them were the Cantrells, all three of whom adored her. Eulalie, free yet always capricious in her physical affections, reciprocated Tom and Martha's ardour sparingly, but majestically, and she made young Frankie her particular favourite.

Frankie worshipped her with all the fervour he'd later bring to bear to his rather eccentric perception of God: he thrilled in her beauty and basked in her indulgence, drinking in the torrent of ideas and art that she channelled around her.

According to the histories of hippie-era San Francisco, it was the SFPD's Narcotics Division whose raid in 1969 put an end to the Black Queen's reign, and incidentally propelled Frankie Cantrell into the care of his straitlaced, religious-minded aunt and uncle in San Diego. Few have wondered why Goldenchild's in particular should have been singled out from the many drug-using communes in the neighbourhood, but some conspiracy-minded researchers have suggested something more sinister, a CIA propaganda operation to shut down a high-profile nest of radical subversives. For them, Eulalie would have represented a moral weak spot in the network of black civil rights activists, and a more acceptable target than her paler hippie peers.

It may indeed be that the CIA were involved. But none of these historians have yet identified the true principals of the raid on the Black Queen's court – and up to now, Franklin Cantrell was the only person living who knew its cause.

One day when each of them, for different reasons, had become bored with the antics of her hangers-on, Eulalie had taken Frankie aside and shown him one of her greatest treasures: an old book bound in blue leather and embossed in gold. She read to him from it the story of a beautiful black woman called Calafia, the caliph of the Amazons, who sent her griffins to intervene in the siege of Constantinople, and fell in love with a Christian knight.

'It's just a story,' Eulalie told Frankie. 'I read it first when I was no older than you. Calafia was never real, but that legend of hers sure lasted. When some Spanish people were sailing round the West Coast and found what they thought was an island here, they named it *California*, just like her homeland.'

Ten-year-old Frankie was impressed. Even then, he had a sharp eye for a mythic parallel, though his theology was kind of eclectic. He asked, 'Eulalie, are you Queen Calafia's reincarnation?'

Eulalie granted him a secret smile. 'Honey, how could someone who never lived be reincarnated?' she asked, and refused to say any more.

They came for her a few weeks later, as they do eventually for all the legends that refuse to conform to the America they founded. The heroes of the establishment of the United States, the Agents of Benjamin Franklin and Paul Revere, Davy Crockett and Daniel Boone, Wyatt Earp and Bill Hickok; these upright white men, sheriffs and lawmen, alert for any encroachment on their conceptual frontier; they came for Calafia and her followers as they had for the other deviants, for Lizzie Borden and Belle Starr, for John the Conqueror the trickster slave, for Geronimo and Sitting Bull, Aunt Nancy and Coyote. They came with laws and statues, guns and badges, cuffs and paddy-wagons; and in one night they broke the power of the Queen of California.

They took her for possession and use of drugs, for civil disobedience and property damage, and – most devastatingly – for fraud. They proved, to a court's satisfaction and with the relatives' collusion, that her dead benefactor had never meant to leave her his house, and that it should belong to some distant cousins of his. They confiscated her assets, imprisoned her followers and impounded all her art and books.

Three months later – her wealth gone, her court scattered, stripped of all her dignity, treated as the chattel that her ancestors had been taken for – Eulalie Goldenchild took her own life in the medical wing of the California women's prison.

* * *

Cantrell sighs. 'I won't bore you with the details of my personal journey after that, 'cause it was complicated, and a lot of it was kind of dull even at the time. But I knew I couldn't stay in the States. I may not have known the name "Founding Frontiersmen" back then, but I knew the government had killed my best friend just 'cause she was different, and I knew I was different too. By the time I was ordained in the Christian church I was seriously looking into missionary work in Haiti, because of how I'd heard voodoo let a person ally themselves with a spirit out of folklore. That sounded like something I could relate to.

'Then I heard something else… from Mom, as it happens. When Dad got out of jail he kept his hair short and got taken on as a bank clerk in Sacramento, but Mom went right back to the hippie scene. At the first Burning Man festival she got talking to this woman who'd met the Stones at Altamont in '69. It seems they'd told her that they knew this guy who'd told *them* the ghosts of Robin Hood and his Merry Men were alive and active here in England.'

He smiles. 'Bottom line is, if our friend Brian hadn't

been so eager to impress his rockstar buddies, I wouldn't be here today.'

* * *

'Oh, very affecting,' Ron sneers after a short silence. 'Very fucking poignant. And on the basis of your suspiciously apposite autobiographical ramblings we're supposed to jump back into bed with Taylor, are we? Because some Frontiersmen sixty years ago expunged some arabesque Conquistador fable nobody's heard of, we're supposed to stop them bringing down King Arthur?'

Rev shakes his head. 'Nobody hearing of her was the whole idea, Ron. Wiping out the writing in the margins is what they do. What d'you think Herne the Hunter is to them? Come to that, what d'you think Robin Hood is? A thief, an agitator, a terrorist. A commie, and what's more a commie who hangs out with Muslims. Hey – he wears skins too, hunts with arrows, camps in a forest – sounds kind of *tribal*, don't you think? You give those fuckers a foothold here in Britain, and in a generation we'll all be living on reservations.'

There's some nodding of heads going on by now. Over the past few years the Chapel have got used to Ron's logorrhoeic rhetoric, and Cantrell's straight talking's coming as a breath of fresh air. He's always been a powerful preacher, and in this instance he's got a compelling point.

Ron looks around in scorn. 'You're not permitting this old fart to sway you, are you? He doesn't know his cubital hinge from his gluteus maximus. Which is he, Green Chapel or Circle? Is it Robin Hood he cares about, or this Calafia woman? Is he even Friar Tuck any more, or does he think he's some pound-shop Merlin now? The dichotomies are fucking excoriating.'

Zara says, 'If all you can say is abuse, Ron –'

'Oh, I've got more to declare than that,' says Ron. 'A whole cavalcade of more. I speak for Herne the Hunter in this. You put the cure of the Chapel's souls in his hands, remember? His and mine. And he says that the land itself is ailing. It's been maimed and mutilated by that tinpot despot. The only way to rectify that abuse is with an *oblation*. It's the oldest rubric in the codex: if the king fails the people, the people must sacrifice the king.'

'Christ, is *that* what this is about?' groans Scar. 'More pagan shite?'

'It's mandatory,' Ron insists. 'We rub his blood into the sickly weal. Only with the decanted corpuscles of a monarch can the land be revivified.'

There's a long silence, during which Tania in particular takes great care not to call herself to anyone's attention. Then Zara says, 'I believe I agree with Scar. Our decision must be based in something more solid than magical ritual.'

'Yeah, because Herne knows all about kings, huh Ron?' Rev suggests. 'A king at Windsor had him hanged, after all. I'll bet he wants revenge for that. He just wants to see the Pendragon run, am I right? To make him the quarry for his hunt? Any blood-soaked pagan ritual takes a back seat to his revenge.'

'Immaterial,' Ron snaps. 'The propitiation's indispensable. If the Green Chapel won't embrace that objective, Herne will endorse whoever will. Can you afford to lose us, Zara? Me and Herne?'

Zara takes a moment to survey her comrades-in-arms. Chaz, Jo and HazMat, the new blood, are looking upset and conflicted. They're used to accepting what Ron says without reservation, but this wild talk of sacrifice is something else. Besides, Cantrell's story affected them as much as anyone. Janene is glaring disgustedly at Ron, so her opinion's clear. Scar's face is always less expressive, but as she meets her lover's gaze she gives her a sharp nod. Lee and Ahmed, who've returned from the forest during Rev's story, are looking equally resolved.

Zara nods quickly to herself, then says, 'Ron, what you do is yours to decide. The Green Chapel fight to defend Britain. Not because we don't support the Irish against the Circle, but because this is the wrong way to resolve the question. With the Frontiersmen on their way, we must unite against the greater threat. Refusing that because of your personal religious beliefs is your choice: for us to do it with you would be suicidal. If you stay we'll be glad of your guidance. Leave if you want to, but if you join the enemy then we will fight you.'

It's common sense rather than visionary rabble-rousing, but it gets her a ragged surge of applause even so.

'You're being fatuous, Zara.' Ron knows he's beaten. He stares around the straggly circle of faces, but finds no solace in them. 'This... is distinctly injudicious. Herne can be... volatile. Vindictive. Inexorable. He's a perilous adversary to contend with.'

'Stay, Ron,' Cantrell says, his voice full of compassion for the lad he once knew. 'Please. This Herne thing's done a number on you worse than any ally I've seen, but maybe we can help. There must be some way we can find to send it back wherever the hell it came from.'

Ron glares at him, all words forgotten now, then dips his head and spits at Cantrell's feet. The he turns and stalks away into the naked forest, antlers bobbing until they're lost among the branches.

* * *

'So what about us?' Eoin MacNeill asks the ensuing silence. 'Will you tell High King Jordan we're with the Chapel, Rev? Will you send Knights here to drag us back?'

'They already know we took you,' Janene offers. 'They just don't know where.'

'They know?' Tania's alarmed. 'How?'

'We left a note,' Zara admits. 'A boast.' She shrugs. 'It's what Robin Hood would have done.'

'Oh great,' says Eoin. 'So now all they need to do is search every wood in southern England for a great big camp of people?'

'It's harder than you might think,' says Tania. 'But even so...'

'If they were onto us, we'd know,' says Scar. 'Same way we knew they were onto you. We've got a guy who tells us stuff.'

Eoin persists. 'But if Rev tells the High King where he's been ...'

'We move on,' Zara says calmly. 'We've done it many times before.'

'Could be wise,' Rev Cantrell says. 'But don't on my account. I won't be telling HK anything. My place is here now with all of you, if you'll have me. I hear you have a vacancy for a holy man.'

Zara smiles. 'The selection process is quite rigorous. You may not make the grade.' Her relief at being rid of Ron and the malignant device inside him is palpable.

Tania, meanwhile, is still staring at the tablet Ron left behind when he stalked off.

Eurostar services have been suspended as the army blockades the Channel Tunnel at Dover...

Irish units under Fianna command are reported to be massing on the Ulster border...

There have been reports of an exchange of fire between NATO's North Atlantic fleet and the Royal Navy...

As RAF fighters scrambled to shoot down unmanned spy planes encroaching on UK airspace...

The Circle has called up its reservist men-at-arms and all retired Knights...

'I should go back,' she blurts out suddenly.
Most people stare at her, though more than one pair

351

of eyes is rolled. Eoin looks betrayed. 'What are you talking about?' he demands. 'We only just got here.'

Woodville gestures at the screen. 'They'll whack us with everything they've got, and that includes devs. Fianna, Frontiersmen, Paladins... the Head's going to need his best Knights. Sir Gawain's gone rogue, Sir Lancelot has a disability, Sir Galahad's nearly sixty. The High King needs Sir Tristan.'

'The *country* needs Sir Tristan, not the High King,' Cantrell says. 'As far as the Circle's concerned, you've gone rogue yourself. You go back to the Fastness now, they'll give you no end of grief, maybe a court martial. The Circle does love its honour code, even in wartime. Stay here with us and you can fight freely, outside the Circle's code if you can stand to. You still feel guilty once all this is over, you can give yourself up then. Though why you'd do that, with this handsome guy to think of, I can't imagine.'

He claps Eoin heartily on the back, then transfixes Woodville with a look. 'That's if you're ready to make it count,' he says. 'If you're too busy playing the lovesick teen, I'll put that call through to Windsor now.'

Tania lets out a breath. 'Oh,' she says, 'it'll count, Rev. You have my word as a Knight.'

She wonders as she says it just how much, now she's betrayed her vows to the High King and the Circle, her word as a Knight might be worth.

19. SIR LANCELOT

'We have a leak, sir.' Paul Parsons has always had a gift for stating the obvious. 'Someone with history with the Green Chapel. Woodville's had nothing to do with them in the past – I don't think she could have contacted them in a day, do you? Someone in the Circle let them in on the details of our quest. Or the Device Squad, I suppose,' he concedes.

Sir David Stafford purses his lips. 'You're assuming that note was genuine,' he points out. 'It could have been faked to throw us off the scent. Woodville and MacNeill might not be with the Chapel. They might never have been in that lodge.'

The two of them are in the Seneschal's office in the Fastness keep. Crisp winter sunlight diffuses in through the glass roof and lights up the white cliffs of paperwork in his in-tray. (Despite all modernising drives, the Circle still insist on using paper for secure admin – a hopelessly archaic approach which just happens to align with the recommended best practice for keeping data secure. It's certainly looking rather shrewd as NATO forces with access to data-killing EMP weaponry prepare for an invasion.)

Paul's sceptical. 'Anyone on the Woodville estate would have been able to spell the family name, surely. No sir, that poster felt real to me. It's just the sort of childish one-upmanship the Chapel revel in.'

'Well, even so,' says David, reserving judgement on the

evidential value of Paul's feelings, 'we've other things to worry about at present. With Woodville and Montalban out there, our intelligence is already thoroughly compromised.'

The Circle's quest to trace Oli has been unfruitful so far, although the resources they've been able to spare have been understandably limited. Some of the more hysterical Knights are suggesting that she, too, has gone to the Green Chapel; that the Chapel are now operating an underground railroad smuggling rogue Knights out of the country. Quite where they might be sending them, that would take both a Fianna sympathiser and the butcher of the Irish Embassy, is a point of further contention.

'Respectfully, sir,' says Paul, 'I disagree. This is a major security breach, and we can't afford even one of those at present. Request permission to investigate.' Jason Smith's still under the High King's protection, and the Seneschal's loyalty to the Head is unimpeachable. For the moment he doesn't want to tell Sir David what he thinks he knows.

'Permission denied.' Sir David shakes his head sympathetically. 'I'm sorry Paul, but you're one of our best remaining Knights.' (He'd be *the* best, easily, if it wasn't for his hand; as it is, Percival's bondsman Cornish has the edge.) 'We need you combat-ready now, not wasting your talents on investigative work. Leave the Chief Superintendent to do her job while we do ours.'

'But sir...' As yet Parsons can't quite articulate, even to himself, his sense that this whole debacle, domestic as well as global, could still be averted if only... well, *something*. As I say, he can't articulate it. It's there, though, a shape hanging in his mind ready for the light of realisation that will eventually illuminate it.

He's aware he sounds like a whining child, though, so he tries one last gambit. 'With respect, sir, Kinsey doesn't have the whole picture.'

The Seneschal looks at him sharply. 'If you know anything special about this, Paul, you should share it with her at once. Also with me.'

'You misunderstand me, sir,' Paul says hastily. 'All I mean is that she's not an insider. To plug a leak in the Circle, she'll need someone who knows the Circle well.'

'Yes, that's a fair point,' Stafford nods. 'I'll suggest she consults with Mahama. He's eager to get back to work, and clearly we can't use him in combat.' The surgeons have reattached Josh's arm, but it will take weeks of close observation to know whether the severed nerves are likely to recover.

'Very good, sir,' Paul says through gritted teeth.

It's only after he's left the Seneschal's office that he realises he's just, for the first time in his life, lied to his commanding officer.

* * *

Doug Felton, carrying the starred-and-striped shield of Sir Lionel, is enthusiastically training in the courtyard along with most of the Knights remaining at the Fastness. Sweat trickles down his visored face as he bobs and weaves around a squire armed with approximations of a Fianna shield and spear.

Everyone in the Circle is aware, of course, that the Children of Oisín may not be their most dangerous enemies. The retired professors of jurisprudence who advise the Circle on the interpretation of the honour code are looking carefully at how the Knights' no-projectile-weapons rule should best be applied when facing an enemy devicial order whose weapons of choice are muskets and six-shooters. While they ponder, this training for close-quarters combat continues.

'Felton,' calls Paul as he crosses the swing-bridge across the moat of the inner keep. 'A word?'

'Five minutes' break,' Felton tells his squire, and goes to follow Paul.

During the war, Doug Felton and the late Nick Frith – respectively the bondsmen of Sir Lancelot's cousin and his uncle, Sir Bors – acted as Paul's unofficial aides-de-camp (or, if you were with the Green Chapel, his henchmen). Since the war, with the Circle's command structures normalised once more under Sir David, Parsons and Felton have seen less of each other, but as with many bearers of devices related by kinship, the bonds between the two of them remain strong. The two Knights stroll a short distance across the training-ground, past a shooting-range where men-at-arms fire Webley 2020s at cardboard cutouts in Irish army combat uniforms.

'Felton,' says Parsons grimly, 'we have a rat. A rotten apple in the Circle itself. It's up to you and me, and anyone else we can persuade, to flush him out.'

Doug Felton doesn't have the imagination to question Parsons' patchwork use of metaphor. Instead he says, 'It's a priority though, right? We've all been told we can't get distracted now.'

'Listen,' Paul tells him urgently, 'the Seneschal's got that all wrong. He's missing the bigger picture. If I'm right' – and he once again avoids giving too much thought to how exactly this might be true – 'there needn't be a war at all. Once we've got rid of this traitor, we can go back to the way things used to be. The way they *ought* to be.'

Felton shrugs. 'Sounds all right, then.' He's not a man given to loquaciousness.

'Thing is,' says Paul, lowering his voice instinctively – despite the nearby sound of practice fire, and the fact that the idea of the Fastness' inner courtyard being bugged is more absurd by far than anything he's consciously suggesting – 'the chap may not be alone. I'd arrest him myself, but he might have help, you know?'

Paul's not lying now, of course. A lack of physical courage has never been his problem, but even he knows he can't take on the Green Chapel... (and even as he thinks the next word, a fury he'd thought long-healed bursts open) ... single-handed.

Controlling himself, Parsons continues: 'If he calls in his friends and slips through our... fingers, the whole thing's useless and we have to fight this filthy war anyway. We need the fellow alive, to tell us what he knows and to attest to it in court.' Again, his brain slides off what exactly this might entail.

(If Paul was a clearer thinker, he might recall an earlier occasion when his mind was occluded, far more obviously than this, when for a period of months he was barely able to think at all, and he might then remember what had been done to him on that occasion. But then, if he was thinking clearly, he wouldn't need to.)

He says, 'I need you to round up fellows we can trust. Ones who'll be happy to take on whoever we need them to. Farnsworth's sound enough, but it should mostly be the old guard.' Frank Farnsworth is a younger Knight, Frith's replacement as the bondsman of Sir Bors. 'Reliable types, though – not Busman or Mukherjee.'

Felton's nodding. 'That should be doable. Where are we going?'

'Tud House,' says Parsons shortly. He still doesn't want to give too much away, in case the Knights Felton sounds out are less on board with this side-quest than he hopes. 'Oh, and Felton...'

'Yes?' Felton waits for his instructions, just like old times.

He says, 'After that dreadful thing with Montalban, and the Woodville business too, I think no women would be safest as well, yeah?'

* * *

They're waiting for Jason Smith when he's discharged from the Circle's medical facility the next day. Though Paul would like to suspect his fellow Knight of malingering, the attention he's received from the trauma doctors has made it clear that the internal injuries he suffered in his beating – consensual or otherwise – were real.

Smith grins to see Parsons as he emerges from the doors of the facility. The frost is taking a day off, and instead it's raining an aggressive, persistent splatter onto the tarmacked car park.

'Paul, mate!' says Jason. 'You should have said, I needn't have booked a taxi.'

His smile slips as he registers that Paul's in armour and carrying the shield of Sir Lancelot. The three blood-red bends cut across the flesh-white blazon like clawmarks. Jason glances over to the cab that's waiting for him, its wipers swishing in the rain, then back.

'Blimey,' he says. 'Something formal happening, is it? What, is the Seneschal going to decorate me?'

At this point he realises that Paul is backed up by Felton and about a dozen others, all on foot but also in armour, and bearing the shields proper to their devices. Across Tud House's car park, a moist-looking squire tends to a pair of armoured horses as they crop the damp grass verge. 'Fuck me,' says Jason unhappily.

'That's right, Smith,' Parsons tells him boldly. 'The game's up.'

'What's up?' asks Jason. 'What game? What the hell, Paul? What the sodding arse is going on?'

'We need you to come with us,' Paul tells him. 'We know all about you and the Green Chapel. The High King...' he pauses. 'The High King can't protect you this time,' he concludes.

'Me and the Chapel?' Jason's quite indignant. 'They beat me up, you ponce. Where d'you think I've just been, bloody Butlins?'

'Come off it, Smith,' Paul jeers. 'We know that was a put-up job. They overdid it a bit, worse luck for you, but it was all so we wouldn't suspect, wasn't it? We know why you were so insistent on getting all the updates on the quest for Woodville and MacNeill. You tipped the Chapel off to find them at the lodge, didn't you?'

Jason stares at him. 'Paul,' he says carefully, 'you're off your trolley, mate. I don't know what's made you think all this bollocks, and I don't know why you think you need a small army to come and get me. But unless you're going to arrest me in the name of the Circle and its Head, I'm getting in that taxi, going home and spending the evening with my Debbie and a beer. So are you lot going to sod off out of my way, or what?'

'Felton,' says Parsons, and Lionel's bondsman comes forward hefting an enormous holdall. The squire leads the two horses over as Felton unzips the bag to reveal a sword, a suit of armour and a shield bearing Sir Gareth's red-barred, double-headed purple eagle.

Smith stares at the shield, then at the horses, then at Paul. 'You cannot be fucking serious,' he says.

'Get it on quickly,' Paul says shortly. 'If you won't come quietly we'll have it out, man to man.'

Jason looks justifiably alarmed. The story-blindness is a curse most Knights – the ones who aren't actually pathological, anyway – struggle with as best they can. One fact from the myths which they can generally be relied on to remember on demand (though, like so much else, it can elude them under stress or in the heat of the moment) is how their devicial patron dies.

Some Knights, like Theo Harte or Sir Marrok's bondsman Nigel Roth, have sponsors dull or obscure enough that no death is recorded for them. Others, like Woodville, get multiple-choice options: depending who you ask, Sir Tristan may have been killed by a jealous King Mark (possibly using a poisoned lance supplied by Morgan le Fay), or executed by the King of France for refusing to marry the wrong Iseult, or died of despair when wrongly convinced that his own Iseult had abandoned him. Then there are those devices whose demises are unambiguous, but seem quite easily avoided: Sir Bors, for instance, died fighting the Saracens in Jerusalem, which must have seemed unlikely to trouble Nick Frith right up to the point when he found himself engaging a Green Chapel force including Zara and Ahmed at the Ye Olde Trip to Jerusalem inn in Nottingham.

And then there are those who can only cross their fingers

and hope – like the device-bearers of Sir Gareth, killed in the *Morte D'Arthur* by Sir Lancelot when Gareth found the older knight shagging Queen Guinevere, and precipitating by his death a feud which tore apart the fellowship of the Round Table and left Britain wide open to the depredations of Sir Mordred.

The last seventy or so bondsmen of Sir Gareth have been lucky to avoid that fate (if by 'lucky' you mean, say, being run over and killed by a British Beasts motorcycle instead), but that run of good fortune had to break at some point.

Smith says, 'I'm not gonna fight you, Parsons. Tell you what, if you're looking for a Chapel mole, I reckon you might want to look in the Device Squad. Naming no names, but there's one of Kinsey's lot I know the Chapel used to have some contact with.'

'Oh, that's rich, Smith,' sneers Parsons. 'Trying to deflect the blame now, are we?' You're forgetting, I *know*.'

Smith looks at him. 'Don't be a twat. We'll go to Sir David together and talk to him about this. Or the Head if you like.'

'Oh yes, you'd like that, wouldn't you?' Paul puts in. 'You'd be safe with them, yeah?'

Smith shakes his head. His hair's wet now, and he sprays slightly. 'Whatever. We'll do it first thing tomorrow. Right now I'm going home to my pregnant girlfriend and putting my feet up.' He makes to walk towards his taxi, but finds his way blocked by Parson's sword.

'Fight me,' demands Paul. 'If you're innocent, then prove it.'

'Oh, we've gone back to trial by combat now, have we?' Jason asks. 'I'm not fighting anyone just 'cause you've gone bleeding mental.'

'Fight me!' repeats Paul Parsons. 'Or are you an even bigger coward than you look, Smith?'

'Sod,' insists Jason emphatically, 'off.'

Paul shifts his sword into his left hand. Then he lifts an armoured gauntlet, clenches his fist and punches Jason in the face.

Parsons' prosthetic hand is sophisticated enough that it's much the same weight and resilience as an organic one. It's the gauntlet that really does the damage. Smith goes reeling backwards, hand clutched to his face, blood pouring from the smashed skin above his right eye.

'Fight me, you spying traitor!' yells Paul, his bloodlust up now. 'You quisling! You snotty little oik!'

Jason pulls his bloody hand away from his brow and glares at Parsons. Then he jumps on him, legs around his armoured waist, pummelling at his unprotected face. 'Come on, then!' he yells. 'You want this, you stuck-up bastard? Is this what you wanted, then?' His hands come away bruised from the edge of Paul's visor, but he's doing some damage to his eyes and nose nonetheless.

Paul's supporters look at one another. Hands wander across sword-hilts, but everyone's too well-bred to actually draw their weapons, even in the face of this unconventional form of single combat. Parsons has the presence of his mind to drop his own sword, with the unfair advantage it brings (not to mention the danger of killing Smith when he's still needed). He staggers under the onslaught of Smith's fists, but finally succeeds in pushing the younger man off him. Smith falls on his knees in a puddle, where Parsons lands a good kick in his chest.

Jason's riled now. 'All *right*,' he snaps. He rolls to one side, grabs Paul's sword from the ground and swings it at the older Knight's face.

Paul steps back, blocking with his shield. He holds out his hand impatiently, and Felton sticks a second sword into it. Frank Farnsworth meanwhile is pressing the eagle shield on Jason, who's staring at it disbelievingly.

'Suit up,' Parsons insists again. 'No point you fighting at a disadvantage.' No honour in it for Paul, either, if he beats an unarmoured man.

'Fuck's sake,' says Jason, remembering himself. 'There's no point fighting *at all*.' He straightens out of his defensive crouch. 'What the hell's got into you, Paul?' He tosses the sword aside.

'You'll come quietly, then?' Parsons shouts.

'Will I arse,' says Jason. 'Jesus. I mean, I don't know where any of this comes from, but *I* got over the Green Chapel quite a long time ago, OK? If I hadn't, I would've after the bastards kicked the shit right out of me. It doesn't sound to me like you *ever* got over them. You still hate them just as much as ever, right? Even all the time there was that truce on, I bet that missing hand of yours still pissed you off.' He takes a step towards Parsons.

'That's enough, Smith,' warns Felton. He's seen the expression on Paul's face, and knows that Jason's heading into dangerous territory here.

But Jason's too angry now to stop. He takes another step. 'And who d'you think shot that exploding arrow into your arm, eh? I bet you've always wanted to find out, haven't you? That's what all this is about, just getting them back for that, isn't it? Well, *I* know who it was.'

'Smith, shut your mouth!' Felton tells him sharply.

'And d'you know what, you prancing toff?' Jason yells. 'I'm *never* going to fucking tell you! You'll die not knowing, you upper-class *tit*, so stick that up your –'

He cuts off, as Paul's sword skewers his torso. Blood trickles down his parka and onto his wet jeans and boots.

'It doesn't matter,' Paul tells Smith's suddenly gasping face. 'I don't care who it was. I'm long past revenge. All I want is to protect the Circle, and this country, from the likes of you. You and your feckless, treacherous, unproductive, unwashed, unpatriotic, degenerate friends. And you can stick *that* in your pipe and smoke it, Smith.'

Placing a hand on Jason's chest, he pulls the sword free, and his adversary collapses.

Squig's dead before he even hits the watery ground.

* * *

There's a troubled silence among the assembled Knights. Whatever spin you put on it – and their minds are doing tumble-dryer cycles right now – Paul's just killed a defenceless man. Not only that, he's set Knight's hand against Knight on the eve of perhaps the greatest war the Circle has known since the Battle of Camlann itself.

Eventually Felton breaks the silence. 'So… he was a traitor, then?' he asks hopefully. On the sodden tarmac of the car park, Jason lies silent and inert. A small puddle of blood, diluted by rain, spreads out around his torso.

'He was,' says Parsons. He's breathing heavily, but somehow his voice is calm and level. He understands what's going on now. He's confident of his own rightness as he never has been before – and for Paul Parsons, that's really saying something. 'He was collaborating with the Green Chapel all along. Following their agenda. Betraying the Circle and its values. Selling out Britain itself to our enemies. He has been for years, they all have.'

'All?' asks Felton. Overhead, two RAF Wyvern fighter-planes shriek eastward, to engage a NATO spy plane over the North Sea.

'Yeah,' Paul agrees. 'All of them.' He's finally permitted himself – or been permitted – to complete the thought that makes sense of all of this. '

Smith,' he says. 'David Stafford,' he continues.

'And,' he concludes, 'Jordan Taylor.'

* * *

Parsons doesn't lead his followers back to the Fastness. Instead, he takes them to a Circle armament depot in Luton, where he sends out a message on every communications channel the Knights have access to. It's a simple web link, leading to a video file where Paul sets out his somewhat surprising call to arms.

'Most of you know me, yeah?' he starts, disguising his awkwardness before the webcam with his usual lazy drawl.

'My name's Paul Parsons, and I'm the bondsman of Sir Lancelot. You know that Lancelot was King Arthur's closest friend, and I'm pretty sure there's no-one in the Circle more loyal to the Pendragon than me.

'Time was, though, when that would have gone without saying. These days, sadly, there are so-called Knights within the Circle who are far from loyal. Names like Olivia Montalban and Tania Woodville spring to mind – but they're not the only ones.

'It's my sad duty to tell you that High King Jordan's special envoy himself, Jason Smith – the supposed bondsman of Sir Gareth – has been working for the Green Chapel. He's been deceiving us for years, even during the War of the Devices. Recently he passed on information about Woodville's whereabouts to his Chapel friends, and helped her avoid capture. He tried to cover his tracks by subjecting himself to a realistic beating at the Chapel's hands, but we were wise to him I'm afraid.

'I regret to say Jason Smith died today, resisting arrest by his brother Knights.

'You may well be surprised that Smith was allowed to continue his subversive activities for so long. You may wonder, indeed, how High King Jordan could have been ignorant of such a betrayal by one of his most trusted men.

'There's only one answer to that – and it's not an easy one to hear. Remember though, our loyalty is to the device of King Arthur, the Circle's Head. Any man who may – or may not – bear that device is at best a temporary vessel.

'It pains me to tell you then, my brother Knights, that we've been disastrously misled. Our so-called Pendragon is as false and treacherous as his envoy – and so is his choice as Seneschal, a former Green Chapel leader. It's pretty clear now that Jordan Taylor, David Stafford and Jason Smith between them staged the War of the Devices specifically to bring Taylor into power.

'As High King, far from bringing peace, Jordan Taylor has been continuing the war by other means – manipulating us, and Britain itself, by pretending to hold the device which above all must command our loyalty, love and respect. In fact, he's exactly what we thought he was, before he somehow made us forget – the avatar of an outlaw, traitor and master trickster, Robin Hood. The immigrant woman who we thought carried that device is just another misdirection on his part, I'm afraid.

'Through Smith, and through the traitor Edward Wendiman, Taylor's been in touch with his ex-lover Malory Wendiman – the woman who bears the worst device in all our mythos, Morgan le Fay. Even while our foreign enemies are rattling our doors, our enemies within have been conspiring against us.

'This explains so much, of course – when a traitor is acclaimed as king, the damage he can do is practically unlimited. Without our so-called High King arranging it all, would the legitimate royal succession have been suspended? Would Scotland have been allowed to leave the Union? Would women *really* have been permitted to serve as Knights of the Circle?

'In our hearts, my brother Knights, I think we all know the answers to these questions.'

* * *

With Jory's collusion (Paul goes onto insist) women 'so-called Knights' like Woodville, Montalban and Laing have destabilised the Circle and the social order: smearing the reputation of the legitimate heir to the throne, freeing vital prisoners who happen to be Paul's ex-girlfriend, provoking a war which threatens to destroy Britain itself – all to serve Robin Hood's insidious agenda. Even Merlin, the only device who might have unmasked the false Pendragon, was conveniently removed from the picture, leaving the ally of Friar Tuck as the High King's most senior remaining advisor – now, like Smith, returned to the Chapel where he feels most at home.

For any loyal Knight, continuing to serve under such a despot is clearly out of the question. So until such time as a new Seneschal can be legitimately appointed by a rightful monarch, Parsons is assuming that authority himself.

He outlines the quest awaiting the loyal (and, by definition, male) Knights, squires, pages and men-at-arms of the Circle who rally to the cause of the true Pendragon: to seize control of Circle resources from the treacherous Stafford and his lackeys; to regroup and proceed to Windsor, there to take the Castle and place the false High King under house arrest; finally, to hand the deposed tyrant into the custody of the NATO forces – after which they'll hopefully go away and stop bothering everyone, leaving the country under the temporary command of the Circle's acting Seneschal.

Paul may not be a credit to the Lancelot device, but he isn't – and I've said this before, I know – a bad man. He's a weak man, easily manipulated, but one who believes he's strong. He's a man who takes a firm line on morality, despite possessing very limited moral insight. He's a man with so little self-awareness that he mistakes his internal dislikes – of Jason, of David, of Jory, of the Green Chapel – for principled stances.

In many ways, he's a natural politician.

* * *

The rebel faction make their move the next morning. Partly because Paul's rallying-cry was available on open channels for all the Knights to see, and partly because of who he managed to convince – generally the old, the hidebound, the partisan, the senselessly belligerent or rampantly misogynist – it's a bit rubbish.

The rebel Knights and their squires turn up, in full armour and waving their swords, at the Seneschal's office, the Fastness armouries, the various regional garrisons, to find loyal Knights and squires already there waiting to defend them. A few blows are exchanged – there are even casualties, though no deaths as yet – but mostly these confrontations consist of frank exchanges of views. Most of the rogue Knights opt for tactical withdrawal: those at the Fastness try to get out through the car park, and end up locked in there by the Seneschal's loyalists.

Of the Windsor Castle garrison, only one Knight is remotely tempted to join Parsons' mutiny, and he wakes up that morning to find himself locked in his bunkroom with all his weaponry and armour missing, and also his clothes and shoes. When protecting her High King, Bonnie Laing doesn't mess about.

Sir David takes stock of his remaining complement of Knights: the young, the women (because girls aren't allowed to be in Paul's gang, whatever their political preferences) and those men like Obote and Harte whose allegiance and judgement of character remain sound. Mukherjee reports for duty as usual, his loyalty to the Seneschal outweighing the impulse to follow Sir Palamedes in joining Sir Lancelot's original, fateful rebellion.

Because that's clearly what's being recapitulated here. Sir Lancelot's device has effortlessly overcome the absence of a Guinevere, and found a way to split the Circle anyway. Sir Gareth's dead, and now Lancelot's fled Camelot, taking half of Arthur's knights with him.

This is, unless it can be sorted out quickly, the point in the Round Table legend where all the wheels come off.

* * *

Stafford puts in a call to the Fastness's R&D division and politely suggests they start working with great urgency on device-recognition software for the Knights' AR specs, to allow for speedy distinction between friend and foe in battlefield conditions. Although he imagines the Knights' unique symbolic blazons will be ideal fodder for an optical recognition system, it's not something he's previously considered he'd need.

As an honourable gesture, Parsons returns Jason Smith's body to the Fastness in a rented hearse, respectfully dressed in full ceremonial armour. On seeing this his girlfriend Debbie, who's been camping out in reception awaiting news of her unborn child's father, understandably makes a scene: at first distraught, she quickly progresses to shrilly denouncing the Circle, the High King and the devices generally.

The distraction this provides allows the mutineers to escape the car park. It later transpires that they pushed a van close to the portcullis, set fire to it and let the petrol tank blow it open for them.

They bugger off to join the main body of Parsons's forces, and leave David facing the prospect of a war against multiple enemies. At home: the Green Chapel and the supporters of Sir Lancelot. Abroad: the Children of Oisín, and the other NATO forces, including the Founding Frontiersmen, who'll almost certainly be using them as a bridgehead. And that's not mentioning Woodville and Montalban, who Stafford has to assume have been up to *something* while they've been off the Circle's radar.

Sir David's a veteran of the War of the Devices, and of the mopping-up campaigns that followed it – not to mention nearly fifteen years in charge of the peacetime Circle – but these are too many strategic variables for him. On the basis that, if anyone in Britain can fight a war on so many separate fronts, it will be the man bearing the device of the greatest military leader in the nation's history, he puts through a call to the Pendragon.

But what the High King says to him is, 'David, I've just had a call from the mac Cumhail, O'Leary. He warned me NATO will be airdropping paratroopers into the Castle grounds within two hours. How soon can you get your people here, do you think?'

20. MORGAN LE FAY

'Good luck to you, General,' says Henry O'Leary.

During his half a century as the *aithgin* of one of the most powerful archetypes in western Europe, O'Leary's been a terror to the rogue devices of the Fenian Cycle – from the avatar of Aillén mac Midgna, equally in love with heavy metal music and murderous arson attacks, to the rogue vivisectionist *aithgin* of the Fear Doirich. He's an old man now, something near Rev Cantrell's age, with the knotted muscle of an old soldier who still works out regularly and exactingly – though also, increasingly, very carefully.

'Normally,' he adds, 'I'd say you won't need it, but we all know what you're going up against over there.'

O'Leary's well over six feet tall and still unstooped; his eyes are bright black diamonds, cutting through all they see. Some of the legends of Fionn mac Cumhail ascribe to him gigantic size – building the Giant's Causeway so he wouldn't get his feet wet walking to Scotland, for instance – and looking at this old man it's easy to see why. His towering presence, as pent with power as the waiting USAF Chinook helicopters, could overwhelm a lesser man than General Alec Kreiss – or a more self-aware one.

'Oh, I got the measure of King Arthur,' Kreiss flatters himself. In an airfield full of soldiers, he's the only person more imposing than O'Leary – a massive rhino of a man with shoulders that look like they could heft a steamroller. Behind him, on the runway of the Irish Air Corps' Casement Aerodrome, paratroops from half a dozen NATO countries file aboard the troop transports. Humpbacked and squat, the great khaki machines look like whales decked out in unconvincing fairy wings. Their fighter escorts, sixth-generation Lockheed-Boeing F-42 Wolverines, surround them like pilot fish.

Before the UK's great industrial resurgence, and Westland's development of the equivalent Catuvellauni, these twin-rotored giant helicopters were used by the RAF, too. Nearly twenty years ago, the Circle used one to recapture an unwilling Jory Taylor from the Green Chapel.

'Just don't underestimate him,' suggests the mac Cumhail. 'Remember how few people have heard of your original, or mine, then think on how many know the name of his.'

This isn't how O'Leary wanted things to play out. He's known, since long before his counterparts in Paris and Berlin and Oslo, that the USA was going to have its war with New Arthurian Britain one way or another – and that it wouldn't be a war in which the rest of Europe was allowed to stand by and remain neutral. By now he should have had all the intelligence he needed to ensure that Irish casualties, at least, were kept to a minimum in the fallout from the Founding Frontiersmen's crusade.

And yet... all his meticulous analysis, his impeccable strategy, his move-by-move planning, have come to nothing. The queen he sent out across the board took his opponent's knight – then vanished from play. For all his wisdom, O'Leary failed to foresee the single most predictable event in this entire intricate scenario: that the Grainne device would, given half an opportunity, betray her Fionn.

And so the story-blindness takes us all, he thinks, *even me. For all my cunning I'm a stupid old man, and my people will suffer for it.*

'Yeah?' Kreiss says, oblivious. 'Back home a lot of people know my guy's name. A hell of a lot. Finn McCool's too, I guess,' he adds generously.

'In the States, maybe,' O'Leary agrees pleasantly, setting aside his gloomy musings. 'In England, maybe not.'

The continental plates of Kreiss's scalp and eyebrows together, throwing up mountains. 'Does how near they are matter?'

The mac Cumhail chews his thumb thoughtfully. 'Maybe not,' he admits. 'The research isn't conclusive.'

'Well, then,' laughs Kreiss. 'They'll find the Founding Frontiersmen don't scare so easy. Your men neither,' he adds, nodding to where a war-band of twenty or so Fianna is standing, waiting to accompany the mac Cumhail in the second wave of the attack. 'We're gonna whup that stuck-up limey's ass, however famous he thinks he is.'

An assortment of device-bearers – Paladins for the most part, but including some Nibelungentreue and a couple more Frontiersmen – are already aboard the lead Chinook waiting to leave. Although Denmark, Norway and Iceland belong to NATO, the Swedish runeholder of the shieldmaiden Lagertha, who currently chairs the Ragnars Synir, has supplied a string of impeccably plausible excuses for why her people all need to be elsewhere today. Still, with the Nibelungentreue in attendance, O'Leary supposes they've got the Norse angle covered all right.

'Right so,' the mac Cumhail replies. 'And speaking as a downtrodden mick, I'm rooting for you all the way. Be careful, is all I'm saying. I'll see you on the other side, General.'

He salutes, and the General returns it. O'Leary watches as the soldier's sofa-wide back recedes towards the waiting aircraft.

'And by then we'll know if you're wrong,' he murmurs, and turns back towards the mess-hall.

* * *

In his disconcertingly pod-shaped study at Windsor, the High King disconnects the call on his desk screen and sighs.

'David's sending everyone he can,' he tells me and Bonnie.

371

'They're overstretched already, though, so I don't suppose they'll be here in time. Meanwhile, it looks like the entire country's shagged. Bonnie, you'd better start evacuating the non-military staff. And do we have a Knight who can escort Izzy away safely somewhere? I'm thinking Orkney might be safest, or possibly the Hebrides. Wherever it is, don't tell me.'

The Pendragon's always taken care to give his daughter minimal significance in the life of the realm: in theory it would be absurd for any emerging resistance movement to adopt her as a symbol when the country's dominated by living, breathing symbols, but it doesn't do to underestimate human perverseness.

'I'll get on it, my lord,' says Laing, and tramps off towards her office.

The Pendragon stares restlessly out of the circular window for a moment, then says, 'Dale, if you end up chronicling this later, don't use the word "shagged", OK?'

(Yeah, I know. But what's he going to do about it now, sue me?)

'That other call,' I begin cautiously.

'The one I sent you out of the room for?' he says. 'I'm sorry, Dale, I can't tell you any more about that.' Which is fair enough, obviously – he's a head of state, he's entitled to have state secrets – though being me I'm still curious.

'Not that one,' I say. 'The mac Cumhail's warning. He's obviously trying to spook you.'

The High King steeples his fingers. 'Not necessarily,' he says judiciously. 'It's possible he's as dismayed with the Frontiersmen coming in and taking over the show as we are. Well, not *as* dismayed, probably. But a bit.'

'Even so,' I say. 'Whatever his reasons, he wants you to run. It's better propaganda for them that way.'

The High King nods. 'I know. But what are my options? I run, or I surrender, or I fight and die. None of those are going to look good on the CV. Besides – hello sweetheart, are you OK?'

It's Izzy at the doorway. The High King's daughter is

wearing a long white dress with one of those waistcoat things that tie up like a corset in front and sweep down into a train at the back, in dark burgundy.

She has a peculiar look on her face, as well she might if she's been listening in. 'Hi Dad,' she says. 'Bonnie said you needed to see me.'

'That's right,' her father says sombrely, standing up and going over to her. 'Listen Izzy, it looks like there's going to be an attack on the Castle. I'm considering my options, but I need to keep a clear head, and for that I have to be sure you're well away from here. Bonnie's finding a Knight to go with you –'

'Dad,' she says again. 'I can't make sense of the news, it's all over the place, but I've been talking to people. They've been saying Jason's dead. Is that right?'

Jory long ago resolved to make it a rule to only lie to his daughter about certain very specific things. 'I'm afraid so, love,' he says gently.

'They're saying Paul killed him,' she says. 'Like Lancelot and Gareth. They're saying the Circle's split because of it.'

Jory sighs. 'That's right. It's going to make handling this a lot more difficult. That's why I need to know you're somewhere safe.'

'And now NATO are sending in the paratroops?' Izzy persists. 'I mean, we'd have heard by now if they'd landed a ground force. I suppose they could bomb us, but they wouldn't want to destroy the Castle, would they? Not if they're pretending this is a mission of liberation. And Bonnie has, what, fifteen Knights to protect you? Fourteen once she's sent one away with me.' She giggles suddenly, then claps a hand over her mouth.

'Well, yes,' the Pendragon says helplessly. 'I don't think we can hold the Castle, honestly.'

'Oh, I can see that, Dad.' Izzy says. 'You've got into a war you didn't want, your right-hand men are gone, and you've only got a fragmented Circle to protect you. It's like history's repeating itself, isn't it?'

'That's not really very helpful,' Jory says. Then, as Izzy starts to laugh more openly he adds in alarm, 'Are you all right, love?'

'I'm fine,' says Izzy, then she's off in peals again. She doesn't sound hysterical, though, just deeply amused.

'What's up, sweetheart? What's the matter?' her father asks, seriously concerned now.

She bites her hand to stop the laughter. 'Oh, Dad,' she sniggers. 'Who do you think started the war? Who do you think broke your precious Circle for you?'

So she tells us.

* * *

Seventeen years ago, a young mother named Katja Kollwitz was sitting with her daughter Bella, assembling a jigsaw puzzle on the floor of a squat in Bristol where they lived with some of Katja's friends, when their world fell in. Fourteen men-at-arms and three Knights of the Circle kicked the front and back doors down, and marched in to take possession of young Bella's house and of her life.

The house was known as Mystic Villas, and the Knights were Paul Parsons, Doug Felton and Nick Frith. They separated the terrified mother and child, searched them, arrested Katja and the other adults, and took Bella and two other children into Circle custody. Bella was only four years old.

Paul was there to arrest Rev Cantrell, Laney Wardsley and Liss Dashwood, who were using Mystic Villas as a temporary safe house, and the welfare of the squat's regular inhabitants was not his primary concern – especially after the unfortunate incident which led almost immediately to Dashwood's death.

He was quite clear, though, that Mystic Villas was no environment for a child. The floors weren't clean; the bedrooms were overcrowded; there was drug paraphernalia about the place. No responsible mother would bring up a child there, and anyway Katja wasn't even out of her teens.

374

He signed the papers to make the three children wards of the Circle – effectively meaning that they entered the social care system like any other child in care, but with regular reports sent to Sir Charles Raymond – and thought no more about it, except for a brief glow of self-justification when he heard that, after being denied access to her daughter on her release from prison, Katja Kollwitz had overdosed on heroin and been pronounced dead on arrival at Bristol Royal Infirmary.

A short while later, when an unmarried Knight named Craig McCutcheon was feeling broody, he talked to Sir Charles about adoption options, and Raymond dug up Isabella Kollwitz's name from the files.

* * *

'I didn't know that,' the Pendragon admits. 'I knew your birth name, and that you were a ward of the Circle when Craig adopted you, but I hadn't realised why. I didn't think you'd even remember any more.'

'Yes, Dad, I remember,' says Izzy. 'I loved my Mum. She was all the family I needed – just her and me against the world. I know she used drugs, but she never let it get in the way of looking after me. We'd lived in squats my whole life, but she'd always kept me safe and comfortable and fed, even when she suffered for it. She was only fourteen when she had me, but she was a better mum than some women three times that age. And then the Circle broke us apart with a pen-stroke.'

* * *

Izzy was six when her new Dad, Craig, went off to fight in the War of the Devices. He hadn't wanted to send her off to boarding-school so young, but his military duties didn't give her a lot of choice. He drove her with her luggage to the school near Wells, comfortably within Circle-controlled territory, helped her unpack in her new dormitory, then kissed her goodbye and drove away.

The school was pretty much like being in care again – the lack of personal space, the petty unimaginative vindictiveness, the intense friendships so vulnerable to betrayal. In both cases the adults were kindly and well-meaning, though the teachers at the school were sterner than the always harried care workers at the home. Even at their best, though, they couldn't have stamped out the children's propensity to be vile little bullies to one another, especially in their shared spaces when all the adults had withdrawn.

At Mystic Villas, her mum had been an ever-present buffer, protecting Izzy from the worst excesses of adult behaviour. At the home, she'd had to get by through befriending an older girl who was prepared to subject her to milder physical abuse than the rest. It had taken her a long time to learn to trust her new Dad not to do the same – and now he, too, had been taken away from her.

Meanwhile, the country was tearing itself apart over this new thing – or rather, not a new thing at all (because her new Dad had had one for years, apparently), but a previously-secret thing – called the devices. When the early rumours started flying, wild talk of schizophrenia and brainwashing and ghosts and possession, Craig had taken her aside and told her calmly what exactly the devices were. They were, he told her, living stories, no more or less than that; people made bargains with them, gaining strength and protection in return for their service.

It was a simple power transaction, of the kind her life had prepared young Izzy well to understand. Granted, she didn't know Arthurian myth, but Katja had taught her to read early, and she'd always been a fast learner. She was warming to Craig, who certainly adored her, and he'd told her that he was the bondsman of Sir Accolon. Although it was known from the Green Chapel that women could theoretically take on male devices, within the Circle's sphere of influence this

376

was considered a perversion, which limited the pool of options available.

All in all, it didn't take a lot of thought for Izzy to decide which Arthurian character she should be.

The tricky part was working out how to invoke the device. She considered various rituals – burning candles, chalking out five-pointed stars, sacrificing animals – but none of those seemed to fit. In the end, after reading carefully about her chosen legendary figure, she settled on sabotaging the communal showers.

An older girl – docile and plumply pretty, and called, in a happy coincidence, Ellie – was in the habit of bathing early, before the others were awake, so she could exercise away her puppy-fat with a run around the playing-fields before breakfast. Careful and covert observation revealed to Izzy that Ellie never checked the state of the mixer tap in the cubicle before turning on the water, which often led to her leaping out of the cubicle and swearing dully as she adjusted a too-hot or too-cold stream.

Izzy joined a shopping-trip into Wells led by a teacher, and when she wasn't looking shoplifted a tube of superglue.

At four o'clock in the morning, Izzy set the mixer-tap in Ellie's favourite cubicle to maximum heat – which was reliably scalding – and glued it in position, before going to sit by the door of Ellie's dorm and listening for sounds of the older girl rousing herself. Just as she was clambering out of bed, Izzy ran down and applied two long vertical lines of superglue to the cubicle door and frame. Then she flushed the tube down a toilet, rushed back to bed and pretended to be roused, like the other girls, by the screams.

As some of her peers rushed to help, to get a teacher or just to stare through the billowing steam at the shrieking naked figure of their classmate as her flesh darkened from pink to red, Izzy stayed huddled in bed next to those girls too frightened, surly or cool to involve themselves in such crises, and reread in TH White's *The Once and Future King* the story of Elaine of Corbenic, 'the boiled girl', imprisoned for five years in a perpetually seething bath by Morgan le Fay.

* * *

'And then she came,' says Izzy now. 'It was it was like nothing I'd ever felt before. Like I was Dorothy being picked up by the tornado. Like a snail being grabbed by a raven and carried off into the sky. I could still feel the bed under me, but I was *flying*. I felt her poking and probing me as we flew, checking and assessing to see how I'd shape up as a vessel. I felt like, if she dropped me, I'd shatter and stay broken, a soft crawling thing writhing in pain before being stamped on or gobbled up.

'And then it was as though she said, *You'll do*. It was grudging, but I could tell she respected what I'd done to Ellie, just to get her attention. So she put me back on the bed, and then she poured herself into me. She filled me up until I was full to the brim, and then she just kept on pouring. I could feel my mind *stretching*, just to fit it all in.

'And when she finished... I was Morgan le Fay the enchantress, daughter of Duke Gorlois and Igraine, half-sister and enemy of King Arthur... and she was me. There was no way to tell us apart any more.'

'We all thought Merry Wendiman was Morgan,' I say, inconsequentially. By this point in this awkward family confrontation I have to admit I'm feeling rather surplus to requirements – and besides, there's still an imminent assault by some of the best-trained troops in the western world to worry about. Even so, I clearly can't walk out and leave my High King alone at the mercy of the bondswoman of Morgan le Fay.

Izzy laughs again. 'I know you did! The Circle spent all those years looking for her. It was hilarious.'

She calms her giggles. 'At first I just wanted to hurt the Circle, however I could. I knew where my Dad worked. It was pretty easy to google and find out that everyone thought the scientists there were making devicial weaponry. With him being the bondsman of Sir Accolon and me being Morgan le Fay, it was pretty obvious what I needed to do.'

* * *

Morgan protected Izzy, after she came to her that morning in the dorm room. After that Izzy found she knew things a six-year-old really shouldn't have. She knew what to say to someone to get them to be friends with her, or to persuade them she wasn't worth victimising, or to change their mind about giving her detention. She could get the younger girls to love her, and the older girls to leave her alone... and middle-aged men in an emotionally vulnerable state to want to do anything they could to protect her.

She played on her first adopted father each school holiday, tweaking his misgivings and insecurities at Morgan's instruction and behest, and with the active co-operation of the Sir Accolon device. Together the three of them built his initially microscopic reservations about the new High King, first into full-blown suspicion, then into a passionate (though private) rejection of his kingship.

Then they hinted and insinuated and implied, until he had a clear idea in his mind about what to do about it.

If you'd asked him, McCutcheon would have said that chatting to his daughter cleared his head, took him out of himself, helped him to think more clearly about things. In fact, of course, it was doing just the opposite.

It took Izzy years to weaponise Craig McCutcheon against the Pendragon, and years more before the Knight was in a position to act on his plans. It took the High King less than half an hour to kill him.

Izzy's grief was quite unfeigned: she'd never known her biological father, and had come, over the years, to love her adoptive Dad. But there was anger and frustration in there too – as there would have been with normal grief, of course. In her adolescent naivety, she'd assumed that Craig would kill the Pendragon as Sir Accolon had failed to do, and would be hailed for saving Britain from a tyrant. It had never occurred to her that Craig, like Accolon before him, would come to grief in the attempt.

It's pretty rare for children to acquire devices at all, and most people – other than children, obviously – would agree that this is for the best. They're horribly ill-equipped either to overcome their story-blindness or to cope with the inevitable horrific consequences.

In that respect, Izzy was exceptional – and Morgan gave her precisely no time to recover before embarking on further plotting. As soon as the initial shock had passed, Izzy realised her mistake. All she'd been doing over the past seven years was shepherding a story to its predetermined ending – a tragic one, as far as her late Dad was concerned.

What she should have done was simply pick a story whose outcome was the one she wanted.

Before, she'd just hoped to hurt the Circle, and anything else had seemed a means to that end. Now, though, she had a clear target in mind. And *his* demise was so well-charted they'd named a book after it.

* * *

'I needed you to trust me,' Izzy says. 'Like Arthur trusted Morgan before she betrayed him. She was his sister, so becoming your daughter worked for me. I might even be able to use your story-blindness against you – hide in your device's blind spot about the people close to him betraying him. But I knew there'd be others who might be suspicious. So I was always the fond, doting daughter, affectionate and obedient, helping out her Daddy, quite regardless of the fact that he happened to be the most powerful man in the country. Did I play the part well, Dad?'

Jory's sitting down now in one of the pine-and-canvas armchairs, looking shellshocked. God knows I'm feeling appalled enough, and she's not my daughter.

I've no idea where Bonnie's got to – given the malevolence and power of the Morgan device, Izzy could have done anything from arranging a distraction elsewhere in the Castle to cutting her throat in her office. No-one's walked past the door to the corridor in ages – too busy preparing to defend the Castle, I suppose – and we can hardly look for help from the High King's bedroom.

If anyone's going to defend the Pendragon from the serpent in his bosom, it's going to have to be me.

Unfortunately I can't think of a thing to do. It feels like I'm paralysed with crippling indecision, except I don't even have options to decide between. It's like my mind's been cryogenically frozen.

* * *

Izzy was young, and the seven years she'd spent preparing Craig McCutcheon for his mutiny felt like a lifetime to her – but Morgan had been waiting fifteen hundred years, and she was in no hurry. Once again, they opted for the long-term approach.

Izzy sought out someone who would one day become a Knight, someone malleable who she could shape according to Morgan's will. She took the High King's page Olivia Montalban under her wing, and spent years tainting her with the subtlest of psychological poisons, mixed in with cheerful teenage talk of boys and hair and music. Through Izzy, Morgan ensured that, when Oli stood her vigil and became a Knight, her mind would be the perfect vessel for one device in particular – a device which, thanks to this careful preparation, found a plan to disguise itself as Sir Gawain of Orkney ready and waiting for it.

In a few of the myths, Morgan herself, not Morgause, is Sir Mordred's mother. In this case, *midwife* was probably a better word.

In her spare time, Izzy worked on Paul Parsons: a graceless man, wary of women, his natural self-regard fatally

381

boosted by hosting the device of the best knight in the world, his habitual bitterness armour-plated by his wounding at the hands of the Green Chapel. His mind needed little twisting into shape, but she tweaked and pruned it whenever they met, cultivating it like a bonsai tree.

And all the time, she watched and waited – keeping alert for a time when the very different betrayals of Mordred and Lancelot could be set into motion.

* * *

'And it worked gloriously,' Izzy says. 'I haven't talked to Oli since she came back from The Hague, but it's pretty obvious she stabbed you in the back out there. She must have sold you out to the Frontiersmen – agreed to do something awful that would discredit the Circle and give the Americans an excuse to invade. If it hadn't been Tania Woodville running off with that spy, she'd have found something else to overreact to. She's cleverer than you ever gave her credit for. Which is good – I'd hate to have been stuck with one of the pathetic Mordreds.'

I'm trying to think of something to say, but there's nothing that isn't exactly the kind of moral outrage she'll be dying to hear at this point. In any case, I doubt I could motivate my vocal cords any more than I can the rest of me.

'It's a shame Jason had to die,' she says lightly. 'I actually really liked him, but the myth goes how it goes. I let Paul think he was a Green Chapel agent, and hinted that you might be one as well. By now Paul will have convinced himself he's saving Britain from a tyrant. Which he is, of course,' she smiles.

By now I've sat down too, and am staring up at her as she charmingly harangues her father. At some point, someone's closed the door to the corridor. My memory tells me it might even have been me.

Izzy goes on, 'Because you can run all you want, Dad – the Frontiersmen are coming for you, and your broken Circle

382

can't save you. I picked the right myth this time – the myth to end all myths. The *Morte D'Arthur*.'

'Oh God,' says Jory. His voice is strangulated, but I'm amazed he can speak at all. 'Izzy, she's hurt you so badly. What she's made of you. I had no idea...'

'Oh, dear.' Her giggles overspill again. 'Don't go worrying about *me*, Dad. You're the one who's doomed here. You'll have your last battle, then they'll kill you. Maybe they'll let the myth play out the way it's supposed to, but I wouldn't bet on it. The Frontiersmen have their own myths. They'll hunt you down like Jesse James or Bonnie and Clyde. They'll throw your tea into the harbour, arrest you for tax evasion, then shoot you from a grassy knoll. They'll crush the Circle and your precious Green Chapel forever. And then...'

She doesn't really know where to go after that.

'Then what?' asks someone, and I'm surprised to realise my voice is working after all. 'So Morgan le Fay gets to be the last device standing in a devastated Britain? That doesn't sound much of a victory to me.'

She stares at me, suddenly disinclined to laugh any more. 'You don't know Morgan,' she says quietly.

'That's true,' I say, feeling my eyes widen as I stare over her shoulder at the connecting door to Jory's bedchamber. 'But I bet I know a man who does.'

'Oh, Dale.' She gives me an exasperated look, then lifts a finger and says, 'Stay.' She casts a glance sideways at Jory, who's still slumped dejected in one of his armchairs. Only then does she turn to see Blaze standing at the bedroom door.

He's wearing a loose suit the colour of blue curaçao. His silver dragon ring's on his finger and in his hand he holds his metal pole of power. He's nearly eight years older than when I last saw him, but he's still looking pretty sharp.

'Did you really think Broceliande could hold me, girl?' he asks.

It sounds like he's genuinely interested to know.

21. THE LADY OF THE LAKE

General Alec Kreiss stands in the open doorway of the troop transport, looks northwards across the majestic snow-rimed peaks of Snowdonia, and snorts.

'Call those mountains?' he asks the interior of the helicopter. 'Back at my daddy's house we'd trip on humps like that on our way down to fish at the lake. Guess the people who called those *mountains* had never seen the Rockies, huh? Never seen Mount McKinley, that's for sure.' Kreiss isn't the sort of man to use a Native American name for something when there's a WASP alternative available.

None of the paratroops in the helicopter's metal belly takes it upon themselves to answer him. A massive ball of blackened smoke flies past the window, close enough to warm the skin: the remnant either of one of the escorting Wolverines or the RAF Wyverns that are engaging them ahead.

'Damn right,' Kreiss assures his silent troops. 'Those crumpet-eating medieval tight-asses have no idea how big the world is. We're gonna march in there like an ox trampling an anthill.'

He claps his second-in-command, Agent Frank Mallucci, on the shoulder, then crosses back to his seat and squeezes his huge frame back into the crash-webbing. 'We'll see how long their fairytale castle stands up when I shake it,' he booms.

...What? Don't look at me like that. It's not *my* fault the General's the worst kind of national stereotype.

It's not his fault either, not really. Alec Kreiss – otherwise Agent Kreiss of the Founding Frontiersmen – is a product and expression of his culture. His primary, the folkloric figure whose Agent he is, is a national boast of the precise kind we Brits find so offputting in our transatlantic cousins.

You have to imagine, though, what it must have felt like, those very few centuries ago, to explore, colonise and begin to exploit North America. European minds set loose in a continent that dwarfed their expectations, a continent with no legends of its own – none which seemed believable to Europeans, at any rate – had no choice but to fill it with their own imaginings.

And because the open spaces they sought to fill were so vast, they writ themselves very large indeed.

Which is how we get figures like Paul Bunyan, the giant 'lumberjack king' of North Dakota: if he ever existed, then merely a very large man like the General, but inflated in retelling and exaggeration until he's able to fell a million trees in a winter, drink dry a lake of pea soup, wade through forty-foot snowdrifts and the like. Like Fionn mac Cumhail's, Paul Bunyan's passage – and that of his equally gigantic ox, Babe – is credited with being literally earth-shattering.

It's not exactly surprising, then, that self-deprecation and humility should be difficult to track down in the catalogue of Alec Kreiss's personality traits.

'Less than an hour to Windsor now. Those Brits are gonna welcome us with fireworks and confetti,' he predicts optimistically.

In his imagination, a bullock lows, vast and infrasonic.

* * *

In the High King's study, Izzy's stunned into silence. For a good few seconds as she stares at Blaze she opens her mouth and closes it again like a ruminating cow. Then she says uncertainly, 'Oh, right. And I'm supposed to have forgotten he lost his device years ago? You're lucky I even *recognise...*'

She tails off even as she says it, though – because even that explanation, straw-clutching though it is, still has to mean her revelation just now came as no surprise to the High King. He could hardly have summoned Burn out of retirement during the twenty minutes she's just spent gloating at us.

Besides, she *does* recognise the Merlin device. Anyone would. Blaze may have been out of circulation for years, living as harmless street conjurer Bernard Maddox, but now the arrogant angle of his eyebrows, the timbre of his voice, the absolute self-confidence of his body-language, display the wizard's vital presence like a neon advert. In this moment, his flashy choice of handle seems entirely appropriate: he *blazes* with the wisdom, power and righteous anger of a mage whom this enchantress has personally wronged.

'Oh, you recognise me, kid,' he says. 'You were the one who tried to take it all away from me.'

He's right, of course. Izzy may have used Craig McCutcheon as her instrument, just as McCutcheon used the devicial mine, but it was Morgan who imprisoned Merlin in the oak tree.

Whatever behavioural trigger Izzy used to trigger our fear-paralysis reflex, Merlin's arrival has broken it like a wooden wand. Jory's standing at her side now, a hand on her arm.

'I want you to know,' he said, 'that I loved you anyway. I may have concealed things from you, but I never lied about that. You are my daughter, and that was never a pretence.'

Izzy looks understandably sceptical.

* * *

Seven and a half years ago, or thereabouts, sitting at the big oak desk in the High King's old study a corridor away from here, Blaze pointed at a tablet which was chiming irritatingly to inform his boss of an urgent message, and asked, 'Look, d'you want me to open this or not?'

'Hmm?' the Pendragon asked, distracted still by his thoughts.

'Hold on,' the conjuror added, as the phone in his pocket whistled an equally obnoxious jingle to let him know a text had arrived. 'That might be from Squig.'

'Read it, then,' said the High King, coming over. 'If this is for my eyes only, I suppose I should open it. Although what Freda can have to say that's so –'

And it was at that point – with Blaze facing away from the tablet towards the door and the High King reaching in behind him to press the flashing icon – that the First Fateful Touchscreen Interaction of the Island of Britain occurred.

At the babble of compressed voices and the violently flashing lights Blaze's head whipped round at once, but his view of the screen was obscured by the Pendragon, who recoiled violently into him.

Blaze yelled something sweary and not immediately helpful as he struggled to support the High King's weight, but then his eyes were seduced by the screen. For a moment flickering images threw up flashcard impressions of a burning shield, a fleeing knight, a toppling castle – a stop-motion Tarot of defeat – and then he'd dropped the Pendragon into his chair and was reeling away to bounce off the wall. As the High King slumped forward against the desk, Blaze saw a layer of his boss's identity – a cunning, laughing, generous, righteously indignant layer – stripped away before his eyes. Blaze tried again to go to him, but his legs failed him: he collapsed against the teak panelling, turning his face away from the cackling psychedelic display that threatened to leach away his – or at least Merlin's – soul.

And that's pretty much when I knocked at the door.

* * *

'Robin Hood was gone,' Blaze says. 'That was bloody

obvious just from looking at the boss. Robin had shielded the Pendragon device from the worst of it, but it had burned him right away.'

'One final act of service to his king, perhaps,' Jory suggests sceptically.

Blaze says, 'Merlin, though – he was weak, yeah, took him a long time to recover, but he was there, he was aware, and he was *pissed off*. I didn't get the same faceful as the boss,' he admits.

'Neither of us told you that part, Dale,' Jory says, flashing an apologetic smile in my direction. 'We both knew straight away that that information would be a useful commodity. Not the sort of thing you pass on to a chronicler.'

Offended, I say quietly, 'I could've kept a secret, boss.'

'Probably,' says Blaze. 'We couldn't take the risk though, mate. Up till today we've not told *anybody*.'

'You let us all think…' I say. 'In fact, you *told* McCutcheon, with the news drones listening in…'

'That's right,' says the Pendragon, slightly shamefaced again. 'I'd learned a few tricks, playing the part of Robin Hood. A weapon your opponent thinks you've thrown away is twice as dangerous.'

'It was a relief to me, and all,' Blaze adds. ''Cause we all know the Merlin device has to go away – it's part of the story, innit? Exile, imprisonment, madness, doesn't matter. But this one I knew I could come back from – any time the boss gave me a call. Like when your homegirl totalled the Irish Embassy and he realised the Mordred device was in play,' he adds to Izzy.

'We wanted people to go on thinking I was carrying the Robin device as well,' says Jory. 'We knew my prestige would suffer otherwise. But Zara put an end to that.'

'But what about me?' Izzy asks, her voice small now. 'When did you know about *me?*'

'Pretty much straight away, I'm afraid,' her father says. 'Sir Accolon's motivation is his love for Morgan le Fay, and…

well, it was fairly obvious that there was only one woman in Craig McCutcheon's life.'

* * *

The High King knew when he flew down to Wells that he'd probably be facing the avatar of Morgan le Fay. He wasn't sure what he was expecting, but it was more like the defiant vengeance Izzy presented to him just now than the fearful, tearful child he met that day.

He gauged her carefully as they spoke, probing her fragility for signs of contrition or defiance. Her hatred of the Circle was clear enough, but he didn't get any sense that she was directly dangerous to him. The face she hid behind made him suspect that she'd prefer to work her will behind the scenes as she had with McCutcheon, goading and manipulating rather than getting her hands dirty.

He'd more than half foreseen that he'd decide what he did: that she'd be less of a threat living at the Castle where he could at least keep an eye on her activities. What he hadn't expected, even for a moment, was that he'd be so drawn to her. Even given her relationship with McCutcheon, adoption hadn't been on his mind when he entered her headmistress's study.

What he saw, though, filled him with pity and affection – and, yes, even admiration – for this lost, grieving scrap of a thing and the strength she'd somehow found within herself. If he could be a father to anyone – and that hadn't been a thing he'd thought was possible, not for quite some time – it was to this small girl.

He knew that all this might be a trick of his subconscious – or even, conceivably, hers. Arthur loved his half-sister, after all, at least until she tried to have him killed with his own sword.

He didn't think that was it, though. She was so hurt, so alone, so bereft... yet still her own person utterly, even at thirteen, a woman capable of speaking her mind to a King.

Her honesty and vulnerability reminded him of no-one more than Malory.

* * *

'But... Malory Wendiman!' Izzy exclaims, in what's not quite a wail. 'You were all meant to think it was her!'

'But that's just the thing, sweetheart,' Jory tells her gently. 'The thing is, you see... by the time this happened I hadn't believed in the devices for years. I lost my faith in them, back in the civil war. Of course I believed in the effect they have on people, I'd have been an idiot not to – but I thought they were a fiction. A delusion, like... well, Scar once told me the devices exist in the same way a country does, or money, or God. By consensus. I still thought that was true, but I believed that the consensus was a false one.'

'But...,' Izzy says. Then, as if she's talking to a frustratingly dense child: 'But... you're *the Pendragon*.'

Jory shrugs. 'So everyone believes. I acted according to that consensus, but I wasn't part of it. Blaze thought I'd lost one of my devices, but if he'd told me I'd lost both, it wouldn't have made any difference to me. I had to go on persuading people I was the bondsman of King Arthur, or everything would fall apart.

'There were a few people who'd have realised that – Blaze and Dale, for a start – but nearly all of them worked for me. The only one who didn't,' he says, 'was Malory. I'd talked to her about all this, back at Stonehenge. She of all people would have known there was no point attacking me with a devicial mine. But we knew – or at least we strongly suspected – that Accolon could only have been motivated by Morgan le Fay.

'Which meant,' he explains, 'that Malory wasn't Morgan after all.'

* * *

There's a damn great logical gap there, of course. Merry could have laid the trap anyway, as a bluff, to persuade Jory that she wasn't Morgan le Fay when in fact she was. Or she could have done it to prove to him that the devices were real, by stripping away the ones he had and leaving him defenceless. Or simply because *she* believed his device made a difference to him, whether he did or not.

Or, since we're talking about Malory here, for some other reason that he simply isn't clever enough to guess.

But that relied on Merry being crueller and more devious than he'd ever truly believed. Besides… well, Jory just wasn't prepared to think it through in that level of detail. He'd been running the country for seven years by then, and he knew full well he couldn't keep going without screwing it up eventually. Malory had always been smarter than he was, and her knowledge of the devices and of mythopolitical theory was unparalleled. He needed her wisdom and advice.

And if that doesn't sound like good enough reason, remember that he'd loved her for years. Besides, there was the boy to think of. His other, biological child.

That same night, after flying back from Wells to Windsor and finding Laney Wardsley held prisoner there, after he'd ordered Jason and Bonnie out of the Crimson Drawing-Room, he loomed over her menacingly. She cringed from this towering, threatening figure, bloodstained and armoured, with the power of a kingdom at his back, and even as she prepared her next barbed quip she quailed at what he'd say to her.

But it was, 'So I gather you're working with Malory. Can you get a message to her? From me, I mean?'

And she gasped in relief and said, 'God, I thought you'd never ask.'

…Yeah, so it was Jory who let Laney out, and let the rest of us think there'd been a security breach, the great big twat. He told Laney the only way she was leaving the Castle a free woman was as his messenger, and as it turned out that suited both of them nicely.

That's why the guards would never say who'd given them the drug – the High King himself had ordered them not to. It's why the door was locked and the key put back neatly, too. Jory always was tidy with his own things.

* * *

The first time they met it was awkward, naturally. Not just emotionally, but practically too.

Finding a safe, neutral location had been as tricky as the delicate covert negotiations which had eventually convinced Merry, over the months following McCutcheon's death, of Jory's honest intentions. The High King was in the public eye everywhere he went, and Merry's was still the face of a wanted criminal.

In the end Jory had to resort to the oldest trick in the book: going abroad among his people disguised as an ordinary working man. Although the builders working on the New Quad had all been carefully security-vetted, they were numerous enough that none were surprised at being joined at the end of a shift by a red-bearded brickie they failed to recognise. The other side of the security barriers they went their various ways, which in the new bloke's case involved getting on a bus to Slough, where he checked into the local branch of Premier Inn and waited for a knock on the door.

Merry looked different, too: she wore her hair short now, her natural autumn russet dyed a muddy brown, her pale skin darkened with what had to be fake tan (because Malory didn't tan, she freckled). She wore a severe, though inexpensive, business suit. She looked like the PA to an unusually old-fashioned chief executive.

They looked at each other for a few minutes before Merry said, 'You're wearing a lumberjack shirt, your majesty. And a baseball cap.'

Jory said feebly, 'It's a disguise.'

Malory smirked, and everything he'd ever felt for her came billowing back into his mind.

392

He said, 'Mal, I've been an arse. I'm so, so sorry.'

She said, 'It took you long enough to work that out.'

He said, 'I know. I was… I was upset and angry. I can't even remember what about now.'

'You decided I must be evil,' she reminded him coldly, 'because I admitted to letting my device – the Lady of the Lake device, *not* Morgan le Fay – rule me in a moment of panic. Something that you've done several times, with worse results. It took me a year to cure Dad of the hex I put on him. Remind me, did you ever manage to reattach Shaun Hobson's head?'

'That's fair,' he said. 'You're right, I do remember. I was a judgemental prick. Can you forgive me?'

She sighed – a deep, relieved sigh. 'Oh, Jory,' she said. 'I forgave you long ago, you stupid sod.' She sat in the room's one chair – an uncomfortable wooden one meant for use at the desk – leaving him to settle on the bed. 'Why did you think I set Freda Tate-Hendricks' people on the right track to give you devicial weaponry? Although I never thought you'd be *quite* so dense as to put Sir Accolon's bondsman in charge of security. Honestly, what were you thinking of?'

He smiled; he'd missed this. 'Dale said the same thing,' he told her.

'And I suppose you're here because you've found the real Morgan device,' Merry said. 'That took you long enough as well.'

'We weren't looking in the right place,' he said. 'It's McCutcheon's daughter. She's only thirteen.'

'Oh God.' Malory looked stricken. 'That poor kid.' She'd been thirteen herself, when Edward held the ritual which allied her to Nimue, the Lady of the Lake. From everything she'd told Jory, that had been pretty traumatic even with her father's support – and Nimue's a relatively benevolent device.

'I'm adopting her,' Jory said.

Merry looked carefully at him. 'Why?' she asked.

He said, 'I hope… That way I hope I can contain her. Perhaps help her to get over her Dad's death.'

She shook her head. 'Morgan won't care about that.'

'Izzy does,' Jory insisted. 'I owe it to her, for McCutcheon's sake and hers. Shaun's too, and Shafiq's, and all the others. This time I have a chance to make amends. And... maybe I can help her channel her device. Morgan isn't always evil, even in the original legends. There must be fifty modern retellings where she's a sympathetic character. I'll lend her some books.'

'Oh, Jory.' Malory smiled, quite fondly this time. 'You think she'll read *The Mists of Avalon* and see the error of her ways?'

Doggedly he said, 'It has to be worth a try.'

For a few moments they were silent. Then he said, 'The photo. Did you... Was that...?'

'I left it for you deliberately, yes,' she said. 'You had a right to know.'

He said, 'I hoped... before I adopt Izzy... that I might see him?'

She smiled again, and said, 'Next time perhaps.'

* * *

The next time they met in the Holiday Inn in Maidenhead. The room Jory had taken was marginally more luxurious in that it also had an easy chair, though paradoxically quite a hard one. Malory didn't bring the boy, but she brought an up-to-date photo. A freckly child in a school football kit, with shoulder-length red hair that reminded him achingly of how Malory used to look.

'What's his name?' Jory asked.

She gave him a rueful smile. 'Pendragon,' she admitted. 'Pendragon Wendiman-Taylor. Not that that's the name we're using for now, obviously.'

'And how is... Pendragon?' he asked, feeling the name in his mouth changed by its new significance.

Merry smiled. 'Thriving. Happy. Doing incredibly well at school. Wants to be a journalist, if you can believe that.

Sporty, too – so more like you than me there. Thoroughly bored by Arthurian mythology, which goes to show the power of a well-chosen forename. How's Izzy?'

'Quiet,' said Jory. 'Still mourning, obviously. Friendly enough so far, although I don't know how much of that is an act. I really want to help her if I can, Mal. Protect her from herself, as far as possible. She's just a kid.'

Malory nodded. 'Well, you've set yourself a challenge there.'

He said, 'I hoped I could ask your advice. I can't tell the others – Dale, Rev, David, even Bonnie. I want them to accept her for who she is, not suspect her for the device she's carrying. The only one I can talk to is Blaze, and he's not living at the Castle any more. Besides... well, he's Merlin, obviously, but he doesn't know the devices like you. Nobody does.'

She said, 'OK. Happy to help if I can.'

He frowned, then. 'There was... one thing I wanted to ask first, though. This covert organisation you've set up. With Laney and that woman from the hotel and whoever else. I know it's nothing sinister, but... what does it do?'

She laughed, a little shortly. 'All sorts of things. Protecting you, mostly. Until the MRF can build you an Excalibur, we're all vulnerable. You're on the right track, trying to keep the Morgan device contained, but she was never the only threat to Arthur's realm.'

He said, 'I know that. But the Circle...'

She said, 'You know yourself they're not sufficient. That's why you've kept the Chapel as your secret second line of defence. Well, we're your third. One so secret even you don't know about it.'

'Yeah.' He nodded. 'I thought it must be something like that. What I don't understand is why your double...'

'Claudine,' Malory reminds him.

'That's right,' he said. 'We thought whoever rescued her must have sent her. But you're not working with the Paladins. So it was...'

She laughed again. 'Economics,' she said. 'Mythoeconomics, if you like.'

Just like in the old days, he waited for her to explain.

'We know about your vow of chastity,' she told him. 'Everyone does. It's a perfectly sensible precaution, given that if you marry a Guinevere or impregnate a Morgause, we're all potentially stuffed. But sexual restraint wasn't exactly Arthur's strong suit, was it? Not that he was exceptionally bad, by Camelot standards – sometimes it feels like they were all at it, except Galahad and Percival –' she gives a tiny laugh as she remembers that these were the devices of David Stafford and his long-dead lover Trevor Macnamara '– but still, just making the vow doesn't mean you'll keep it.'

Jory was more than a little aggrieved. 'Christ, Mal, I've managed it so far.'

She smirked. 'I'm sure it's taken superhuman willpower. But we can't let the security of the realm rely on something as flimsy as King Arthur's word. So while you've been making your heroic efforts to control demand, I've been trying to limit supply.'

He stared at her. 'You mean…'

God, he'd missed saying that.

She said, 'Every woman you've been romantically linked with, we've recruited. Starting with me, of course. Laney, Claudine, your old girlfriends from university, the Duke of Cornwall's niece… a bunch of others, some of whom you've never even met.'

She said, 'The Welsh *Triads* reckon Arthur had three wives called Gwynwhyfar. So far we've collected seventeen possibles, and counting.'

* * *

It wasn't until their third meeting, this time at the Novotel in Reading, that Jory met Pendragon Wendiman-Taylor.

By now, Izzy had been living with him for five months, and the paperwork for her adoption was coming through soon.

Of course, as supreme monarch Jory could have decreed it with a word at any time, but he'd felt it best to observe the proprieties. They'd settled into an easy, comfortable relationship, in which Jory's honest – though wary – fondness for the girl seemed to have been reciprocated. He was already thinking of recruiting through the Fastness some female pages of school-leaving age to keep her company.

Seeing this seven-year-old – his biological child, whose true nature had been disguised, even from him, until this moment – he was amazed all over again at his previously unguessed capacity for fatherly love. The kid wore jeans and a Manchester United football shirt, and a knowing smile that was a carbon-copy of Malory's.

'Jory,' said Malory, 'this is Penny. Penny, this is…'

'My Dad,' said Penny. 'I know that, silly Mum. He's always on the telly. I'm so glad it's OK to meet you at last, Dad.'

She came to him where he stood by the mirrored wardrobe, and Jory enfolded his other daughter in his arms.

* * *

A lot of this I won't learn till later, of course. It's not exactly the time or place for Jory to enthuse at his adopted daughter about how fond he is of his secret biological one.

All he says is, 'Malory's been giving me advice for years now. This crisis would have come a lot sooner without her help.'

Izzy snarls, 'Whatever. None of this makes any difference. You're still finished, Dad, with all your Circle and your code of honour and your bloody New Arthurian bloody Britain. Even with Merlin and the Lady of the Lake on your side, you're done for now.'

It's difficult to argue with her there.

22. SIR MORDRED

The first wave of NATO paratroops hits the Castle a short while later. Dropping from the skies like leaves from some unimaginably colossal redwood tree, they settle on roofs and in courtyards, scatter themselves across the Home Park and the nearby streets, drift up against the Round Tower at the Castle's heart.

The two-hundred-odd civilian staff – catering, ancillary, service and clerical – have all been forcibly evacuated by Bonnie and her Knights, as have the pages of the Circle. Remaining are the fourteen Knights, eight squires and twenty men-at-arms quartered at the Castle, plus another forty men-at-arms from the Victoria barracks in Windsor town. They're outnumbered by the incoming airborne forces, but they have the defensive advantage, and for their High King they're prepared to put up the fight of their lives.

They wait patiently, though, obedient as ever to the dictates of honour, watching from window embrasures and battlements as the invaders disentangle themselves from their parachutes and strew hundreds of square metres of silk across the yards and lawns. Then one man-at-arms stands up on the roof, waves his arms and shouts 'Oi!'

The answering volley of machine-gun fire (which he successfully ducks) releases the men-at-arms from the honourable restriction against firing the first shot. They immediately let loose in return, and soon the courtyards are filled with a hailstorm of deadly projectiles. Machine-guns bellow, Victorian leaded glass shatters, and shards explode from centuries-old stone as invaders fall to the defenders' bullets (and a few vice versa).

Alert to the propaganda value of capturing the castle intact and holding it in trust for the British people pending their promised liberation, General Kreiss has ordered that nothing be damaged except from strict operational necessity. The order doesn't last twenty seconds in a combat situation, as the NATO troops frantically force open ground-floor windows and break down doors to avoid the field of fire.

Other parachutists have landed on the roofs, however, or the towers themselves, and it's not long before the men-at-arms positioned there are distracted by their own problems. In the New Quadrangle, NATO troops are climbing the vertical gardens to break into the upper-storey windows. In the older parts of the castle, those who've landed atop the stone towers are setting grenades to blow the doors and hatchways to the stairwells below.

Outside the Castle's bounds, the outliers form up into a geometrically displeasing perimeter taking in Castle Hill and Windsor High Street as well as a straggly loop through the Home Park. A number of locals come out onto the streets to yell at them and throw stuff, but it's going to be a while before the nearest secular army troops – probably local Army Reserve forces – arrive to back them up. However well-prepared the NATO forces may have been for this eventuality, the speed with which a diplomatic incident has escalated into a war has taken everyone in Britain by surprise.

Soon the paratroopers in the courtyards have breached the buildings and are struggling with the men-at-arms in the corridors and chambers of the ancient palace. Soldiers snipe at one another from behind antique chests and suits of armour which their bullets score and dent irreparably, the defenders occasionally mustering a shield-charge which either beats back the invaders or allows them an opening.

Rooms and staircases fall to the enemy and are recaptured… but more often the former than the latter.

Meanwhile, the device-bearers of both forces slug it out in hand-to-hand combat.

Mostly it's Knight against Paladin. On the staircase of the Round Tower, old Darius Beddowes' successor as the bondsman of the Hungarian Round Table Knight, Sir Urre, fences desperately with the *porteur du blason* of Roland's companion Ogier the Dane. Urre's man is strong, but the attacker has the literal upper hand. The Normans built their castles to be defended from the bottom up, not the top down.

In the Grand Vestibule, Queen Victoria's marble statue gazes down primly aghast at Jean Tarrant, the bondswoman of Sir Brandinor, as she slashes urgently at the shield and helm of the *porteuse* of Roland's warrior sister Bradamante. Nearby in the Waterloo Chamber, the device-bearer of the Moorish Sir Morien has locked swords with the *porteur* of Otuel the Saracen; they wrestle grimly, each trying to position themselves for a more decisive blow.

Upstairs in the New Quadrangle, under the glass roof of the banqueting hall, Amal Samadi and Andy Burridge stand nervously in front of the entrance to the royal chambers, swords at the ready, shields hefted, Sir Safir's gold-and-green mathematical tiling next to Sir Brastias' punning armoured arm. Both are determined to defend the Pendragon Tower against all comers, be they Fianna, Paladin, Nibelungentreue or some more exotic legend. The High King's safety depends on it.

At the far end of the hall, the double doors crash open and a figure is outlined there, wearing a bulletproof vest, leather boots and a Stetson bizarrely attached to the top of a standard combat helmet. The moment he sees the Knights, his hands dive for holsters mounted on his left and right hips.

Amal and Andy swear simultaneously. They barely raise their riot-shields in time to deflect the bullets from the twin recoil-operated Smith & Wesson automatic revolvers borne by the Agent of Virgil Earp, Wyatt's lesser-known but somewhat more straitlaced brother.

The last either Amal or Andy heard before today, the Circle's jurisprudes were still working on finding that loophole for Knights facing enemy devices armed with ballistic weapons. Since neither Knight has a gun, it's moot in any case. The best they can manage, as further bullets follow the first, is to charge together at the Frontiersman through the length of the banqueting-hall, holding their shields high to protect their faces and giving voice to full-throated, and frankly terrified, war-cries.

The Agent gets a lucky shot at Andy's knee, piercing the armour at the join between cuisse and greave and sending him toppling, but Amal keeps up the charge. Bullets slam into her own breastplate and cuisses, enough to give her some impressive bruising in a few hours' time, but she presses on until she can engage the man directly.

The Frontiersman falls back as the Knight finally gets within sword range. She slashes at his legs and arms and at his unprotected face, his handguns of little use to him at such close quarters. Amal has little attention to spare for the crashing noises she can hear from the glass hall behind her, the screech and clatter of glass which follows them, or even the crunch of a pair of heavy boots landing amongst shards. She's too busy hacking at the Agent in front of her, who's bleeding now from elbow and thigh, and who shortly collapses onto the floor, desperately trying to bring one of the revolvers to bear.

Behind her, there's a meaty thud and a scream. Andy's voice. Amal can't allow herself any distractions. She slices the gun from the Frontiersman's gloved hand, taking a digit or two along with it. The other weapon must be empty now anyway, but as heavy footsteps approach from behind she stamps on his wrist until he gives it up.

She whirls to face the enemy to her rear. It's a huge lumbering figure in the uniform of a US Army General — not even armoured, she notes in astonishment — carrying a massive metal firefighter's axe as lightly as a rolled-up newspaper.

'Had you figured for a gentleman, Agent Nielsen,' Alec Kreiss booms. 'Ain't like you to give the finger to a lady.' He laughs uproariously at his own joke, as Amal raises her sword and jabs it at him.

He knocks her point aside with the axe's shaft like he was batting away a leaflet advertising feather pillows. She's too slow to parry or duck as his blade returns, slicing – not without some difficulty – through her armour's shoulder joint and severing her left arm.

'I guess it ain't quite an eye for an eye,' he tells her as she loses consciousness, 'but that's asymmetric warfare for you.'

* * *

The Circle loyalist forces under Sir David Stafford, driving from the Fastness on their somewhat belated quest to protect the High King from the NATO attackers, run into the schismatic faction led from Luton by Paul Parsons, whose equally superseded plan is to capture the High King and hand him over to them, at Junction 15 of the M25 orbital motorway where it joins the M4 from London to Windsor. It's all rather embarrassing, and the only way of avoiding the resulting social awkwardness is to violently attack each other.

Both forces consist of long convoys of minivans and horse-boxes, escorted by Brachet armoured personnel carriers and a couple of Castellan tanks. (Stafford at least could have called on helicopters to get some of his people there quicker, but with RAF Wyverns engaging NATO's Chinooks and Wolverines on their approach to Windsor – and presumably, before long, London – air travel didn't seem advisable.) The loyalists' vehicles are all badged with a golden dragon's head in a blue circle. The mutineers have painted theirs out, rather hastily, in white and overlaid it with the three red stripes of Sir Lancelot.

The battle begins when the loyalist vanguard spots the

mutineers emerging from the slip-road ahead of them, at which point the body of the schismatic forces are strung out beneath the loyalist convoy, in the slip road beneath the M4. There's a messy, ugly interlude with vehicles ramming one another or screeching as they pull up short; men-at-arms disgorging from their transports and taking up firing positions; cars, lorries and coaches full of civilians speeding by as quickly as humanly possible; and the outliers of both convoys hastily radioed to throw up barricades which keep any further traffic off the battlefield, and will incidentally cause the worst tailbacks in British motoring history. There are quite a lot of people hoping to leave London today.

The junction consists of a main flyover where the M25 crosses the M4, but also of pairs of slip roads joining the two motorways, which pass above and below that intersection. Parsons' forces, on the slip road routing southbound traffic from the Luton direction eastwards towards Windsor on the M4, are on the lowest of the four levels, while Stafford's, on the M4 proper, are on the level above. This gives the Seneschal's men-at-arms an advantage as gunfire breaks out between them: his men and women, crouched on the hard shoulder and firing over the concrete crash barriers, are almost fully protected from Parsons', who can only cower in the cover of their vehicles and shoot awkwardly upwards. The advantage lasts exactly as long as it takes the rebel forces to send a couple of their Brachets back along the slip road and forward onto the M25 proper, where they can lie on their own hard shoulder and take potshots through railing barriers onto the loyalist troops below.

Before long both roads are an unholy mess of blood and fallen bodies, their surfaces cratered with strewn rubble from the Castellans' attempts to shell each other.

At the vanguard of both forces, the Knights are getting their hands dirty. Spilling across both lanes, they've established an impromptu battlefield stretching from the point where the slip roads join, right back to the junction proper. Saddling up on the hard shoulders, these hectic straggles of hastily-armoured men, women and horses become in short order disciplined ranks, which revert to a chaotic melee as soon as they've charged at one another.

The Knights, of course, bear only their own emblems, with no convenient logos to declare their allegiance. Since the Circle's R&D people have only recently made a start on that emblem recognition software, the Knightly battleground immediately becomes a fiendish test of memory. *Gules, a fox or armed azure* is the device of Sir Melian – but is Crispin Millard one of Parsons' rebels or loyal to the Seneschal? *Quarterly argent and azure* is Sir Galagars – so is Paul's old mentor William Posnett still alive, or has he died and handed his blazon to a younger Knight? Is the latest bearer of the *Argent semy of crescents sable, three bends gules* of Lancelot's cousin Sir Bleoberis a man, so likely loyal to his device's family ties, or a woman and thus blacklisted from the rebel forces?

Is that lion passant or rampant? Is that field azure or vert? Is that serpent winged? It's a minefield – though looking on the bright side, only a metaphorical one.

When they get going properly, though, a full-on battle between conflicting Knights of the Circle is a sight to behold. (Well, assuming you enjoy watching grown men and women beating each other to pulp and occasionally hewing bloody bits off one another.) Armoured horses rear and shy; swords and riot-shields judder; helmets resound with crash after clash, shoulders and fists and arms and knees grow numb from repeated impacts. Blood flies from blades and joints in armour; encumbered bodies fall and roll on the tarmac, or topple over crash barriers into the wooded waste ground separating the motorway from the nearest industrial outlets and sewage works.

Stephen Mukherjee finds himself facing Doug Felton, whose three red stripes adorning a field of black stars explain his device's family affiliations quite clearly. The press and heave of their portion of the battlefield makes their horses useless for manoeuvring, so they stand in their stirrups and exchange great crashing blows until the random chaos separates them again.

Across the melee, David Stafford makes out the emblem of Sir Lancelot, this time emblazoned on a riot-shield, and fights his way towards it. Parsons has spotted him too, and is forcing his way through the melee, punching and slashing at the loyal Knights who stand in his way. Eventually the two men face one another in sight of the overhanging flyovers from which the men-at-arms are still shooting at one another, taking pains to avoid winging any Knights or the few civilians who didn't quite manage to flee before the fighting started. Seeing what's going on the other mounted men and women, loyalist and rebel both, force their own horses back into a ring. They keep on fighting, but they leave a clear space in the carnage in which their leaders can face each other.

Both men's shields are red on white. A cross; three slanting lines: they look like mismatched cards in a telepathy experiment.

* * *

Oli Montalban huddles among the lower, sturdier branches of a tree in Windsor Great Park, a long coat inadequately concealing her Circle armour, listening to the cries and explosions and stutters of gunfire emanating from her former home.

She's been watching since the first helicopters passed above the Castle, the figures pouring from their bellies blossoming with silk as they fell. She's been hiding out somewhere or other since the events at the Embassy – the events she's still managing surprisingly successfully not to think about in any detail, even while their repercussions have been painted across the news outlets she's been scanning for any sign the Circle might be on her tail. The Seneschal and his Knights have other things on their to-do lists, though.

Being Sir Mordred's device-bearer is a rubbish deal by anybody's standards. The really upsetting thing is that they start off with the same idealism and optimism as any other Knight of the Circle. They are, after all, supplicants for Knighthood, hoping to give their lives in service to the chivalric values of the Round Table: for centuries now, anyone who's thinking purely of personal power or self-aggrandisement has been weeded out pretty early in the process. Deprived of such openings, the Mordred device tends to imprint itself upon those whose morals or bravery are compromised by weaknesses it's more difficult to detect and deselect for: those whose conviction and strength of will aren't quite enough to stand up to the temptations it represents.

Most of them begin their Knightly vigils wide-eyed with possibility (Might they end up adopted by one of the big names? Sir Percival perhaps, or Sir Gareth, maybe even Sir Galahad or Sir Lancelot?), and are naturally dismayed to find themselves the bearer of such an ill-starred device. Historically, very few have had the presence of mind to do what Oli did and lie about it – but historically, very few were coached in advance by the bondswomen of Morgan le Fay.

At the beginning, then, most bearers of the *argent, three bends sinister sable* are loyal Knights of the Circle, eager to prove themselves as brave, altruistic and honourable as any of their better-omened comrades. Some, indeed, win out by dying shortly after their acclamation, and are remembered justly as good Knights. For those who live longer, however, the moral flaws the device targeted inevitably reveal themselves – in little deceits or betrayals, shows of malice or cowardice, or full-blown meltdowns of the kind Oli's helpfully demonstrated for us.

At first – persuaded by her friend Izzy that her strength of character meant she could, with effort, overcome her new device's worse nature – Montalban expected to prevail against all the temptations it threw at her. She imagined she'd make herself so invaluable as to supplant Bonnie as the High King's right-hand woman, so irreplaceable by the time her true device was revealed (probably by the real Gawain adopting a new supplicant and denouncing the imposter), that he'd have no choice but to pardon her deception.

I think it's safe to say that Izzy never believed for a moment this was going to happen. Poor Oli did, though, just as she had believed (again encouraged by Izzy) that Knighthood was her rightful station in life.

That was before she met Zara in this very park, and discovered just how far her supposed strength of character extended in the face of deadly threat. After that, she knew she'd fail the High King sooner or later. After that, she understood that she had to turn her failings into strengths.

If she had no choice but to betray the High King, she wasn't going to do it through weakness. She was a modern woman, a Knight no less, and she would take command of her destiny. In a backroom at the Hague she met with Louis Zelinsky, the Agent of the celebrated private detective and sometime Union spy Allan Pinkerton, and offered him a deal.

Zelinsky's side of the bargain, her compensation, was necessary but boring. The interesting part was hers: that she should find a way to discredit the Circle and the High King in the eyes of the international community. Violating international law and killing a bunch of US allies hadn't been what either of them had in mind at the time, but there's no doubt it's done the trick.

Oli understands now that her strength as a Knight is ruthlessness: a willingness to do without compunction (albeit without any exceptional degree of courage) what the other, more rulebound Knights would never for a moment sanction. (She also has a propensity for after-the-fact denial which would have had Freud raising his eyebrows in grudging admiration, but that's more a personal survival skill than a devicial trait.)

This was perhaps an obvious revelation for the device-bearer of Sir Mordred, but for Oli Montalban discovering that she had a strength at all came as something of an epiphany.

Now she sits in the Great Park again, waiting until the flashes and crashes die down, then cease entirely. While she waits she breaks off a straightish, slimmish, narrowish branch of her tree, and strips it of twigs and leaves. Next she pulls out of a coat pocket the plain white tea-towel she bought at the Britomart in Brentford, and ties it to the branch by two of its corners. Then she drops from the tree and starts to walk towards the Castle.

And it's at this point that she suddenly realises, with a heartstopping jolt of shock, that someone in a closely neighbouring tree has been watching her all along – someone who's somehow managed up till now to escape her notice entirely.

Someone whose clothing matches the tree's winter bark, and who appears to have brought along some branches of his own.

'That was quite the sanguinary extravaganza you unleashed back in the Great Wen, Olivia Montalban,' the antlered figure drawls, dropping to the ground in turn. 'I'm appropriately reverential. Now, before you go and welcome our colonial overlords, I'd suggest the brace of us exercise our larynxes in a little conflab. What do you reckon?'

* * *

In the *Morte D'Arthur*, Sir Lancelot and Sir Galahad, his son by Elaine of Corbenic, fight only once. On that occasion Galahad rather embarrassingly unhorses not only his old dad but also Sir Percival, who happens to be in the vicinity at the time.

That situation doesn't really compare with this one, though. It's not a life-or-death struggle, for a start: just a joust that happens more or less in passing while Galahad is – for perfectly good reasons which needn't trouble us for the moment – in disguise. In fact, despite Lancelot being an absentee father for much of Galahad's upbringing, there's little bad feeling between the two knights. They're rivals in the quest for the Holy Grail, but then so's everybody else.

They don't even die in battle. After the Grail quest,

when Galahad's blameless life has allowed him to succeed where his less-than-chaste father failed, he's granted by God the gift of choosing his own time of death and – rather predictably – picks a moment of immense religious rapture. He dies on good terms with Lancelot, and entirely avoids the awkwardness of having to choose between his father and his liege lord when the Round Table splits some years later.

Lancelot, on the other hand, survives his falling-out with Arthur, manages to miss the Battle of Camlann – although in some accounts he mops up Mordred's sons afterwards – and lives out his life as a hermit, eventually becoming a priest. He and Guinevere, who becomes an abbess, see nothing of each other after Arthur's death, but Lancelot officiates at her funeral, dutifully dying afterwards of a broken heart.

Still, as I sometimes have to point out, while the devices can influence our ends they don't determine them – not on their own, at least. If they did, Sir David Stafford, device-bearer of Sir Galahad, wouldn't have survived to be nearly sixty, and Paul Parsons, bondsman of Sir Lancelot, wouldn't be relying on a prosthetic hand, as they square up to each other in the westbound fast lane of the M4.

The Circle's finest pair of Knights spend their first few charges testing one another, swords crashing against shields with a force that could have unseated a lesser rider. Both are shaken in the saddle, but keep their grip as they canter back to the edge of their limited jousting-field and wheel round for another pass.

Above them, a second flight of NATO Chinooks passes ominously, battering the air on a course for central London.

Without the range to build up a decent charge, horseback combat has distinct limitations: there's not a lot two riders can do, tactically speaking, except to keep hitting each other as hard as possible in the hope that one of them falls off before the other. Accordingly Parsons and the Seneschal keep turning and charging, chopping and parrying, neither taking any damage beyond the constant bruising impact, until in the end they fall in the same bout. A particularly strenuous blow from Paul knocks David hard from his saddle, but Parsons unbalances himself in the process and fails to regain it, falling messily and being dragged several metres before separating himself from his horse.

Stafford's rolled, as best he can in armour, and sword in hand, retrieving his shield ready for the inevitable ground fight, he clambers upright like a rearing tortoise.

Paul's up already, though, and the speed and ferocity of his next lunge takes Stafford by surprise. He stumbles aside in time to trip him with his sword. Parsons responds by hacking from the ground at the Seneschal's feet – causing him to leap back – and then is on his own feet again, diving and jabbing, forcing David back towards the hard shoulder, the crash-barrier and the bank beyond.

The Seneschal's footwork is too nimble for that, though. He works his way round anticlockwise until it's Parsons who has his back to the barrier – but Paul responds by pressing him further and further forward until they're fighting in the central reservation, swords still leaping and wheeling and diving in a dance of aggression and defiance.

It's quite some time into the single combat that first blood goes to the Seneschal, who eventually manages to get his blade in behind Paul's guard and jab it into his shoulder, withdrawing it a moment with a crimson streak to match their shields. Paul responds with a renewed ferocity, dissecting the air from all directions, probing for a gap in the Seneschal's defences – a gap which he eventually finds, darting under the overlap of Stafford's cuirass and his cuisses, and twisting his sword before bringing it away bloodier than Stafford's own.

Then a horse, most of its rider still hanging limp from its saddle, bolts between them and knocks both men flying like bowling-pins.

* * *

Half an hour after the assault on Windsor began, General Kreiss is standing in the High King's study, roaring with rage.

The Castle's his now – internally for sure, and so far the perimeter's holding against the reservists the locals have managed to mobilise. The second wave of the attack will be deploying over London now, the news of the Castle's capture fresh in their ears.

The dictator he's here to topple, though, is gone. So are his daughter, his tame storyteller and his bodyguard.

Their clothes are here, they've left behind their phones and tablets and a note addressed to him by name, but the targets themselves have split.

The note's handwritten, evidently in something of a hurry. It reads:

Dear General Kreiss,

I hope you find the Castle to your satisfaction. It's not the Waldorf-Astoria, I know, but the views are very nice, and it should do for what I'm sure will turn out to be a short stay. Please help yourself to wine – I'm told there are eighteen thousand bottles in the cellars, so you should be able to find something to your taste unless you're a beer man, in which case you're out of luck I'm afraid.

I'm sorry not to be here to greet you personally, but I have urgent business elsewhere in the country. I gave my people permission to leave too, but they insisted on staying behind to distract you while my party went on its way. They're very loyal – too loyal, you may feel, and I wouldn't necessarily disagree with you, but I respect the choice they've made. I promise that you will suffer for every one of them who loses their life in this absurd quixotic venture of yours. I fully intend to ensure that you and everything you're working for are destroyed before this business is concluded.

I'm afraid that the birds nesting in the vertical gardens can be annoyingly loud early in the mornings. It's been my

*experience that foam earplugs work very well, but you may
find buggering off back to America suits you better.*

Sincerely yours,

Jordan Pendragon

Kreiss screws the letter into a ball and throws it at the
nearest soldier, yelling at him to go send Agent Mallucci to
him, so he can yell at him to go away again. Then, taking
the view that operational necessity can get to hell, he pounds
down once with two anvil-heavy fists on the Pendragon's
glass-topped desk, shattering it.

Mallucci arrives as requested, though understandably
nervous at disturbing his superior in this mood. '...Sir?' he
asks. The Agent of Daniel Boone carries a Special Operations
Forces Combat Assault Rifle, an Ontario Mark III Navy
knife, and a polished buffalo horn in which he keeps his
rolling tobacco.

'Get the hell out of here, Mallucci, will you?' Kreiss
shouts. It's not as satisfying as he'd hoped.

Mallucci says, 'Sir, there's someone here to see you.'

'To *see* me?' Kreiss is incredulous. 'Ten minutes after we
take the fucking target someone wants to come visit? Tell
them to make an appointment.'

'It's a Circle Knight, sir,' Mallucci elaborates. 'Not one
of the ones we just captured, a different one. She just walked
out of the park and up to the perimeter carrying a white flag.
Says she's on our side.'

Kreiss is alarmed. 'Goddamn it, Mallucci, keep your
voice down, will you?'

Mallucci frowns. 'Sure, sir.'

Kreiss says, 'I guess what you're trying to tell me, Agent,
is that Olivia Montalban, the Circle operative responsible for
the atrocity at the Irish Embassy, is surrendering voluntarily
into our custody, right?'

'I guess, sir.' Mallucci loses his doubts swiftly at the expression on his boss's face. 'I mean sure, that's right, absolutely.'

'Well then, that's different.' Kreiss gives a broad grin. 'In that case, show her in. And get someone in here with a really big broom, will you?'

* * *

Parsons and Stafford scramble to their feet once more – the Seneschal panting hard now, but the younger man still fairly fresh.

'Yield,' Paul suggests, hefting his sword. He has to shout, of course, over the stink and clangour of the struggle surrounding them. 'How many men are dying here? You could end all of this right now, Seneschal.'

'That's not an option... as long as you oppose... the High King,' David tells him breathlessly. 'You... know that, Paul.'

Parsons shrugs, then whirls and cuts at the Seneschal's side in a blow which the older man only just deflects.

They're at it again then, hammer and tongs and any other blacksmithing equipment you might name, each landing more blows than before, but collecting more injuries as battle-fatigue begins to erode their defensive skills. It becomes clear, though, from the trail he's leaving behind, that the Seneschal's losing a lot of blood.

When the end comes, it's through another accident. This time it's a Knight, stunned and weaponless, propelled into their lane by the kick of a horse's hooves, who staggers half-aware into the Seneschal and pitches him to the floor. Paul stands back courteously to let the older man rise, but hampered by the weight of his armour, his shortness of breath and loss of blood, the Seneschal's attempts are abortive.

Parsons stands over him. He pushes back his visor. 'You *have* to yield now,' he says, sounding slightly petulant.

'I won't,' Sir David gasps. 'You're – a traitor. My men – and *women* – need to keep – fighting you.'

Paul says, 'You've got to. You know what I have to do otherwise.' His voice is steady, but the eyes beneath his visor are pleading. For the first time in ages Stafford remembers the young man squired to Jory Taylor, his arrogant self-righteousness a front for deeper insecurities. 'Do the sensible thing for your men, Seneschal. No-one can save Taylor now, but you may be able to save the Circle.'

David shakes his head painfully. 'Do what – you have to,' he tells him.

Paul blinks fiercely, twice. Lightly, affecting weariness, he says, 'I hoped it wouldn't have to come to this, yeah?' He raises his sword, two-handed, high above his head, and reverses his grip so it points downwards at the older man's throat.

The shaft which appears in his own armour, between helmet and gorget, might as well have been spontaneously generated. Yelling in pain, Sir Lancelot's bondsman drops his sword by the fallen Seneschal and scrabbles frantically at his neck, remembering what the last arrow that got lodged in his body did to him.

He's not wrong to be concerned. Paul barely gets a couple of seconds' panic in before the projectile explodes in a gout of flame and greasy smoke, and a light red mist fills the air.

Paul Parsons' body burns from the neck as it staggers slowly and topples sideways. His helmed head leaves a splash mark as it spins to a halt on the opposite carriageway's hard shoulder.

It's not a unique occurrence, as David sees when he at last manages, with the support of Parsons' sword as well as his own, to stagger to his feet. Across the battlefield Knights are falling, arrows pinning their armour: only about one in five then goes on to explode, but that's quite enough to keep the targeted Knights distracted from the battle. As far as he can see, every Knight thus afflicted is one of Parsons' men.

The archers must be using AR targeting software, he thinks – the kind of thing he asked the Fastness technical people for the other day. There are online Circle-watching fora with open-access databases of rebels and loyalists, so it would be easy enough to source the necessary data. Of course, you'd have to have been expecting something like this for a while.

The Seneschal looks up. On the topmost flyover, a tier above the highest level the battle has reached before now, a row of figures stands. Each holds a bow, and from this distance he can just make out their green hoods. They must have climbed up onto the slip road to the south-east of the junction, walked back along the nonexistent direction of traffic, and taken up their positions at the point of maximum strategic advantage while everyone's attention was on the junction's lower tiers.

Sir David finds a vacant horse and scrambles on top of it. He stands up in the stirrups and waves his shield above his head, shouting at the top of his remaining breath.

'Stop...!' he gasps. 'Stop fighting..., all of you! It's over! Surrender... surrender now... and we can all... leave here... alive!'

He slumps back from the effort. Across the battlefield, the confused remnants of the fighting stutter to a close.

On the flyover, the central archer holds up a hand, and her comrades lower their bows.

* * *

Oli is sitting in the Crimson Drawing-Room at Windsor – notionally, and she's increasingly realising actually, under arrest. She's not sat in the precise chair where Laney Wardsley sat nearly eight years ago, because on the whole life isn't that tidy, but there's nothing much to choose between it and the one she's picked.

The NATO troops have treated her well, overall: aware that invading what used to be considered another civilised country is a mission that will be scrutinised intently in the days and years to come, they've generally been on their best behaviour. She's certainly had some filthy looks from the Irish troops in particular, but the one soldier who spat at her was immediately reprimanded by his sergeant. The invaders seem to want to play this by the book... but just to make sure, General Kreiss has set exclusively US troops to guard her here, keeping her well away from the Europeans.

Since Montalban's first, brief interview with the General, Agent Mallucci has been in once to see that she has everything she might need, and she's watched a further wave of helicopters depositing troops and materiel, but on the whole she's been left here on her own to contemplate the proposal Ron Byron made to her back in the Great Park. Time was – very recent time, in fact – when she'd have rejected out of hand anything a Green Chapel member said to her, but recently her life's developed in some novel directions. Britain's politics are changing too, on an almost hourly basis, and Montalban needs to chart a careful course through the currents if she wants to emerge intact on the far side.

Her ruminations are interrupted by the arrival of General Kreiss, all shoulders and geniality. He brings with him the smell of blood, sweat and gunpowder, although he's changed his uniform and washed – his hands, at least – since butchering Andy Burridge and Amal Samadi.

'Hey there, Miss Montalban,' he cries affably from the doorway. 'They treating you OK?'

'Yeah, can't complain,' Oli says politely, and indeed it's perfectly clear that she couldn't even if she wanted to. She glances at the two US Special Forces men who've followed the general in.

Kreiss glances back at them. 'Yeah guys, I'm pretty sure I can take care of myself here. Dismissed.'

The troopers file out, and Kreiss sinks onto a heavy gilded sofa. It creaks under his weight, but holds.

There's an awkward silence for a minute, then he tells her, 'So, I heard from the Fianna. They took your Parliament, and they're working down a list of government buildings on Whitehall. Your army's been trying to get through, but the streets are full of panicking civilians and our air support's keeping them pinned down pretty good. Looks like your Circle guys are kind of busy for now, but we're gonna bomb your Fastness to bits just in case. Central London's ours in a couple of hours max. Then we start in on Edinburgh.'

'You found the new Parliament building OK, then?' Montalban asks sweetly. 'Or are your troops sitting proudly in Westminster Palace Museum?'

Kreiss laughs hugely. 'Our intel runs to buying the *Lonely Planet* app,' he says. 'Listen, Miss Montalban,' he continues, looking serious again. 'I'm having trouble figuring out what to do with you. Long term there's no question – we honour the commitment Agent Zelinsky made. We set you up somewhere comfortable – here or in the US, depending on political contingency – provide for all your needs, you never need to work again. For now you're pretty much our prisoner, and it has to keep looking that way. What you did at the Embassy... hell, I respect it, but it sure as shit wasn't pretty. A lot of people are out for your blood.'

Oli nods carefully. Just now she doesn't trust herself to actually comment.

Kreiss says, 'Now, this place was a strategic target while Taylor was living here, but right now it's strictly symbolic, see? London's where the action's at, and our guys need me there. So I'm thinking – yeah, I could take you down there with me, get you put under house arrest somewhere comfortable – but you'd be kind of high-profile, you get me? Difficult for the world to forget about you, difficult for us to get you any special privileges, or spirit you away when the time comes.

'So what I'm thinking instead, I leave Agent Nielsen in command here and you stay behind with the NATO garrison. Like I say – long term, sure, we get you out of here,' Kreiss breezes, 'meantime, you get the run of the place. A one-woman prison for NATO's Public Enemy Number One. Like Hess in Spandau – except this isn't a jail, it's a royal palace. So more like that Lord of Cornwall guy.' Oli knows from the newsfeeds that the ex-Duke has refused to condemn the NATO invasion – indeed, some pundits are expecting his family to benefit from it, perhaps to the extent of getting their throne back. As Blaze once said, the Frontiersmen would rather sell Mount Rushmore than work with the British royals, but that doesn't mean they can't make use of them. 'What do you say?' Kreiss asks.

Oli considers. 'Yeah, no,' she says. 'I don't think so.'

Kreiss looks put out. 'What, you want the London option ? Like I say, it won't exactly be –'

'No,' Oli says again. 'Not that.'

'What then?' Kreiss isn't a man with effortless control of his temper, and it's showing.

Montalban says, 'You know I'm carrying Sir Mordred's dev, yeah? You can use that. I'm like basically King Arthur's nemesis. Why shut me up in prison when you could be sending me out to track down the High King?'

Kreiss looks aggrieved. 'Like I say, missy –'

She says, 'I stay your prisoner, troth. But you make me an operational asset. Send a squad of soldiers after him, with me to advise them. Put someone else in command, but tell them they'd bloody better listen to what I say, yeah?'

Kreiss laughs brutally. 'And have the Children of Oisín say we had the Irish Embassy killer in our hands and let her go? Not gonna happen, lady.' A thoughtful look crosses his face for just a moment, though, amidst the bluster.

'What, you think I'm going to run off again?' asks Oli scornfully. 'I came here, didn't I?'

'Sure you did,' says Kreiss. 'And maybe once you've found out all you can about us, you're gonna run back to your Circle and buy yourself a pardon with that intelligence.'

'Oh yeah, that'd work,' sneers Oli.

She sighs. She hoped she wasn't going to have to do it this way – apart from anything else, she's terrified the General might snap her neck on the spot and damn the consequences – but she'd rather risk that than decades of enforced captivity spent waiting for the mac Cumhail's people to catch up with her.

She says, 'So, you don't want people wondering too much about me, yeah? So how would it look to the Children and everyone else if a bunch of journalists in every NATO country got anonymous mail saying that Agent Zelinsky recruited me in The Hague, and that I was working for you when... that stuff happened... at the Embassy that day? OK, maybe most of them would just delete it, but some would check up. They'd see Zelinsky and I met all right. There are already people out there saying the Embassy was a false flag operation.' The conspiracy theories were inevitable, of course, but their development is something she's monitored carefully over the past two days. 'It would give them a lot more credibility.'

Kreiss says nothing, contenting himself with glaring at her thunderously.

Montalban says, 'I can still stop the emails going out. All I need's a working tablet sometime in the next... um, twenty hours. That's if your people haven't blown up the internet. But I'll only do that if you go along with my plan.'

Reluctantly, Kreiss is thinking about it. 'It's not such a stupid idea, I guess,' he eventually grumbles. Like you say, your principal's gotta follow its function, and if it gets us to Taylor... let's just say we wouldn't publicise your part in it. I'm guessing you could live with that?'

'Yeah, happy to,' Oli says hastily.

Kreiss makes a great show of considering his alternatives, but they both know he's committed now. 'All right, lady,' he says at last. 'You go with Agent Nielsen. He's in command, you advise. The men and women obey him, not you. He tells them to shoot you in the head, they ask how many times. Got it?'

Montalban smiles. Despite her massive swimmy feeling of relief, she's careful not to turn it into a grin. 'Got it.'

'And I'll get you that tablet,' Kreiss says.

'When we set out,' says Oli.

Kreiss nods with grudging respect. 'Just don't forget,' he says. 'You're a tabloid supserstar. The Circle's very own

419

war criminal. *Everyone* out there hates you. Brits, Europeans, Americans… you're not gonna get a warm welcome this side of the Middle East. Except what I hear, the jihadis are still kinda down on other people's myths. We're the only friends you've got left in this world, lady, and don't you forget it.'

Oli stares out of the window, beyond the men and women unshipping crated missile-launchers and armoured cars from the third flight of Chinooks, at the Great Park and its denuded trees, which branch against the winter sky like antlers above their bark-brown trunks.

'Yeah,' she says at length. 'I'd be crazy to think otherwise, wouldn't I?'

* * *

In the aftermath of the M25 battle – the first to be fought between rival British forces since the War of the Devices, and one which will go down in history as the Battle of Harmondsworth – there's a paradoxical feeling of solidarity, even camaraderie, between the Circle loyalists and their Green Chapel allies. *Yes*, the Knights seem to be thinking, *you may have killed a pile of our ex-colleagues, but you kept a lot of them alive too. And at least you're not trying to kill us.*

And unlike the War of the Devices, this time the two great bodies of British devices are – broadly speaking – on the same side, which is a massive relief for all concerned.

That includes the rebels of the Circle, those that survive at least. The mutineers are paraded before Sir David while the Seneschal has his wounds dressed, and given the option of joining the march on Windsor or being locked in the troop vans and left for NATO. All but a stubborn vanload opt for the former.

Doug Felton isn't one of them. 'No hard feelings, Mukherjee,' he informs Stephen, with a confidence the latter suspects he doesn't feel. 'You know how it is – Parsons was my CO back in the war – the last war, I should say. Blood's thicker than water, all that.'

Stephen nods shortly, knowing that however he feels about it personally, the Seneschal's decision is the right one. 'No hard feelings,' he replies, but he takes care not to notice the hand that Felton's holding out to him.

The news from London is very bad, from what he hears, and from Windsor too. Parliament's Pankhurst House has fallen to a targeted airdrop of NATO paratroopers led by the Children of Oisín. The Fastness is under sustained aerial assault. Worst of all, Windsor Castle itself is in foreign hands: the media footage shows the NATO flag flying over the Round Tower, a white compass-rose against a dark blue field. There's been no confirmation yet that the High King is in custody.

Stephen presses forward through the press of Circle men-at-arms and Knights, heading for the knot of Green Chapel bowmen and bowwomen who are busy having their hands clasped and being hailed as long-lost comrades. For a moment Scar emerges from the crowd, a beer-can in her hand, a pair of AR specs pushed up on her forehead. She shouts, 'Stephen, you great hairy fanny!'

Mukherjee's not in a celebratory mood, but he has to smile at this. 'Scar, old girl. Good work back there. You certainly saved our skins.' The two of them worked together with Jory during the last war, both considered traitors to their causes as they tried to minimise the damage to the country from the War of the Devices. The older woman claps the Knight a comradely clunk on the shoulder, and drags him into the greater mass. He shakes hands with Zara, accepts a celebratory kiss from Janene and gives Rev a manly hug before being introduced to Chaz, Jo and HazMat, emitting polite platitudes all the while.

Released, he presses on towards the Chapel's non-combatant contingent – the camp followers who handed out the arrows, watched the perimeter and troubleshot the targeting software. There are few faces he recognises there – most of them would be too young – but rather to his surprise he does see Barry Jenkins, one of Superintendent Kinsey's sergeants. The man's in a plan green hoodie and bears no sign of his police identity. Either he's undercover – which seems unlikely, given that many of the Chapel met him during a jailbreak eighteen years ago – or he's the leak who told the Chapel where to find Woodville and…

'Steve!' an Irish voice cries, and Stephen smiles with delight as Eoin MacNeill appears in front of him.

'Eoin,' he says, 'good work old man, good work indeed.'

Eoin grins infectiously. 'Never thought I'd be in a battle. Guess things have changed now, hey?' He gives the Knight a hug, and – much to the latter's surprise and embarrassment – a quick peck on the lips.

'That was some jolly impressive archery back there,' Stephen blusters. 'A few arrows went astray, I'm sorry to say, but our medics tells me virtually all the injured were on the other side.'

'Yeah, some fellow called Eric's been working on the targeting software, they tell me,' says Eoin. 'He borrowed the specs from some university department somewhere. He thought the time might come when the Chapel would need to get choosy about which Knights they shot.'

'Prescient chap,' says Stephen, looking around them awkwardly. 'Is… Woodville here?' he asks, a little diffidently. He didn't see her with the fighters – archery's not something Knights have ever been trained in anyway – but he can't imagine her meekly taking her place among the support staff either.

He looks back to see Eoin looking stricken. 'Oh, Steve,' he says. 'She's gone.'

'What – *gone?*' Stephen asks stupidly. 'Surely you don't mean…'

'Oh, Christ, no!' Eoin says. 'At least… well, I hope not. But she's gone off on this… fecking crusade of her own. Rev told her it was her holy duty, or some such shite. I'm… God, Steve, I'm so worried. I couldn't bear it if she got herself killed, now we've finally found each other.'

Stephen swallows.

The Saracen Sir Palamedes, the fall guy for so many Medieval prejudices, adores Iseult with a love passionate but unrequited. Though well aware that she has eyes only for Tristan, his obsession nevertheless inspires him to great deeds of heroism and knightly courage – though also to such base acts as kidnapping her after he rescues her handmaiden.

This sours relations between him and Tristan, who after defeating him in a joust grants his life on condition that he can't bear arms for a year and a day. Even more humiliatingly, Iseult has him take a message to Guinevere informing her that the only true lovers in the kingdom are Guinevere and Lancelot, and Iseult and Tristan. It's breathtakingly passive-aggressive (though of course Arthurian ladies didn't get much scope for more direct aggression), and in a modern context difficult not to read as racist, or at least Islamophobic.

One thing about being Palamedes' bondsman, Stephen reflects, is that it certainly prepares you for disappointment.

He asks Eoin, 'Where's she gone? Perhaps I can help.'

23. HERNE THE HUNTER

An observer standing at a safe distance from Kelliwick House – on the north bank of the River Thames, say, somewhere in the vicinity of Billingsgate – would have a privileged view of the Circle's Fastness as the notorious concrete monstrosity succumbs to the ministrations of NATO's airborne forces.

The reinforced glass roof shattered – not that anyone really expected otherwise – with the first pass of a US combat UAV. The anti-aircraft gun emplacements, even after seventy years of disuse, would have been as useful as ever against a Junkers bomber or a Messerschmitt, but no-one in the '60s really thought in terms of unmanned aerial drones with precision-targeted air-to-ground missiles. There's no way the men-at-arms manning the guns can keep up with their multiple-G approach curves.

That first missile's only an exploratory volley, but even so, it takes out a chunk of the curtain wall as well. Fortunately, the outer shell of the building's been evacuated since the first strikes on London targets, the doors to reception and the car park locked up tight. Harte, Busman and the other personnel still in the central keep have ample time to decamp to the underground bunkers, where they'll be safe unless the invaders lose the plot completely and opt for a nuclear strike.

The Fastness's surface structure, though, isn't long for this world. As the first drone comes back with two friends in tow, it targets the curtain wall more accurately. Two missiles hit, and what one of them hits is the sixth-floor armoury. A massive detonation follows, which the putative observer would feel in the soles of their feet as well as their eardrums. As the first billow of smoke clears, what's left of the Fastness is looking more like the Coliseum – although unlike the Coliseum (since the middle years of the Severan dynasty at least), it's also on fire.

Beneath the slender keep which still rises up intact in the centre of the conflagration, Harte and the rest are holed up in the deep shelters, hoping that some at least of the upper subterranean levels (the Fastness archives, in particular, with their priceless collection of rare Arthurian texts) survive – but mostly hoping they do themselves. Their walls and ceiling are so deep and so heavily insulated that even the armoury's explosion came as just a gentle thud and tremor.

Far above them, the UAVs soar west and bank somewhere over Hyde Park before returning for another go. This time they successfully demolish the last of the curtain wall, leaving the keep standing proud within the flames, like an obelisk designed by someone who's heard of Freudian symbolism and thinks it's a lot of foreign nonsense. Surrounding it is a gargantuan ring of piled cement boulders, fused glass and the twisted wreckage of furniture and portcullises, occasionally erupting in subsidiary explosions as more of the contents of the armouries contribute to the destruction.

The drones turn again, high over Greenwich, and home in on the Fastness like malevolent pigeons.

By now, a pair of RAF Wyverns, scarred survivors of skirmishes with the NATO Wolverines, have noticed and are moving to intercept. They spurt out air-to-air missiles at these interloping robots who are muscling in on their element.

One drone explodes in the air. Another, whose teleoperator back at the Pentagon is more bloody-minded than the rest, takes a hit but keeps moving, angling its flight path towards that of the nearer RAF plane. They meet in an explosion of dark oily smog, which wipes out millions of dollars' worth of equipment and a thirty-one-year-old pilot.

The third drone – as it happens also the first on the scene – survives, to home in on the keep of the Fastness. As the remaining Wyvern banks and returns in pursuit, the UAV empties its remaining air-to-surface arsenal at the base of the tower, then screams away at several times the speed of sound.

The column billows out in a puffball skirt of smoke and flame, and then it falls. The Knights' quarters and office space, the reserve armoury, the boardroom, the Seneschal's office, the Heraldry Corps's design studio – even the tenth-floor chapel where once the future High King of Britain stood vigil to become a Knight, and was surprised by the arrival of a nude Malory Wendiman – are all crushed to rubble.

The NATO drones have compressed the centuries-long process of ruination which claims all castles and fortresses in the end, into a quarter of an hour. All the Fastness needs now is ivy, and a once-hideous building will have become Britain's latest picturesque ruin.

(It'll never happen, of course. Five years from now they'll have cleared the rubble and planted a memorial garden, and London will be missing another piece of her history.)

For now, though, from the smoking ashes that were the Circle's headquarters, two semicircles protrude like the halves of a crashed flying saucer: the wreckage of the giant, wooden boardroom table.

* * *

Although it's high up NATO's priority target list – after Windsor, Pankhurst House, Whitehall, the Fastness and Holyrood, but before Chequers, Balmoral, the Cardiff Senedd, the Stormont Estate and the six English regional assemblies – the Mythopolitical Research Facility was never built to be defensible in time of war. Its security infrastructure's designed to be proof against leaks and theft in peacetime, not a siege by a small battalion of NATO infantry commanded by three Nibelungentreue officers carrying the devices of the Valkyries Waltraute, Helmwige and Rossweisse.

Still, Johnny Quayle, the bondsman of Sir Lucan the Butler, retains one major strategic advantage: the intruders know the building's full of civilian researchers, and are bound by orders and personal inclination to try to recover them alive. In particular, retrieving Ernst Schmidt – a German national snatched from under the Nibelungentreue's noses at the precise point in mythopolitical history when he would have become of strategic value – is a long-delayed priority, which is why the Nibelungentreue insisted on command of this particular mission.

So when Johnny peremptorily insists, over the tannoy system his men-at-arms hastily rigged up while waiting for the attackers to arrive, that the NATO soldiers keep their distance and he'll send out the academics, the three ringbearers order their troops to halt their advance, and to spread out and surround the building at a respectful remove.

Johnny sends out the researchers one at a time, at ten-minute intervals, each escorted by a Circle man-at-arms who immediately surrenders to the NATO troops, while inside his rapidly diminishing team scurries about shredding documents, degaussing hard discs and making various other preparations. First he hands over the undeviced academics who happen to be in the building today – the handful who've been too wrapped up in their studies to realise that the MRF is an obvious target for the invaders (or, in a couple of extreme cases, that there's an invasion happening at all). Freda Tate-Hendricks is not among their number.

This buys him fifty minutes, after which he dispatches, at the same intervals (and to much impatient Germanic tutting), Dr Kawasima, Thora Yrsasdottir, Ben Ben-Ari, and Cécile Lazard. Only Ben-Ari surrenders with good grace: the others have spent the interim getting loudly and objectionably drunk.

Finally, Quayle himself vacates the building, walking beside Ernst Schmidt's electric wheelchair. When they reach the NATO lines, he tells Lorena Eisler, the ringbearer of Waltraute, 'Cheers for that. I'd just fall back another fifty metres if I were you, to be on the safe side.'

Cursing, the Nibelungentreue gives the order. Two minutes later her troops watch from a safe distance as the demolition charges placed by Quayle's team thunderously reduce the building to a ruin of billowing brick-dust.

'Where is Professor Tate-Hendricks?' Eisler demands of Johnny after the noise dies down. 'We expected her here. Was she inside?'

Johnny smiles grimly. 'John Sebastian Quayle. Knight of the Circle. They don't give us service numbers, but you can have my National Insurance if you like.'

'Do any of you know where is Director Tate-Hendricks?' Eisler asks the assembled researchers.

Kawasima spits, while Ben-Ari shakes his head mutely. Cécile demands in French that Eisler does several mutually incompatible obscene things, and brings her a packet of cigarettes when she's finished.

Thora belches and says, 'Beer from the south, a joint from the north, cured meats from the countryside. The highway makes the meal; the walker eats. The one you seek joins the feast.' Which isn't, perhaps, as helpful as it could have been.

Then Ernst Schmidt – whose device plays along with his captor for as long as it's expedient to, but extracts a particularly horrible revenge thereafter – well, does the best he can, although compared with Wayland raping King Niðhad's daughter and turning his sons into jewellery, it's a bit tame.

Schmidt says, *'Ich glaube sie ist in Winchester. Sie trifft sich dort mit Hochkönig Jordan.'*

* * *

Bonnie and I don't know about any of this, of course. We just know that the High King's spending more time hanging around the Roadchef services at Sutton Scotney – on the

A34 in Hampshire about eight miles north of Winchester –
than strikes either of us as entirely prudent.

We've mostly been taking the smaller roads since
leaving Windsor, though we've spent some time walking
cross-country as well. From Ascot to Bagshot we took the
train, we got on a local bus from Fleet to Winchfield, and
we hitchhiked from Alton to Petersfield. Sometimes we've
struck off at right angles or even doubled back on ourselves
–breaking up the journey, covering our tracks.

Now here we are at a service station – a small one,
admittedly, not on a motorway, but still serving a major
A-road, and definitely somewhere that waiting around for too
long will start to make us look conspicuous. We've done our
best to offset that: Bonnie's in civvies, though I assume that
big rucksack of hers holds her sword and shield; I've given
myself a rubbish haircut (yeah, a different one) and stopped
shaving; and Jory… well, being the most recognisable of us
by far, he got Blaze to give him a thorough make-up job in a
deserted gents at Legoland Windsor, where we broke in after
hours that first evening. He looks maybe twenty years older
and significantly darker-haired, with a much fuller beard that
hasn't yet started peeling away at the edges.

Legoland is also where we sent Izzy on her way with
Blaze. We don't know where they've gone – the High King
insisted on keeping it that way – but Blaze insists he knows
of somewhere safe where he can work on the Morgan le Fay
device, try out ways of keeping it contained in future.

Even so, splitting up and changing our appearances
are such basic precautions that the invaders would be more
confused if we didn't take them. There's also the problem
of Jory's device, which gives him a presence and gravitas
that compel attention whatever he looks like: we've got
recognised several times that way already, though fortunately
it looks like those most likely to spot him are the ones who
are the most devoted to him. Frankly, I'm suspecting that
the only reason we're getting away with this at all is that all
three of us have spent time with the Green Chapel, and are

still benefiting from the concealing power of the Sherwood distributed devicial emanation.

In short, staying put for even five or ten minutes after finishing our burgers and fries is starting to make Bonnie and me feel pretty jumpy. From inside the Roadchef we can't see the road outside, or we'd be still more nervous, since in the last few minutes a convoy of US Army Armoured Multi-Purpose Vehicles passed by heading south to Winchester, but for the moment we're in blissful ignorance of that. What doesn't help is Freda Tate-Hendricks strolling up wearing a half-hearted headscarf and saying, 'Blimey, my lor – oh shit, sorry – I mean, blimey, I hardly recognised you.'

'Fuck's sake Freda,' Bonnie hisses. 'Sit down and shut up.' She's looking around outside to make sure the Director came here unaccompanied.

'Freda,' the Pendragon smiles. He's been almost supernaturally calm throughout this whole frantic road trip, content to leave all the necessary fretting, stressing and panicking to Bonnie and me. 'It's good to see you. I'm very much hoping that we can finally sign off on the job I hired you for.'

Tate-Hendricks gives a momentary satisfied smile. 'I bloody hope so,' she says. All she's carrying is a small handbag, certainly nothing that you could fit something a sword into. 'It turns out Ernst's had a working prototype for months now – well, one that tests out OK under laboratory conditions. He's been stalling for time, the wily old bastard.'

The High King frowns. 'You're sure he hasn't shared it with anyone else?'

Freda shakes her head emphatically. 'Johnny's had the place locked down tighter than a duck's arse, my lo – shit, sorry – than a duck's arse. He's certain nothing could have been sent out. How much Ernst can keep in his head is another matter, but even if he defects I reckon it'll take him at least six months to replicate the work. Till then' – she lowers her voice – 'Excalibur's yours, my lord.'

From her handbag, she brings out a thumbnail-sized pin

– an ordinary datatack that you could stick in any phone or tablet. These days an extended family can fit all their favourite books, films, music and TV shows on one of them, to be conveniently lost down the back of the sofa or eaten by the dog.

'What, he's still got to *build* it?' I ask incredulously. 'What use is that?'

'Hush, Dale,' Jory says. To Bonnie, who's also looking dubious, he adds: 'I'll explain later, I promise. I assume it's all self-explanatory?' he asks Tate-Hendricks.

She shrugs. 'For someone who already knows what they're doing, sure.'

'That's good,' he smiles. 'I've got someone lined up. You'd best be going, Freda. I'm not sure any of us are safe just at the moment.'

'Bloody right,' she says. 'I'm booked out of Heathrow under a false name later today. I've been channelling half my salary into a farm in New Zealand for years. I'm going to shear sheep, go to *Lord of the Rings* re-enactments and write books. Not memoirs,' she adds hastily. 'More of the romances. I've had a five-book deal on hold with my Australian publishers.'

Jory looks miffed. 'You've been planning for this,' he says.

'As a contingency?' she says. 'Christ yes, I'm not an idiot. I'm not betraying you – you already know I can keep secrets, that's not going to change. I'm grateful for the work – it's been really interesting, though frankly you can be a shitty boss at times. If you survive the next couple of weeks, maybe you could work on your management style? Anyway, the work's been OK, yeah, but fighting Uncle Sam isn't what I signed up for. Good luck with it, though.'

She doesn't wait for a reply before standing and hurrying out.

* * *

Meanwhile, in NATO-occupied London…

431

…Hang on, I'd better explain Thora Yrsasdottir's riddle. If I don't it always comes up in the questions afterwards.

The MRF staff have always spied on one another – all part of the internal politics of the place – but some of them are better at it than others. Schmidt's gathered that Tate-Hendricks' rendezvous with the Pendragon is happening somewhere in the Winchester vicinity, but Thora got the precise details off her encrypted tablet.

Because, say what you like about the Icelandic saga hero Ref the Sly, he tends to know what he's talking about – even when whoever he's talking *to* doesn't have a bleeding clue. With typical cunning, he allowed Thora to avoid betraying Jory while still being able to claim she told the Valkyries his exact location, hampered only by the unavoidable circuitousness of her device. If she'd told them directly, Agent Nielsen's manhunt operation would have turned up while we were still waiting for Freda, whereas with only Schmidt's vague clue to go on we're gone an hour before they send one of the AMPVs north to check the place.

…The place being, as I say, Sutton Scotney services. Sutton as in 'south ton' – 'ton' meaning town here, but alternatively a kind of beer-barrel: *beer from the south*. *A joint from the north* is, ahem, Scot-knee, while *cured meats from the countryside* obviously means Ham-shire. Specifically, we're in the Roadchef, hence *the highway makes a meal*. Then there's *the walker eats*: as I say, our party's done a certain amount of literal walking, but also 'High King' sounds quite a lot like 'hiking'.

You see? Simple, really. I guess putting in something that meant 'A34' would have made it too obvious.

* * *

Anyway. In NATO-occupied London, General Kreiss has booked himself into Claridge's Hotel, on the grounds that if you're going to conquer – sorry, liberate – a nation, you might as well take advantage of the opportunities to do it in style. The Camelot Suite – a penthouse apartment which the management have been hasty to assure the General will be renamed any day now – is vast and spacious, furnished in the New Arthurian style of a decade or so ago. Bright patterned rugs cover bare stone flooring, abstract tapestries hang from the walls and braziers in wall-mounted stanchions bear bright neon tubes.

Kreiss receives Henry O'Leary in the drawing-room. He stands with his back to a giant open fireplace, above which a pair of heraldically decorated riot-shields has been mounted (their blazons carefully chosen to have no actual Knightly connotations). Between them, a pair of Circle-issue polymer-steel swords are crossed in an empty symbolism of combat.

O'Leary's kept his personal involvement in the fighting to a minimum, a prudent precaution at his age and one which his Fianna understand – although perhaps some of them half-hoped to see him fall in battle so a younger and more virile mac Cumhail could arise in his place. *They'll just have to wait a little while longer*, he thinks.

'O'Leary!' The General is in expansive mood, chomping on a fine cigar (not Cuban) and toasting the mac Cumhail's arrival with a glass of expensive Scottish single malt. 'It's going pretty good, huh?' A maid follows O'Leary in with a tray bearing two champagne flutes and a bottle in an ice-bucket.

The mac Cumhail composes a cautious response. 'So far we're getting on well, right enough. But there's a way to go yet you know, General.'

Kreiss waves this aside along with his cigar smoke. 'That's just the detail. Hey – get some life into the fire, will you?' he tells the maid. 'The sidewalks in this city are covered in shattered brass monkey balls.'

'Yes, sir.' She crosses to the fire and starts stacking anthracite blocks in the grate.

'Like I say,' Kreiss tells O'Leary, 'details. We got London, we got Edinburgh, we got those other pissant towns they call capitals. We got Windsor Castle and the Research Facility.

What is there left? The goddamn spaceport? You think they'll be calling up reinforcements from Mars?'

O'Leary frowns. 'I just think we need to keep our wits about us.'

'You know your problem, O'Leary?' the General asks, waving a hand and slopping his expensive scotch. 'You're too goddamn cautious. Difference between you and me,' he adds, warming to his theme, 'you don't take enough joy in the way things are. We're *giants*, O'Leary, trampling this tiny island. Paul Bunyan and Finn McCool.'

'Fionn mac Cumhail,' O'Leary replies sharply, but the General's not to be deflected.

'We should *think* like giants,' he goes on. 'We change the landscape, you know? Your guy built the Giant's Pathway or whatever they call it, mine scraped out the Grand Canyon. We throw a stone, the little guys get a new mountain. We take a piss – hey, there's a new river. Today we're gonna build a new nation right here, and who's gonna stop us?'

'We missed the High King in Winchester,' O'Leary points out gently. 'The Circle still has an army.'

'The Circle's broken,' the General says. 'They managed that themselves before we even got here. Now we've bombed their Fastness till it looks like Stonehenge. Sure there's a force out there, but they're a mess. What can they do to us now?'

'And Taylor?' the mac Cumhail asks.

'Got my best man on it,' the General grins. 'Along with an honest-to-God native guide. We'll hunt the bastard down, don't worry.'

'Let's hope,' O'Leary replies gravely. *What native?* He wonders. He makes to nibble at his thumbnail, but it can wait. 'In the meantime, we need to consolidate our hold, here and in the other capitals. The Circle may not be a threat, but there's the Green Chapel too. They're used to guerrilla warfare. Resistance against a superior force is their specialty.'

'The Green Chapel?' Kreiss roars with laughter. 'We brought down King Arthur and his goddamn Knights, and you're worried about a bunch of guys in green tights? What's Robin Hood gonna do, folk-dance us to death?'

The mac Cumhail sighs. There's not much to be gained by reasoning with the General in this mood. Or, he's beginning to suspect, at all. He says, 'It's not the thing to underestimate any myth, General. They wouldn't be myths otherwise. Do you not know the current bearer of the Robin Hood ally's a radical Muslim?' *Both radical and Muslim anyway,* he thinks, *even if she's not radical in her Islam.* At this point he'll take whatever gets the General's attention.

The General barks a laugh. 'The US has occupied countries full of radical Muslims. What's one more or less?'

O'Leary rolls his eyes. Then he frowns. There's something different about the wall behind where General Kreiss is standing.

'So tell me, O'Leary,' Kreiss insists. He's getting belligerent now. 'I want to know. What can one woman do against men like us?'

'General –' the mac Cumhail says, urgently.

But the General's not listening to him. Something else has attracted his attention. Something that's genuinely surprised him. He stares down at it, spluttering. Some of the whisky he's just swallowed comes back up, mixed with a little blood.

It's the point of a Circle sword, emerging from his huge chest just below his sternum. O'Leary's mildly surprised that it was long enough to go all the way through.

'This ain't...' Kreiss begins indignantly. He tries to swivel to see who's standing behind him. O'Leary turns too, and without looking back dashes across the suite to the door.

The maid's locked it, of course. He spins back in time to see the General's bulk crash to the floor, shaking the room, and revealing the slight figure standing behind him. She holds both swords, still: one clean, one slimy with Kreiss's gore.

'You stupid sods,' says Tania Woodville. 'Didn't anyone *tell* you what we do to giants in this country?'

* * *

The NATO taskforce under Agent Brad Nielsen is passing through the outskirts of Harewood Forest when things start to come unstuck.

Before they both left Windsor Castle, General Kreiss assigned Nielsen four AMPVs, twenty secular troops – of both sexes and various nationalities, though none of them Irish – and custody of the war-criminal-cum-intelligence-asset Olivia Montalban. Thus far the manhunt has been hampered by the general uncertainty over such fundamental questions as what transport the High King might be using, how many supporters he has with him, and his likely destination. A strategy of questioning locals at gunpoint hasn't been making them wildly popular, and some of the US troops in particular have been getting rather demoralised at the ingratitude these Brits are displaying.

Montalban – who has little to go on other than her strong preference for not ending up at the side of the road with a bullet in her head – has argued that the High King is likely heading for the Celtic heartlands of Wales or Cornwall, but her intuition hasn't convinced Nielsen. An early investigation of the countryside near Windsor – including those broken-into loos at Legoland – was interrupted by the intelligence supplied by Ernst Schmidt, which galvanised them into an afternoon of fruitless footling-about in Winchester. At last, though, a positive sighting at Sutton Scotney services – where, as I say, we made it difficult for people to miss us – has set them on something approaching a trail.

Nielsen, bearing up stoically under the absence of his left middle and index fingers, has turned the AMPVs westward in the direction the High King was seen leaving – which leads to, or at least passes, Stonehenge – when the convoy encounters the hitch.

The specific form it takes is that of a crude home-made landmine, consisting of high-yield explosive crammed into a cellulose fast-food carton, glued shut and placed carefully as if randomly chucked onto the largely deserted road. As the leading AMPV rolls over it, it goes off with a percussive slam, turning the vehicle into a seared twist of scrap metal from which only one trooper emerges, on fire and screaming.

Forbidden by protocol to run out into what might be an ambush, his comrades can only watch helplessly as he rushes off into the undergrowth and rolls frantically to extinguish the flames.

The three remaining vehicles huddle tightly to await the follow-up, but none is forthcoming: the presumed Pendragonist resistance forces appear to have played their hand. Eventually, loading the injured man aboard, the remaining AMPVs hurry ahead, leaving the bodies of Agent Nielsen and five of his troops behind for later recovery.

Oli Montalban, riding in the rearmost car, is unscathed.

* * *

Stephen Mukherjee pulls up his Triumph round the back of Claridge's in Brooks Mews. It's a civilian model commandeered from a showroom in Slough (though he was careful to write the owner a receipt), because he's not quite such a colossal chump as drive a Circle bike through the centre of occupied London. Keeping his helmet on for the mo (because it wouldn't do to be recognised, after all), he sits and considers.

Most of those news outlets which are both reliable and still functioning agree that General Alec Kreiss booked into the hotel this morning, and has been holding court there ever since. Just half an hour ago, according to those same sources (mostly foreign correspondents for news sites in the NATO countries, backed up by local civilian bloggers), Henry O'Leary the mac Cumhail turned up too, and is now closeted with the General. All of which makes it pretty likely, based on what Eoin told Stephen at Harmondsworth, that Woodville is either inside already or is planning to be soon.

Stephen's promised Eoin that he'll try and help her not get killed, by physically preventing her carrying out her plan if necessary. (Assassination's shockingly unworthy of a Knight of the Circle in any case, and is liable to get her court-

437

martialled if the Seneschal hears of it.) If that happens, though, he's not planning on bringing MacNeill's name into it. Better to let Woodville think her plans were ruined by blundering old Mukherjee chucking his oar in, than that her boyfriend thought she couldn't do her job properly.

Stephen remembers that kiss, though – the friction of Eoin's slightly stubbly lips on his, the unexpected *normality* of it. If he wasn't a man of his word... which he *is*, of course... well. He feels a cad for even thinking it, of course, but if it *should* turn out he's got here too late and she's been killed already, MacNeill won't want for someone willing to take care of him in Woodville's absence.

...Which is quite enough of *that* kind of maudlin thinking, thank you very much.

Stephen dismounts and surveys the backstreet. It's narrow as London thoroughfares go, but still the width of several cars. Claridge's takes up most of its block, rising to a height of five or six storeys, of which he suspects the General will be ensconced on one of the uppermost. Many of the rooms have helpful balconies, some of them close to a potentially shinnable drainpipe.

The adjoining building is some kind of absurd upmarket gym with pretensions to being a private gentlemen's club: certainly far outside Stephen's price range on a Knight's salary... even assuming the Circle had a payroll department left, or a functioning economy to move the money around in.

Best not to think about that either, just now. Stephen shakes his head to clear it, and briskly runs through his options.

Plan A: Walk in and brazen it out, using some pretext to track down Woodville or at least the General's room. Hugely risky, since the lobby – and presumably the service entrances – will be crawling with NATO personnel.

Plan B: Climb up the outside of the hotel, peering in at windows as he goes, until he comes across Kreiss's suite and sees what's going on inside. Better – because he could hopefully get inside to help Woodville if need be – but dangerous, labour-intensive, and hugely conspicuous.

Plans C and D ('Set off a fire alarm and have a word with Tania on her way out' and 'Abseil heroically in from the expensive luxury flats opposite') he quickly dismisses, which leaves Plan E: Disguise. Even if the invaders have had time to print up decks of cards backed with the faces of prominent Knights, they won't be expecting him specifically, and a uniform – whether of the hotel staff or a fellow NATO soldier – will make them less inclined to look closely.

A soldier would be best, of course, but the staff – who surely can't all be traitors – are more likely to be amenable to the idea.

All of which means that Stephen's pretty much hit on the plan which Tania herself put into practice half an hour ago, when she unexpectedly appears above him, carrying out his rejected plan B in reverse.

She's not looking in a good way. She's clambering painfully down the drainpipe, when any self-respecting escaping assassin would be scurrying. Her grip looks none too secure; a couple of times she fumbles and almost slips before hugging herself tightly to the pipe.

She's leaving a trail of red along the paintwork as she descends.

'Crikey,' Stephen gasps. Whipping off his helmet, he hurries to the bottom of the drainpipe. She doesn't see him – she's glaring grimly at the pipe, not looking down – and he daren't call up in case he distracts her, or attracts the wrong kind of attention.

As Woodville crawls painfully toward the ground, Stephen's mind dashes off in all directions. How badly is she hurt? Where can he possibly take her? Did she manage what she came here to do? Has the alarm been raised? Will every NATO soldier in London be out for still more of her blood?

What on earth will he tell Eoin if she doesn't make it?

Three floors above him, Woodville slips again, and this time slides a foot or two before coming to a halt. She pauses, then begins weakly to try to clamber from the drainpipe onto the nearest balcony. Again she slips; her blood-slick hands fail to regain her grip, and she falls.

It's not exactly the prodigious leap from the cliffside chapel at Roche which Sir Tristan made to escape being executed by King Mark, but... well, you know how these things work by now.

Without a thought, Stephen raises his arms and catches her before she hits the ground. She's not a heavy woman, but she's moving fast and she's a dead weight: without his device to help him, he'd be in a bit of bother. As it is he staggers a bit, but keeps his footing.

Woodville's breath is coming in quick gasps. A large gash in her side is letting out an awful lot of blood: the maid's uniform she's wearing is painted with the stuff.

Her eyelids flutter open, and she gasps, 'Mukherjee?'

'It's me,' Stephen agrees. He adds, 'Hullo.'

She groans, 'I took them out. Kreiss *and* O'Leary. But O'Leary fought back.'

'Good work, Woodville,' says Stephen, because now isn't the time for recriminations. He carries her quickly across to the bike. 'Can you hold on to me while I drive?' he asks, but he doesn't get an answer.

He stands there, holding the limp, unconscious, oozing woman, and wonders what he can possibly do next.

From far above his head there comes a yell of outrage and alarm.

* * *

The NATO taskforce regroups a few miles down the road in Andover, where they sequester an area of street outside a pub named – presumably sometime in the past decade and a half – the Golden Dragon. Sergeant Hoyt, the Frontiersman footsoldier who's been left in charge by the deaths of Agent Nielsen and the others, radios London to report the fact, and to request a medevac for the burned man, Lavelle. He's being treated by the team's medic inside the pub.

When Hoyt emerges from the AMPV, he finds that the cluster of fifteen men and women standing alertly between the three vehicles have their attention focussed on a newcomer.

'He's a friend,' Olivia Montalban insists quickly, hoping it's true. 'A Green Chapel deserter, yeah? He's offered to be our guide. Agent Nielsen knew all about it.'

'He didn't tell me, ma'am,' Sergeant Hoyt replies curtly.

'His choice, sergeant,' she replies. 'Probably "need to know" or some shit. Mr Byron has skills we need now, haven't you Ron?'

The brown-hooded man – who's not wearing his antlers today in deference to delicate foreign sensibilities, although their outermost tines peek from the top of his rucksack – nods. 'I'm here to lend my virtuosity in huntsmanship to your endeavours, gentlemen. Like Ms Montalban says, my archetypal sponsor is of the venatorial persuasion, and purposes to adopt as his quarry none other than our erstwhile potentate.'

'What's that in English?' the sergeant snaps.

Ron looks annoyed. 'Are you defective or something?' he asks. 'That fucking *was* English.'

'Maybe slide back a bit on the thesaurus, varl,' Oli suggests.

'Oh, very well.' Ron sighs elaborately. 'A gloss, then, as a sop to the hard of cogitation. My devicial principal, gentlemen, is Herne the Hunter, the leader – one of the purported leaders, at any rate – of the Wild Hunt. Now, those of you of northern American origins, who spend your leisure time trolling out into the copious wildernesses of your continent to shoot, stuff and mount various quadrupeds – and I should clarify that I *did* envisage a comma there – may find that unremarkable. But let me assure you that in here in Albion our conception of hunting is a rather more upmarket one, and so are our myths about it. If Herne of the Hunt undertakes to lead you to a quarry, that quarry will be found.

441

'I don't need to explain "quarry", do I?' he asks Oli in an extravagant aside. 'They won't start asking about stone production?'

'No, I think you're solid there,' Oli mutters.

Sergeant Hoyt's irritated by this whole situation, but he's used to dealing with the Frontiersmen, some of whom are just as eccentric. A long-term assignee to the Agency – the Frontiersmen's equivalent of a sergeant-at-arms in fact, although their command structure's rather different – he's in the habit of deferring to such people. And Agent Nielsen told him from the get-go that they were all under orders to respect Miss Montalban's expertise.

So if she says they need this pompous-ass freak... 'You reckon we can use this guy?' he asks wearily.

'Troth,' she says. 'Agent Nielsen was sure of it. Poacher-turned-gamekeeper, yeah? To catch a device you need a device.'

'I thought that was your job,' Hoyt replies.

She says, 'A good leader makes use of the resources available. Mordred couldn't have killed Arthur otherwise. We need to do the same.'

The sergeant sighs. 'I need to call the General personally to authorise it,' he says.

* * *

Unlike the Mythopolitical Research Facility, Windsor Castle *was* built to withstand attack. Admittedly the Victorian modifications and the New Quadrangle have compromised that vision (as General Kreiss demonstrated, you don't put a glass roof on a building you want to fortify), but a full-on assault – especially with a NATO garrison in possession – would still be a formidable challenge.

Kreiss's forces only managed it because they had access to a technology – aircraft and parachutes – which understandably didn't figure in the original defensive plans. The Circle's options in that direction are limited, especially since blowing the place up with lots of high explosive would make for unfortunate symbolism (and could be disastrous for any prisoners held within, including, possibly, the High King himself) – but with the Green Chapel on their side, they have the option to sidestep the ordinary rules of combat in ways William the Conqueror's architects might not have anticipated.

It's night-time – a near-moonless winter night of frost and high-blown cloud – when a figure cloaked in vegetative green slips from the avenue of trees that sentinel the Long Walk and darts across the lawns, unseen between patrols of guards, to stand beneath the New Quadrangle's Turbine Tower. The wind tonight is chill but gentle, and the blades' revolution is a majestic slow wave worthy of the premises' last-but-one owner. In its silence, an owl's hoot oboes through the chilly night.

With businesslike precision, the hooded figure draws from her backpack a reel of cord which she clips onto a buckle at her waist. The slim rope is braided from carbon nanotubing and is strong enough to lift a dinosaur, provided it was decked out in a harness of the kind she wears beneath her cloak.

She pulls an arrow from her backpack, which she snaps into a special clasp at the rope's far end. Then she unshoulders a powerful compound bow, nocks the arrow, and in a fluid movement leans back, draws it and fires directly upward at the turbine sails.

She fails, twice, the arrow falling back to earth and having to be hastily reeled in… but those who bear the allies and devices are used to that. She knows she has a good five minutes between patrols. On her third attempt, she succeeds in getting the arrow to loop around one of the great blades and back, to be gripped by its own cord as the turbine's stately movement pulls it taut.

The vast drum turns. The plaited filament is wound around it like spaghetti on a fork. The woman places a preparatory foot on the wall of the tower.

Then the cord's tight, yanking at the harness around her waist, and all at once she's running up the tapering but still near-vertical wall of the tower, exulting – heartily but silently – at her own skill and daring.

As she reaches a particular window halfway up the structure, she hits the quick-release on the buckle, and tumbles into the embrace of its embrasure. Above her, the monofilament cord whips away upwards, like an electric flex mysteriously vanishing into a vacuum cleaner.

Poising herself on the window-ledge, she pulls a circular diamond saw from her backpack and carefully screws a hole into the glass. She reaches in, deftly picks the lock on the window-catch, then faces nothing more awkward than a potentially deadly scramble around the outward-opening pane before she's inside.

She selects a torch from her backpack and flicks it on, confirming that she is indeed inside the New Quadrangle's Upper Armoury, located on the sixth floor of the Turbine Tower to keep it safe from burglars. Surrounding her are racks of Circle-issue swords, unblazoned riot-shields, armour, tasers, dazzlers, fuddlers, smoke grenades, flash grenades, actual exploding grenades, pistols, sub-machine guns and machine-guns, and a pair of modest shoulder-mounted rocket-launchers.

Zara allows herself a quiet but merry laugh.

* * *

While Zara's spearheading the joint Circle-Chapel assault on the Castle, the Green Chapel's non-fighting contingent and the injured of the Circle are setting up camp, with a guard squad of able-bodied men-at-arms, in the Long Wood in the far south of Windsor Great Park. Given the need for stealth, a riotous party's out of the question tonight, so like most of the rest of the encampment, Eoin MacNeill spends the evening sitting in his tent huddled in his layers of clothes, blanket and sleeping-bag, listening to music on the smartwatch Tania bought him and doing his best not to worry.

In fact the retaking of the Castle holds little interest for him, but he can't help thinking about Tania and what may well turn out to be her suicide mission. Truth be told, he's feeling a little guilty for sending Steve Mukherjee after her. If he saves Tania it'll be worth it, no question, but if they both die... well, he'll have lost two people he's come to care about, and that's a hard thing to look forward to.

It's a massive relief, then, when he hears a self-deprecating, 'Knock knock?' and the flap of his tent unzips to reveal Steve himself outside, bending and peering in.

Eoin's face lights up with a grin. 'Steve!' He fumbles to turn off the music. 'Did you find her?'

'Can I come in?' asks Stephen. Eoin gestures, and he does so, zipping up the flap after him. He sits on the hard groundsheet and says, 'Yes, old boy, I found her.' There's something different about him – something uneasy, even haunted. 'She's hurt, I'm afraid, too poorly to bring here but she'll pull through. She got the buggers all right, though – Kreiss and O'Leary both.'

'That's my girl!' Eoin punches the air. 'That old bastard's had it coming to him for years. Kreiss too, the arrogant fecker. You say she's hurt, though?' His face falls. 'How bad is it? Where's she now?'

'Probably best if I tell you from the beginning, old chap,' says Stephen, and gives him a swift recap of Woodville's escape from Claridge's Pendragon suite.

'I had to lie her across my lap and drive the bike as best I could without her falling off,' says Stephen, grimacing. 'I couldn't keep it up for long, of course, but it got us far enough away that I could... well, steal a car,' he admits, shamefaced.

Eoin giggles. 'Sorry,' he says. 'But your face! C'mon, Steve, it was only a car. Tania's life was at stake.'

Stephen looks upset again. 'Well, yes,' he says. 'I managed to get her to the flat of one of the Fastness's secular medics, and our luck held enough that she was at home. Well, with the Fastness bombed to bits and London under martial law she could hardly go to work, I suppose. She's treating Tania there – on the QT, of course. She can get the supplies the needs from the hospital her other half works at.' He says it as if distracted, as if there's something far more pressing on his mind. 'So, I – well, you know. Saved her life, I suppose. Just like you asked.'

'Oh Steve, that's brilliant!' cries Eoin, and gives him a massive hug. Mukherjee holds him tight.

'That's great,' Eoin repeats. 'Really, Steve, that's great.'

He looks into his eyes. They carry on holding one another.

'Steve,' he says seriously, 'you wouldn't be shitting me now, would you? Telling me something I want to hear because you think I can't handle the truth? 'Cause you know I wouldn't want that.'

Mukherjee shakes his head. 'Cross my heart,' he says weakly. 'Honour as a Knight.'

And then Eoin's kissing him, their tongues entwining, lips sliding across one another as they fall onto the pillows, fumbling and straining to undo the sleeping-bag's zip, hands insinuating, stroking, grasping, gasping and whimpering.

After a moment, Stephen pulls away. 'I can't,' he says. 'You and W– Tania. It wouldn't be –'

'Hey, I'll be the judge of that,' Eoin tells him seriously. 'That's not your problem, OK? Now, come here.'

He pulls him closer, kissing him more tenderly this time, one hand gripping his neck while the other makes quick and expert work of his belt-buckle and fly. 'Oh, Steve,' he says, kissing his face now and his neck, and working his way down, 'you hero, you fecking hero you. You great big brave old muscled Knight in armour. My great big fucking hero.'

Then his head reaches Stephen's groin, and doesn't say anything else for quite some time.

* * *

'You told us you'd explain, my lord,' Bonnie reminds the High King that night, as we settle down to sleep. 'You said.'

'You did, boss,' I agree. We're sharing a room for safety, although for appearances' sake we've taken three. The landlady's two floors up and deaf, so she's unlikely to notice. The B&B's a frankly grotty one at Winterbourne Stoke, just down the road from Stonehenge and not twenty miles from the pub in Andover where our hunters are overnighting.

Jory thinks we can reach our destination – wherever that is – the next day: he says we can travel faster now he's got what he needed from Tate-Hendricks. For a while I thought Stonehenge itself might be where we were going, that the Pendragon intended to make his stand where his reign began fifteen years ago – but no, he just glared at the stones as the couple we'd hitched a lift with drove on past, as if the past decade and a half are entirely their fault.

(And, in a sense… well, let's not get into that now.)

The High King sighs. 'Can it not wait till the morning?' he asks, but Bonnie and I are adamant. Apart from anything else, he had us take some serious risks to get hold of that datatack.

'All right, then.' He sits up, gathering the duvet about him against the scarcely-moderated chill of the night outside. The B&B owner doesn't seem to believe in heating, which is another persuasive reason for us all to share a room.

'Excalibur,' I remind him. 'It's not a sword, is it?'

He shakes his head. 'We called it that to mislead people. Though in the end, I'm not sure anyone outside the building even heard the name. It's my ultimate weapon, as Excalibur was Arthur's – that's the idea, anyway – but no, it's nothing so simple as a sword.'

'What, then?' asks Bonnie. 'How long's it take to get it off of that tack and into real life? What you going to do, print it?'

'No need,' says Jory. 'The data is the weapon. Excalibur's a devicial WMD. Like the devicial mine McCutcheon used on me, but… bigger. Very much bigger indeed.'

Bonnie whistles. 'Big enough to get the Frontiersmen and the Fianna in one go?'

'It doesn't work quite like that,' says Jory, hesitantly. 'It works on a culture, not on individuals. The way Freda explained it to me, it's actually more a metadevice, in that it's driven by people's expectations and beliefs about the devices. New ideas, new technologies usher in social revolutions. The printing press, the telephone, the internet – they all changed how people think in fundamental ways. Subconsciously, people expect the same from the devices – some kind of radical social shift. This draws on that expectation to bootstrap the revolution itself.'

'But boss,' I say, 'there's already *been* a devicial revolution, fifteen years ago. Lots of stuff got blown up, people got killed. You were very upset about it.'

'Not like this one,' Jory says. 'This breaks the devices' hold across an entire culture. Their stranglehold on people's politics and thinking, their... *hegemony*'s the word Freda used – the Excalibur Program shatters it to pieces. No more strict devicial schools wielding the devices as instruments of control. No more selection processes, no more out-groups, no more suppression of devices that don't fit the formula. No more Wars of the Devices, because no more sides to have the wars between. Just... people, fulfilling their ordinary human potential, outside the shadow of oppressive groups like the Founding Frontiersmen. Compared with what we're used to, it would be a utopia.'

'Shag me,' says Bonnie. 'And 'cause the data doesn't get used up, you can do it again and again. After you've done the Frontiersmen you can use it on the Fianna and the Paladins and the Nibelingythingy. And anyone else who won't leave us in peace.'

'Peace is the aim,' Jory agrees. 'But I'm not going to use it. Malory is. Now go to sleep.'

He lies down, and refuses to say any more that night.

* * *

The morning after Zara's breached the walls of Windsor Castle, the Pendragon flag is once more flying over the Round Tower, and the Seneschal of the Circle and the ally of Robin Hood are walking in the New Quadrangle.

The Castle's liberation was at the same time an act of great valour and heroism, and also pretty much a walk in the park. After the insanely risky trick it took to penetrate the armoury, Zara just armed herself with two pistols, stuck half a dozen more in her backpack and went hunting for the nearest guards. She found a pair of them, and persuaded them to tell her where to find the nearest prisoners while being dangled out of a fourth-story window. Release the prisoners, arm them, then repeat. By the time she threw open the Castle's gates to Sir David's forces, she had nine Knights, seven squires and thirty-three men-at-arms at her back. The Castle's defenders – a mere hundred NATO troops under the sole command of Guillaume Ficheur, the *porteur* of the blood-steeped warrior-archbishop Turpin – didn't stand a chance.

By sunrise, the Circle's wounded – who'd been given effective enough short-term care by the NATO medics – were being rushed to hospital in Slough, Jean Tarrant and the other intact Knights were greeting their old comrades, and the unfortunate Ficheur – an actual Catholic priest, as it happens – was confined to the chapel vestry and having Rev Cantrell's theological objections to the just war theory explained to him at length.

Despite a total loss of nine men and women on both sides it's not a bad night's work, and David and Zara toasted it gravely together that morning in the High King's study, with a glass of vintage sherry from the Castle cellars.

They have a pressing question still on their minds, though. Tarrant and the others have confirmed the High King's departure shortly before the assault: he and Izzy left accompanied by Bonnie, me and – surprisingly to David and Zara, who aren't up to speed on this part – Blaze.

Since neither David nor Zara considers Jory a complete

idiot, they're less surprised to discover that he didn't tell the people he left behind to face the enemy where he'd going.

'If he'd been arrested or – you know – we'd have heard by now,' David says nervously. He really doesn't like to think about the likelihood of *you know*, but he's well aware of how things usually go for the heads of state of countries NATO forces invade. 'Mind you, Kreiss has been quiet since yesterday.'

Zara nods judiciously. 'Still, I think so,' she says. 'They'd have nothing to gain from letting us believe he was alive and free if they'd captured him. I'm surprised they haven't tried to claim it anyway.'

'Difficult, with his device,' says David. 'They couldn't palm us off with a lookalike. Unless the lookalike had some kind of shapeshifter device, perhaps,' he muses.

Zara shrugs. 'If he was dead, I think we *all* might feel it.'

'Perhaps.' Stafford shakes his head. 'This is uncharted territory for us all.' He bends to peer at a vertical flowerbed in the nearest wall. In the unexpectedly warm morning sun, a few of the plants are beginning to sprout tiny white buds. He doesn't give much for their chance of survival, honestly.

He asks her, 'I assume we're agreed about what we need to do next?'

Zara smiles. 'You go first.'

Sir David nods. 'All right. We have more devices than the NATO troops – for the moment, at least – but we can't count on the secular armed forces to back us up. Too many of them are deployed at the land border in Northern Ireland, and with these rumours about the ex-Duke of Cornwall supporting the invasion… well, there's still a substantial old-school royalist contingent among the senior officers. With the Pendragon missing from the equation, I'm afraid old loyalties may out.'

'We need to find HK,' Zara agrees. 'He needs our protection, and the country needs his… leadership. Even a popular rebellion needs a leader, and –' she makes a wry smile '– a country that has known King Arthur will not unite behind Robin Hood.'

The Seneschal smiles too. 'I'm so glad you agree. So... all we need to do is work out where on earth he's going. Hang on,' he adds as his tablet starts chiming, 'I'd better get this.'

As he thumbs the answer icon he looks at the caller ID, and his eyebrows rocket.

'Ms Wendiman,' he says. 'This is a little unexpected.'

* * *

Although the whole Green Chapel camp awoke exultant at dawn – when the only slightly exaggerated news arrived that Zara had taken back the Castle single-handed – it took some time before anyone thought to bring Eoin MacNeill up to speed. In fact it's Rev Cantrell who thinks of checking on him, aware that there's still been no news from Eoin's girlfriend, and worried that everyone else's jubilation may be distressing the guy.

When he stops by Eoin's tent later that morning, though, the kid's gone, taking all his stuff with him – and leaving just some rumpled bedclothes that Rev's long-practiced eye can tell have been involved in a protracted session of carnal enjoyment.

'Hey,' he asks the nearest Circle man-at-arms, 'who did Eoin have with him last night? Did Tania make it back?'

The man asks around, and comes back with the news that Stephen Mukherjee arrived shortly before midnight, asking for directions to MacNeill's tent.

'Steve Mukherjee?' Cantrell barks out a laugh. 'Now who'd have thought that. He always turned me down, anyway. Hey, guys,' he asks the encampment at large, 'Has anyone seen Steve or Eoin today?'

But nobody has.

When Rev eventually gets round to asking some slightly more searching questions, it turns out no-one anywhere has any idea what's happened to Tania Woodville, either.

* * *

Meanwhile in Andover, Ron's busily pontificating. 'The watering-hole of Sutton Scotney was a mere waystation for his former majesty. He'll be striking out for Camlann, the prototypical Pendragon's ultimate battle, or my name's not Ronald Alfred Byron. He'll be homing like an Atlantic salmon for the locale where Arthur's and Mordred's forces faced one another, and the High King and his ill-considered progeny exchanged reciprocally mortal blows. We'll try to avoid that eventuality this time round, Oli,' he adds, hardly reassuringly.

The NATO troops are gathered round a cluster of tables in the Golden Dragon, enjoying the landlord's full English breakfast. Ron has dug out a twenty-year-old AA road map from behind the bar and is flicking through its pages.

Sergeant Hoyt hasn't been able to get through to the General, of course. When finally, after hours of trying, he got sixty seconds with a distracted Frank Mallucci, Daniel Boone's Agent said he couldn't spare the manpower to relieve Hoyt, and hazarded that although it was goddamn irregular, for the moment the taskforce should consider itself under Miss Montalban's command.

And since Montalban herself seems to be deferring to this Ron guy...

Still, that doesn't mean Hoyt can't ask questions. 'Why would he do that?' he asks. 'Why'd he go somewhere he knows he's gonna die?'

'If my surmise is sufficiently hydroretentive,' says Ron, 'our recent autocrat won't be able to restrain himself. Arthurian history's recapitulating itself apace: Sir Lancelot's betrayed his king, Sir Gareth's bench-pressing the daisies, and it would seem the avatar of Morgan le Fay is abroad. By now the Pendragon archetype, its hour come round at last, will be slouching towards Camlann to be killed.'

'Yeah, but Ron,' Oli objects, 'nobody knows where Camlann *is*, do they? The location's been lost, like Camelot. Like most of the places in the myths. If the High King knows, he hasn't told the rest of us.'

Ron nods. 'It's my supposition,' he says, 'that his device

452

can no more authenticate the locale in question than any other source. Of the multiplicity of candidate sites for the theatre of combat, the compelling issue won't be which is the authentic Camlann, but which one meets the present needs of his device. Wherever our one-time lord and master's betaking himself, though, I'll wager it's not the River Camel in Cornwall, nor to Castlesteads in Cumbria. It won't be to Camelon in Falkirkshire that his particular way's being wended. Even Cwm Llan on Mount Snowdon will not, I'll aver, lie at the far end of any beeline he finds himself compelled to lay down.'

Montalban stops rolling her eyes. Dutifully, because she's twigged by now that playing along is the only way of actually getting any relevant information out of Herne's ally, she asks him, 'Where, then?'

'Before I vouchsafe that particular datum,' Ron tells them all gravely, 'I need to be assured we're of a unified understanding on this. If we're to shepherd the lifespan of his ex-majesty to its natural surcease, we all need to be chanting from the same psalter.'

'That's our job, Mr Byron,' Hoyt confirms. 'If you can point us to him, we can take him.' Realising what Ron probably just said, he adds, 'But our orders are to take him alive if possible.'

Ron nods. 'Oh, doubtless, doubtless. Nevertheless, Sergeant, if we were to fall short of that estimable aspiration – by, for instance, *tearing the fucker to shreds and filming it on our phones* – it would be my contention that the tidings and attendant footage would find your respective kingpins, bigwigs and honchos in a regretful yet lenient mood. Provided the great work of liberation is brought to completion, the specific mechanism is to some degree moot, innit?'

Sergeant Hoyt's lips are dry. He licks them. Although not normally a brutal man, he finds Ron's bloodthirsty imagery unexpectedly refreshing. This is a war, after all, and war is hell. Agent Nielsen and the others discovered that for themselves already, and he can't see why Jordan Taylor shouldn't get a taste of it. The dictator's the reason they're here at all, after all. It's no worse than he deserves, after the Irish Embassy.

Glancing at Oli Montalban, Hoyt realises there's something about that thought that doesn't quite hang together. He quietly puts it aside to think about later.

Around them the troops are holding back a little, waiting for his lead. He can feel their eagerness, though. This Ron's got their blood up. For a moment he thinks he maybe hears one of them growl.

Hoyt says, 'I guess we decide that later.' He knows full well that when they find the High King there'll be no time for anything so considered. 'For now... this asshole thinks he can get away from us? I say no way, José. I say we run the fucker down.'

Montalban's looking mildly perturbed, but Ron acknowledges the sentiment.

'A hunt, then,' he says gravely. 'That would be wild.'

24. THE PENDRAGON

Just south of the A303 as it passes through Somerset, there's an Iron Age hill fort called Cadbury Castle. The archaeologists reckon that it was built around a thousand years before what we think of King Arthur's sixth-century heyday. A thousand years later still, though, an antiquary named John Leland decided (perhaps unilaterally) that the earthworks were the site of 'Camelot, sometime a famous town or castle,' adding – in case we missed the point – that 'The people can tell nothing there but that they have heard say Arthur much resorted to Camelot'. (Actually he used spellings like 'Arture' and 'Camallate', but you get the gist.)

Most scholars are sceptical about the Cadbury-Camelot connection, and many suspect that Leland made the whole thing up. Even if he was writing about a genuine sixteenth-century tradition, Cadbury's only one of many candidates in Britain for the site of Arthur's castle. (It's not even the only Cadbury in the West Country, the name having once meant 'battle-fort', though it's pretty clear Leland thought he was talking about this one.)

Even so, this particular putative Camelot has a couple of interesting features. At one time there was an ancient bridleway called King Arthur's Lane, long since disappeared under the hoof-, plough- and tyre-tracks of the local farmers, along which Arthur himself was rumoured to ride out hunting every midwinter with his phantom hounds.

And then there's the River Cam – not the Cambridge one obviously, 'Cam' also being a surprisingly common name for rivers as it once meant 'bendy' – which runs close by the hill fort, and whose nearby banks are widely touted as the location of the Battle of Camlann. ('Camlann' means either 'banks of the Cam' or – less conclusively – 'bendy banks'.) Local lore claims that a bunch of farm labourers once dug up a mass grave of male skeletons there, and while both identifications remain dodgy, it would make a certain amount of sense if Arthur's last stand had been made just outside his primary stronghold.

In any case, associations with Arthur's kingship, his downfall and – just incidentally – a tradition bearing a strong similarity to the legends of the Wild Hunt, give the countryside which this particular stretch of dual carriageway is passing through a certain significance. Malory probably has a term for it, a 'geomythical devicial nexus' or something equally unpronounceable, but in her absence let's just say it's somewhere it wouldn't be all that surprising for surprising stuff to happen.

This particular surprising thing happens while Bonnie's driving us westward in the battered Mini Magus which our increasingly reckless High King bought this morning for three times its value from the first person in Winterbourne who recognised him. (His name was Duncan, and although he really wanted – begged, in fact – to give it to us for free, Jory insisted on paying in cash, which is the sort of thing the people whose heads go on the money can afford to do.)

Taking her cue from her High King's newfound willingness to make himself conspicuous, Bonnie surprised me by unpacking from her rucksack a suit of the Circle's latest lightweight foldable armour, made from some new plastic-like metamaterial whose precise name escapes me. She's wearing it now – it's flexible enough for her to drive in, and even with the heating in the car turned up she doesn't seem too uncomfortable, though maybe that's just the stoicism they teach them at the Fastness.

We're within sight of the so-called Castle – which from here just looks like a long flat mound with trees growing up the sides – when without any warning a blocky fortified van, all camo paint and Batmobile facets and bearing a NATO badge on its bonnet, trundles out from the side-road up ahead and comes to a halt across our two-lane carriageway, blocking it completely.

Bonnie swears violently and screeches to a stop, as men and women in women in combat fatigues start climbing out of the vehicle. Their faces are painted green and brown with camouflage makeup, and their heads are adorned with leaf-bare tree-branches.

'Schoolboy error,' Jory notes calmly. 'Turn round, Bonnie.'

Bonnie doesn't need a second bidding. She executes a hasty yet impressively controlled three-point turn in the deserted carriageway, and hares back along it the way we came. Behind us, the yelling men and women turn and scurry angrily back towards their vehicle.

A moment later, Jory says, 'Or maybe not,' and Bonnie yells 'Cocktwats!'

Looking forward, I see what's caught their attention: up ahead, a second NATO Armoured Multi-Purpose Vehicle is parked on a road bridge. Men and women in combat gear are dropping from it at the end of lines, all dressed in bits of tree like it's Macbeth they've come here to hunt down.

On the road the other side of the bridge a third wheeled khaki block is also disgorging troops. Atop it stand two more distinctive figures: one stock-still like a sentinel, the other capering wildly and shouting encouragement. That one wears a brown top, the hood thrown back across his shoulders, and is waving some sort of staff above the branching tines of the antlers he wears.

'Is that… Ron?' I ask as Bonnie slams on the brakes. It's been years since I last saw the lad. I get a vivid flash of the chirpy, blithely confident adolescent who introduced himself to us with such aplomb at the Green Chapel's Trafalgar Square rally on the eve of the War of the Devices, as I stare at the demented dance of the man ahead of us.

Nobody seems especially interested in that question, though, because the other figure, the stiller one, is in Circle armour and carries a shield which shows every sign of having been hand-painted. It's white: across it, from our lower left to upper right, run three parallel black stripes.

'Oli Montalban,' Jory concludes grimly.

The branch-headed soldiers charge us. They're emitting… well, I suppose you'd call it a battle-cry. A whoop, a collective yell.

To us, just at that moment, it sounds an awful lot like the baying of a pack of hounds.

Behind us, the first AMPV is fast approaching. Well, I say *fast* – the thing's top speed is probably about fifty miles per hour. Judging by our journey here, Duncan's knackered old Mini can manage rather better than that, but not as much as you might hope.

Bonnie takes the brakes off and guns the engine, roaring alarmingly towards the approaching soldiers before throwing the car into a screaming handbrake-turn. This sends us hurtling back the way we were going in the first place, towards the first AMPV. The driver starts to slew it across the road, but those things aren't exactly the most manoeuvrable, and there the Magus does have the advantage.

Bonnie just manages to fit between the front edge of the advancing vehicle and the central metal barrier, scraping the paint all down the side of the car as she squeezes us past – and then we're through and off again, heading westward away from the notional site of Camelot and Camlann, but this time with the hounds of the Wild Hunt on our tail.

* * *

'Come off at the next junction, Bonnie,' the High King suggests.

'The nearest one's off the other carriageway,' I say, pawing desperately at the scrolling map on my tablet. 'There's no exit from this side.' Behind us, the first AMPV is in pursuit, its occupants yawping and yapping at us through its built-in PA systems. (They're not shooting though, which, while mystifying, comes as something of a relief.) We're gaining, but not fast enough for my liking. Behind the vehicle, its siblings will be picking up their own speed.

'Bonnie?' repeats the Pendragon.

'On it, my lord,' she replies.

'What? But you can't,' I say, waving the map. 'Look.'

'Christ, Dale, you're so *negative*,' Bonnie says, as she brings the car to a sudden, juddering halt opposite the exit on the other carriageway. Between us and it stands the central reservation, fenced with a low but sturdy aluminium barriers. 'Those things get broken all the time.' She reverses in a screeching arc until we're directly facing the central line, then guns the engine.

'What, *really?*' I say, glancing right. The AMPV driver's already worked out what we're at, and is slowly moving across to the other carriageway. The vehicle's treads flatten the reservation barrier like origami, which I suppose supports Bonnie's point.

'Let's find out,' Bonnie growls, and releases the brake. The Magus surges ahead, experiences an almighty, jarring jolt, a scream of mangling metal – and then we're over, hurtling towards the exit road with the AMPV still a good ten metres away.

The cry of the hunt recedes as they lose sight of us: their vehicle was going flat-out to try and catch us, so I imagine it'll take a minute or so for them to brake, back up and take the side-road.

We reach a junction opposite some weird buildings that look like a cross between a motel and a bus station – I'll later discover it's a giant motoring museum, stuck out here in the middle of the countryside – and Bonnie takes a left.

'Shit,' she mutters. I can feel it too – the Mini isn't handling so well since its encounter with the metal wall. It's perceptibly slower, and it's making an unpleasant graunching noise.

We burrow back under a square concrete bridge that carries the A-road over our heads, then take a right across a railway bridge and double back immediately, to pass underneath again on the other side. We're now heading north, away from the NATO manhunt. The Mini could fail us at any moment, but for the moment it's keeping up a steady fifty MPH. We haven't seen an AMPV for a couple of minutes.

'So, where are we going, boss?' I ask. The railway's on our right, the motor museum's grounds beyond it, though the road veers off to the left up ahead. The tablet tells me it'll amble for several miles across the countryside before joining the A37 somewhere called Lydford-on-Fosse. 'And can we get there before the car conks out?'

Just at that point one of the armoured vehicle bursts through onto the bend ahead, collecting some bits of fence in the process. I realise that the AMPV's actually driven over the railway tracks, after presumably breaking through from the motoring museum car park. Men and woman leap into the road ahead of us, bellowing triumphantly.

Bonnie yells something with words in it even I haven't heard before, floors the accelerator and steers us left through a hedge. She cuts across a grassy field, the Magus bumping and jouncing like a microlight in a hurricane, while the foremost hunters run howling to cross our path.

Jory's been ferreting about in Bonnie's backpack, which has been sitting in his footwell. Now he opens up his window and leans out holding her sword in his left hand, pointing it ahead of us to impale a NATO soldier who's crossed our path. Another goes under the wheels with a revolting crunch before we're through another hedge and back on the road again, comfortably ahead of the pursuing AMPV.

It's at this point that one of the hunters loses patience and starts shooting at us. The rear windscreen shatters and I scream and duck, but after a moment the gunfire ceases. I wonder whether Ron's had a sharp word about the sanctity of the hunt or something similar, although pursuing the quarry in an armoured car hardly seems within the spirit of the thing either.

'Twatting hell,' mutters Bonnie. 'That was *too* close. Good work with the sword, my lord.

'My lord?' she adds, glancing aside. 'Oh. Oh *shit*.'

I sit up again. The High King's slumped sideways in his seat, blood trickling from the side of his head.

'Jesus bollocks Christ,' Bonnie groans, and I can hardly disagree.

* * *

And so begins one of the most stressful and terrifying experiences I can remember. Bonnie coaxing the failing car down increasingly cramped roads, around bends and through tiny hamlets, in constant terror – well, *she* may not be, but I am – of meeting something coming the other way or getting stuck suddenly behind a tractor or a flock of sheep; me doing my best to stop Jory's head from getting knocked about too badly, and all the time that yelping behemoth – and, as they slowly catch us up, its two companions – lumbering along behind us, always in sight, never falling behind, never gaining: like a monster in a nightmare, only a lot more vivid and solid, capable of crushing us under its treads without a moment's hesitation when the Mini's engine finally gives up the ghost.

Even if we stopped now and surrendered, I wouldn't give much for our survival. I don't think the pursuing troops are following the NATO rules of engagement any more. I think they've been subverted by the animal charisma of Ron's out-of-control device, seconded to his Wild Hunt, with King Arthur as their quarry rather than their leader. I guess Merry would call it a devicial emanation, like the one that lets the unallied Green Chapel members blend into the background like the Merry Men. I've not seen anything like it since the British Beasts.

It's not Midwinter any more, of course, but that doesn't seem to be stopping the Hunt. It's the fifteenth of January – a date which, to us as to everybody else in the country, has no particular significance as yet.

The other two can be forgiven for their inattention to the devicial ramifications of our predicament, of course. Bonnie's trying to keep the car under control – and I can feel how the steering's suffered worse than the rest of it – while Jory's unconscious, breathing shallowly, with a bloody bullet-graze in his right temple. I've been dabbing frantically at it with a windscreen cloth – like a lot of head wounds, it's bleeding more than seems healthy or reasonable – but there's a limit to the triage you can perform while being jolted frantically along in a moving car.

'Did he even tell you where we're going?' I ask Bonnie, who only grunts in reply.

She seems to have some idea, though – at least, whenever we reach a junction she takes one road or the other, and she hasn't yet driven us into a dead end or someone's farmyard. The AMPVs take longer to negotiate the forks and bends, which is all that's kept us ahead of them so far, but we can't stay on these tiny country roads forever.

* * *

After about ten minutes of this, Jory comes to with a groan and says, 'Good God. I though my head had come off.'

"Fraid not, my lord,' says Bonnie. 'You're stuck with this.' *And so are we,* she loyally doesn't add.

I pass him a cloth – the sixth I've used, as Duncan considerately left us with a whole packet – and he holds it groggily to his temple. I keep expecting more shots, and the dilemma of following my instinct to duck or trying somehow to shelter the High King from further injury, but so far the hunt's resolve to do this the old-fashioned way – give or take the motorised transport – seems to be holding.

It's just as we're approaching another railway bridge that the Magus finally cashes in its chips. The engine coughs and shrugs, then apologetically stops supplying us with motive power. The car coasts forward while Bonnie and I swear and panic for a bit. The lead AMPV's about fifty metres behind us.

'Out, out, out!' Jory's shouting, or trying to shout at least – his voice is pretty weak. He passes Bonnie her sword and Sir Bedivere's red-and-gold gonfanon shield. As we roll level with the bridge she wrenches on the handbrake and throws open her door. Jory leaves the car as well, but almost immediately he staggers and collapses. By then I'm out too, and quickly I help him up.

'I'm OK,' he assures me, shaking off my hand and standing determinedly. 'Just the loss of blood, I expect.'

'*Just?*' I say. 'Boss, honestly…'

But the Hunt's approaching, and it's not the time. We leg it up the road, the High King shrugging off my help and Bonnie's, though he's weaving woozily at first.

Bonnie was always a smart kid, and she's a smart woman now. Leaving the Mini blocking the bridge was a clever move: crushing a ton or so of small family hatchback under your treads isn't a quick process, even for an AMPV. We dash along the road until we get to a junction with a bigger one, and Jory shouts at us to go left.

I hare after Bonnie and the Pendragon, worrying what the sudden exertion must be doing to his system after that bullet-graze, and trying to ignore everything I can feel it doing to mine. The High King's making a game go of it –he's taken pains to keep himself in trim these past fifteen years – but he's still giddy, and Bonnie's having to steer him in the right direction occasionally. She may not be a kid any more, but she's young still, and without her middle-aged monarch in tow I can tell she'd be running a hell of a lot faster.

As for me… well, I was sixty last birthday, and I didn't

exactly put in the hours in the gym even at Bonnie's age. Knowing I'm running literally for my life is keeping me going so far, but there's no way a tubby elderly ex-folk-singer can keep this up for long.

A tiny single-rotor camera drone – a personal model, not one of the ones the media use – appears along the road in front of us, flying low. It buzzes a couple of feet above our heads, circles us once as we run and then carries on towards the hunt.

'That... wasn't... military,' I gasp as we run.

'It's a friend,' pants Jory. 'At least... I hope so.'

Behind us one of the AMPVs has found a route across the railway line, and is churning a muddy trail across the fields to the left of us. Ahead is one of those small hamlets, a line along the road of pretty flint-grey houses with red clay-tiled roofs, low stone walls surrounding their neatly trimmed lawns. They're only on the north of the road, though: to the south there's no obstruction to the fort on wheels that's trundling towards us.

Something from the map's been bothering me, but I'm aware I'm not thinking straight, and I've hardly got the time now to call it up on the tablet and have a closer look.

As we past the first few houses there's an almighty thud and a crashing, roaring sound. Not daring to stop, I look back over my shoulder, and see the AMPV juddering to a standstill, smoke pouring from its front. The cab's smashed to pieces, and from the brief glimpse I get so is its driver. The doors fly open and out stagger branch-headed soldiers, coughing and choking.

I don't have the leisure to wonder what the hell's happened, though. The other two vehicles are coming, though – one over the fields, the other, after presumably crushing the Mini, along the road behind us. I keep going, but I keep glancing back as well.

From behind one of the houses, a Castellan tank emerges, British army issue but badged with a gold dragon

464

on a blue circle. As my ears clear from the explosion, I can hear thundering hooves from the fields behind it.

Behind the ridges of the roofs, clearly visible from our angle, figures are lying: green-hooded men and women, their bows and arrows at the ready.

'Keep going!' Jory gasps at the pair of us, urging us further on through the village, past an old red phone box and a pub.

'But –' I say, trying to ignore the excruciating cramp my right side. Living the cliché: *I'm getting too old for this shit.* Frankly I never much enjoyed it in the first place. 'But boss – we can stop now. The Circle – the Chapel – they're here!' Behind us now, there's the sound of gunfire, and the occasional booming of the tank's heavier ordnance.

'They'll – distract them,' the Pendragon agrees. 'Slow them – down.'

We scramble on, and soon we're at a crossroads – I realise this must be Lydford-on-Fosse, in fact. Behind us there comes a long, repeated yelp, as of a single hound, and I turn to see Ron, a long way behind us but running full tilt. His face has been painted like the others, and he's waving that stick – *good God,* I realise, *it's a spear* – above his antlered head.

'I'll bloody distract *him*,' says Bonnie, drawing her sword, but Jory drags her on.

'No, Bonnie,' he insists. 'I need you with me.'

After the crossroads there are a few more houses, then open countryside. Before long, Jory's hustling us along a footpath off to the right, and then before us in the distance we can see our destination.

'Oh shit,' I say, stopping dead. 'No way, boss. No way are we going *there.*'

My brain's finally realised what was nagging at it, and has joined the dots.

Oli Montalban. Cadbury Castle. A battle.

The Excalibur Program, Bonnie here with us... and this.

He frowns at me. 'We've no choice, Dale,' he says. 'That's where this ends, one way or another.'

Ron's shrieks again, that whooping, barking war-cry. He's showing no sign of slowing down. The Circle and the Chapel are evidently occupied elsewhere.

So, wearily, I turn, and we stumble on towards the marshy shores of Lake Glastonbury.

* * *

Behind us, on the far side of the village, the NATO troops suborned by Ron and Oli have been diverted into a pitched battle against the joint Circle-Chapel forces. Men and women with the compass-rose logo on their shoulders crouch now behind their armoured vehicles, shooting at the Knights who are charging towards them. One AMPV's still moving, trying to run down the oncoming horses, but it's under constant threat from the munitions the Castellan is dropping nearby, and shortly it's become another smoking ruin. Every time the NATO men and women pop up to fire, they run the risk of getting an arrow in the eye or the gun-arm from the archers giving the Knights cover from the roofs.

Nor does the enemy's borrowed devicial emanation from the Wild Hunt help them – it's distracting them from the fight in fact, urging them constantly to chase after their departed quarry. Meanwhile, the riders bearing down on them carry devices they're fully in tune with, who completely support their aims in this battle.

A few of the pack make a break for it towards the crossroads, Oli Montalban and Sergeant Hoyt at their head. A volley of arrows from Scar and Janene, positioned on a house at the western perimeter of the action, drops the lot of them, and Mordred's bondswoman falls with the rest.

* * *

Ron catches up with us on the margin of the artificial lake, a boggy borderland where the grass and scrubland of abandoned fields gives way to reeds and sedge. Though most of them have been felled by now, a few dead trees stand out in the water, decomposing picturesquely, and the occasional outcrop of an undemolished house reminds us how recently this area was populated. Looking down the long sweep of this lobe of the lake, the vista's broken by a tiny wooded island to the left, and to the right the spit of land that was once the A361 at Havyat – but the view is clear down to the island town of Glastonbury, and rising up from it the warm, motherly shape of the Tor and tower.

We turn – at bay, I suppose – at the water's edge, and face the Hunter.

His spear's a vicious-looking thing – clearly modern, presumably designed for hunting, the sort of thing survivalists order over the internet then practice shoving into animal carcasses while railing against the left-wing liberal media. Its head is stainless steel, three fingers thick with a razor edge. The handle's black, some kind of fibreglass perhaps, with a rubberised grip. There's not much doubt that it could kill someone pretty effectively.

Bonnie steps up, sword ready to protect the High King, but he says, 'No, Bonnie. Leave this to me.'

'He's got a giant fucking *skewer*, my lord,' she says, but she stands obediently aside.

Ron's breathing heavily, but nowhere near so out of breath as Jory and me. 'So here we are, old man,' he says, and he doesn't mean it the way Stephen would say *old man*, as a friendly endearment. '*In extremis*, you might say. Just your good self and mine.'

'Well, actually –' I begin, but Jory shushes me.

'You two vamoose, scram, scat, make like trees, leave, take a hike and get the fuck out of here,' Ron tells Bonnie and me. 'This is between the *former* High King and myself.'

'It's OK,' the Pendragon asserts implausibly, and Bonnie and I move a little way away.

'Further,' says Ron, and we back off further.

'What's this about, Ron?' Jory asks. Forgetting his wound, he rubs the side of his head, then winces. His hand comes away sticky with blood. He says, 'I don't even know what your grudge against me is. Do you? Or are you being driven completely by your ally now?'

'Oh, I've got all the objections,' Ron avers. 'Devicial, political *and* philosophical. I abominate monarchs every iota as utterly as Herne does. As much as the Chapel used to, before you made them all your worshipful lap-dogs.'

'You're not the only republican in the country,' Jory reminds him. 'But the rest of them don't seem to be taking it to quite the same extremes. What's so objectionable about me specifically?'

'Oh, it's not personal,' Ron sneers. 'You're damaged, but so are all kings – spiked by their crowns, impaled by their very sceptres. All wounds corrupt, and an incurable wound corrupts incurably. You came to heal the nation, yet here we stand, our gaping lesions wrenched ever further apart. I don't know what your private traumas may be, Taylor, but a maimed king makes for a mutilated land. And you're as cognisant as I of how that's to be palliated.'

'By human sacrifice? The old king dying so a new one can be born?' Jory actually seems to consider the point. 'No Ron, I don't think so. I think Britain's had its share of miraculous rebirths. I don't imagine there'll be another High King after me.'

'Don't mire up the *aqua* fucking *pura* with me,' Ron barks. 'All kings are crippled, I said. The *realm's* to be revivified, not its monarch. Your demise is to vitalise the land; your blood will fructify the seeds of our new commonwealth. From Camelot's cinders a republic will arise. Any queries?'

Jory smiles patiently, gently even. 'Was it Rev, Ron?' he asks.

Next to me, Bonnie says 'Bollocks,' and starts running.

'Were you in love with him?' asks Jory. 'And I took him away from you? Because that's all I can –'

'Shut your flapping cavity!' Ron yells, and leaps wildly at the Pendragon, spear raised. Jory's taken by surprise, and stumbles backwards into the reedy marsh. Roaring incoherently, Ron puts his foot on his chest and pushes him down into the water, then raises his weapon to thrust down into the High King's body.

Bonnie's long run-up reaches him then and, with a wild two-handed swing of her sword, she takes his head off.

It splashes as it falls, rolls to one side under the weight of an antler, presents the other to the sky like the dead trees out in the lake. The rest of him flops down onto the Pendragon, and has to be heaved off by Bonnie's booted foot.

She helps him up. 'Bonnie,' he gasps angrily as I run up to join them both, 'what did you do that for? I was still talking to him.'

"S my job, my lord,' says Bonnie, quite unrepentant. 'Always has been. He wanted to kill you.'

'Yes,' the High King agrees, 'but that just shows I was getting through to him. I never will now. You can't just go round beheading people whenever they annoy you, Bonnie.'

'You used to,' Bonnie reminds him.

* * *

The Battle of Lydford's a short and unequal one. The NATO troops have guns and the protection of their armoured cars, but the Circle have bulletproof armour, archery support, Knightly devices and a bloody great tank. Before long the taskforce's shelter has been shelled into pieces, and they're being sliced, trampled and pierced through the soft parts by the Knights and their Chapel allies.

Sir David's supervising the arrest of the few survivors, and the counting of the bodies, when Zara and her party come loping over from the houses.

'Was that your drone we saw just now?' Rev Cantrell asks him, pretending hard not to be out of breath. 'We thought it was these guys', but it seems they didn't see us.'

'Not ours,' Stafford says. 'I thought it was yours.'

'Perhaps it belongs to Merry,' Zara suggests, joining them.

David gazes round at the enemy, alive and dead. The live ones look faintly concussed, and aren't talking. 'Who do these people think they are?' he asks, not rhetorically. He points at some of the flags on their shoulders above the NATO compass-rose. 'Americans, Germans, Poles, Hungarians, but all wearing those branches on their heads. I know devicial contamination when I see it. Who are they supposed to be?'

'I think,' says Zara, 'what they really wanted to wear was antlers. This was the nearest they could get.'

'It's Ron,' Rev tells David sadly, and the Seneschal's face falls. 'He did this to them. We let him down, all of us. We let the Herne the Hunter ally take him. Which one is he?' he sighs, looking around for a body whose antlers are more convincing that the rest.

Scar approaches in a hurry from the far end of the battlefield. 'Janene's gone after HK,' she says breathlessly. 'There's no fucking dead Knight.'

The Seneschal smiles. 'Fortunately not,' he says. 'We've a couple of injuries, but nothing major.'

'No yours, you daft sod,' Scar tells him. 'I'm talking about the lot we shot running after HK. We just checked – there's three dead NATO soldiers and a sergeant who's still alive, but the lassie with the black and white stripes has buggered off.'

* * *

'Poor Ron,' the High King's saying, shaking his head sadly as he gazes down at the body of Herne's ally. Bonnie and I exchange an awkward look and wonder whether we can all go back to the village now. Personally I'm hoping there might be somewhere that does cream teas.

The Pendragon says, 'We could probably still have done something for him. It's not even the worst case of devicial psychosis I've seen. You should have seen James Ribbens, or Alfred Noake. The Benwick Institute have techniques now that...'

He stops with a grunt, as Oli Montalban comes dashing

up out of the scrub, an arrow still embedded in her armour's shoulder-joint, and, weeping silently, runs him through the midriff with her sword.

* * *

In those days there were Three Dolorous Blows struck against the High King Jordan of Britain.

The third was the blow of Olivia Montalban, who transfixed the High King with her sword of British steel; and that was struck in the last year of his reign, close by the shores of Lake Glastonbury.

The second was the blow of Craig McCutcheon, who stole his greatest weapon, the device of the laughing archer; and that blow was struck at the Castle of Windsor in the seventh year of his reign.

Yet the most dolorous of all was the first, the blow of Malory Wendiman, which out of his love for her wounded him worse than all the others; and that blow was struck at Stonehenge, in the year of the War of the Devices.

From none of them did the High King ever heal.

* * *

'*Stop, Bonnie!*' Jory gasps as he falls to his knees, clutching at the bloody rent piercing his abdomen.

Bonnie unwillingly halts her sword as it's about to swing down on the immobile, uncomplaining Oli. 'You're fucking kidding me, my lord,' she suggests. But she holds her blade steady.

'Don't kill her,' the High King gasps. 'Not this time.'

Oli Montalban stares at him. 'But —' she says, then her face shows understanding. 'Oh, right, you want to do it yourself. That's fine. That's how it goes, isn't it? King Arthur and Sir Mordred kill each other. OK, that's fine. You'd better hurry, though, High King, I don't think you've got long.'

471

'Nobody's killing anybody,' Jory insists, although the evidence is against him there. 'Oli, I forgive you.'

'*What?*' Oli's flabbergasted.

I hear the distant sound of a motor. It takes me a moment to realise it's coming from the lake.

In the distance, out across the water, a boat's approaching. A red-headed woman sits in its bows, her hand on the tiller. Behind her a much younger woman – no, a girl, tall like her mother and just as russet-haired – is doing something complicated with a phone.

'You can't *forgive* me!' Montalban wails. 'It's not part of the story!'

* * *

'Whatever,' Izzy snarled, nearly a week ago at Windsor. 'None of this makes any difference. You're still finished, Dad, with all your Circle and your code of honour and your bloody New Arthurian bloody Britain. Even with Merlin and the Lady of the Lake, you're done for.'

You could tell her heart wasn't really in it, though. Before, her gloating had been gleeful, now it felt… just dutiful. As if she was doing it for form's sake. The revelation that her dad, at least, had seen through her deception all along – and that it hadn't stopped him caring about her – had taken all the joy out of it for her.

It was hard not to feel for the kid, to be honest. At least until I remembered Squig was dead because of her.

Jory sighed. 'I know, love. That story's coming to an end. It's time. But we don't have to let it take us along with it. Whatever Morgan le Fay is, whatever she's done to you, she's only a story. That's all the devices are – just stories – and we don't have to follow those old stories if we don't want to.

'Lancelot doesn't have to kill Gareth,' he said. 'Tristan doesn't have to run off with Iseult. Gawain doesn't have to behead the Green Knight. Even in the stories, they didn't have to do those things. Lancelot could have surrendered to the High King's justice; Tristan could have left Cornwall and never come back; Gawain could have bitten his tongue and let the Green Knight ride away disappointed. The stories come from the choices they made, but only because they made them freely.

'You picked Morgan le Fay as your protector,' he reminded her, 'at a time when you desperately needed one – but *you* get to choose what that story means. You can be the Morgan who's a healer, who welcomes Arthur to Avalon. You can be the Morgan who's always loyal to her half-brother, but is cruelly slandered by others. You can be the Morgan who just wants to be left to worship her own gods her own way.

'Or you can make up a new Morgan to be. People tell stories, not the other way round. The devices forget that we made them, not they us. I've tried to teach you all of this,' he sighed, 'but I suppose I wasn't clear enough.

'In any case,' he said, 'I choose to be the Arthur who forgives. I'll forgive Lancelot and Tristan if I get the chance. Mordred even, if Oli will let me. And I'll forgive Morgan le Fay, too. I'll forgive you, Izzy.'

Izzy glared dismally at him. 'I never wanted your forgiveness,' she said dully. 'Or your love, though I liked it when it came. I wanted *revenge*.'

'I know,' he said again. 'I forgive you for that, too.'

'You can't,' she insisted. 'Those people Oli killed. Poor Jason Smith. I caused those deaths, and all the others that come out of this. You can say Paul and Oli didn't have to follow their stories, but I gave them those stories. I set them on those paths. The only one who's chosen their own path in all of this is me. How can you forgive me that? What gives you the *right?*'

The High King said, 'If you believe in Morgan le Fay, then you believe in Arthur. As High King, I *have* that right. And if you don't... well then, you're just Izzy Taylor, and I'm your Dad who loves you. And I forgive you, too – whatever happens. Whoever dies because of this, even me – even my daughter, who I love – I forgive you. Whatever you make of

473

the rest of your life, I forgive you. I'm your Dad, Izzy. And I'm not going to die if I can help it.'

She stared at him from wet hollows. Finally she said, 'You killed my Dad.'

He sighed, and shook his head. 'I know. Arthur didn't have to kill Accolon either. I could have forgiven Craig, too. I'm so sorry, love.'

She said, 'I miss him.' Then, almost too quiet to hear, she said, 'I killed him too.'

He nodded again. 'Perhaps we can forgive each other.'

* * *

The boat with Malory and Penny in it is drawing nearer. Oli seems docile for now. The distant sound of gunfire and shelling appears to have stopped.

And Jory's dying.

We've helped him up out of the marsh, propped him up against a hummock to watch as the boat arrives. The Circle and the Chapel must be out looking for us by now. Bonnie's produced a pay-as-you-go mobile she must have bought somewhere along the way here and called an ambulance. But none of us is under any illusion now as to how this is going to end.

The Pendragon reaches painfully into a pocket, and pulls out the datatack Freda Tate-Hendricks gave him at the service station. The datatack containing the output of the Excalibur Program.

'Bonnie,' he says, then see the tears in her eyes.

'Not Bonnie,' she says dully. 'Sir Bedivere. That's right, isn't it? That's why you kept me around all these years.' She gestures at the lake. 'You needed me for *this*.'

'Oh, Bonnie, *no*,' the High King gasps. 'You were my best, my bravest, my most loyal... I couldn't have got here without you, Bonnie. I never could have.'

Her face crumples. 'And that's supposed to make me feel better,' she mutters.

474

'Take it,' says Jory. 'Please. Throw it out to Malory. There may be more NATO troops around. The Wild Hunt may have called in reinforcements. She mustn't risk coming in to shore, it's too dangerous.'

'Good luck persuading her of that,' I say.

Bonnie takes the tack from Jory and steps forward to the margin of the Lake. She hefts it in her hand.

Her phone rings. She looks across at Jory, and he sighs and nods. Out on the boat, Malory is holding her daughter's phone.

'Yeah?' says Bonnie into her own. 'Oh. Right. OK.'

She cuts the connection and puts the phone away, then hands the datatack back to the High King.

'She told me, "Don't you bloody dare",' Bonnie reports.

* * *

'Where are you both living now?' Jory asked Malory, some seven years ago.

'Glastonbury,' she told him, trusting him again. 'They've built up some excellent flood defences in the past seven years. Our flat's just round the corner from the New Age tat shop Dad used to run – do you remember, the Tree in the Well? They've turned it into a fishing-tackle shop now.'

They were in a room at the Travelodge in Bracknell, lying comfortably together on the bed – both fully clothed, of course. Even if Jory's chastity hadn't been a matter of honour, neither of them were prepared to risk the consequences if he broke it. Not even for each other.

Jory laughed easily. 'I remember. Crystals and dowsing rods and pendulums for measuring ley lines. You were very scathing about it, as I recall.'

'I was,' she said. For a few moments she was silent, trying to put something into the right words for him. Eventually she said, 'Do you still think the devices are a daft pseudo-science, Jory?'

He winced. 'I'm so sorry I said that.' It was another of

the stupid things he'd said to her at Stonehenge. He'd thought they were past all that now.

Malory said, 'No my love, that's not what I mean. I just want to know if that's still what you think.'

It was his turn to consider. After a while he said, 'I do feel different, since the devicial mine. But then a lot of things changed that day. Blaze, McCutcheon, Izzy... I felt different back when I was carrying Sir Gawain's shield, too. But that was before I met the Chapel. Before you and I... well, you know.'

Malory laughed. 'Down boy.'

Jory said, 'And then when I became a Knight... that was a big change in my life too. What I mean is, big things have been happening to me at the same time, every time my device has supposedly changed. The day I'm supposed to have taken on the Pendragon device, I stopped a war. That would have affected the way I felt about myself whatever. How do I know whether the different *me*s I remember, looking back to those times, were changed by the devices or just by my experience?'

She said, 'But what's it like subjectively? Being Arthur?'

He remembered her double, Claudine, in that other hotel room, asking the same question. *How does it feel? To carry* that *device?*

He said, 'I think... The thing is, Arthur himself never expected to be High King. He didn't know his heritage until the day he stumbled across the sword in the stone. He grew up as the foster-child of a minor knight, then suddenly he was consorting with wizards and fighting rival kings, directing knights and planning battle strategy and being asked what God thought about it all. I don't suppose he ever really got used to it.

'I think,' said Jory, 'King Arthur must have spent most of his reign feeling as if he was faking it.'

'Is,' said Malory, 'the right answer.' She squeezed his arm.

She paused for a few moments, and then said, 'I'm going to tell you something, Jory. Something I've had a lot of trouble accepting myself.'

'OK,' he said, puzzled.

She said, 'You know I've always said the devices don't grant magic powers? That all their effects happen within the normal operation of the human mind and body? That there's nothing supernatural about them at all?'

Jory said, 'Of course. That's why I basically think there's nothing there.'

'And yet,' said Malory. 'No two device-holders – Circle or Chapel or any other devicial group I've been able to research the history of – have ever held the same device at the same time. Do you remember when you lost the Robin Hood device?'

'Of course,' said Jory. 'Like I say, it felt a bit different, but…'

'You didn't tell a soul, not even Dale,' she said. 'Blaze didn't either. And yet that same day – the *same day*, Jory – Zara found Robin taking root inside her. You lost the device in the morning, and by midnight she was shooting arrows from a roof and swordfighting on the stairs. How did she know, Jory?'

'Well,' Jory began, then stopped. He thought for quite a while. 'A lot of people watched my fight with McCutcheon. I suppose if I subconsciously *believed* I'd lost the Robin device, it might have affected my behaviour, my body-language…'

'On a tiny screen?' Merry said incredulously. 'With you in full armour? It's not like that's the only example either, I've got a spreadsheet full of them.'

'All right,' said Jory. 'Just tell me. I know you're dying to.'

She shrugged. 'It can't be explained. Not by conventional science. I didn't want to admit it to myself for ages, but it just can't. It's evidence of telepathy, if not of the supernatural.

'But if even telepathy exists,' she said, 'if the devices don't just occupy a single mind, shaped by the shared cultural heritage, but can move across the whole population of minds like a fish in a sea… well then, the devices transcend the individual. They lead an independent existence. When we talk about a device, we're talking about something that's real.'

Jory lay quietly for a while – absorbing this new information, yes, but also taking comfort, such as he could given the short time they had, in the breathing warmth of Malory next to him.

Eventually he smiled. 'They're still just stories, even so,' he said.

* * *

When Janene Long finally catches up with us, crashing through the sedge like a strangely graceful moose to find the little huddle of us standing by the water's edge, she stops and stares, the warnings she was bringing instantly forgotten. She knows exactly what she's looking at, and it's the worst thing she can imagine.

She sees me and Bonnie standing at the lakeside, keeping a tight hold on Oli Montalban's unresisting upper arms. We're staring out across the water, so she doesn't immediately see the tears dripping down our faces. Nearby and unregarded, Ron's sad remains bloody the marshy waters.

A little way ahead, but picking up speed as its outboard motor grumbles, is a small boat helmed by a tall red-headed girl. She stares out resolutely across the lake, her face hidden to us. Next to her, by the tiller, lie her phone and a cheap camera drone.

Behind her lies the High King of Britain, the Pendragon, Jordan Taylor, his head in Malory Wendiman's lap. Merry's head is bowed and she's weeping, hair trailing across the face of Arthur's bondsman like autumn leaves.

In tears herself now, Janene watches as the girl sets a course across the lake to the distant island, the old town with its tower, its holy well, its ancient abbey. Away in the distance, a church bell tolls.

Janene recognises what she's seeing. How could she not? By this point in history, anyone in Britain would.

Of course she knows Jory's dead – Janene's a realist. This

High King's never coming back, time of Britain's greatest need or no.

But still, she understands, as do the rest of us, that this story is far from being over.

JERUSALEM

25. ALAN A'DALE

The old man sighed wearily. 'I'm don't think I can tell you much more, though,' he said.

He was exhausted. Every evening for a week, he had been telling instalments of the same perennial story to this audience of hungry ears, eager eyes and agog faces, all hanging on his words. As always, it had involved reliving all the greatest deeds of his life, but also the worst moments. Both had been so very draining to recall.

Now it was nearly at an end, again.

Wearily, the old man shook his head. 'It's all so long ago, now,' he said. 'And... well, he commissioned me to be *his* chronicler. That's the job I did for him, and it's the job I've been doing ever since. Telling the story of his life, his reign and his death. Beyond that... well, like the historians say, it's not my period.'

He stared defiantly at the audience filling the hall, eight hundred faces taking in his words, and felt their disappointment. These people cared nothing for his limitations, nor for whether he had told this tale a thousand times before or ten thousand. Some of them had heard it before, certainly, many times perhaps; but not all of them, and never this exact audience. They needed him to finish what he had started, and they knew as well as he that this tale did not end with High King Jordan's death.

The old man sighed. 'Beyond that... well, I lived through it, obviously, but I don't exactly understand it. I'm not sure anyone does, except Malory.

'The mythopolitical theory's beyond me, certainly. I could tell you how it felt at the time, but like most people who'd known Jory I was too busy feeling numb. So many individual stories could be told about that time, as rich and complex as the one I've been telling you here this week. But not by me.

'The best I can do is give you the overall shape of the events. Retell them as a myth, I suppose. It's what I do best, after all.'

The old man allowed himself a moment to gather his thoughts. 'So where've we got to?' he asked rhetorically. 'The Pendragon's dead, of course. But so are the mac Cumhail, and the Agent of Paul Bunyan. Both armies have been beheaded, and the invasion's stalled.

'So, Sir David Stafford contacts NATO HQ in The Hague, and asks for a ceasefire...'

* * *

'Sir David Stafford contacts NATO HQ in The Hague, and asks for a ceasefire, so both sides can bury their dead. Kreiss and O'Leary's bodies are returned home with all the appropriate honours, and Malory and Penny bring the High King's body in a van from Glastonbury up to London. I'm waiting there by then, with Bonnie and David and Rev and Janene and the rest. Blaze and Izzy turn up shortly afterwards.

'Izzy's in pieces, poor kid – no matter what she did, she's lost another father. Penny is grave and sorrowful, but Jory was an occasional visitor in her life; she didn't know him like Izzy did. She doesn't seem to hold a grudge against her sister.

'Malory... Malory is quiet, controlled, efficient. Her grief for him isn't for public consumption.

'Between us we have a lot of future to plan for, but first there are the funeral arrangements to make.

'The High King lies in state in the ruins of the Fastness,

the lower levels where Theo, Nate and the others sheltered from the bombing, now thrown open to the public for the first time. The Circle archive survived in the end, and in lieu of the pulverised chapel the High King lies for viewing there in the library, surrounded by stories. (That was my idea, I admit.)

'After three days his coffin is loaded aboard an open-backed hearse, a black electric Bentley flying the Pendragon flag. Malory and his daughters ride along with him, the other mourners following in other cars. An honour guard of Knights on motorbikes accompanies the cortege.

'The procession crosses London Bridge and passes through the City and the West End, past Buckingham Palace and Pankhurst House, to Westminster Abbey. The streets are bannered with black like London's been colonised by roosting bats, and the flags on all the buildings – the dragon's head, the Union Jack, even the compass rose – are flown at half-mast.

'At the Abbey, Jory's family step out of the hearse. With six other women, the High King's lover and his daughters lift his coffin smoothly onto their shoulders, and carry it inside. Janene, Scar and Zara are there on behalf of the Green Chapel. Jade Kinsey represents the Device Squad, having gatecrashed the coffin detail by swearing at us all and only shutting up when we agreed – protesting all the time that she'd never liked the deceased much anyway.

'There would have been ten pallbearers, but no-one's been able to track down Tania Woodville – or Stephen or Eoin, for that matter. The Circle's represented by just two Knights, Bonnie and Oli – the latter hardly an uncontroversial choice, under the circumstances, but having seen how much forgiving her meant to the High King, I insisted. He got to go to Craig McCutcheon's funeral, after all.

'There are reasons why nine's a better number, in any case, for this particular task.

'The service is an ordeal, as you'd expect. The Archbishop of Canterbury's presiding, but she confines herself to the liturgical bits. The prayers are delivered by Bishop Sally

Marvell, St Dubricius' bondswoman, and the sermon… well, let's just say Rev Cantrell's not taking any prisoners.

'The terms in which he excoriates the NATO invaders, the late General Kreiss and the Founding Frontiersmen are so forthright that two churchwardens are taken unexpectedly ill and a verger resigns on the spot. But he saves his special opprobrium for the devices. *They* did this – not just to Jory but to his killers, Ron and Oli, and to those like Izzy who they induced to conspire against him. *They* brought the country to this pass – and the world too, not only Britain but Ireland, France, America and every other country where their pernicious influence has been allowed to prosper. The devices are inimical to humanity, he tells us, upstart creations who've set themselves up as gods of this world. It's time for them to *fall*.

'There in the pulpit, in front of two thousand mourners, Rev abjures the ally of Friar Tuck, who's been with him for forty-five years, and walks out of the Abbey a free man.

'The rest of us have to stay and sit through it all – the prayers, the eulogies, the creeds. The singing of the High King's favourite hymn – silently amended back into its original, far superior, form. Nobody here today has the heart for New Arthurian propaganda.

'And then his body's placed into the vault, where Anish Kapoor's famous memorial sculpture will one day stand – no crusader-style recumbent statues for our Jory, just an organic metal teardrop with a corkscrew-shaped hollow leading down into the vault itself – and the plaque's unveiled with the famous inscription from the *Morte D'Arthur*.

'Then, in accordance with Green Chapel tradition, we all go to St James's Park where a sound system's been set up, and get riotously drunk.

'And then the next morning, tearful and sore, we get up and face the history of Britain once again.'

* * *

'The ceasefire holds at first, but its foundations were always pretty shaky. In theory, the threat to the NATO member states ended with the life of the Pendragon himself, so now the peacekeeping force can pack up and go home.

'In reality, of course, the army of occupation is here to stay. After what Woodville did – not that she can be traced anywhere, but by now NATO have identified her as a Circle operative with Green Chapel backing – the Fianna and the Frontiersmen both want blood.

'The sticking-point comes, as Malory always predicted, with the succession. In Jory Taylor's absence the rule of the Republic of Scotland falls to its President, who's swift to pledge her country's neutrality in this and future conflicts; but the United Kingdom of Southern Britain and Northern Ireland needs a head of state too. The Circle want Sir David appointed Regent; the Chapel want a short-term executive appointed by a nationwide network of co-operative communes, except for those who don't; some of the populace want an elected President like Scotland's; others just want the old Queen's grandson to inherit. Pretty much everyone's agreed that NATO's preferred solution – the octogenarian rebel ex-Duke of Cornwall as their biddable, malleable client king – is unacceptable.

'So, with the ex-Duke's heavily-guarded coronation at the Abbey – now once more in NATO hands – the détente breaks, and the Second War of the Devices starts in earnest.

'The Chapel are the first to attack the NATO forces, using fire arrows to burn down their encampment in Hyde Park. In reprisal the occupiers attack the Circle's interim HQ at Windsor, and soon the whole country's in spasms. For a while it doesn't go badly for the home team – the Circle have hundreds of Knights to call on, and the Chapel are practiced guerrilla fighters. NATO has links with a dozen foreign devicial orders, but few of them are willing to send more than a handful of their agents abroad on such a thankless mission. It almost seems that the Round Table and the Merry

Men might prevail, and defend Britain from this latest round of invaders.

'But over the sea in Washington, the Director of the Founding Frontiersmen, the Agent of Honest Abe Lincoln, has one final ace up his sleeve. He sends in the big guns – in fact, in devicial terms, the nuclear option.

'Since the invasion he's been busy pulling every string he can find at the State Department, and the USA has worked its arse off to earn itself one mighty favour from one tiny foreign ally – one which, despite its venerable history as the cradle of democracy, is in every respect but this one an obscure, impoverished player on the world stage.

'And so, the Greeks break the habit of fifty lifetimes and send abroad the heroes who've stayed quietly at home since their long-awaited return from the siege of Troy. Once more, the plumed helms bob, the leaf-shaped swords flash, the round shields resound with the rhythmic clatter of spears, as they come for the descendants of those they long ago displaced.'

* * *

'You have to admit, we brought it on ourselves. Our legends proudly proclaim our foundation by Brutus, Corineus and their compatriots – legitimising the Matter of Britain by appealing to the older and more venerable myths of the classical world.

'It's there in black and white: our legends are important – because they derive from theirs. Did it never occur to us that the Greeks might turn up one day to finish the job?

'Because, make no mistake, their mythos trumps even ours.

'Oh yes, Sir Galahad's a name to conjure with; Merlin and Sir Lancelot – even when attached to a new young Knight – even more so. Sir Percival, Sir Bedivere, Sir Mordred even – and Robin Hood, of course – all these names have lived in myth for centuries.

'But... Perseus. Theseus. Jason. Odysseus. *Hercules*... Those names are twice as old, and better known even now. Those names are myth itself.

'In Arthur's absence, how could any heroically doomed Round Table, any band of jolly outlaws, hope to stand against such men – or against the women they bring with them: Atalanta, Medea, Hippolyta and their like?

'And so they fall – the Circle, the Chapel, the British secular armed forces – to the most successful invasion of these lands since 1066. Behind Greek generals wearing the helm of Perseus, the armour of Achilles, the lion-skin of Herakles, the invaders are unstoppable. Across the lands of England, Wales and Northern Ireland, our forces at their best are routed and flee.

'David Stafford loses his life in the Battle of Cerne Abbas, killed by Herakles' *aegis*-bearer at the site where Romano-British colonists once worshipped the demigod. Oli Montalban redeems herself in battle after battle, and dies a hero, fighting off a mob of Maenads at Dover. Our sole victory's at Newcastle, where Zara manages to take out Achilles' bondsman with a high-explosive arrow to the heel, losing a leg of her own in the ensuing carnage.

'No new Pendragon steps forward to relieve us at this time of need. The omens seem pretty clear. From now on Britain will be a mere vassal state, ruled on behalf of Athens and Olympus by the puppet king so ineffectually claiming Brutus's mantle.

'(Yes, Athens – all the signs point to Greece as the emerging superpower of the new millennium. No-one's thinking of Washington now, and the Founding Frontiersmen are in a state of panic at their loss of control. Once invoked, the heroes of Hellas can't be so easily controlled.)

'And then, three months after Jory Taylor's death in the Battle of Lydford, Malory Wendiman deploys Excalibur.

'And nothing's ever the same again.'

26. THE DEVICES

The old man faltered again, baulking at the magnitude of the narrative task facing him. 'Excalibur…' he began, and stopped. Practiced and polished though most of his recitation always was, he had spent years trying to find ways to describe the weapon, to make sense of its effects, and had never quite succeeded.

His listeners gazed at him still, expectation in all their eyes. Row after row of seating filled the Great Hall, crammed in between the triangular stage in front of its black curtain, and the rear wall with the faded ocean mural. The paintwork had been carefully restored all those years ago following the incident with the bondsman of Sir Garlon the Red, but close up those who knew where to look could still see where the man-at-arms' bullets had hit it. The old man's eyes were sharp still, for his age, but from this distance the mural was the soothing sea-green blur its painter had intended.

He said, 'The output of the Excalibur Program…'

Impatient now, but respectfully polite, they waited: some in elaborate costumes and makeup, others sporting more modest brooches, badges and tattoos, the myriad symbols of the new order he now must somehow explain to them. This was his task, which sometimes he believed was his curse: to wander the world like the Ancient Mariner, telling of death and of mysterious happenings beyond his ability to elucidate.

He knew an Ancient Mariner, he recalled, a member of a storytelling circle he had attended a few times near Durham. The girl showed promise.

He said, 'The output of the Excalibur Program goes out on every British TV channel…'

* * *

'The output of the Excalibur Program goes out on every British TV channel within a three-minute window, those under NATO control as well as the few we've managed to keep hold of. At the same time it's leaked across a hundred internet locations, mostly ones with .uk and .scot domains, where those who missed the broadcasts can watch it and catch up.

'The BBC, whose newsrooms are now mouthpieces of Washington but whose other programming has continued with only minor tampering, has its output hijacked five minutes into an episode of *EastEnders* where teenage Ollie Carter, who previously wanted to join up with the Circle, considers instead throwing in his lot with Major Husek, the sympathetic NATO peacekeeper billeted with the Fowlers. The sabotage is eventually traced back to a junior member of the soap's production team: an obscure minor royal, a niece of the new king no less, who's been working quietly at the Beeb without distinction since her graduation six years previously. At every broadcast outlet in the UK and Scotland similar disruptions occur.

'What the viewer sees at first is a brief flash of station logo, accompanied by Laney Wardsley's voice saying, "We interrupt this programme…" It's followed by a thirteen-second flicker of imagery, text and babbling voices, all coming far too fast for conscious minds to process, but capturing the attention sufficiently to stop most of them from switching off. It's the payload of the *Enola Gay* to a firecracker, but it follows essentially the same principles used in the inframemetic interface of Craig McCutcheon's devicial mine.

'It's not the output that's taken Malory all this time to prepare – that was effectively complete when Freda Tate-Hendricks handed Jory the datatack. It's the delivery, the sheer logistics of intercepting and subverting so many separate signals at once. It involves a vast network of hackers, infiltrators and burglars who it's taken Merry fifteen years to assemble. Since the funeral Merry herself has been under close watch by NATO forces, who've realised how potentially dangerous she is: it's only by deploying a decoy who closely resembles her that she's able to get away for long enough to send the "go" signal.

'And... well, as I say, everything changes.

'Excalibur does all that Jory promised us, those months ago in that chilly bedroom in Winterbourne. Within the swiftly-expanding sphere of those who've received the trigger signal, the devices' constricting dominance is shattered. It's the trojan to end all Trojans.

'The invaders' strength crumbles immediately, New World pioneers and heroes of ancient city-states alike. All at once there's no power here for them to usurp, no devicial awe in the British collective unconscious for them to get traction on. Abruptly they're reduced to their unenhanced states, mere men and women with none of their originals' epic stature. Like the Fianna, Paladins and Frontiersmen, the Achaeans and Argonauts in Britain find themselves with no special mastery.

'And yes – the grip of the Circle and the Chapel is broken too. Not just for this generation (which NATO had been managing pretty effectively by itself), but definitively and forever. No more will Knights crusade to suppress the rogue devices, no more will outlaws preach ideological dogma. Never again will we fight a War of the Devices. We have no reason to, not now.

'You see, Excalibur has done exactly what Merry and Jory hoped – it's broken the devices' strength, deprived them of the ability to control. No longer can they use human beings as their tools – no, that relationship's been completely reversed.

'Because the devices of Britain haven't been destroyed, just fragmented. Their monolithic structures are demolished, rendered back into their raw materials, and scattered.

'Distributed, in fact, across the entire population.'

* * *

'As the signal propagates, everyone in Britain who's ever identified with a knight or a merry man – which, given our recent history, is millions of us – is granted a piece of that device. In thirteen seconds, we gain ten thousand Lancelots, ten thousand Guineveres, ten thousand Merlins.

'Twenty thousand Robin Hoods. A hundred thousand King Arthurs.

'I'm pulling figures out of my backside, obviously, but you get the idea. In that moment, what used to be tiny minorities become whole demographics – and those are just the devices that existed before. In that moment, we become a nation of heroes like no other in history.

'Of course NATO withdraw, they'd be suicidal not to. The devices they've deployed here – their remnants that is, because they're as fragmented as our own – are powerless against this revolution in their sphere.

'Besides, those videos on the web go viral straight away, spreading the inframemetic signal way beyond Britain's borders: soon every nation in the world begins to feel the bite of Excalibur. As they begin to recall their troops in panic, the withdrawal becomes confused and farcical.

'Not all of the invaders even leave. Some of them have *become* those Galahads, those Little Johns, those Ladies of the Lake. Some of them go home even so, and tell their stories there, hastening the spread of the viral signal. Others stay behind here, and the rest of us make them welcome.

'Our cost has been huge, but the invasion's over, and the

493

danger with it. The only task we face now is rebuilding our society in our new image.'

* * *

'It takes some constitutional finagling, but with the old order in tatters in any case, there's little resistance to Malory Wendiman being appointed Lady Protector of the United Kingdom.

'There's perhaps no-one else in the realm who could have followed High King Jordan without being abysmally unpopular, but with Blaze and Zara as her advisors, Malory manages it. Even with thousands of other Nimues, Merlins and Robin Hoods out in the world, their unique combination of knowledge and experience is what's needed to shepherd a nation of extraordinary individuals into this new, and radically changed, mid-twenty-first century.

'By now of course, other countries are facing their own upheavals, but they're lagging behind. Under the Pendragon, Britain has had a massive head start. Now we have undreamed-of talent waiting on tap, and Malory intends that everyone should have the opportunity to fulfil it. Her guiding principle is that all citizens should have the right to make the most of their potential without infringing the rights of others – and she's been planning how to put that into practice for a long time.

'Within a few years we've become a beacon to the world, loaning out our expertise and talent to other countries to assist them in their birth-pangs.

'At home, the old structures aren't so tenable any more. The Circle simply hasn't the human resources to run an order encompassing all the followers of Arthurian knights – especially when any former man-at-arms might now share the device of Percival, Gawain, or Arthur himself. In the face of equality so wide-ranging, even the Round Table is insufficient. The Circle becomes a vague network of associations between like-minded individuals, no more organised than *Telegraph* readers or Manchester United fans. Between them they accept quiet Theo Harte as Seneschal, but from now on his position will only ever be a ceremonial one.

'The Green Chapel was already pretty much like that, of course: now it's just far larger. With Zara hampered by her new disability, and much of her time taken up helping Merry run the country, she and Scar make way for younger Robins and Marians. Now, though, the Chapel have less clear structures to define themselves against: with no King's men to fight, no barons to rob, no fat abbots to taunt, they're free to focus on what they do best, the charitable work of helping the poor and needy.

'At the Device Squad, Jade Kinsey's predictably furious about the whole thing. She's trained herself and her people to ferret out exceptional criminals among a mundane population, and suddenly *everyone's* exceptional. It doesn't help – well, naturally it doesn't – that, after so many years' scorn for the idea, she's somehow acquired a device herself, the ancient British warrior-queen Boudicca.

'Bonnie and Janene are among those who gained part of the Pendragon device in the grand reshuffle. Without a High King to protect, Bonnie puts her abilities to use leading a team of firefighters, and saves a great many lives before succumbing to smoke inhalation during a fire at a youth hostel. Janene becomes a backbench MP, serving her constituents wisely and with good humour. She adopts two children with a bloke called Ray – an avatar of her first ally Adam Bell, although she insists that isn't what attracted her to him.

'Politics is a nobler pursuit now anyway: while there's still plenty of scope for disagreement, it's far more difficult to be cynical about the motives of politicians when that Tory MP strives humbly to live up to the example of Sir Galahad, or that union leader gains his inspiration from Little John. Not that every device is benevolent, of course... but strangely, few people are over-eager to vote for a candidate who identifies with Mordred or the Sheriff of Nottingham.

'Meanwhile there's a great resurgence in religion, since most devices date from times when faith was commoner. Archaic forms of Christianity resurface, as do still more ancient faiths. The leader of a growing Druid sect, Isabella Kollwitz-McCutcheon-Taylor collects about herself all the other Morgan le Fays she can discover, teaching them Blaze's meditation techniques to steer them away from the more alarming expressions of their archetype.

'Rev Cantrell, who was always religious, never joins any of the impressively determined dissenter sects who reject all manifestations of the devices as evil, or at least dangerous: instead, remembering always what happened to Ron, he sets up a foundation for the care of those suffering from devicial psychosis, and to research a cure. When he dies, not many years later, thousands turn up to his funeral. A disproportionate number of them are muscular young men.

'Penny Wendiman-Taylor never does acquire a device of her own – and after everything she's seen them do to her family, you can hardly blame her. For a while the dissenters try to recruit her too, but she makes it unflinchingly clear she isn't interested in that either. She wants to be a photojournalist, and she becomes a good one, documenting the new forms of society emerging in Britain and across the globe.'

* * *

'Nobody ever does find out what happened to Tania Woodville, Stephen Mukherjee or Eoin MacNeill. It's regarded, by the tedious people who keep track of that sort of thing, as one of the great unsolved mysteries of the twenty-first century.

'Most of their biographers – one of whom will get a lip-reader to interpret the CCTV footage from behind Claridge's, while another manages to track down a Chapel member who overheard the conversation in Eoin's tent that night in the Long Wood – will come to agree that Tania died of her wounds in London, and that Stephen lied to Eoin about it. Perhaps, some speculate, he even let her die, in some peculiar cross-contamination from the legend of the death of Diarmuid. When Eoin found out, he either murdered Stephen in revenge, or simply left the Knight alone with his guilt and grief, returning home across the Irish Sea while Mukherjee found his own end in his own way.

'For quite a long time, and with sadness, I'll believe them.

'But then, years later – quite recently, in fact, as I'm talking to you now – I'll come across someone who tells a different story.

'This woman's a delivery rider, a minor knight – Sir Helin the White or someone, I forget – taking parcels across the Scottish Highlands, and her motorbike comes a cropper on a road that passes through a forest. Her tablet's broken in the crash, so she can't call for a lift. She has to walk, and on the way she meets a handsome middle-aged man with a trace of an Irish accent, who invites her to come and use his wife's phone.

'She joins them at what seems to be a charcoal-burners' bothy. Now there's not much call these days for hand-burned charcoal, but more people are reviving the old crafts, and some buyers will pay over the odds for their product, so our friend doesn't think it's overly odd.

'The man introduces her to his wife – an older Englishwoman, muscular from all the outdoor work, grey-haired with a few streaks of blonde – and to their husband, who's an elderly, but sprightly, British Asian man. Three-way marriages still aren't all that popular in rural Scotland, so she can see why they live out in the middle of the countryside like this – but our friend's from Edinburgh and pretty open-minded, so she's happy to accept their hospitality.

'She contacts the nearest garage, but they're all busy at a motorway pile-up and they can't get to her till the morning. So she accepts the old triple's offer to stay with them in their bothy. They feed her, let her have the most comfortable camp-bed and so on, and the four of them stay up late into the night, drinking whisky together.

'I'm sure you can all guess where this is going. She wakes up in the morning and they're gone. They've left the phone behind, and enough food for her breakfast, and a bottle of water with a sticky note reminding her she'll need hydrating.

'She can't remember much of the night before – which she comes to suspect was deliberate on her hosts' part – but one thing the elderly man said stuck in her mind.

'"Excalibur passed us by," he said, in answer to a comment she made. "The three of us were out of circulation at the time, and have been since. But, you know, there are other ways to escape from following our stories. A good one's love."

'That's what she tells me, anyway. And maybe she's a storyteller, like so many of us these days, trying to start a legend of her own. But maybe she's not.

'And that, my friends,' the old man said, 'is all I've got for you.'

* * *

The question-and-answer session was mercifully brief, whether because of the comprehensiveness of his account or out of respect for his age: a few researchers, Merlins mainly, filling out the footnotes of their theses; a breathless wimpled Guinevere, no older than fifteen, wanting to know what Jory Taylor was *really* like, as if the evening, the week and his entire latter career had not been dedicated to answering that very question.

Before long, the audience were filing out of the venue and he was running the gauntlet of dignitaries and fans: shaking hands with Kate Blackwood, the new Seneschal, suited and with a discreet white-on-purple lion shield on her lapel; having his cheek kissed by a pair of teenage Morgan le Fays, all black feathers and eyeliner; submitting to a selfie with an over-jovial Friar Tuck in full habit and tonsure.

Generally, he reflected, it was the younger ones who adopted the most elaborate costumes: this middle-aged man must be, or possibly should be, committed.

At length, firmly rejecting all offers of a curry or a swift pint at the Hunter's Head, the man who claimed the name of Dale the Tale escaped from the National Centre for Oral Storytelling and set out for a stroll along the South Bank of the Thames, towards the Fastness Memorial Gardens and his hotel nearby.

He faced a respite now, after his gruelling week. This weekend he would spend in London, seeing a few old friends (as if he had any other kind left), before, on Monday morning, setting off once more on his travels. There must, he felt sure, be a handful of people in Birmingham who had not yet heard him speak.

He smiled to see two teenagers, a leaf-bedecked Peter Pan and an alice-banded Alice in Wonderland, walking arm in arm, steering well clear of a drunken, though slightly scrawny, Beowulf in full Viking rig. The old man would relish the quiet of the weekend, but for now, after the attention of all those eyes upon him in the Great Hall, he appreciated being anonymous among this swarming crowd of humanity, taking in the evening air and famous skyline on this summer night.

Two earnest young men, one in an Inverness cape and deerstalker, the other in a long dark double-breasted coat with wide lapels, strolled past in animated conversation. They must be hot, the old man reflected: it was far warmer outside than he had guessed inside the air-conditioned Centre. The Godiva shooting by on a folding bicycle was more appropriately dressed.

Most of the audience in the Great Hall had been die-hard Arthurians or Robinistas, eager to hear the stories of their heroes; but the Excalibur Program had liberated more myths than just those of Hood and the Pendragon.

The old man strolled eastward along the bank of the river, smiling to himself. Though many would disagree, it was not for nothing that he had called the Lady Protector's new world order a utopia. Though there were dissenters still (and having known Franklin Cantrell and Penny Wendiman-Taylor he respected them greatly), any man or woman could hold any device they wished. While British ones predominated here in London (even among the tourists, reflecting the prominence of British culture in the world), that, too, was no stricture: from where he was standing, one quick glance identified for him a Hua Mulan, a Shaka Zulu and a Barbarella.

All of them, provided they did not impinge on others' freedoms, were permitted and encouraged to fulfil their greatest possible potential. Britain produced the best detectives, the best spies, and the best gentleman and gentlewoman dilettantes in any number of fields, while the nation's skilled domestic servants were in the highest demand across the globe. Except for those who felt called to it, though, drudgery was a thing of the past: the automated industrial processes created by inventor archetypes from James Stevenson to Ada Lovelace had seen to that.

Once, what these people did, setting out masked in the identities of fictions and legends, would have occurred only on special occasions, and would have been referred to as 'carnival' or 'cosplay'. Today, it was simply everyday life.

A woman nearby was wearing a Guy Fawkes hat and moustache, but no mask. Intrigued, the old man wondered whether she was a follower of the original, or of his later imitator.

He counted himself lucky to have lived to see such a world. So many of his friends had not: he remembered Shaun Hobson, Shafiq Rashid, Alice Dashwood, Jack Bennett, Jason Smith and so many others. He smiled again, sadly this time, thinking of how Fiona Quinn would have been in her element.

A woman gave a delighted cry, and many heads turned. A bright light was climbing steadily skyward through the twilight to the east of the city. 'Is that a Quatermass VI?' said the woman, who wore a replica of a World War One flying-helmet. 'I say, she's a beauty, isn't she? Look at her go.'

'It'll have launched from Canvey Island,' a young man with a dog on a lead observed, nodding wisely to himself. 'Heading towards Dare Station I should think, wouldn't you Rover?' He wore a long, striped scarf and a broad-brimmed floppy hat.

The old man continued on his way. He would sit, he thought, in the Memorial Gardens and remember his fallen comrades, one by one.

'Excuse me,' said a voice, too young by far to be a friend of the old man's, and yet with something familiar in its timbre. 'But is your name Dale?'

The old man took a moment to gather his wits. His storytelling sessions took so much out of him, these days, that meeting a fan outside their confines felt like a quite unreasonable imposition. He assembled a smile nevertheless, and turned to see a boy of eighteen or nineteen, incongruously smart in a dark suit and pale tie. He wore a lapel-pin which the old man took a moment, in the fading light, to identify as a golden dragon's head.

A Pendragon, then. One of the many Arthurs. No wonder the young man recognised him: he had probably come to one or other of his storytelling sessions, perhaps even tonight's. 'That's me,' the old man said with forced cheer. 'Dale the Tale, if you want to get all bardic about it.'

'I saw you talk at the Connaught Theatre in Worthing,' the teenager said eagerly. 'Years ago now, when I was ten. That's when I got my device. I'd never really cared much about Arthurian legend, but then my dad dragged me along and... well. Your story had me hooked.'

Of course, the old man thought, it happened. Young people had to get their inspiration one way or another. 'Well, I'm pleased to hear it,' he said. He paused for a moment, feeling that more was needed, then reached for a familiar pleasantry. 'Glad I could be your sword in the stone.'

The boy looked confused for a moment, then his frown cleared. 'Oh no,' he said. 'Like I said, I'm not really interested in Arthurian myth. Modern history, though... that's much

501

more exciting. You really inspired me that day. I'm here to study at High King's College – Neo-Arthurian History and Mythopolitics. This is such an exciting time to be alive. Any one of us could change the world for the better, and... well, I suppose it's natural that I'd want it to be me. Everyone does, I guess.'

The boy thrust a hand out. 'My name's Ali, Ali Harper. And I carry the device...'

'It's all right, I know,' said old man, because he had recognised him at last.

After all, Malory had always said that the devices might reproduce.

'You carry the device,' he concluded, taking the young man's hand, 'of Jory Taylor. I'm very pleased to meet you, Ali Harper.'

THE END

Yet some men say in many parts of England that King Arthur is not dead, but had by the will of our lord Jesu into another place; and men say that he shall come again, and he shall win the holy cross. I will not say that it shall be so, but rather I will say: here in this world, he changed his life.

But many men say that there is written upon his tomb this verse: HIC IACET ARTHURUS, REX QUONDAM REXQUE FUTURUS.

Sir Thomas Malory, *Le Morte d'Arthur*

Nothing's forgotten… nothing is ever forgotten.

Richard Carpenter, *Robin of Sherwood: The Time of the Wolf*

ACKNOWLEDGEMENTS

While I hope it may be a 'true story' in the ways that myths can be true, *Trojans* is absolutely a work of fiction. In particular the various public figures who appear in the book are fictional characters, acting to suit its plot and themes rather than conforming to the personalities of any real people. It would be a grave mistake to infer, from the behaviour in this book of the near-future Duke of Cornwall and his relatives, anything relating to any real individuals in the United Kingdom of 2016.

Similarly, despite recent examples of flooding on the Somerset Levels, Glastonbury's return to a permanent island state is highly unlikely without a rise in sea-level more extreme than any currently predicted. For the sake of the story I've opted to ignore this awkward fact.

As in *The Pendragon Protocol* and *The Locksley Exploit*, I've drawn liberally on multiple versions of the King Arthur and Robin Hood myths, from Nennius to Errol Flynn. The best source for the early Trojan occupation of the British Isles (by which I mean the most inventive, as reliability's not really a concept that applies here) is Geoffrey of Monmouth's *History of the Kings of Britain*. Herne the Hunter and the Wild Hunt are marginal figures in British folklore, first brought to my attention in three outstanding fantasies for children: Alan Garner's *The Moon of Gomrath*, Susan Cooper's *The Dark is*

Rising and John Masefield's *The Box of Delights* (known to my generation from the BBC adaptation starring Patrick Troughton). Two books in particular have been useful sources for the other myths on which *Trojans* so promiscuously draws: *The Faber Book of Northern Legends*, edited by Kevin Crossley-Holland, and Rosemary Sutcliffe's *The High Deeds of Finn Mac Cool*.

The poem 'And did those feet in ancient time', generally known as 'Jerusalem', was written by William Blake in 1804 as the preface to his epic poem *Milton*. It's sung (in church, at sporting events, at the last night of the Proms and at the annual conference of the Labour Party) to a tune written in 1916 by Sir Hubert Parry. Dale's misgivings about the hubris of amending it entirely echo my own.

I'm grateful to Richard Carpenter's estate for permission to quote from his *Robin of Sherwood* novelisation. Sir Thomas Malory died 238 years before the invention of copyright, but I'm grateful to him nevertheless for providing the novel's other epigraph.

I'm indebted to Helen Angove, Simon Bucher-Jones, Rachel Churcher, Finn Clark, Stuart Douglas and Dale Smith for their wise and helpful comments on the manuscript; to Ian Mond, and Finn again, for advice on deploying specific mythologies; to Des Fischer for linguistic assistance; to Barnaby Eaton-Jones for his help with copyright; to Blair Bidmead for website artwork; and to Emma Barnes, Anna Torborg and everyone at Snowbooks for their superlative work on bringing this book, and the *Devices* trilogy as a whole, to its fruition.

That I'm also immensely grateful to my wife and son for their love, tolerance and support, goes without saying. This is lucky, because my debt to them is greater than I can possibly describe.

LIST OF CHARACTERS IN TROJANS

Jordan Taylor, *device-bearer of King Arthur and ally of Robin Hood; former bondsman of Sir Gawain and, briefly, Sir Mordred; now High King of Britain*

Malory Wendiman, *former device-bearer of the Lady of the Lake and ally of Maid Marian; now believed to be the bondswoman of Morgan le Fay; High King Jordan's former lover*

Dale, *ally of Alan a'Dale and device-bearer of Taliesin; High King Jordan's chronicler; the narrator*

The Circle

Bernard 'Blaze' Maddox, *device-bearer of Merlin; advisor to High King Jordan*

Sir David Stafford, *device-bearer of Sir Galahad; former ally of Richard the Lionheart; Knight, Seneschal of the Circle and advisor to High King Jordan*

Sir Charles Raymond, *device-bearer of Sir Kay; retired Knight and former Seneschal of the Circle*

Stephen Mukherjee, *device-bearer of Sir Palamedes; Knight*

Tania Woodville, *device-bearer of Sir Tristan; Knight*

Bonnie Laing, *device-bearer of Sir Bedivere; Knight, formerly of the Green Chapel*

Paul Parsons, *device-bearer of Sir Lancelot; Knight, once squire to Jordan Taylor*

Jason 'Squig' Smith, *device-bearer of Sir Gareth; former ally of Much the Miller's Son; Knight and High King Jordan's roving envoy*

Theo Harte, *device-bearer of Sir Ector; Knight and the Seneschal's adjutant*

Nate Busman, *device-bearer of Sir Kahedins; Knight and later Warden of the Fastness*

Patrick Sullivan, *device-bearer of Sir Marhaus; Knight assigned to the Duchy of Cornwall*

Craig McCutcheon, *device-bearer of Sir Accolon; Knight in charge of security at the Mythopolitical Research Facility*

Olivia Montalban, *newly-acclaimed device-bearer of Sir Gawain; Knight and great-niece of 'Monty' Montalban*

George 'Monty' Montalban, *device-bearer of Sir Sagramore; Knight and Oli Montalban's great-uncle*

Amal Samadi, *device-bearer of Sir Safir; Knight*

Johnny Quayle, *device-bearer of Sir Lucan; Knight*

Andy Burridge, *device-bearer of Sir Brastias; Knight*

Hugh Stein, *device-bearer of Sir Sadoc; Knight assigned to the Duchy of Cornwall*

Ken Rudge, *device-bearer of Sir Licanor; Knight assigned to the Duchy of Cornwall*

Sandy Hithers, *device-bearer of Sir Andret; Knight assigned to the Duchy of Cornwall*

Freddie Obote, *device-bearer of Sir Ywain the Bastard; Knight*

Doug Felton, *device-bearer of Sir Lionel; Knight and former aide to Paul Parsons*

Frank Farnsworth, *device-bearer of Sir Bors; Knight*

Ross Cornish, *device-bearer of Sir Percival; Knight*

Christopher Timms, *device-bearer of Sir Aglavale; Knight*

Nigel Roth, *device-bearer of Sir Marrok; Knight*

Kate Blackwood, *device-bearer of Sir Lamorak; Knight*

Josh Mahama, *device-bearer of Sir Agravaine; Knight*

Harold Lenton, *device-bearer of Sir Griflet; Knight*

Jerry Transom, *device-bearer of Sir Lavaine; Knight*

Harry Plaice, *device-bearer of Sir Geraint; Knight*

Zoe Bramwell, *device-bearer of Sir Menw son of Teirwaedd; Knight*

Ed Lambert, *device-bearer of Sir Leondegrance; Knight and director of the Benwick Institute*

Jean Tarrant, *device-bearer of Sir Brandinor; Knight*

William Posnett, *device-bearer of Sir Galagars; retired Knight*

Darius Beddowes, *device-bearer of Sir Urre; retired Knight*

Rt Rev Sally Marvell, *device-bearer of St Dubricius; Bishop of Lichfield*

Bob Thackett, *sergeant-at-arms, head of the Circle's Regal Protection Detail*

Roy Stavers, *man-at-arms*

Jacqui Parkes, *man-at-arms*

THE GREEN CHAPEL

Franklin 'Rev' Cantrell, *ally of Friar Tuck; advisor to High King Jordan*

Janene Long, *ally of Little John; former ally of Adam Bell*

Marianne 'Scar' Millar, *ally of Will Scarlet; Zara's partner*

Zara, *ally of the Saracen; Scar's partner*

Ron Byron, *ally of Much the Miller's Son*

Lee, *ally of Gilbert Whitehand*

Ahmed, *ally of Arthur a'Bland*

Shell, *ally of David of Doncaster*

Eric, *ally of Will Stuteley*

Chaz, *Scar's successor as the ally of Will Scarlet*

Jo, *Zara's successor as the ally of the Saracen*

Hannah 'HazMat' Matthews, *Ron's successor as the ally of Much the Miller's Son*

Vicks, *unallied Chapel member and explosives expert*

Twink, *unallied Chapel member*

CHILDREN OF OISÍN

Henry O'Leary, *aithgin of Fionn mac Cumhail; the mac Cumhail, leader of the Children of Oisín*

Dermot Healey, *aithgin of Conán mac Morna*

Eugene Molloy, *aithgin of Fianchad*

Eamonn Costello, *aithgin of Diarmuid Ua Duibhne*

Eoin MacNeill, *spy for the Children of Oisín*

PALADINS DE LA RÉPUBLIQUE

Marie-Odile Laclos, *porteuse du blason of Huon of Bordeaux*

Guillaume Ficheur, *porteur du blason of Archbishop Turpin*

Claudine, *Paladin spy*

FOUNDING FRONTIERSMEN

Harding Steele, *Agent of Hank Morgan*

General Alec Kreiss, *Agent of Paul Bunyan*

Frank Mallucci, *Agent of Daniel Boone*

Brad Nielsen, *Agent of Virgil Earp*

Louis Zelinksy, *Agent of Allan Pinkerton*

Sergeant Hoyt, *footsoldier*

NIBELUGENTREUE

Ernst Schmidt, *ringbearer of Wayland Smith*

Lorena Eisler, *ringbearer of the Valkyrie Waltraute*

OTHER FOREIGN DEVICIAL ORDERS

Dr Kawasima, *kamon-bearer of Muramasa*

Benjamin Ben-Ari, *carrying the ruach of Tubal-Cain*

Thora Yrsasdottir, *runeholder of Ref the Sly*

Cécile, *mambo of Ogoun Ferraille*

THE ROYAL FAMILY

The Queen *of the United Kingdom*

The Duke of Cornwall, *the Queen's son, heir to the throne; putative device-bearer of Corineus*

A prince, the Duke of Cornwall's son

The Duke of Cornwall's niece

OTHER

Chief Superintendent Jade Kinsey *of the Device Squad; advisor to High King Jordan*

Laney Wardsley, *putative device-bearer of Elaine of Corbenic; former Green Chapel member*

Edward Wendiman, *Blaze's predecessor as device-bearer of Merlin, and previously of Sir Menw son of Teirwaedd*

Freda Tate-Hendricks, *Director of the Mythopolitical Research Facility*

Izzy McCutcheon, *Craig McCutcheon's daughter*

Valentine Brewster, *device-bearer of Sir Garlon the Red*

Roberto Schultz, *American evangelist*

Chad Schumacher, *American armaments salesman*

Mrs Eunice Tang *of Strathclyde*

The President *of the Republic of Scotland*

President Gomez *of the United States*

Sharon Brain, *device-bearer of Hellawes*

Bretwalda Ward, *device-bearer of Rowena; former leader of the Saxon Shield*

Dr Chisholm, *Member of Parliament*

Debbie Charner, *Squig's girlfriend*

Sergeant Barry Jenkins *of the Device Squad*

Bill Spink, *British evangelical preacher; device-bearer of St Gildas*

Mark 'Adze' Addis, *device-bearer of the Questing Beast and later of the Camlann Adder; former leader of the British Beasts*

Duncan, *a resident of Winterbourne Stoke*

DECEASED

Shafiq Rashid, *Jordan's predecessor as the ally of Robin Hood aka the Green Knight; formerly Zara's predecessor as the ally of the Saracen*

Shaun Hobson, *Shafiq's predecessor as the ally of Robin Hood aka the Green Knight*

Jack Bennett, *Janene's predecessor as the ally of Little John*

Brian, *Eric's predecessor as the ally of Will Stuteley*

Fiona 'Finn' Quinn, *Squig's successor and Ron's predecessor as the ally of Much the Miller's Son*

Liss Dashwood, *member of the Green Chapel; Laney Wardsley's best friend*

Trevor Macnamara, *Cornish's predecessor as the device-bearer of Sir Percival; Knight of the Circle and partner of David Stafford*

Nick Frith, *Farnsworth's predecessor as the device-bearer of Sir Bors; Knight of the Circle*

Fr Hywel Evans, *Marvell's predecessor as the device-bearer of St Dubricius*

James Ribbens, *device-bearer of Retho of Arvaius; serial killer*

Alfred Noake, *device-bearer of Hengist; Bretwalda's predecessor as leader of the Saxon Shield*

Eulalie Goldenchild, *ally of Calafia; the 'Black Queen of the Upper Haight'*

LIST OF DEVICES IN TROJANS

THE MATTER OF BRITAIN

King Arthur Pendragon, *High King of Britain*

Queen Guinevere, *Arthur's wife*

Morgan le Fay, *Arthur's half-sister; a sorceress*

Sir Mordred, *Knight of the Round Table; Arthur's villainous bastard son*

Merlin, *Arthur's wizard*

Nimue, *the Lady of the Lake*

Taliesin, *Arthur's bard*

St Dubricius, *Bishop of Caerleon and Llandaff; Arthur's chaplain*

Brutus, *Trojan refugee and legendary founder of Britain*

Corineus, *Trojan refugee and legendary founder of Cornwall*

Sir Gawain, *Knight of the Round Table; Arthur's nephew and one of his finest knights*

Sir Gareth, *Knight of the Round Table; Gawain's brother*

Sir Agravaine, *Knight of the Round Table; Gawain's brother*

Queen Morgause, *Arthur's half-sister; mother of Gawain, Agravaine, Gaheris and Gareth, sometimes also of Mordred*

Sir Kay, *Knight of the Round Table; Arthur's foster-brother*

Sir Ector, *Knight of the Round Table; Arthur's foster-father*

Sir Lancelot, *Knight of the Round Table; Arthur's best friend and best knight, lover of Guinevere*

Sir Galahad, *Knight of the Round Table; Lancelot's son, a knight of renowned purity*

Elaine of Corbenic, *Galahad's mother; later Lancelot's wife*

Sir Bors, *Knight of the Round Table; Lancelot's uncle*

Sir Lionel, *Knight of the Round Table; Lancelot's cousin*

Sir Bleoberis, *Knight of the Round Table; Lancelot's cousin*

King Mark, *King of Cornwall under Arthur*

Sir Tristan, *Cornish Knight of the Round Table; King Mark's nephew and lover of La Belle Iseult*

La Belle Iseult, *wife of Mark and lover of Tristan*

Sir Marhaus (*aka* 'the Morholt'), *Irish Knight of the Round Table; Iseult's uncle*

Sir Palamedes, *Saracen Knight of the Round Table; also in love with Iseult*

Sir Safir, *Saracen Knight of the Round Table; Palamedes' brother*

Sir Sagramore, *Knight of the Round Table; friend to Tristan*

Sir Dinadan, *Knight of the Round Table; friend to Tristan*

Sir Kahedins, *Knight of the Round Table; Tristan's brother-in-law, also in love with Iseult*

Sir Sadoc, *Cornish Knight of the Round Table*

Sir Licanor, *Cornish Knight of the Round Table*

Sir Andret, *Cornish Knight of the Round Table*

Sir Bedivere, *Knight of the Round Table; Arthur's marshal*

Sir Percival, *Knight of the Round Table; a virtuous knight*

Sir Accolon, *Knight of the Round Table; Morgan le Fay's lover*

Sir Lucan, *Knight of the Round Table; Arthur's butler*

Sir Marrok, *Knight of the Round Table and occasional werewolf*

Sir Menw son of Teirwaedd, *Knight of the Round Table and magician*

Sir Geraint, *Knight of the Round Table and jealous husband*

Enid, *Geraint's wife*

Sir Mador de la Porte, *Knight of the Round Table; Arthur's doorkeeper*

Sir Urre, *Hungarian Knight of the Round Table*

Sir Morien, *Moorish Knight of the Round Table*

Sir Brastias, *Knight of the Round Table*

Sir Lanval, *Knight of the Round Table*

Sir Ywain the Bastard, *Knight of the Round Table*

Sir Aglavale, *Knight of the Round Table*

Sir Lamorak, *Knight of the Round Table*

Sir Griflet, *Knight of the Round Table*

Sir Lavaine, *Knight of the Round Table*

Sir Leondegrance, *Knight of the Round Table*

Sir Galagars, *Knight of the Round Table*

Sir Brandinor, *Knight of the Round Table*

Sir Melian, *Knight of the Round Table*

Sir Helin the White, *Knight of the Round Table*

The Green Knight, *a cursed nobleman or nature spirit in conflict with Sir Gawain; identified with Robin Hood*

Sir Garlon the Red, *an invisible knight*

Hellawes, *a sorceress*

St Gildas, *a critic of Arthur*

Hengist, *a Saxon warlord*

Rowena, *Hengist's daughter*

The Questing Beast, *a fabulous creature*

Hank Morgan, *a time-traveller from nineteenth-century Connecticut*

ROBIN HOOD AND HIS MERRY MEN

Robin Hood, *a merry outlaw; identified with the Green Knight*

Maid Marian, *Robin's lover*

Little John, *Robin's lieutenant*

Friar Tuck, *a jolly cleric*

Will Scarlet, *a thug with a penchant for red*

Much the Miller's Son, *a young outlaw*

The Saracen, *a Muslim outlaw of inconstant identity*

Alan a'Dale, *a minstrel*

Gilbert Whitehand, *a skilled archer*

Arthur a'Bland, *a pugnacious outlaw*

David of Doncaster, *a young outlaw*

Will Stuteley, *an elderly outlaw*

Herne the Hunter, *a ghost or nature spirit; Robin's spiritual adviser in some sources*

Adam Bell, *another legendary outlaw; Robin's predecessor in some sources*

Richard the Lionheart, *the king in exile*

THE FENIAN CYCLE

Fionn mac Cumhail, *leader of the Fianna*

Gráinne, *Fionn's fiancée*

Diarmuid Ua Duibhne *of the Love Spot; member of the Fianna; Grainne's lover*

Conán mac Morna, *member of the Fianna; a joker*

Caílte mac Rónáin, *member of the Fianna; a runner*

Diorruing mac Doba, *member of the Fianna; a seer*

Lughaidh Stronghand, *member of the Fianna; a sorcerer*

Fianchad, *member of the Fianna; Fionn's doorkeeper*

THE MATTER OF FRANCE

Huon of Bordeaux, *a Paladin*

Ogier the Dane, *a Paladin*

Otuel, *a Saracen Paladin*

Bradamante, *a female Paladin*

Turpin, *a Paladin and archbishop*

GERMANIC MYTH

Wayland Smith, *the master blacksmith*

Waltraute, *a Valkyrie*

Helmwige, *a Valkyrie*

Rossweisse, *a Valkyrie*

US FOLKLORE

Paul Bunyan, *giant lumberjack of North Dakota*

Daniel Boone, *frontier pioneer and trapper*

Virgil Earp, *Arizona lawman, brother of Wyatt Earp*

Allan Pinkerton, *founder of Pinkerton's detective agency*

Abe Lincoln, *sixteenth President of the United States*

THE NORSE SAGAS

Ivar the Boneless, *a Viking leader, son of Ragnar Loðbrók*

Sigurd Snake-in-the-Eye, *a Viking leader, son of Ragnar Loðbrók*

Ref the Sly, *Icelandic saga hero, trickster and inventor*

CLASSICAL MYTH

Herakles *aka* Hercules, *son of Zeus; demigod and greatest of the Greek heroes*

Perseus, *son of Zeus; Herakles' great-grandfather; slayer of Medusa*

Achilles, *great-grandson of Zeus; hero of the Trojan War*

OTHER

Muramasa, *Japanese katana-maker*

Tubal-Cain, *Old Testament inventor of metalwork*

Ogoun Ferraille, *blacksmith loa in Haitian vodoun*

Calafia, *Queen of the Amazons in Spanish literature*